DEREK R[...]   [...]lvertising
in London and [...]   [...]adcaster for radio
and television, a[...] [...] [...] [...] [...] [...] [...]r thirty years. His
novel *Goshawk Squadron* was shortlisted for the Booker Prize in 1971.

"Rob[...]on sho[...]d b[...] [...]oned in the same breath as Mailer, Ba[...]   [...]
Heller. A masterpiece"   *Express*

"Tough, taut prose that pulls you through the book like a steel cable . . .
great"   *Guardian*

"Robinson writes with tireless enthusiasm which never sacrifices detail to
pace, or vice versa . . . terrific"   JENNIFER SELWAY, *Observer*

"Derek Robinson has developed a brand of 'ripping-yarn' all his own
. . . hard-bitten stuff, anti-Newbolt and anti-Biggles"
                                               Times Literary Supplement

"Robinson is a better storyteller than Jeffrey Archer, Ken Follett or Wilbur
Smith . . . His is a rare achievement, difficult to attain and one not much
striven for in the current literary output, the creation of poetry in fiction"
                                               TIBOR FISCHER, *The Times*

"Robinson has a narrative gift that sets up the hackles of involvement.
A rare quality"   PAUL SCOTT

"Nobody writes about war quite like Derek Robinson. He has a way of
carrying you along with the excitement of it all before suddenly disposing
of a character with a casual, laconic ruthlessness that is shockingly realistic
. . . As a bonus, he writes of the random, chaotic *comedy* of war better than
anyone since Evelyn Waugh"   MIKE PETTY, *The Independent*

"If the argument that book reviews sell more books is ever proven, then
reviews of Robinson's books should be posted on every wall, hydrant and
lease-expired storefront. They should be free with your breakfast cereal.
They should be dropped from planes – for the only purpose of reviewing
in Robinson's case is to persuade readers who have yet to pick up a
Robinson novel to do so in their millions" JULIAN EVANS, *Weekend Post*

Novels by Derek Robinson

* Available from MacLehose Press from 2012/13
* * To be published in ebook by MacLehose Press

Derek Robinson

HORNET'S STING

MACLEHOSE PRESS
QUERCUS · LONDON

First published in Great Britain in 1999 by The Harvill Press
This edition published in 2013 by

MacLehose Press
an imprint of Quercus
55 Baker Street
7th Floor, South Block
London W1U 8EW

A CIP catalogue record for this book is available
from the British Library

ISBN 978 08 5705 225 4

2 4 6 8 10 9 7 5 3 1

Designed and typeset in Minion by Libanus Press, Marlborough
Printed and bound in Great Britain by Clays Ltd, St Ives plc

For Q and Joan

EARTHQUAKE STRENGTH 1:

Tremors not felt by persons.

It had snowed in the night, and from five thousand feet the Western Front looked almost pretty. The tens of thousands of shell craters made a plain of white dimples. The trenches, so often just brown zigzags that blurred into the mud, were as crisp as black stitching on linen. "Makes a nice change," Captain Lynch said aloud. It was January 1917.

He often talked to himself; it helped him stay alert during long patrols. He was leading "B" Flight of Hornet Squadron, six Sopwith Pups in a loose diamond formation. With men guarding his flanks and his tail, he could afford the luxury of taking a long look at the ground. Everything was clean. Even the ruins had the decency to be snowcapped. "Jolly Christmassy," Lynch said. "Well done. Stand the men at ease, sergeant major." There were no men to be seen, of course. Fifty thousand British infantry were hidden in this stretch. A man could spend a year in the trenches and never see his enemy. Then there might be an attack, and he would go over the top, and still he might never see his enemy. "Fritz would see him, though," Lynch said. "Fritz couldn't miss him, could he?"

He turned the flight away from the German Lines, just as the first blots of anti-aircraft fire appeared, and he kept climbing and turning, or sometimes not, until the Archie lost interest. By then the Pups were at eleven thousand feet. He led them east, still climbing, and levelled out at fourteen thousand. The glare of the winter sun bleached the sky.

Not hot, he thought. If he opened his mouth at this height the blast of air would freeze his teeth. He looked at each of the Pups in turn, making sure the pilots were searching the sky. Cold and monotony were great killers.

Nothing happened for forty minutes. Then a tiny patch of specks appeared, in the northeast, far away. Lynch felt the familiar rush of excitement.

They turned out to be four Fokker single-seaters, painted a swirling purple and green. They came up and took a good look at the Pups but they declined to fight. When Lynch got within a quarter of a mile of them, they turned away. At full throttle, the Pups gained very little and were being led deeper into German airspace. Lynch stopped the chase and turned north. The Fokkers turned and flew parallel with him. Were they decoys? He held up his hand to blot out the sun, and searched for an ambush hiding in the glare. Nothing. It was all rather pointless. The enemy formation was untidy. New boys, he decided. Someone's teaching them lesson one: Don't get killed. Very sensible. He wheeled the Pups around and headed back to the Lines.

By now a pair of German observation balloons were up. A little shelling was taking place down there, Lynch could see small flowerings of explosion spoiling the snow, and an occasional dot of flame as a gun took a pot at the enemy battery. It was probably just a bit of long-range sniping to keep the gunners in practice. Perhaps it would kill a few men, perhaps not. Boys played with their toys and sometimes it ended in tears. That was nothing to do with Hornet Squadron. But Lynch was bored.

He steered his flight towards the action. He was still so high that the balloons looked no bigger than peas on a plate, but he knew that somebody down there was watching his Pups through binoculars. At the right moment, when the angle would be steep but not vertical, he tipped them into a dive. Halfway down, with the wires screaming like gulls, he pulled out. The balloons were on the ground. The Archie had anticipated his move and now there were dirty blotches all around. It took him five minutes of twisting and climbing to get his flight clear of the filth.

There was still half an hour to kill. He flew south. He hadn't visited this stretch of the Front for a long time. It might be worth seeing. Maybe the Russian Army had broken through and was giving the Hun what-ho from the rear. That would make a nice change.

But nothing had changed. The lines of trenches still wandered away into the misty distance. Specks could be seen in the sky, but none was interested in joining combat with six Pups. Then Lynch saw another German balloon. Immediately he turned away from it and flew east.

He led the flight three miles into Hunland and signalled to his deputy leader to take command of two machines and go home. That left Lynch with the other two Pups. They began a long dive, curling westward.

A mile short of the balloon they were hedge-hopping, racing across fields, dipping so low that propeller-wash blew snow off the grass. Once they even jumped some troops at rest, too startled to find their rifles. Even so, the balloon was being hauled down fast. Lynch climbed at it and opened fire and saw his bullets make a puckering slash in the tight fabric, and he tipped the Pup on its side to sheer away from dangling ropes. Streaks of tracer, red and yellow, searched for him as heavy machine guns opened up. He imitated the jack rabbit: dodged and bucked and swerved, and crossed the Lines with holes in his wings but his skin intact. The other Pups survived too: the gunners' aim had been divided by three. Behind them, the balloon was burning like a Viking sacrifice.

* * *

"Brigade want to know . . ." Captain Brazier, adjutant of Hornet Squadron, put on his glasses. The message was faint; it had been hammered through an old, tired typewriter ribbon. "They want to know why we haven't made our monthly return of plum jam, in pounds (a) supplied, (b) consumed and (c) remaining in store." He looked up. "Is this more of your wickedness, Lacey?"

"Just put *Nil Return*, sir."

Brazier dipped his pen in the ink, and hesitated. "What if Brigade tell us we ordered two hundred pounds of plum jam?"

"We say the quartermaster delivered three hundred pounds of strawberry jam in error and we sent it all back."

"That doesn't answer their question."

"No, sir. But it gives them something different to worry about."

Brazier wrote *Nil Return* three times, and shouted for the despatch rider. The man saluted, took the paper, saluted again, and marched out. "Plum jam," Brazier said. "Why not black boot polish?"

"They're saving boot polish for next week," Lacey said. "You can't rush a war. You're too impetuous, sir. It was always your fatal flaw, if I may say so."

Brazier slowly relaxed. "This war has ruined soldiering. If you'd spoken to me like that in India, you'd have been doubling around the parade ground under a full pack and rifle until you were just a small pool of sweat evaporating beneath the merciless midday sun." He felt better for having said that. "Anyway, what the deuce do you know of my fatal flaws?"

"I typed them out, sir. When you joined the squadron, the C.O. asked for a précis of your Service record. He had no time to read the full document, rich in the clash of combat though it is."

That amused Brazier. Lacey watched his lips shape the phrase: the clash of combat.

They were a curious couple. Sergeant Lacey was in charge of the orderly room. He had been expensively educated at Sherborne and could have had a commission if he wanted; but Lacey had studied history at school and when this war broke out he was not surprised that nothing went according to plan. He knew that sooner or later the army would take him and so he anticipated the move by learning typing and short-hand. Infantry were plentiful, but a soldier with his skills was invaluable. There had never been any danger that Lacey would go to the Front.

He had been with the squadron ever since it formed and he had developed a talent for barter and bribery that kept the squadron supplied with coal and bedsheets and toilet paper and Daddies Sauce; little luxuries that made war not only tolerable but sometimes enjoyable. He was slim and spruce, aged somewhere between twenty and thirty – a neat, thick moustache made it difficult to guess – and his uniforms were more smartly tailored than those of the officers. He made Brazier look like a bear. The adjutant didn't realize this.

Brazier was six foot four and so broad-shouldered that sometimes he had to edge through a doorway. He hadn't joined the army to peacock around in tight trousers but to fight. He had a chin like a wooden mallet, a nose like a steel wedge, and bright blue eyes, a combination that many men found alarming when they first met him. He didn't alarm Sergeant Lacey. Brazier was nearly fifty and only a captain. Lacey knew what flaw had brought him down from a major's rank and sent him out of the trenches to an R.F.C. squadron when he knew nothing of flying. During an especially bloody battle, Brazier had smelt panic and shot a couple of his men as an example to the others. No more panic, the enemy was thrown back, the line was held. It had happened more than once. Brazier never tried to hide his actions; he believed they were correct. Others didn't. Bang went his major's crown. In certain lights, its outline was still faintly visible on his epaulettes. Brazier believed that, once you went to war, defeat was unthinkable. Otherwise why be a soldier? Brazier was a good soldier. Too good for some.

"Brooms," he said. He was reading another message. "Brooms, bristle, stiff, latrine, men's, for the use of. Wing H.Q. say our requirements are ten and we've been issued with forty. Why?"

"Leave it to me, sir. I'll take care of it."

"Yes. You already have, haven't you? What did you get? Lino? Fish paste? California syrup of figs?"

"Canadian bacon. The Calgary Battalion was desperately short of disinfectant, and . . ." Lacey paused, and looked out of the window. "It's rather complicated," he said. "And you have more important things to worry about than domestic trivia."

"Right. You sort it out. But no crime; understand?"

"Crime requires a victim. I ensure that everyone benefits."

"You'll never get rich that way, Lacey."

"My fatal flaw, sir." He stood as the adjutant heaved himself up and put his cap on. Suddenly the room looked much smaller. "Lunch," Brazier said.

* * *

You could see England from the cockpit of a Sopwith Pup, on a clear day, provided the Pup was at fifteen thousand feet or more. Futile reminders like this made France all the more foreign. Hornet Squadron had been at Pepriac, which was a scruffy little village, since the spring of 1916.

In those days, the squadron flew a strange aeroplane called the FE2b. It looked like an elongated bathtub, with the gunner sitting in front of the pilot, and the engine and the propeller behind them both.

The FE2b had two advantages – it provided a fine view of the oncoming enemy, and its bullets did not have to travel through the propeller arc – but it flew like what it was, a two-man bathtub with an engine and wings bolted to its backside. Hornet Squadron was not sorry to swap it for the Sopwith Pup.

The Pup was well-named, being small and nimble and not tremendously fast, and it didn't have as big a bite as its opponents; but the pilots thought it was a great improvement on the FE2b. So did the German Air Force. Much work was done at the drawing boards of Fokker and Aviatik and Pfalz and Albatros and other companies.

Meanwhile, the battle of the Somme had dragged to an end like some great hulk of a beast that takes too long to die. In twenty weeks the two sides had mown down or blown up or drowned or incinerated more than a million men. The cost was probably fairly evenly divided. About a quarter of the casualties were dead or dying. It takes a long time to bury a quarter of a million men, so there would not be another battle for a while. And in any case, it was winter. Field Marshal Mud was in command, assisted by General Freeze.

* * *

Major Cleve-Cutler was C.O. of Hornet Squadron. He looked perky and optimistic, but this was because a flying accident had redesigned his face: since the doctors had stitched it together, one corner of his mouth went up where it used to go down, and one eyebrow had a challenging kink to it. This new face was a useful disguise, except at funerals. Perky optimism did not suit funerals.

Twice a week he met his flight commanders to make sure everyone was winning the war properly. Captain Gerrish led "A" Flight. He was nicknamed "Plug" because he was so ugly; he was also tall and powerful and sombre. Only his friends used the name to his face. "B" Flight was led by Captain Tim Lynch, M.C.: slim, softspoken and carefully groomed. Captain Ogilvy had "C" Flight. His family lived in Ireland, so he was called "Spud".

"Dull week everywhere," the C.O. said. "Average casualties and no new types reported, so Wing says. Weather hasn't helped."

"If the weather stays lousy, the Hun won't be flying," Gerrish said. "Got more brains."

"It's not the Hun I'm worried about, it's landing accidents," Cleve-Cutler said. "One stunt like Pocock's is enough for me." Pocock had touched down on a stretch of grass so soggy with rain that it clogged his wheels. The nose dipped, the tail rose, and the Pup somersaulted and fell onto its back. Pocock broke his neck, the petrol tank split open, and two mechanics got burned while bravely failing to drag out a body which they did not know was dead.

"It's depressing to see that black scorch-mark every time you land." Cleve-Cutler said. "The grass won't grow for ages."

"We could plant a tree," Lynch said. He seemed to be serious. Cleve-Cutler watched him, thoughtfully, but Lynch had no more to say.

"Morale's not a problem in my flight, sir," Gerrish said. "Knocking down a couple of Huns would cheer everyone up, but nobody's complaining."

"Guns are a problem," Ogilvy said. "I like the Vickers when it fires. When it jams, it's bloody maddening."

"On second thoughts, a tree is not a good idea," Lynch said.

"Well, that's all," Cleve-Cutler said. "We carry on giving the enemy his medicine. More offensive patrols. I need a word with Tim."

Gerrish and Ogilvy left.

"You got a balloon this morning, I hear."

"Yes, sir. Cooper and Simms and me."

"But not in your patrol line."

Cleve-Cutler went to a wall map of the British stretch of the Western

Front. At the bottom he pencilled a neat cross. "Any further south and you would have been in the French sector," he said.

"Golly."

"A Colonel Merrivale's been on the phone. Pop down and see him, would you? There's a landing ground nearby. It's all here." He gave Lynch a sheet of paper. "And take someone with you, why don't you? For company."

Lynch and Lieutenant Simms flew to the landing ground. A car was waiting for them. It was mid-afternoon, and the sky had the scrubbed, pale blueness that France gets only in winter.

They drove for about five miles, to a smashed village. Troops were everywhere: cooking, washing, sleeping, parading. "This is as far as I go, sir," the driver said. "They're diggin' up the road ahead."

Simms believed him. "What on earth for?" he asked.

"Not buried treasure, sir, so it must be sheer bloody spite."

He went away and came back with their guide, a stubby corporal, muddy to the knees. The corporal gave them steel helmets and said: "Run when I run. The Jerry gunners got regular habits, thank God."

The road soon became a track and the track made little detours around flooded shell-holes. The snow had been trampled into a dirty sludge. Few men were about, and those few were all in a hurry; nobody paused to salute the officers. All around, the land was flat and empty except for a few shattered trees and patches of tired black smoke.

The corporal stopped at a heap of rubble. "Colonel's dugout's over there, sir," he said, and pointed. Lynch saw nothing.

While they walked, there had been distant bangs and crashes. Now a soft, slow whistle suddenly magnified into a howl that became a scream, like an express bolting out of a tunnel. The pilots fell flat. The shell burst two hundred yards away and created a fountain of mud that did not want to come down. The corporal had not moved; he helped them to their feet. "Thanks awfully," Simms said. The fountain was collapsing, leaving behind a stain of smoke.

"Quick as you can, sir!" the corporal snapped, and ran. The pilots skidded and stumbled. They were carrying pounds of mud on each boot.

The steel helmets were flopping around their necks. The corporal was waiting at the dugout entrance, shouting at them. He hustled them down some wooden steps. They stood where they were put and made a lot of noise, gasping for breath. After the sharp sunlight their eyes were nearly useless. There were two candles. Presently someone said, "Thank you, corporal." The man saluted, and left.

Lynch's eyes began to work again. He saw a colonel: a tall man with a face that made a brave start with a big, boney nose, then fell away to a thin mouth and a nothing of a chin. "You must be the fearless aviators," he said. There was Yorkshire in his voice.

"I'm Lynch, sir. This is Lieutenant Simms."

"You attacked the German balloon? Set it on fire?"

"Yes, sir."

"Why did you do that?"

The question was so strange that Lynch looked around, hoping for clues. All he saw was dirt walls, a corrugated-iron roof, a telephonist sitting in one corner, a sergeant and a captain in another, boxes for seats, and the usual military litter: weapons, belts, tinned food, plates, maps, blankets, bottles, binoculars. "It was an enemy balloon, sir," he said.

"Who told you to destroy it?"

"Nobody, sir. But—"

"What harm was it doing?"

"Well, sir, presumably the Hun observers were spying on our trenches, and on any activity behind—"

"They're not *your* trenches, Mr Lynch. You know nothing about what goes on here. These are *my* trenches, and *my* men. Come with me."

They went back up the steps and into the dazzling daylight. Now and then the remote boom of artillery could be heard, and the gloomy crump of a shellburst.

"Look around," Merrivale said. "What do you see?"

To the horizon, the landscape was empty, streaked with snow, abandoned. "Nothing, sir," Lynch said.

"Nothing worth shelling? Correct. Shells are expensive," Merrivale said. "Here comes one now." The express rushed out of the tunnel, but this time it landed much further away, and the explosion merely buffeted their ears. "I've lost twenty men this afternoon. Twenty good men gone and nothing gained. Not counting the wounded. Harry!" The captain came up from the dugout. "Harry, be a good chap and take these officers over to Major Gibbons' batteries."

It was another long slog through the same sort of mud. Sometimes the shellfire died out entirely for long minutes; sometimes it awoke and barked furiously. Harry said little. Simms looked at the naked landscape and said: "Must get jolly chilly here."

"I don't suppose you brought any whisky."

"Actually, no."

The batteries were of field guns. Empty shellcases lay tumbled in heaps: it had been a busy afternoon. Major Gibbons turned out to be a thickset, red-headed Irishman. He looked cheerful, but that was just the face he had been born with. "Jesus wept!" he said. "I knew you flying idiots were all absolute maniacs, but is it utterly necessary for you to inflict your lunatic insanity on us? Eh?"

"I'm sorry, sir," Lynch said. "Evidently I miscalculated."

"*We* miscalculated. We should have blown your idiot heads off when we had the chance. We've got a nice, well-managed war going on here. Stay away!"

Simms was baffled. "Well-managed, sir? I don't see . . ."

But Major Gibbons had put his fingers in his ears. Simms looked at Lynch. Lynch shrugged. Then the battery fired. When the pilots turned to look, guns were recoiling and ejecting shellcases and exhaling smoke, and men were scrambling to reload. "Beautiful bang, isn't it?" Gibbons said. "I don't suppose you brought any whisky."

"Afraid not."

"Buzz off, then. Fly away. Harry, show them to Tommy Skinner. I doubt he's had much to laugh at today."

"Oh, thanks awfully," Harry said flatly.

They followed him across more snow-speckled mud, to the beginnings of the trench system. It was late in the afternoon, and the sun had lost whatever little warmth it had had. "This is frightfully good of you," Lynch said. "I hope we aren't ruining your afternoon."

"It was ruined already."

They trudged along communication trenches and into reserve trenches, squeezing past soldiers whose khaki had long since turned to the colour of mud. The men wore greatcoats, mufflers, woollen gloves; many smoked pipes; all wore steel helmets. They had the slack, resigned air of travellers waiting for a train that has been cancelled so often that it might never arrive. The occasional whistle of a shell or the fizz of a bullet did not disturb them. They were at home. It was filthy, cold and lice-infested, but it was home.

Tommy Skinner turned out to be another major, in another dugout. He wore a balaclava under his cap, two greatcoats and thigh-length rubber boots. He was listening on a field-telephone, and grunting every five seconds. Finally he yawned, and said: "Do my best. Can't say more." He handed the phone to a signaller. "My compliments to Mr Arbuthnott, and I need a lieutenant and six men for a raid." He turned to his visitors.

"They're Flying Corps, sir," Harry said. "They shot down the Hun balloon."

"Idiot bastards," Skinner said. "Bastard idiots."

"It was a mistake, sir," Lynch said quickly.

"Wrong again," Skinner said. "It was a crime. We have a tacit agreement with the enemy. Tacit means silent. Silent means they don't shell us and we don't shell them."

Simms said, "With respect, sir, that's not war."

"Of course it's not! And I'll tell you something else: *war* isn't war, either. Not all the time." He fished a Colt revolver from a greatcoat pocket. "I am strongly minded to kill you two sparrows. Nobody would know, would they, Trotter?"

"No, sir," said the signaller.

"Just a couple of bodies. Add 'em to the pile. Yes?"

"Got hit by shrapnel, I expect, sir."

"War isn't war?" Lynch said. "Too deep for me, sir. I'm just a simple sparrow."

"That Hun balloon," the major said. "It went up every day, took a dekko behind our Lines, saw nothing doing, came down. Likewise with our balloon. Then you winged pricks turn up. Fritz thinks: they popped my balloon, they've got something to hide! An offensive, maybe! So he pops *our* balloon and he shells us like buggery, just in case." He put the revolver muzzle in Lynch's ear. "How long is the British Front?"

"Sixty or seventy miles."

He took the muzzle away. "Lucky guess. Can you have a sixty-mile battlefront on the boil, all year round?" He put the muzzle back to the ear.

"No, sir."

"So why didn't you think of that?" Skinner roared. A rat scampered across the dugout floor and ran up the steps and he shot at it and missed. "See? Even the bloody rats can't stand you."

Lynch smiled. "What are you grinning at?" Skinner demanded.

"Well . . . here you are, sir, threatening to shoot me for being too warlike. I was just thinking how odd that was."

"*Thinking?* Sparrows don't think. You flap about the sky and you shit on the poor bloody infantry and that makes you a golden eagle. Well, go and see the troops. Find out what they think! Harry, take them up to B-Company. Find Captain Vine." As they climbed the steps, he added: "And next time you visit the Lines, bring some whisky."

The trenches became more crowded as they moved forward. In places the trench-wall had been smashed by shellfire; the chemical stink hung in the air; men in sheepskin jerkins were repairing the damage, shovelling dirt into sandbags. The pilots made room for stretcher-bearers, who were in no hurry; blankets covered the heads and bodies but not the boots. The boots were exposed and angled at forty-five degrees to each other, just as the drill sergeant had taught. Simms touched a boot as it went past, and wished he hadn't.

Captain Vine was in the first trench, waiting for the dusk stand-to. Ice had begun to form.

"What the deuce does Jerry think he's playing at?" Vine complained. "Nobody starts an attack in January, for God's sake. This is just a damnfool temper-tantrum."

Lynch said, "I'm sorry, we bust their balloon and we won't do it again."

To everyone's surprise, Vine found that very funny. "Take a squint at this."

Lynch climbed onto the step of the parapet and looked through binoculars, past a fuzzy fringe of barbed wire, across the wide wasteland to the German wire. Behind this was a notice, painted red on white. The setting sun picked it out beautifully: TELL YOUR FUCKING FLYING CORPS TO LEAVE US ALONE. WE ARE SAXONS.

"Sorry about the whisky," Lynch said. He gave the binoculars to Simms.

"The odd thing is they're *not* Saxons," Vine said. "One of them deserted, the other night. They're Bavarians."

"That completes the Cook's Tour of the Front," Harry said. "Unless you want to look in on our Advanced Casualty Clearing Station?"

"Another time, perhaps," Lynch said.

"Well, think of us, under the stars," Vine said, "when your servant is tucking you up in your feather bed."

But by the time they had walked to the smashed village, and waited for transport, it was black night. They finally scrounged a ride to the landing ground and slept in blankets on the hangar floor. Next morning, unwashed and unshaven, they flew back to Pepriac.

*   *   *

There were three guests at lunch in the mess. Nobody was surprised to see Colonel Bliss, from Wing H.Q. The other two were strangers, in strange uniforms: their breeches were baggier and their tunics shorter than the British Army's style. One man had a small beard, which the British Army forbade. They were young and they wore more medals than a general would collect if he spent his entire career in the cannon's mouth.

The padre said grace. Brown soup was served.

"Wops," Spud Ogilvy guessed. "Wops from Italy."

Gerrish shook his head. "One's got blue eyes."

"You can't possibly see that from here," said Dando, the doctor. "Can you?" The day was gloomy and the mess was dim. He envied their eyesight.

"The Italian Army is fighting splendidly," the padre said. He was the tallest man in the squadron, and the most enthusiastic. "The Italians will stand no nonsense from the Austrians."

"If they're not wops, they're Greeks," Ogilvy said. "Lots of fighting in Salonika. Is that in Greece?"

"Ask young Mr Hamilton," Gerrish said. "He was at school last year, so he should know. Where's Salonika, Mr Hamilton?"

Hamilton hated having people stare at him. "Geography wasn't all that important at Rugby," he muttered.

"Well, I don't suppose they play much rugby in Salonika," the doctor said. "So you're quits."

The soup plates were cleared. Mutton chops arrived. Lynch, who had been listening carefully, said: "I know who that chap with the beard is. I just can't remember his name."

"How about the fellow next to him?" Gerrish said.

"Ah, that's Cleve-Cutler. Claims to be C.O. here. Can't make up his mind. One day he wants you to go balloon-busting, next day he doesn't. Bet you wouldn't have put up with him at Salonika," he said to Hamilton. "Eh?" Hamilton stopped eating, and his eyes flickered in panic from Lynch to Gerrish, who merely shook his head. Lynch sawed a chunk off his chop and waggled it on his fork. "Say no more." He was silent for the rest of the meal. Gerrish was glad of this. He found Lynch's jokes unfunny. If they *were* jokes. How could anyone tell?

* * *

The visiting officers came from Russia. Colonel Bliss told the C.O. and the adjutant that they were on secondment from the Imperial Russian Air Force and they were now attached to Hornet Squadron, to gain experience. "Did you know there is a Russian regiment already in the Lines?" Bliss said.

"No? Well, there is. Maybe the Tsar plans to send us a squadron of his latest scouts, too."

After lunch, Captain Brazier took the Russians on a tour of the aerodrome, while Bliss and Cleve-Cutler went to the C.O.'s office for a chat.

"I'm told they don't speak a word of English," Bliss said, "which doesn't mean they can't understand it. Totally unpronounceable names, by the way. At Wing we called them Steak and Kidney. The beard is Kidney."

"How did they get all those medals? They look about my age."

"Younger. They're related to the Tsar, distantly. Steak is a grand duke and Kidney's a marquee or a flower show or something. I expect the medals came with the titles. Top Marks for Pluck. Cossack Order of Chastity, Third Class. Best Geranium in Show, that sort of thing. You know what the Russian court is like."

"No."

"Treat them like any other officer."

"How well can they fly?"

"That's for you to find out, old chap." Bliss was looking out at the drab, dank afternoon. "This would be considered a bright, sunny day in Russia, so they should feel quite at home here . . . Now then. About Captain Lynch."

"We've sent Colonel Merrivale a case of whisky."

"Send him a dozen, he won't forgive you." Bliss put on his glasses, looked hard at Cleve-Cutler, then took them off. "The Corps is not universally popular, you know, Hugh. London gets bombed by Zeppelins while we buzz about like flies in a thunderstorm. Some people in high places think the money would be better spent on more anti-aircraft guns. Don't bugger-up the infantry. Bugger-up the Hun. Otherwise you'll never get a better Pup."

"Let me get this straight, Colonel," Cleve-Cutler said. "To prove that they need a better machine, my chaps must first succeed with an inferior fighter. Have I got it right?"

Bliss shrugged on his British Warm and picked up his hat and stick. He put a hand on Cleve-Cutler's shoulder and leaned forward until his mouth was near the C.O.'s ear. "Don't tell them," he whispered, "and they'll probably never find out."

*   *   *

Captain Vine had been right: nobody launches an attack in January. The wind moaned over his stretch of trench and from time to time rain pattered or bucketed or lashed down on his men. Their boots churned the mud to a clinging, sucking liquid that made walking a drudgery and running an impossibility.

Pepriac too was wet and windy, but smoke raced from the stove pipes, the billets were dry, the beds were warm and the food was hot. Every night, Wing H.Q. sent its orders for the coming day. Usually it wanted deep offensive patrols, and usually its orders were cancelled before breakfast. The pilots relaxed again. They settled down to a day of letter-writing and poker, of drowsing in battered leather armchairs while mishit ping-pong balls ricocheted past their heads, of winding up the gramophone to play songs from *Chu-Chin-Chow* or *The Bing Boys Are Here*.

A mess servant brought Plug Gerrish a postcard datemarked London. He read: *Bumped into Frank Foster in Piccadilly. Calls himself Timms now and has grown a ginger moustache. Very shifty behaviour. I informed Military Intelligence but M.I. is not what it's cracked up to be. Cordially, Frank O'Neill.*

Gerrish made a sour face, and tossed the card to Spud Ogilvy. "Hilarious," he said. Ogilvy read it and grunted.

Later, an amiable, chubby lieutenant called Munday followed the duckboards to the orderly room. Sergeant Lacey was refilling his fountain pen while listening to a Souza march on his gramophone. It ended with a crash.

"Such swagger," Lacey said. "I am preparing myself spiritually for the Americans to enter the war. They wear cowboy hats, you know, like the Boy Scouts. So debonair, so refreshing, so irresistible to flying shrapnel. I see you have read Captain O'Neill's postcard."

Munday gave it to him. "Can you translate? It gave off a bad smell in the mess."

"Captain Foster was a flight commander. He had been at Eton with another pilot, Lieutenant Yeo. When Yeo was killed, Foster removed himself to a tent, took up the clarinet and blew his brains out."

"My stars!"

"The whole episode was self-indulgent in a middle-aged way, but then Eton is a self-indulgent and middle-aged school. You can't dress school-boys like stockbrokers without damaging their minds."

"Captain Ogilvy picked on the phrase 'not what it's cracked up to be.'"

"Foster's last words. Nothing, he said, was what it was cracked up to be. A flimsy reason for suicide, don't you think?" He returned the postcard.

"So what on earth is Captain O'Neill up to?"

"Who knows?" Lacey said. "Be sure to read our next gripping instalment."

* * *

Spud Ogilvy's parents had a big house in the west of Ireland and Cleve-Cutler thought he looked Irish: plenty of wavy black hair, a snub nose, a quick smile that revealed a couple of chipped teeth. In fact Ogilvy's parents were Scottish and he had been educated in England – at Eton, like the late Frank Foster – and his speech and habits were thoroughly English; he had damaged his teeth playing cricket. But the C.O. felt that the two Russians needed to be handled with a bit of Irish charm, so he put them into "C" Flight.

Ogilvy found them in their room: half a hut, which was rather more space than two new pilots got. Ogilvy had read some of the exciting bits of *War and Peace*, so he knew that Russian nobles spoke French. "*Bonjour*" he said. "*Je suis votre chef.*"

"Is a long way to Tipperary," the clean-shaven man said. "Everyone says. Why?"

"I haven't the foggiest. But I do know that it's customary on this squadron for new pilots to put their hats on and salute their flight commander and call him 'sir.'"

"Is customary in Imperial Russian Air Force to call me 'Highness,'" the clean-shaven Russian said. "Old soldiers kneel and kiss my boots." He spoke casually: it was not a contest. "But not in Russia now, so . . ." They put their caps on and saluted.

Ogilvy returned the salute. "Tell me your names, please."

They gave him their cards. The clean-shaven man was Lieutenant the Duke Nikolai Dolgorankov-Orlovensky-Vladimirovich. The bearded man was Lieutenant Count Andrei Kolchak-Romishevsky. Ogilvy was impressed by their extreme good looks. So many pilots came and went that he usually paid little attention to faces, but these two held his attention, like fine young actors. And their build was short and slim, which added to the sense of neatness. Most pilots were a bit grubby, a bit untidy: the result of long patrols with oil splattering back from the engine and whale-grease on the face. The Russians looked immaculate.

"I'm told you're here to get experience on Pups," he said.

"No. Here to kill German pilots," the duke said. "I promise Tsar I kill twenty-five by Easter. I swear this on crucifix of Tsar."

"Duke Nikolai is distant cousin of Tsar," the count said.

"And Count Andrei is distant cousin of me. Tsar chose us. We pledge our blood, which is also blood of cousin, Holy Emperor the Tsar."

"My goodness." Ogilvy felt a need to keep pace with all this loyalty. "How is the Tsar?" he asked.

"Very tired," the duke said. "He carries pain and suffering of Holy Russia on his back."

"Also in right shoulder some rheumatism, I think," the count said.

The discussion left them silent and brooding. Ogilvy said briskly: "Well, I'm sure you'll soon settle in here. A servant will be allocated to you and then—"

"Two servants," the duke said.

"One shared servant is customary."

"Not in Imperial Russian Air Force. Two servants each."

"The British Army has definite rules."

"Not in Imperial Russian Air Force."

"I'm afraid my hands are tied."

"Not in Imperial Russian Air Force."

Their bodies had stiffened, their faces were blank. "Need two servants," the count said. "Otherwise filth and squalor. Insult to Tsar."

"Put your hats on," Ogilvy said. "We'll see the C.O. about it." They put their caps on and saluted. "Not now," he said. They looked at each other. "Never mind," he said.

It was a long walk to Cleve-Cutler's office. Halfway there, the duke pointed out that their boots were already very muddy. "Need servants in war," he said.

"Tell me something," Ogilvy said. "Why didn't you speak English when you were at Wing H.Q., with Colonel Bliss?"

"Wing said nothing worth answer."

"Ah. I should have thought of that." They plodded on in silence.

Cleve-Cutler was polite but firm: officers of junior rank were entitled to half a servant each. The Russians thought this absurd: how could an officer be shaved by half a servant? What would the other half do? What if *both* officers needed immediate attention? "One must wait," the C.O. said.

"Not in Imperial Russian Air Force," the duke said.

"This is the Royal Flying Corps." The C.O. sent for the adjutant. Captain Brazier came with a well-thumbed copy of *King's Regulations*. The duke pointed out that King George V was a first cousin of Tsar Nicholas II because their mothers were sisters. What was more, the Tsarina Alexandra was also a cousin of King George, both being grandchildren of Queen Victoria. He himself, as Duke of Dolgorankov etcetera, was a cousin of the Tsar and therefore a part of the British royal family.

"Bully for you, lad," Brazier said. "But it earns you no special privileges here."

"*King's Regulations*," said the count, picking up the book and slamming it shut, "cannot regulate king."

The discussion went on for half an hour. Cleve-Cutler didn't want to impose his rank, but the Russians seemed ready to argue all day. The longer they talked, the more chopped and staccato their speech became. In the end, he offered a compromise: one servant each now, and a second each when it could be arranged.

They talked in Russian, long enough for the adjutant to clean and assemble his pipe.

"Is agreed," the duke said. He and the count stood, put their caps on, saluted, and left.

"God's bollocks!" the C.O. roared. "And that's positively my last word on the subject."

* * *

Ogilvy took the Russians into a hangar and showed them a Pup engine on a workbench.

"As you can see, it's a rotary," he said. "Now—"

"Is too small," the duke said.

"Well, rotary engines don't have to be big. A rotary doesn't work like a car engine, what we call an 'in-line'. An in-line engine is fixed to the frame and the cylinders go up and down and make the crankshaft go round and round, which turns the wheels. Well, forget all that. A rotary engine is totally different. The crankshaft is fixed to the front of the aeroplane. See?" He showed them a Pup with no engine. The crankshaft stuck out like the stub of a unicorn's horn. "Won't turn. *Can't* turn. What turns is the *engine*. The entire engine whizzes round the crankshaft. All nine cylinders."

They moved on to a Pup from which the cowlings had been removed to expose the engine. "The propeller is bolted to the engine. When the engine turns, the propeller turns. Turn it fast enough and the machine flies. See for yourself."

The duke cautiously pulled the propeller through a half-circle. The engine breathed as the pistons slid in their chambers, and one after the other the pushrods opened and shut the outlet valves.

"Exhaust comes out there," Ogilvy said. "Now look: petrol and air and oil arrive *here*, at the back, and they go in *there*, into the heart of the beast. Petrol and air mix and vaporise and the mixture gets into the cylinders by some technical magic that needn't bother you now. The oil does *not* mix, because it's castor oil, and it's needed to lubricate the bearings. The bearings are what make it possible for the engine to whizz round and round at a phenomenal rate. There's a magneto *here* that feeds the plug that makes the spark that fires the mixture that kick-starts the cylinder that . . . But you understand all that."

"No," the duke said.

"Which bit?"

"All."

Ogilvy took them through it all again, twice. No flicker of understanding showed. He decided to move on.

He went through the pre-flight routine. "Test the struts. The struts are all you've got to hold the top wing to the bottom wing. Test the wires." He plucked one and made it sing. "Count the wheels. Check the control surfaces." He reached into the cockpit and jiggled the joystick. "If your elevators go *down* when you want them *up*, then maybe some dozy rigger has got the cables crossed. Maybe he lost a screwdriver in your fuselage. Always check that things move correctly. It's your life. Not his. Understand?"

The duke nodded. "Now we fly?"

"No. Now we start the engine. Flying the Pup is easy. She flies like a bird. Making the engine do what you want is the problem. Treat it nicely and it'll be nice to you. Treat it badly and it'll sulk. Might even cut out. Just think: there's a Hun on your tail. You've been beastly to your engine. It stops. Silence. What do you hear next?"

"Nothing," the count said. "Dead."

For the first time, Ogilvy felt slightly encouraged. He led them through the start-up routine.

Pressure in the petrol tank pumped up to 2½ pounds per square inch. Check the magneto switch is off, the fuel lever closed, the air lever closed. Mechanic turns propeller and squirts a little fuel into each cylinder as its exhaust valve opens. Main petrol tap on. Mechanic gets prop into a comfortable position for swinging. Now the tricky bit: setting the air and petrol levers. They control the mixture going into the cylinders. Set the air lever first. The exact point on the quadrant depends on the weather. A cold day – make it halfway. Warm day, a bit less. Leave the fuel lever alone. Check the petrol tank pressure again. Too high and she'll never start, no matter what you do. Your mechanic says, "Switch on," and you switch on the magneto and say, "Contact," and he swings the prop. With luck she fires at once and goes straight up to maximum revs.

"And that's the point where you do absolutely nothing," Ogilvy said.

They nodded. "Is not difficult," the duke said.

"Is *very* difficult. It's very tempting to open the fuel lever when she fires. Fatal. Do that and you flood the engine and it dies. You must *wait*. Wait while the prime – that's the petrol that got squirted into the cylinders – the prime gets burned off. When you hear the engine start to cut, gently bring up the fuel lever, always *behind* the air lever. The fuel takes a second or two to reach the cylinders. Don't worry. The engine's spinning like a flywheel. You've got time. She'll pick up."

"Where is gun?" the duke asked.

Ogilvy thought he misheard. "Where is *what?*"

"Gun. For killing Hun."

Ogilvy shut one eye and looked up at the rafters. "Forget gun," he said. "First we'll attempt a start-up."

A Pup was waiting outside the hangar. Ogilvy told the duke to put on his helmet and goggles. A mechanic guided his boot into the footstep cut into the fuselage, and helped him into the seat. Ogilvy took the duke through the start-up sequence again. "Tighten your goggles," he said. "Really tight." The mechanic primed the cylinders. "Check fuel pressure," Ogilvy said. "And don't rush it." He walked away

"Switch on."

The duke switched on. "Is contact," he said.

The mechanic swung the prop and the engine exploded into life like a small bomb. Black smoke blasted out and was instantly hurled back. In seconds the propeller had reached more than a thousand revs a minute and the whole machine was rocking and shaking and threatening to rotate the opposite way. The noise was painful; brutal. Prop-wash hammered the grass flat. The Pup's wheels shuddered against their chocks. The duke's goggles got ripped off by the gale and vanished. And then the engine quit. A fragile silence returned, scared out of its wits.

"You rushed it," Ogilvy said.

The duke climbed down. His eyes were watering and he dabbed them with a silk handkerchief.

"I told you to wait for her to use up the prime," Ogilvy said. "You didn't wait."

The duke spoke in Russian to the count. They walked to the nose and examined what they could see of the engine. It stank of petrol. Petrol dribbled from an open exhaust valve.

Ogilvy had gone to look inside the cockpit. The switch was still on; he turned it off. The fuel lever was fully forward. "You drowned the poor bitch." He ducked underneath the wing. "Have you ever flown a rotary-engined scout?"

A mechanic was handing the duke his goggles. "Never," the count said.

"Never. I see. Look: you are pilots, aren't you?"

"Not pilots," the duke said. One lens of his goggles was broken; he poked his finger through it.

"Captains of aeroplane," the count explained. "In Imperial Russian Air Force, sergeant is pilot. Officer is observer. And captain."

"Oh, for Christ's sake," Ogilvy said. He kicked a wheel.

"Like navy," the duke said. "Captain does not steer ship."

"So you've only flown in two-seaters?"

"Russian two-seaters best in world."

"But our Pups are single-seaters."

The Russians looked at each other and shrugged. Ogilvy went in search of Cleve-Cutler.

* * *

Next day, the War Office sent an Avro 504 to Pepriac. The 504 was a stable, docile two-seater and the R.F.C.'s best trainer. With it came an instructor and two mechanics and a truckload of spares.

For the next two weeks the Russians took turns to cruise round and round the airfield while the elements of flying were hammered into them. When it was too wet to fly, they sat in a Pup and taxied it the length of the field. Airmen in shining oilskins turned it, and then ran alongside and kept the wingtips from scraping the ground as it was taxied to the other end. When it was too wet and windy for that, the Russians walked to the butts and fired a Vickers machine gun until it was so hot that rain sizzled on its barrel.

On the tenth day, the instructor telephoned Colonel Bliss. "I can't make them any better, sir," he said.

"Then they might as well solo," Bliss said. "Don't call me again unless they kill themselves."

Cleve-Cutler had the two oldest, most patched-up Pups in the squadron fuelled and ready. This was standard routine for new pilots; pointless wasting good equipment on novices. Everyone turned out to watch. Nothing morbid about that. All pilots took a professional interest in the ability of someone who might soon be flying in tight formation with them. The Hun was not the only killer in the sky.

The Russians survived their solo flights in Pups. The ambulance and the crash-wagon drove away. The pilots went back indoors.

"Congratulations," Ogilvy said.

"Where is gun?" Duke Nikolai asked.

"We take it off for solo flights, in case you hit your head on the butt."

"Hit Hun with gun. Not head."

"Come and have a drink."

By now they were popular in the mess. They brightened up the rainy days. The duke played Russian ragtime on the piano: some of his bars had more beats than others, some had fewer, but this only added to the novelty. He liked poker. He played fast, gambled with total unpredictability, and won and lost with equal relish. He favoured a Russian variation which he called blind poker: if a player never looked at his cards until the hand was finished, and he won, then the pot was doubled. "Rasputin taught me," he said.

"The Mad Monk?" said Simms. "Did you know him?"

"Godfather. Very hairy, very smelly. Had three balls." It wasn't easy to silence the mess, but Nikolai achieved it. "Is one franc to play." He shuffled the pack. "From Siberia. Empress Alexandra saw Rasputin, thought: ah! is special. Like Jesus Christ had no navel. Because of Virgin Birth."

Simms said, "I can't imagine that sort of carry-on in England. If our local vicar started playing fast and loose, the bishop would have him on the carpet, pronto."

"Look here," Munday said to Nikolai. "Are you sure you got that right, about Christ not having a navel?" Nikolai shrugged.

"Bishop has vicar on carpet?" Andrei said.

"I'm pretty sure I've seen a belly button in paintings," Munday said.

"On carpet." Andrei was still puzzled. "Is maybe penance?"

"It's a figure of speech," Hamilton said. He was awkward, and he understood little of the conversation, so he forced himself to say something or he would have felt completely excluded. "I met the Archbishop of Canterbury once," he added, daringly.

"That's nothing. I bumped into St Peter last month," said a Canadian called Snow. "He told me to come back later when he wasn't so busy." A few pilots chuckled. Hamilton grinned but didn't understand. Ten minutes later he worked it out, but that was too late to laugh, and besides he didn't think it was so very funny.

* * *

The rain cleared, the wind dropped. Plug Gerrish led "A" Flight on a Deep Offensive Patrol. They were at ten thousand feet and still climbing when they crossed the Lines. Black smudges of Archie sprang into being as suddenly as raindrops on a pavement, and as harmlessly; the German gunners were out of practice. From two miles high their gun-flashes were yellow pinpoints, as pretty as fireflies.

Gerrish kept climbing. There was no cloud cover and the air was well below freezing. Each pilot was layered with sweaters inside his sheepskin jacket. Mufflers sealed his neck, whale-grease coated his face. His head was tucked down, out of the blast of the slipstream, but by the time Gerrish had topped fifteen thousand the iron grip of the cold was inside boots and gloves and flying helmet. Apart from the eternal searching of the sky, there was nothing to do but sit and suffer. The Pup was little and light, less than twenty-seven feet in wingspan, less than twenty feet long. A restless pilot, always shifting his weight, would make his Pup sidle and twitch and lose place in the formation. Hamilton was restless.

He was bony because he was so young that he hadn't had time to put flesh on his bones. Hamilton was still a month under eighteen; he had lied about his age to get into the R.F.C. After the wastage of 1916 the army was not too fussy, especially if a chap was keen and tall. But he felt the cold in his lanky, unpadded body, and this made him restless. Gerrish had put him at the tail of the formation, where his twitching was less of a threat to others.

The flight was nudging twenty thousand feet and everyone was breathing hard, dragging in lungfuls of thin air. Gerrish liked height; it gave an unbeatable view of any Huns climbing to attack, and height could always be translated to speed. Hamilton did not like height, certainly not this height. His lungs could not work on the air he gave them. His heart made a painful, erratic thud. His mind sometimes drifted, and his brain was slow to carry out his orders. His Pup wallowed, because it too was unhappy in such thin air, and he knew he ought to make adjustments to the throttle. The decision was enormously difficult, and not helped by specks of light wandering across his eyes. He tried to see where they went. When he looked up, the rest of the flight was two hundred yards ahead. That didn't seem terribly important. The important thing was to get some sleep. That was essential. His hand slipped off the control column. Once he'd got some sleep he'd be better. His eyes closed. The Pup gently toppled sideways.

Nobody saw him leave. It was not the best Pup in the squadron (he was a new boy with an old aeroplane) and its long and vertical power-dive set up a shuddering vibration in the wings. The Pup became unbalanced and began to spin. It spun so hard that one wing cracked and blew away. None of the rest of the flight saw that either. By then Hamilton was three miles down and out of sight.

* * *

Harry Simms was a handsome lad. He wasn't a deep thinker; not even a shallow thinker; his life had been perfectly satisfactory, so he saw no need to question it.

His father had inherited twenty-six farms in Hampshire. The rents allowed him to raise a large family in comfort and to wander his fields with a butterfly net. He had passed on his charm and good looks to his children, and that (he believed) was as much as any reasonable person could expect of a man.

Harry came out best in the breeding stakes. His features were neat and clean-cut; his eyes were dark; his hair was a rich chestnut with enough of a curl to make women sick with envy; and he had the finest calves in the county. It was for his calves that he had joined the Dragoon Guards: their narrow trousers showed off the legs superbly. He kept the regimental uniform when, for a bet, he transferred to the Royal Flying Corps.

His instructors were surprised how quickly and how well he learned to fly. "He's too stupid to realize how hard it is," one of them said. This was only partly true. Harry Simms had spent much of his youth riding a horse or sailing a racing dinghy. Flying an aeroplane was simply sailing on the air with the help of some horsepower. The understanding between balance and speed and steering came naturally to him. Arithmetic did not. "Suppose you've got seventeen gallons of fuel," his instructor said. "She does twenty-three miles to the gallon. How far can you fly?"

"One of the mechanics is sure to know," Simms said confidently.

The day after Hamilton failed to return, a gale roared down from the North Sea. Simms was sitting in his hut at Pepriac, toasting crumpets at the stove, when Ogilvy came in. "Here's your new chum," Ogilvy said. "He's called Dash. Funny name. Not his fault, I suppose. Where did those come from?"

"Salisbury, sir. Martin's Bakery, in the High Street. My mother sent me them. Best crumpets in the world. Have one."

Ogilvy plucked the crumpet from the toasting fork. "Got any jam?"

"Strawberry. Made by my sister Lucy's own fair hand." Simms spooned jam onto the crumpet. "Any word from Wing, sir?"

"Stand-down until tomorrow noon. Don't get blotto."

Ogilvy went out and kicked the door shut behind him. Dash took off his cap. It left a sharp red line across his forehead, which was heavily freckled over white skin. His hair was as straight and as yellow as straw. His greatcoat seemed too big and too heavy for him. "Frightful weather," he said.

Simms forked another crumpet. "Wrong. Frightful weather is when Wing makes us fly. Now *this* weather is perfect. Even the generals dare not send us up in a storm, much as they would like to."

"Oh."

"What school did you go to?"

"Monmouth."

"Bad luck. I was at Winchester. And what regiment is that?"

"Hereford Yeomanry."

"Oh dear. Well, keep quiet about it and people will soon forget. We're a very democratic lot in the Corps. Except the servants, of course. Private Bugler looks after you and me. Bugler's a raging snob."

Dash unbuttoned his greatcoat and sat on his bed. He had spent most of the day travelling from the depot. He was stiff and hungry and tired, otherwise he wouldn't have asked: "What happened to the chap who was here before me?"

"Nothing special," Simms said. "Want half a crumpet?"

When they went to the mess, Dash stood awkwardly and silently and waited for Simms or Ogilvy to introduce him to somebody. They ignored him. Everyone ignored him. Conversation at dinner was all about people or places he didn't know or jokes he didn't understand. He went to bed early. He was fairly sure this was the bed of the man he was replacing, and very sure that the man was dead. What a rotten way to join a squadron: shunted across France, made to wait, ignored, treated like an unwanted parcel. The wind howled in the chimney.

Next day was no better. The gale brought rain, and flying was impossible. Simms played poker, endlessly. Dash read magazines and waited for someone to speak to him. Nobody did. When dusk fell he went to his hut and lay on his bed. He read a letter from his mother. She ended by asking him what he wanted for his nineteenth birthday. To his horror he found himself on the edge of tears. He wanted friendship, popularity, success, all the things he'd had at home and at school. A bit of fun would be nice, too. Simms came in. "For God's sake . . . The stove's gone out," he said. "Bloody arctic in here."

Dash shrugged. "I don't care."

"Well, I do. Bugler's a lazy tick. Someone's got to boot his backside, and you don't look very busy."

Resentment flared, and sent blood tingling to Dash's face. "Tell you what," he said. "Let's both kick Bugler's backside. Take it in turns. Bugler won't mind. He's not very busy either."

To his surprise, Simms laughed. "I've got a better idea," he said. "Let's go to Rosie's Bar and get slightly pickled."

"It's bucketing down."

"McWatters has a car. I expect Munday will come as well. He likes McWatters, God knows why, the man's all mouth and no brains. Still, he does have a car."

The only building that mattered in Pepriac village was an *estaminet* called *Roses d'Or*, known by British soldiers as Rosie's an 'ore and abbreviated to Rosie's. It had a large upstairs room where there was a separate bar for officers. "The prices are higher but the stench is less," Simms told Dash as they went in. "And the glasses are washed once a month, whether they need it or not." The ceiling was dun from the stain of smoke, the carpet was a uniform mud-colour, and pictures of pretty girls, torn from *La Vie Parisienne*, lined the walls. Someone had gone around with a cigarette and burned out all the eyes. From time to time the electric lights flickered as the diesel generator outside missed a beat.

The place was empty except for a bored gunnery captain, playing patience.

"Met a chap the other day," the gunner said, "who told me this Red Baron the newspapers keep writing about is actually a woman."

"He can't be a woman," McWatters said firmly.

"He's a sportsman, by all accounts," Simms said. "Chap I know got into a scrap with the Baron, ran out of ammo, thought his number was up, but the Baron just waved and toddled off home. Wouldn't shoot a sitting duck, you see."

"He can't be a woman 'cos women can't fly," McWatters said. "Their bodies are all wrong."

"I reckon your pal was just lucky," the gunner told Simms. "I reckon the Baron ran out of ammunition too."

Simms shook his head. "It's a matter of chivalry," he said, looking at the ceiling. "If you don't understand, I'm afraid I can't explain it."

"Basically, their plumbing lets them down," McWatters said, when there was sudden uproar nearby. It came from the kitchen: shouting, banging, a scream. Simms made a long arm and opened the door. A man scurried through, cowering away from an angry woman with a meat cleaver. He was safe: she would not enter the officers' bar. He sheltered behind Munday, who was taller by a head. She flashed her eyes and fired off a volley of French. *Voleur* sounded frequently. Also *fromage*.

"Thief," the gunner said. "She caught him pinching the Cheddar."

McWatters fluttered his fingers at her. "Restrain yourself, madam," he said. "The British Army will subdue this blackguard. Be about your duties." He clicked his fingers, and she turned and closed the door, quietly. Dash was hugely impressed. Masterly, he thought. *Head* masterly.

"Come out where we can see you," Simms ordered. "*Marchez-vous pronto*, chum." The man just blinked and gaped.

"Alley-oop!" McWatters said. He rapped on the table and pointed. The man scrambled up. "Stand easy."

He was small and slight and olive-skinned; but for the fuzz of stubble he might have been a boy. He wore a sort of uniform: not khaki, and not the soft blue of some French units; it was a biscuity-brown, faded in places almost to white. The fabric was as thin as pyjamas. The tunic gaped where buttons were missing and it showed stomach muscles clenched tight. Only his boots, big and heavy, looked military. They had no laces.

"The court will come to order," McWatters announced. He pounded on the table with a wine bottle. The man gave a little moan, so McWatters pounded some more. "Cheese-stealing," he declared, "is the stealing of cheese! And I put it to you, ladies and gentlemen—"

"What ladies? Where?" said Munday.

"The Red Baron is hiding in the cupboard," McWatters told him.

"I see no cupboard," Simms said.

"The prisoner is also charged with stealing a cupboard," McWatters said. "How do you plead, prisoner?"

They were all sprawled in chairs, looking up at him. He didn't know what to do with his hands. In the end he hid them in his armpits.

"I submit that the prisoner is mute of malice," Simms said.

"Dumb insolence," Munday said. "Let's flog him until he tells us where he hid the cupboard. And the baron. And the cheese."

"Which may be inside one another," Dash said. "In reverse order." McWatters scowled at him. "Or perhaps not," Dash said. McWatters grabbed Dash by the ear, and twisted. "If you don't damn well know, then stay out of the conversation," he said. Dash was shocked. His ear hurt. He massaged it a little, but that hurt too.

"I want more wine," Munday said. "Look: maybe he's a civilian. Nothing to do with us. What?"

"He's a spy," Simms said. "*Vous êtes un espion,*" he told him. "Don't deny it." The man was trembling.

"Maybe he's a genuine mute," Dash said. He had moved well away from McWatters.

"Well, why doesn't he say so?" Simms took the corkscrew and poked the man in the back of the leg. He gave a little yelp. "Not mute," Simms said.

"He's not a confounded spy," Munday scoffed. "Did you ever see anything that looked less like a spy?"

McWatters went into the kitchen.

"Well, what's to be done with him?" Munday said.

"Give him some cheese," the gunner said. "Poor devil looks half-starved."

McWatters came back with a carving knife. "I bet he's got the British Army's Order of Battle secreted about his swarthy body," he said. "Tattooed on his spleen, I shouldn't wonder." The man dropped to his knees and began gabbling. "You can do better than that, laddy," McWatters said. His knife slid inside the gaping tunic and chopped off the surviving buttons.

"Steady on, Mac," Munday said.

The tunic had fallen open. The hammering of the man's heartbeat made a fast flutter on his skin. McWatters touched it with the knifepoint. "Absolutely nothing to worry about, old man," he said. "I happen to be a fully qualified vet."

That was when the top of the man's trousers started to change colour. The biscuity-brown turned dark, almost black, and this blackness spread downwards and outwards.

"Rotten spy," McWatters said. "Not even house-trained." The man gasped. A bead of blood appeared on his chest.

Dash picked up his cap. "Too rich for my taste," he murmured.

McWatters sniffed the knifepoint, and then tasted it, delicately, with the tip of his tongue. "Not at all rich," he said. "A simple peasant flavour."

Dash left.

The rain had stopped. A damp half-moon was enough to show the way home, and he strode briskly, wanting to get far away from McWatters and his terrified victim. Bullying of a more painful kind had been commonplace at Dash's school; he had suffered from it, he had inflicted it, too. But that was then and this was now. This was war, and Dash knew that there was a huge difference between mere bullying and going into battle. War was death or glory; everyone said so. All the same, he wondered how he would behave if he came across a crippled Hun machine, miles high, pouring smoke, guns jammed. Would he do his patriotic duty and kill the pilot? Probably. But where was the glory in that?

He walked even faster to leave this problem behind, and came across a lorry that was going nowhere. The bonnet was up and he could dimly see the driver heaving on the starting handle.

The effort seemed half-hearted. The engine did not respond.

"Trouble?" Dash said.

"Brute force," she said wearily. "That's the only thing this beast under-stands."

"I see." What he could see was that she was in uniform and pretty. Perhaps very pretty. Smears of oil made it hard to say. "Well, I got top marks in brute force at Sunday school. May I try?"

"Keep your thumbs out of the way or she'll rip them off. She kicks like a pack of mules."

He took a deep breath and heaved on the handle. It was like stirring concrete. "I suppose she is in neutral?" he said.

"Yes. The oil's too thick. It's this awful weather."

He braced his legs and tried again. His fingers began to ache. At the fifth attempt the engine coughed and the handle jumped. It was a false dawn, but it encouraged him. At the twelfth attempt the engine fired and the exhaust backfired, and they cheered. Too soon. It died. But on the sixteenth swing it gave in and roared like the beast it was. She fiddled with the controls and tamed it.

"You're an absolute poppet," she said. "I've been swinging her for twenty minutes. You deserve a medal. Who are you?"

"Charles Dash, Royal Flying Corps."

"Sarah Beverley, First Aid Nursing Yeomanry, commonly called Fanny. The least I can do is give you a ride for being such a poppet."

"I disagree. The very least you can do is give me a ride and let me take you out to dinner quite soon." He surprised himself by his own mastery of language.

"Dinner! Well . . . What a poppet you are." In the headlights she was more than pretty. "And I'm such a wreck. You'd better jump in before she changes her stupid mind again."

Sarah Beverley dropped him at the gates to the airfield. He kissed her hand. She called him a poppet. That made four poppets. He knew where she lived, they were definitely going to dine together, she was an absolute corker. Life was looking up, and about bloody time, too.

* * *

The weather cleared, and Ogilvy got the Russians into the air again. They could fly, but not well. They bullied the Pup. They flew too fast, especially when they came in to land. Ogilvy stood on the airfield and fired red flares into the sky to signal that they should make another circuit. So many flares went up that an infantry regiment camped nearby sent a man on a motorbike to ask if the squadron needed help.

Finally Duke Nikolai made a half-decent approach and touched down. Ogilvy, watching through binoculars, saw him take his gloves off and rub his eyes while his Pup's wheels were racing and her tail was still high. Ogilvy felt ill. It was a breezy day. A gust could easily blow the tail sideways. Then the wheels would try to go one way while the machine went another and in the blink of an eye the whole kit and caboodle would be performing somersaults on its wingtips.

Luckily the breeze had other plans. Nikolai climbed down, put his cap on and saluted. He looked pleased with himself. "The count is less fast than me," he said. Andrei's Pup was still circling.

"It's not a damned race," Ogilvy said. "Carry on like this and I'll end up in front of a court of inquiry, lousy with generals, all wanting to know why I allowed the Tsar's relatives to break their necks. Land slowly, can't you?"

"Is nice little machine. In Russia we have much bigger machines."

"So you've told me. Now will you for God's sake do what I tell you?"

"These generals," the duke said, "on court of inquiry. Tell me names, I have English cousins in your War Office, dukes, only small dukes but—"

"Shut up." Ogilvy shoved the Russian in the chest and sent him staggering. "Shut up! Until you learn to land properly I will not permit you to go on patrol. Hear me? Now go up and do it properly."

Nikolai was blinking as if he had dust in his eyes. "This is serious matter."

"Life and death."

"I am cousin of Nicholas sent by God to be Tsar of Holy Russia. When you strike me, you strike face of God."

"Good," Ogilvy said. "Maybe God will wake up and decide which side he's on. He hasn't been doing your cousin any favours lately, has he?"

The duke was shocked. Ogilvy realized he had gone too far. He walked away. Andrei was coming in to land, far too fast. Ogilvy rammed another cartridge into the pistol and fired a red flare. Andrei flew past, waving cheerily.

* * *

Major Cleve-Cutler sat in his office, watching Captain Dando make his report on the health of the squadron.

Since the surgeons had reassembled his face, it was hard to tell what the C.O. was thinking, but Dando knew he wasn't listening because his eyes had gone out of focus. "No sickness among the mechanics," Dando said. "The man with influenza has recovered."

The C.O. grunted.

"All's well in the cookhouse, apart from a spot of botulism, maybe a touch of anthrax. High mortality rate, of course, but then so was the Somme."

The C.O. grunted.

"Look," Dando said, "if you're not listening, I might as well go and lance a boil on somebody's backside."

Cleve-Cutler got up and wandered away from his desk. He stared at the floor. "Rats," he said. "Hear them?"

Dando held his breath and heard a faint squeaking. "No," he said.

"Little bastards couldn't stand the shelling at the Somme. Ran like mad. Didn't stop until they got here." He stamped, and raised straight lines of dust.

"What the British Army calls a planned withdrawal to a superior defensive position," Dando said. "I remember doing it at Mons in 1914."

The C.O. was kneeling. He pulled a champagne cork from a knothole, put his mouth to the hole and shouted: "Go away!"

"Waste of time," Dando said. "You know what French rats are like, they pretend they don't understand."

"This lot are Huns. I can speak Hun." Cleve-Cutler got up and took a

41

revolver from a desk drawer and was back at the knothole when Dando said, "Think of the smell if you hit. Think of the shame if you miss."

The C.O. squatted on his heels while he thought of that. Then he hammered on the floor with the butt. "You haven't heard the last of this!" he shouted into the hole.

"Exactly what I told General von Kluck at Mons," Dando said. "And that really put the wind up him, that did."

The C.O. went back to his chair. "Mons," he said. He scratched the back of his head with the revolver sight. "What a lot has happened since then."

"No, it hasn't," Dando said. "The same stupid thing has happened again and again and again."

"Buzz off, doctor."

"This war's going to run longer than Chu-Chin-Chow."

As Dando got his papers together, there was a knock and the adjutant came in. With him was a young man who had to duck to get through the door. "Lieutenant Morkel, sir," he said. "From South Africa. Replacement pilot." Morkel saluted.

"My goodness," Cleve-Cutler said. "A replacement and a half." Morkel was as tall as Brazier. He had a bushy blond moustache and intensely blue eyes. A fading tan made the most of teeth that were startlingly white. "Welcome to Hornet Squadron," the C.O. said. "What can I tell you about us? Let me see . . ." Dando cleaned his fingernails; he had heard this speech before, many times. "If you wish to play ping-pong, there is ping-pong to be played," the C.O. said. "If you wish to fly an aeroplane, we have the incomparable Pup. And if you wish to kill Huns, there is an endless supply of eager victims."

"When can I start, sir?"

Cleve-Cutler looked at his watch. "If it doesn't rain, you can start in two hours. You're in 'A' Flight. Captain Gerrish is your commander. The adjutant will introduce you. Good luck."

Morkel saluted and the adjutant took him away.

"What are you hanging around for?" the C.O. asked.

"When did you begin talking to the rats?" Dando said.

"We're all rats," Cleve-Cutler said. "We all scuttle and squeak and breed in the dark. Try to understand that, doctor, and don't ask such bloody silly questions. Sometimes I think you're starting to lose your nerve. How old are you?"

"Thirty-one."

Cleve-Cutler nodded wisely. "Ga-ga," he said.

* * *

Either from winding the starting handle, or from sitting in Sarah Beverley's lorry, Charles Dash had got stains on his best uniform. He had also lost his hat: probably left in the cab. His servant, Private Bugler, was more concerned with removing the stains.

"Never saw nothin' like this before," he complained. He sniffed cautiously. "Smells like 'orse but looks like blood. Was you in contact with a bleedin' 'orse, sir?"

"Just do the best you can."

"That's easy for you to say, sir, but different stains need treatin' different."

Dash gave him five francs.

"You can't go around without an 'at," Bugler said. "Go an' see Sergeant Lacey in the orderly room."

Lacey was reading a letter. "My aunt in County Cork is in despair," he told Dash. "She thinks the entire British war cabinet should be shot for treason. Without trial."

"Good Lord." Dash was taken aback; sergeants didn't usually talk like this. "Why?"

"She feels they blundered by exposing the Zimmermann telegram." Lacey saw Dash frown. "German Secretary of State," Lacey said. "Sent a telegram. Germany offered to help Mexico invade the U.S.A. and recapture New Mexico."

"Yes? Pretty dotty idea."

"My aunt believes the British government should have secretly encouraged the plan. We should have offered to ship the entire German Army to Mexico, where it would sink in a bog of dago intrigue, corruption and folly. Her words."

Dash felt that he was being patronized. "Sergeant," he said, leaning a little on the word, "I need a hat. Private Bugler seems to think . . ."

Lacey pulled open a filing cabinet. It was full of officers' caps, representing Guards and county regiments, gunners and engineers, Australian and Canadian units. There was even a bright Glengarry. "Nothing here from the Herefordshire Yeomanry," he said. "But try this one: North Somerset Yeomanry. Somerset's quite adjacent, isn't it?"

Dash tried it on. "Too tight," he said.

"That's odd," Lacey said. "Jessop complained that it was too loose." He took back the cap and removed a strip of folded blotting paper from inside the lining. Dash tried again. Perfect fit. "Who was Jessop?" he asked.

Lacey shut the filing cabinet.

"I don't suppose it matters," Dash said. He took off the cap and looked at the name written inside. It was J.B.K. Rickman-Ellis. "Jolly handy, these spares," he said. "In case a chap loses his hat."

Lacey nodded.

"Any charge," Dash said, "put it on my mess bill."

"Compliments of the management," Lacey said. "However . . . may I ask: does anyone in your family manufacture or distribute cigars, whisky or gramophone records?"

"No."

"*Quel dommage.*" Lacey turned away.

"There's a cousin in Worcester," Dash said. "His factory makes pork sausages."

"Does it, indeed? Here in France your genuine pork sausage is a currency worth more than diamonds. Kindly ask him to send you ten pounds in weight, urgently."

"Alright. Look: where's the adjutant?" Dash didn't want the adjutant; he just wanted to change the conversation from hats and sausages to something more military.

"Captain Brazier is drilling the burial squad," Lacey said. "He feels their slow march is not up to snuff. Nor is their quick march."

"Who is being buried?"

"Nobody," Lacey said, "but the adjutant never lets a little thing like that stand in his way."

EARTHQUAKE STRENGTH 2:

Tremors felt by persons at rest.

The rain held off, and Plug Gerrish took Morkel on patrol, together with Lieutenant Heeley.

Heeley was a veteran of two months. He had fired at the enemy perhaps a dozen times, and claimed a share in one Fokker which "A" Flight might have destroyed, or which might have disintegrated under the strain of violent combat manoeuvres. Or a bit of both. At any rate, Heeley had seen his bullets raise a string of rosettes in the fabric of the Fokker, and then one of its wings had crumpled, so that was good enough. He was nineteen and he thought it unlikely that he would reach twenty, but he kept such thoughts to himself. His sole ambition was to score one kill that was undeniably his alone. Sometimes he wondered why this killing should matter so much to him, a chorister at Salisbury cathedral until he joined the army shortly before the army would have claimed him anyway. But he had other discoveries to wonder at, whisky and women being the most exciting, and so he took his life a day at a time. That, after all, was how death operated, and death was doing very well.

There was a delay while a search was made for flying gear that was big enough for Morkel.

"I have three rules," Gerrish told him. "The first is: stay in formation. So are the other two. If you lag behind I won't come back for you, and the odds are you won't come back at all. The Huns love stragglers. How many hours have you done solo?"

"Fifteen, sir."

"On Pups?"

"Eight."

"Air-firing?"

"None, sir. It was foggy, so—"

"I don't care. It doesn't matter." Gerrish went off to select an old and unloved Pup for Morkel to fly.

"Don't mind Plug," Heeley said. "He was born with a rat up his arse. You're from South Africa?"

"Yes. The Transvaal, if that means anything."

"I must say it's jolly decent of you to come all this way to rally round the old country."

"I have shot every kind of animal that exists in Africa. It is time to shoot some Germans."

Heeley found that amusing. Morkel smiled gently.

"Is that what you told them," Heeley said, "when you applied to join the R.F.C.?"

"No. I said I had played a lot of rugby football. They seemed impressed."

"The Kaiser was an absolute duffer at rugger," Heeley said. "Poor devil hasn't got a hope, has he?"

Three sweaters, a sheepskin flying coat, fur-lined gauntlets and thigh-length flying boots made Morkel look as big as a gorilla. The Pup creaked and groaned when he got into the cockpit. Gerrish told him to take off, and stood well clear to watch. Morkel used up almost all the runway just getting off the ground. When he had done two circuits without crashing, Gerrish and Heeley followed him into the air. The three Pups droned eastward.

Cleve-Cutler had watched, too. He felt grateful to Morkel for not crashing on or near the airfield. A pilot who made a nonsense of his take-off was like a Guardsman who fainted on parade. The C.O. went back to his office and found Duke Nikolai waiting at the door.

The Russian saluted. He said nothing until they were inside. His face was as stiff as a statue. He read from a piece of paper. "It gives me pain to report," he said, "that Captain Ogilvy has insulted His Imperial Majesty, the Tsar of Holy Russia, to whom I have sworn allegiance."

"Something Spud said? A slip of the tongue, no doubt. A misinterpretation."

"He struck me. I am Tsar's representative. Therefore struck Tsar."

"Bit far-fetched, that."

"Struck me. I am Tsar's—"

"Yes, yes." Cleve-Cutler knew the Russian's powers of repetition. "Point taken."

Nikolai relaxed slightly. "We agree. Tsar demands satisfaction."

"In Russia, perhaps. Here, in the British Army, duelling is illegal."

"Honour has no boundaries, major. I know my duty. I shall do it." He glanced modestly at his shining boots. "Not for first time."

"Duelling is illegal in the British Army. And Captain Ogilvy has sworn an oath of loyalty to *his* monarch. If he duels with you, he breaks his oath."

"I kill him quickly. Then he avoids disgrace."

Suddenly Cleve-Cutler was tired of the whole stupid argument. "You can't have a duel without seconds, can you?" Nikolai nodded. "Well, I'll find a second for Spud. I'll also decide the time and place. *And* the weapons. It may take rather a long time. I'm frightfully busy. The war, you know."

Nikolai saluted.

"Where did he hit you? I don't see any sign of damage."

"Honour was damaged," Nikolai said.

"Honour, eh?" Cleve-Cutler opened the door for him. "Fragile stuff. They don't make it like they used to, do they?" he said.

*   *   *

Morkel had grown up on the *veldt*, where space was vast and every day a friendly sun rose in an optimistic sky, and nothing was impossible. He had come to Europe because the war wouldn't last for ever. Now was the time to seize its challenges.

When the English taught him to fly, he went no higher than two thousand feet, where it was still possible to make out teams of horses drawing ploughs across fields, and smoke from chimneys, and sheep scattered like snowflakes. Now Plug Gerrish took the patrol up to twelve thousand feet, into a wilderness of cloud. Sky and earth were lost. The air was frigid. In Africa and in England, Morkel's big strong body had performed everything he asked of it, but now he discovered that it was not made for a Pup cockpit at twelve thousand. The windscreen was tiny; his head stuck out in the arctic battering of the airstream until it ached with cold and he beat his fist against his flying helmet. After an hour blundering through the gloom of canyons in the cloud, searching tattered gaps that changed shape as he looked, Morkel was lost. He had no idea where they were, or what they were looking for, or what they would do if they found it. Staying in formation was a waking nightmare.

He was constantly fiddling with the throttle-adjustment, which meant looking down, and when he looked up the aircraft was wandering, either sliding towards a collision or drifting into a hill of cloud. For the first time in his life, his size and strength were not enough; the effort of flying sapped his brain and the battering cold had no pity. Despair began to win, and the enemy did the rest.

Gerrish, his head rotating like an owl, saw them high above and behind the Pups: a cluster of biplanes, falling fast. He fired a couple of rounds to alert his wingman and wheeled the formation to face the attack. Morkel, head down, heard nothing, saw nothing. He looked up and was alone. For a long moment he was too weary to be surprised. White-hot eruptions of pain in his right leg changed all that. Bullets had ripped his calf, smashed his shin and his ankle. He collapsed onto the joystick and the Pup dived, which saved it from the guns of the next Huns. By the time they turned, Morkel was circling inside a large cloud, not because he wanted to but because his right foot was jammed on the rudder pedal. By gripping the leg with both hands he dragged the foot free. When the Pup flew into clear air he got the machine level and he pointed it at a glimpse of sunshine, which he knew must be west. Morkel was a better pilot than he knew. He was also more badly wounded than he knew. A bullet had nicked an artery. Blood pulsed into his flying boot until it leaked out of the bullet holes. Morkel flew the Pup until he fainted. After that it flew itself into the ground, which happened to be a flooded shell-hole. Nothing special about that. There were a million shell-holes, and all flooded.

* * *

The adjutant waited three hours before he told Wing, and Wing ordered the standard telegram to the next of kin, regretting to inform and so on. Morkel had not had time to unpack, and his batman was an old sweat who always left the bags on the bed until he saw the new pilot back from patrol.

Heeley was lying on the other bed, chewing on an unlit pipe, when Brazier arrived with a soldier to collect the bags. "You didn't lend him anything?" the adjutant said. "Toothbrush, pyjamas, money?"

"No."

"He didn't give a letter to post? You know what I mean."

Heeley made a sour face. "Rotten job you've got, Uncle."

"You don't give a tinker's cuss about my job." The adjutant had opened Morkel's valise and was looking for a diary or pornographic pictures or a military secret: anything the family should not see. He tossed a pair of goggles to Heeley. "Those won't be any use to anyone in South Africa." He shut the valise and gave it to the soldier and they went out.

Heeley put the goggles on and looked at the other bed. Morkel had been its third occupant in eight weeks. Flying was good fun; Heeley liked every minute of it. Coming back to earth wasn't so enjoyable.

Still, these were jolly good goggles. Heeley cheered up. Time for drinks, dinner, some poker, a bit of a singsong, and clean sheets in a warm, dry bed, which was more than the Poor Bloody Infantry got in their squalid trenches.

* * *

The weather stayed dry but very cold. All three flights went on Deep Offensive Patrols. Nobody died. If a flight was not on patrol, it went up and practised close-formation flying and manoeuvring by hand signal and how to attack in arrowhead or echelon or line-astern. One Pup lost a piston. Another overheated because of an oil leak. Both got down safely.

"A quiet day," the adjutant said aloud as he wrote up the squadron diary. "It seems the Hun fliers have no stomach for the fight."

"Possibly," Lacey said. "But on the whole I feel they are more likely to be on leave in Frankfurt."

"All of them? In Frankfurt? What on earth for?"

"For the opera. Paul Hindemith is conducting a new production of *Der Rosenkavalier*. The reviews have been ecstatic."

The adjutant leaned back and linked his muscular hands behind his heavy head. "Ecstatic . . . I don't believe I've ever met an ecstatic Hun. Not much to laugh about when you've got half a yard of bayonet through your giblets."

"That reminds me. Mr Dash's cousin sent him a large box of best Worcester pork sausages. We are lucky that the sergeant at the fuel depot has a passion for English sausages. He gave me five hundred gallons of diesel. The generator will carry on making electricity for another month."

"If I got you a Hun, sergeant, a nice fat Hun, would you bayonet him?"

"Only if he had tickets to *Rosenkavalier*, sir."

Brazier made a sour face. "You're not much of a fighting man, are you? Sausages and diesel, instead of blood and guts."

"True. But then, you're not shaving by candlelight, sir."

They sat and stared at each other across the adjutant's desk.

"This war has ruined the army," Brazier growled. "I should be at the Front, not listening to cocky little pricks like you."

"Well, every prick serves its purpose," Lacey said mildly. "Otherwise none of us would be in this world. Not even you, sir."

"*What?*" Brazier flung the squadron diary at him, and missed. Lacey was out of the office before Brazier could untangle his legs. Lacey kept going. His assistant, a corporal clerk, grabbed his cap and followed. "You mustn't say things like that, sarge," he said. "Honest."

"It was irresistible. Besides, I know where to get soft toilet paper for the officers' mess, and Cleve-Cutler has piles, and Brazier knows it."

"Strewth," the corporal said.

"He has the bayonet," Lacey said, "but I have the bog-roll. The way to the C.O.'s heart is through his sphincter."

* * *

Next day the sun came up as dull as a counterfeit sovereign. It was only ground mist that dulled it, and half of "A" Flight took off to make the first patrol. The other half followed after breakfast. Now the sky was blue as a lagoon. The barometer was high and steady. It was a good day for a spot of high-flying slaughter. By noon, "B" and "C" Flights had done their stint and nobody had fired a shot except to keep the guns from freezing. It was odd. Even the German Archie lost interest after a few inaccurate rounds. The squadron sat down to lunch with nothing to boast or bitch about.

"What do we eat today?" the count asked a servant.

"Brown soup, sir. Mutton. Steamed treacle pudding."

"Oh." His shoulders slumped. "Brown and brown and brown. All English cooking is brown."

"Steady on," Munday said. "Burnt toast isn't brown. And what about porridge?"

"Porridge is the revenge of the Scots upon the English," McWatters said.

"Come to Russia," the duke said. "We give you soused herring, smoked eel, quails' eggs with paprika, red cabbage, white cabbage, green cabbage, baby venison stuffed with . . . stuffed with . . ." He looked at the count.

"Russian stuffing. Impossible to describe."

Soup was served. "Also vodka," the duke said. "Russia has three hundred different kinds of vodka."

"Which is best?" Simms asked.

"All are best."

McWatters sniffed. "I bet the average serf doesn't eat too many five-course meals washed down with buckets of vodka."

"No serfs in Russia," the count said. "Serfs abolished. All free."

McWatters was taken aback. "Free," he said. "You mean free as in a democracy?"

"Not in Russia," the duke said firmly.

"If Russian people need democracy, Tsar will decide," the count said.

"Don't need," the duke said. "Tsar told me."

Cleve-Cutler had coffee in the anteroom with Spud Ogilvy and the duke.

"This duel has to be settled," he said. "I have decided on the time, the place and the weapons." Ogilvy frowned at the sugarbowl. The duke was impassive. "Your weapons will be Sopwith Pups. The place will be the sky. The time will be thirty minutes from now."

The duke did his best to be calm. He nodded, and he stirred his coffee until he made it overflow, and then he abandoned it. "Very well," he said. He put his hat on and saluted and went away.

"I do wish he'd stop doing that," the C.O. said.

"What d'you want me to do?" Ogilvy asked. "Apart from not kill him."

"Look, Spud. Wing says Brigade says the politicos say we've got to keep the Russians happy. So he must have a duel to save the precious honour of his Tsar. This is the best I can think of. Put on a show. Maybe he'll settle for a draw."

"Maybe he'll die of fright."

Cleve-Cutler finished his coffee, and drank the duke's coffee too "I wish I'd never taken this bloody silly job," he said. "The war's alright, but the people are impossible."

*　*　*

The two Pups took off, side by side. At two hundred feet, the duke swung away and came around in a full circle, seeking an early chance to attack. Ogilvy was not there. He was climbing hard. A job-lot of broken cloud was drifting in from the northwest, and Ogilvy wanted to take advantage of it. The duke climbed after him, but he lacked Ogilvy's cleverness at the controls and he was always lagging behind.

The rest of the squadron was out, watching. "This is just makebelieve," the C.O. told the adjutant.

"What if a make-believe bullet kills someone stone dead?"

"Dunno. What do *King's Regulations* say?"

"They call it sacrilege. It comes somewhere between sabotage and sodomy."

"Very uncomfortable." The C.O. aimed his binoculars at the sky. "Hullo, action."

The pop-pop-pop of a Vickers sounded faintly.

"That's the Russian," Gerrish said. "Miles out of range. No patience."

Ogilvy had levelled out at four thousand feet. He throttled back and flew a wide circle to let the duke catch up. He could see the man's head moving as he looked up and down, fussing and fiddling with the controls, peering through the telescopic Aldis sight, ducking again to search for more power. Ogilvy reversed his turn and offered his Pup as a distant target. The Russian fired, made no allowance for bullet-drop or deflection or the price of apples, and missed by a street.

Ogilvy shook his head. He persisted with his turn until he was pointing straight at the other Pup. The closing speed was about two hundred miles an hour.

In only a few seconds the duke saw Ogilvy's machine charging and enlarging, and almost upon him. Instinctively he raised his arm in defence, and saw the underside of wings and fuselage flash above his head. Ogilvy knew the clearance was a comfortable ten feet; but the duke was startled by the extra roar, and felt his aeroplane wallow in the wash, and was amazed that they had not collided. He dragged his Pup around in the hope of getting a snap shot as Ogilvy went away. The sky was empty. Again.

It could not be true, and it wasn't. As Ogilvy hurdled the duke, he tipped the Pup onto its wingtips and let it fall away. He lost five hundred feet but gained such impetus that when he pulled out and climbed again, the little fighter went up as if it were weightless. Within a minute he was cruising along, two lengths behind the other Pup and slightly below it. The machines wandered about the sky, one trailing the other like a faithful dog.

On the ground, this earned applause.

"Why?" the count asked.

"Captain Ogilvy is sitting in a blind spot," Gerrish said. "The duke can't see him."

"That is not a duel."

"Be thankful. Spud could have blown his head off a dozen times."

The duke dipped his wings to help him search left and right. He was puzzled, and he felt cheated, and also mocked by some childish English joke, sending him up here for no purpose. Then a red signal flare fizzed past him and soared away. It came from behind. He twisted in his seat and saw nothing. Ogilvy reloaded the flare pistol. This time the streak of red was even closer. The duke swore, and dived away. Ogilvy followed.

For ten minutes, Ogilvy chased him all over the sky. No matter how abruptly the Russian skidded or rolled or plunged, Ogilvy was always there. It was a circus act. People on the ground were laughing. The duke looked up when a shadow darkened his cockpit, and saw Ogilvy's Pup exactly above him. He could have hit the wheels with a billiard cue. This was a mockery. And then clouds came and saved him.

His Pup charged into the biggest cloud and he relished the blessed grey oblivion. He came out, one wing down, and made for the next nearest hiding place, and the next. When he popped out, nose up, engine straining, he was into dazzling sunshine.

No sign of the frightful Ogilvy. Excellent.

He cruised around for a couple of minutes. The duel had turned into a farce. So that was a second insult to add to the first.

The clouds parted and he looked down and saw Ogilvy's Pup a thousand feet below. Perhaps the duel wasn't over yet. He shoved the stick forward and said a short Russian prayer. It was time for God, who blessed the Tsar, to do a little something now for the Tsar's cousin.

* * *

Ogilvy landed in a break between the showers.

"I didn't kill him, sir," he said, "but he's not back, so I don't know what's happened." They were in the C.O.'s office, drinking coffee.

"You put up a hell of a show, Spud. You had him by the throat, and he must know that. Honour is satisfied, for God's sake."

"Honour may be. What about pride?"

Cleve-Cutler grunted, and went to the window. Clouds the colour of coal dust were gathering. "Winter isn't good for aeroplanes," he said. "Mildew in the canvas, rot in the spars, rust in the cables . . ." The telephone rang.

He answered it, and said, "Yes, he's one of mine." He listened some more, and said, "I'm sorry he bothered you. Can you put him on the line?" After that he did a lot of listening and grunting. "I see . . . Well, refuel and return. That's all." He hung up.

"Where is he?" Ogilvy asked.

"Deux-Églises. 42 Squadron. Says he got lost and landed there to ask the way. Also says he shot you down. Profound apologies etcetera. God save the Tsar and all his relations." Cleve-Cutler stooped and pulled the cork from a knothole in the floor. "Stand to attention down there!" he shouted. He replaced the cork.

"I'm fairly sure nobody shot me down," Ogilvy said.

"Oh, I think they did, Spud. Fortunately, he didn't see you crash. Too much cloud. Brilliant flying got you home, albeit your machine was holed like a colander."

"*Albeit?*" Ogilvy cocked his head. "Is that what you just said?"

"Yes, dammit. Albeit. I want this idiocy ended, even if I have to talk like a tombstone to do it. Now, we need a bust-up Pup."

"Well, there's what's left of Stone-Franklin's bus, after he tried to fly through a tree."

They found the wreckage in the back of a hangar and had it dragged out. When the duke landed, in gathering dusk, Cleve-Cutler and Ogilvy were examining it, with a sergeant mechanic. The duke came over and saluted. He looked from the wreck to his flight commander and back again. His eyes were wider than usual. Other than that, his face gave nothing away.

"A good landing is one you can walk away from," the C.O. said. "Right, sergeant?"

"Right, sir."

Ogilvy prodded a piece of tail-fin with his foot. "Can't you salvage anything, sergeant?"

"Afraid not, sir."

"Oh, well. You know best. Carry on." The sergeant saluted, and his boots crunched on the wet tarmac.

Cleve-Cutler and Ogilvy strolled slowly around the wrecked Pup.

"Brilliant flying," the C.O. said, "albeit for the loss of a much-loved aeroplane."

"Thank you, sir."

Cleve-Cutler turned to the duke. "Now then, lieutenant. Have you anything to report?"

"I regret—"

"Wait a moment," Ogilvy said. "Things may be different in Russia, but here in the Royal Flying Corps, when an affair of honour is settled, we never discuss it. Never."

"I have nothing to report, sir."

When he had gone, Ogilvy said: "Presumably he took a pot at someone, thinking it was me. And missed."

"He'd better do better than that when you take him over the Lines."

They strolled back to the mess. The first flakes of snow speckled their uniforms. By nightfall the field was white.

EARTHQUAKE STRENGTH 3:

Hanging objects swing.

Snow fell, and ended flying. Cleve-Cutler searched for ways to keep the pilots fit. The adjutant suggested bayonet-fighting. "The bayonet is on the rifle," he explained. "There are certain moves and countermoves. It's very similar to sword-fighting." A space was cleared in a hangar, and within the hour two men were being stitched up by Dando. Cleve-Cutler cancelled bayonet-fighting.

Brazier retired to the orderly room in disgust.

"They were only puncture-wounds," he said.

"Rather like the Crucifixion," Lacey said. "And what a fuss people made about *that*."

"You haven't the slightest idea of physical pain, sergeant. One of these days I might perforate your hide with a bayonet, just to educate you."

"Yes, sir. You're strangely interested in mutilating the other ranks, aren't you? Were you whipped a good deal when you were a child?"

"I was never a child, sergeant. I was issued by the War Office in 1891. You can find the military specifications engraved upon my left buttock." He put his glasses on and stared at Lacey. Lacey went away to brew some tea.

Ration wagons trundled up and down the lanes leading to the Front, but otherwise the war virtually stopped. Without aeroplanes and balloons to spot for them, the guns were blind and silent. Brazier hired fifty Chinese labourers to dig a runway across the aerodrome, but snow kept falling. They never gave up, but they made no progress either. The temperature kept falling, too. The ground was iron-hard; trenches were difficult to repair and impossible to dig. "God's a conchie," McWatters said to the padre. "He's decided He's against this war on religious principle, and He's gone off to play with the angels."

"Too deep for me, old man. Very dodgy area, religious principle. Look: which of these cinema films d'you think the chaps would enjoy?"

McWatters glanced at the list. "Get westerns. William S. Hart, Douglas Fairbanks. Lots of violence."

"There's a rather stirring one about the Battle of the Somme. Don't you think . . ."

"Not violent enough."

"Surely—"

"Get westerns. Revolvers and brawls and bars getting bust-up, that's the ticket. Just like a good mess-night party."

"I suppose you're right."

Next day the padre had to report that the mobile cinema was stuck in a snowdrift, miles away, near a place called Beauquesne. Lieutenant Dash immediately volunteered to go and unstick it. Moving pictures didn't excite him, but the name Beauquesne did. It was where Sarah Beverley, of the First Aid Nursing Yeomanry, lived. Ogilvy asked how he proposed to get there, since he certainly wasn't taking any squadron transport. Dash said he would ride; at home, in Herefordshire, he'd ridden all sorts of horses. "I'm glad you're good at something," Ogilvy said, "since you're obviously a tenth-rate pilot." The adjutant phoned a nearby artillery unit and borrowed a horse. It was a huge, shaggy beast, accustomed to hauling field guns over rough country at the hard canter, and it had a mouth like a steel trap.

Sergeant Lacey fed it carrots while Dash got into the saddle and bunched the reins. "Should you come upon a reputable *épicerie*," Lacey said, "the mess is in need of a good Dijon mustard." Brazier slapped the animal's rump and it set off at a sedate trot that kicked up clods of snow like broken plates.

The name on the bridle was Daisy. It didn't suit. The horse was entirely black, and as broad as a sofa; Dash's knees were far apart. Because one eye was milky, the horse led with the other eye, and this caused it to trot obliquely, aiming to the left while moving to the right. Daisy was a gun-carriage horse. It disliked the saddle and it disliked Dash. After half a mile it locked its front legs and tossed him as easily as a farmhand tossing a sheaf of wheat.

He landed in a snowdrift. Daisy trotted on. By the time Dash got his breath back, cleared the snow from his ears and found his hat, Daisy was a small black shape, growing steadily smaller. He chased hard. Daisy would not stop for him. He ran alongside and managed to vault into the saddle. His breeches were slippery with snow. Daisy threw him twice more in the next hundred yards. The second time, there was something hard in the drift: ice or stone or wood; and he crawled out bruised and cursing, ready to quit; but an oncoming ration wagon had seen his trouble and a soldier had jumped off and captured the brute.

They waited for him to limp up to them.

"Bit frisky, is she, sir?" said the sergeant in charge.

"Just a trifle."

"Your nose is bleedin', sir. Rub some snow on it."

Dash tried to laugh. "That's all I've been doing since I set out, sergeant. This isn't a horse, it's a catapult."

"Too frisky, sir. Give 'er a good gallop, make 'er blow a bit. Once she's fucked she won't be so fuckin' frisky, pardon my French. Women are all the fuckin' same."

Dash remounted and banged his heels against the ribs. Daisy went off at a slow canter and nothing changed that. He wished he had worn spurs. He disliked spurs but he loathed Daisy. The horse seemed to be developing a jolting, sideways prance. This did his bruised backside no good at all. On the other hand he was still in the saddle when they reached a cross-roads. Beauquesne was to the right. Daisy had already decided to go left.

"Come right, you bitch!" Dash shouted. He doubled the reins in his fists and dragged hard. His feet were braced against the stirrups. It was like trying to turn one of the lions in Trafalgar Square. Snow was falling, and he felt the flakes melting on his sweating face. The horse was winning. Dash had come all the way to France to fight for his country, and now he was being beaten by a bloody nag. "You lousy whore!" he screamed. Another ration wagon was approaching. He didn't care. He kept the reins in one hand and unbuttoned his holster with the other and took out his service revolver and cocked it and fired a thunderous shot past Daisy's left ear. The horse shied. He fired again, a blast of noise that flung the head to the right. He whacked with his heels. Daisy broke into a gallop. Dash fired at the sky and whooped. Faintly, he heard the ration party cheer.

* * *

Chlöe Legge-Barrington slid back the bolts and heaved on the door of the nunnery of Sainte Croix. "Goodness," she said. "You look like Napoleon's retreat from Moscow."

Dash stood in the night, layered with snow, too tired to shrug it off. Behind him the horse raised its great head, black capped with white, and looked at the young woman; then it let its head droop.

"Is this First Aid Nursing Yeomanry?" Dash said. "Because I'm looking for Sarah Beverley."

"This is F.A.N.Y., but Sarah's in England. Would you like some supper? Lancashire hotpot with apple crumble to follow."

"That's frightfully decent of you."

"Well, frightful decency is something we have rather a lot of, around here."

They stabled Daisy and came back inside. She led Dash to a cheerless bathroom and ran a hot tub for him. "Thank God the nuns had a new boiler put in before they left," she said. "They believed in self-sacrifice but they drew the line at chilblains."

"Where are they now?"

"Orleans." She gave him a pair of workman's overalls. "Best I can do. Bring your things, they'll need drying."

Dash eased his aching body into the bath. The cold retreated from his limbs like a beaten army. It put up a brief resistance in his toes and then surrendered to the heat. He ducked his head and blew a fanfare of bubbles.

He found the kitchen by following the noise. Six stunningly beautiful young women turned and looked at him. All wore smartly tailored uniform. Most were without their tunics. "Golly," one of them said. "*Such* a lot of freckles."

"Sorry." Dash tugged sideways at the overalls and made them look like a blue sack. "I thought it said fancy dress on the invitation."

Chlöe Legge-Barrington took his clothes. "Left to right," she said, "Edith Reynolds, Laura da Silva, Nancy Hicks-Potter, Jane Brackenden, Lucy Knight. You'll never remember them, but don't worry, they're all thoroughly forgettable."

"Charles Dash. This is really awfully—"

"I say!" Chlöe was draping his uniform on a clothes horse and she'd found the wings. "Royal Flying Corps." Again, they all gazed at him.

"Guilty." This time he smiled back. It was an engaging, wide-mouthed smile; he knew this because he had practised in front of a mirror at home. As he smiled he saluted. It had been an exhausting afternoon and the hotpot smelled delicious.

"My stars, a hero," Lucy Knight said. "I must get a clean tablecloth."

"Are you a pilot? How high do you fly?" Laura da Silva asked.

"Oh . . . a mile or two. Or three. Depends where the Huns are."

"How many Huns have you shot down?"

Dash looked away, while honesty fought temptation. "Oh well," he said. "It's a team game, you know. The squadron gets the credit." That wasn't entirely true, but it wasn't a total lie either; and he could see that his modesty impressed them.

Supper was easy. All he had to do was smile – not all the time – and tell funny little stories about flying. He fascinated them, and the more casual he was, the more attentive they were. He mentioned the Mad Major. "He used to fly upside-down, just above the enemy trenches, and pelt them with old beer-bottles." Edith Reynolds asked why. "Dunno. An expression of contempt, I suppose." He spoke of the banned practice of chasing staff cars full of British generals until they drove into the ditch. "Isn't it awfully risky?" Chlöe asked. "Not if they can swim," Dash said, and tried to look puzzled by their laughter. He told of a marvellous chap called Captain Ball (they had all heard of *him*) who developed a frightfully clever trick. "He flies straight into the middle of a flock of Hun scouts, and they daren't fire at him in case they hit each other." Then what does he do? "Oh, he knocks one or two down and streaks home for breakfast." It was easy. He had never met a Mad Major, nor chased a staff car, nor talked tactics with Captain Ball, but he had heard a lot of chatter in the mess, and by the end of the meal, with a couple of glasses of red wine inside him and these wonderful girls all saying *How spiffing!* and *What a corker!* Dash almost believed that he'd done it. Or at least seen it done.

They gave him a second helping of apple crumble and cream. He said they looked awfully smart.

"We're all volunteers, in F.A.N.Y.," Chlöe Legge-Barrington said, "so we buy our own uniforms. A bit like the Red Cross."

"Only much, much more swanky," Lucy Knight said. The others hear-heared. "We don't wait for orders from the army. We knew the troops wanted a cinema, so we bought our own, but Edith drove it into a snow-drift."

"All the same," said Nancy Hicks-Potter, "you mustn't think we're not nurses. We could remove your appendix right here and now, on the kitchen table."

"Bet you sixpence you can't."

She opened a drawer and took out a carving knife.

"It's gone," he said. "Two years ago. Just when I was about to become captain of boats. *C'est la vie.*"

She cocked her head. "Show us the scar."

"*Please,*" Chlöe said. "No shop during meals. Anyway, Charles here is exhausted." He opened his mouth to protest and was overtaken by a yawn.

She took him to his bedroom. It was on the second floor, at the end of a corridor. "Sorry about the mattress," she said. "You know what nuns are like."

"Actually, no."

"Well, you soon will. Here's a nightgown. Best we can do, I'm afraid. Goodnight."

The nightgown carried a faint scent of roses. The mattress was hard, but he scarcely noticed. He was asleep before her footsteps had faded.

He had never learned to swim, and now waking up was like swimming to the surface of a very deep pool: quite impossible, so he stopped trying and just let it happen. He had no idea where he was, or when it was, and there was no point in looking, because everything was black. Only one thing was certain: a very naked mermaid was lifting him, he could feel her breasts on his chest and her legs entwined with his. Sweetly and easily he became fully awake, and his brain informed him that mermaids had no legs, and he told his brain that he didn't care. He hadn't the faintest idea which of the six girls was doing these exciting, inviting, rhythmic things to his body. At first he had nothing to say. Later he had little breath to spare for talk. Eventually he was speechless with delight.

The last thing he remembered was his nightgown being tucked around his legs and the blankets being pulled over him. While he was trying to think of suitable words he fell asleep.

The whole splendid experience happened again, complete with a climactic firework display on the inside of his eyelids. Or did he dream the second event? He woke up in broad daylight to find a mug of tea steaming on the bedside locker. As he sipped it, he wondered: once? Twice? The same person? Two different visitors? And how best to behave when he met them all again?

As it happened, only Chlöe Legge-Barrington was in the kitchen when he went down. The others were all out on duty. He ate porridge and two lots of bacon and eggs, while they chatted about holidays in Cornwall.

There was nothing he could do about the cinema truck: it had a broken rear axle. He saddled Daisy.

"Come again, won't you?" Chlöe said.

He took a risk, and said: "Certainly – if I've got the strength," and smiled as he looked her in the eye. She didn't even blink. Which could mean everything, or nothing.

* * *

The snowstorm slackened and gave way to blue skies. The Chinese squad dug and dug and when two good runways were open, Wing H.Q. ordered a D.O.P. for the following day, at dawn.

Munday hated these early patrols.

He came from a large family, mainly girls, who lived in a Cotswold manor house with no lack of servants. His father had inherited a small coal mine in Nottinghamshire, and so money came naturally out of the ground, not that the boy ever saw it happen. He drifted through school. At home, his sisters ran and fetched for him, laughed at all his jokes and treated him like a young god. In uniform, they said, he was quite stunning. He was eager to win a few medals. Marching came as a nasty shock. His feet ached abominably. The more he saw of the infantry – especially bayonets, which actually had a *channel* for the blood to run out – the more he liked the R.F.C.

But he could never get used to being shaken awake at 4.30 a.m.

He dressed mechanically, shivering as he dragged uniform over pyjamas, and stumbled through icy blackness, a scarf around his mouth. The mess was chilly. He chewed on boiled eggs and bread. Always the same awful food for the early patrol. Why? Nobody knew. Tradition. Hot tea, too, but Munday knew how his bladder would feel about *that* in an hour, at fifteen thousand feet. He would have to take off his gauntlets and his gloves and unbutton two or three outer layers and fumble his way through the flies of his underwear, and by the time his thing had done its stuff it would be dead of frostbite.

There was just enough light to read the instrument panel when "C" Flight took off. Spud Ogilvy led the first three aircraft, with the Russians flanking him. Munday led the others, angled to the right so as to avoid Ogilvy's wash. They settled down to a hard climb, and this soon pumped the sun over the horizon. It began as a sliver of deep red. With every thousand feet it swelled and burned brighter until it was a white-hot disc that made the eyes water. An armada of aircraft could be hiding there; and if they were, they would have seen the Pups by now. There was nothing Ogilvy could do about that except keep on climbing.

They crossed the Lines at about nine thousand feet. Normally the German batteries would be spattering the sky with Archie. Today a silver-grey mist was enough to keep the German gunners indoors. Munday looked down and envied them, especially their warm feet. Cold was seeping up his legs. Already his toes had lost all feeling.

A freezing gale swept past his cockpit, and it was impossible to search the sky without getting hit in the face. Munday searched the sky. There was something colder than the gale, and that was terror.

On his second patrol – weeks ago by now – he had watched from high above as Ogilvy stalked a Hun two-seater, crept closer, and killed it with a five-second burst. Whenever Munday felt himself getting weary, or cocky, or bored, he terrified himself with the memory of that burst of flame, lemon-yellow with a core of red, that jumped out of the two-seater and exploded it in a flurry of wings and body and tail.

Ogilvy took them up to seventeen thousand feet. There they floated, and froze, for an hour.

One of Munday's wingmen was a Canadian called Barnard, very keen, not very bright, too tall for his weight but filling out month by month. Barnard didn't mind the cold but the height bothered him. His ribs were thin. Running made him dizzy. Now, at this height, his Pup wobbled as his lungs laboured to drag in enough thin air, and there was never enough. He knew he was getting sleepy, he knew that was bad. Munday was waving to him, pointing up. Barnard's eyes were watering long before he found a tiny cluster of Albatros scouts, almost transparent against the bleached blue of the sky. Jesus, Barnard thought. How can they breathe up there?

For twenty minutes, nothing changed.

Barnard was no longer sleepy. From somewhere his body had found a reserve of energy and pumped it into his brain, with the message: Stay awake, godammit, that's death floating up there. A muscle in his left thigh was jumping, which was a waste of energy, so he told it to stop, and it ignored him, so he hit it with his fist, and something went *bang!* in the engine. The Pup shuddered violently. Oil sprayed on the windscreen until it overflowed and ragged black gobbets blew into the cockpit. Barnard stuck his head out to see what was wrong. Oil slammed into his face, oil covered his goggles. He was blind and the Pup was shaking like a wet dog. It shook Barnard too. His hands lost the controls and blundered about, found the switch and killed the engine.

Instant, total peace. No racket, no shuddering, just black blindness. He dragged off his goggles and saw the rest of the flight, many hundreds of feet above and ahead, droning away from him. He eased the Pup through a gentle turn and began the long glide home.

You could glide a mile for every thousand feet of height you lost. Seventeen thousand feet should be enough to see him across the Lines, provided nobody interfered, provided the headwind wasn't too bad, and provided all the Hun gunners were blind drunk. Barnard forgot all that nonsense and concentrated on nursing his Pup so that it neither stalled nor dived but simply slid down a slope between the two.

He had fifteen hundred feet in hand as he crossed the Lines. The wind whistled softly in the wires, and everything was so quiet that he could hear men shouting orders, the hoot of a distant locomotive, the whack of someone pounding in stakes. Nobody fired on him. The mist was still too thick. Now that was a fat slice of luck.

Mist, of course, was a two-sided coin. It hid Barnard from the ground and then it hid the ground from Barnard. It hid a company of pioneers who were marching back to their billets after a weary night of digging new reserve trenches. Their boots, and the blanketing fog, dampened the soft whistle of the approaching Pup. When they saw its silhouette charging at them, head-high, they scattered. Barnard saw none of this but he felt the jolt when the right lower wing clipped a running man.

The Pup's speed was about fifty miles an hour, more than enough to break the man's back. Barnard was luckier. His machine left its under-carriage in a stone wall and racketed across a sea of ancient shell-holes.

The pioneers pulled him out of the wreckage, carried him back to the roadway and laid him beside the dead soldier. Barnard's forehead had whacked the gunsight and he was out cold. Of the two men, Barnard – blackened and bloodied – looked far the worse.

* * *

The mist that saved Barnard was the prelude to a week of rain. It dissolved the snow and saturated the Western Front and settled down to a persistent drizzle.

"Not like English rain, is it?" the padre said. "English rain generally has the decency to turn up when needed, do its stuff, maybe with a spot of thunder and lightning to add to the merriment, and then buzz off and rain on somebody else, like the Norwegians. But this French rain . . . I mean, look at it. Day after day. You can't tell me that's proper weather. That's just . . ."

"Incontinence," said Lynch.

"Exactly."

"Stuff and nonsense," Cleve-Cutler said. They were sitting in the mess. At the distant edge of the airfield, a row of Chinese labourers could be dimly seen, digging a drainage trench. He knew it would do no good. Fifty trenches might get rid of the surface water, but one alone was useless. Still, he let them dig on. "Total piffle," he said. "Utter tosh."

"Well, if you're going to baffle us with science," Dando said.

"I grew up in Cornwall. It rained like this all year round. My cousins have got webbed feet."

"Not uncommon in Britain, actually. We are nearer the primeval swamp than we like to think."

"About ten yards away," Lynch said. "At a guess."

Plug Gerrish, dozing in an armchair, yawned hugely and said: "O'Neill sent us another postcard. He wants us to send him cheese. Says you can't get a decent Rocquefort in London now. Scandalous, he says." Gerrish yawned again.

The C.O. watched a soldier on a bicycle raise waves as he cut across a large puddle. "I bet it's pouring in London right now," he said.

"If I were you, sir," Dando said, "I'd go there and see for myself. After all, nothing much is likely to happen here, is it?"

Cleve-Cutler hadn't been to England for a year. He telephoned Wing and got ten days' leave. Within an hour he was in a car, heading for Boulogne.

Charles Dash was given permission to have another stab at rescuing the cinema truck, which was now assumed to be stuck in mud. He took Daisy. As the horse splashed unhurriedly to Beauquesne, there was plenty for Dash to brood over.

It was assumed by both their families that he would marry his cousin Jessica. She looked a little like him: lots of freckles, good strong legs. They had been warm friends for years, taken holidays together (Jessica with Charles' family to Cornwall; Charles with Jessica's family to Norfolk), and they shared an interest in horses and dogs. They knew all about breeding, so Charles' father saw no need to explain the whys and hows of sex to him. You couldn't live in rural Herefordshire without seeing it all around you, bulls and stallions and rams going at it like steam-hammers. Ample time to discuss all that with the boy when marriage loomed; and when suddenly the boy went off and joined the Yeomanry his father merely told him to remember always that he was a gentleman but that not all ladies were, well, ladies. "Aren't they?" Charles said. His father winked and tapped one side of his nose and walked away, duty done. Charles was baffled. He felt sorry for his father, who was forty-four and losing his wits. Well, he'd had a good innings.

Then, when some nameless nymph – well, alright, one of six names, but which? – slid out of the blackness and into his bed and stole his virginity, *twice in one night*, it was not only a delicious experience, it was a severe shock. This wasn't how it was done in Herefordshire. In Herefordshire a chap took a girl to lots of dances and proposed marriage and after much fuss and expense they went off somewhere and had a honeymoon. It all took time, and announcements, and organisation. It didn't happen like a thunderclap in the night. Two thunderclaps. For days afterwards he could think of nothing else.

For his second visit, Dash took his razor kit, toothbrush and pyjamas. Also a bottle of Madeira. This time each of the F.A.N.Y. nurses welcomed him with a kiss on the cheek. Lucy Knight (small, curly black hair, face like a cherub) was the last to kiss him and she saw how flattered and flustered he was. "Life's too short," she told him. "Men are so slow."

"Only because bullets are faster." Did that make sense? It sounded rather clever.

"All the more reason!" she said, cheerfully. "And you can't tell me anything about bullets. I've been up to the elbows in gore all afternoon."

During supper he wondered whether it was Lucy.

He had few clues. One was the memory of the startling sensation of breasts brushing his skin. Lucy certainly had initiative, and a chest that drew his glance like a magnet. To take his mind off it he talked to Chlöe Legge-Barrington. She had an athlete's figure and a restless energy that he found exciting. Nothing wrong with her chest, either. Could it be Chlöe? She urged him to take more cabbage. "Fortifies the blood," she said. A secret signal? He took more cabbage.

After supper they all played whist. When he tried to shuffle the pack, the cards sprayed from his fingers. "I'm not much good at this, I'm afraid," he said. Edith Reynolds said, "Men are only good at two things," which provoked a flurry of comic suggestions. Edith said no more; simply smiled. Wonderful lips. Chest okay, too. Might well be Edith . . . The Madeira went around. Jane Brackenden proposed a toast to women's suffrage. "Equality now!" she cried.

"Onwards!" said Nancy Hicks-Potter.

"And upwards!" said Laura da Silva.

Dash stopped trying to guess. They were all topping girls, all. They all had crystal-clear, expensively educated voices. They all had spiffing chests.

The whist ended. He said goodnight, took his candle, hurried upstairs, got into his pyjamas, then had a better idea and took them off. The bed was so cold that he jumped out and put them on again. He lay awake, occasionally squirming as lust visited his loins. Eventually Madeira overtook lust and he slept.

He awoke smoothly and swiftly when the bed was invaded by a silky tangle of limbs. By now he was a veteran of this business of nocturnal seduction; he knew exactly how to handle it. He did a lot of handling and a steady amount of kissing and he did his level best to prolong the thrill, until his body leapfrogged his good intentions and exploded like a firecracker and left him as limp as yesterday's salad. That was the time to speak. The room was so black that he could make out nothing, not even the shape of her head. What to say? In his mind he rehearsed phrases. May I know your name? Awfully formal. What about: I don't think we've been introduced . . . Not in good taste. He cleared his throat. As he did, she slid out of the sheets. "I say . . ." he whispered. The door clicked shut. Too late.

Twice more, that night.

He awoke feeling fuzzy in the head and stiff in the thighs and bruised about the balls. Everyone was at breakfast, full of chat and bustle. He ate an enormous meal and realized how impossible it was now to ask anyone anything. He should have spoken up at the time, in bed. But if he had done so, she might never have returned. No secret, no sex. He was caught in a wonderful trap.

Nothing he had been taught at Monmouth School had prepared him for this. At Monmouth he had dissected a frog and got the impression that reproduction was all a matter of tubes. Well, clearly that was not an adequate explanation.

It was time to leave. He kissed everyone and said goodbye. Everything was delightfully bewildering.

When Daisy carried him into Pepriac, he was ravenously hungry and so pale that his freckles seemed to float on his skin. He ate, and immediately went to bed. "Give it up," Simms advised. "It's only Charlie Chaplin, after all." But Dash shook his head. "I can't disappoint everyone now. Isn't this what we're fighting for?" Simms stared. "No, it isn't," he said. Dash blinked three times and then his eyes closed.

* * *

Dash got up in time for dinner. With the C.O. away, and the aerodrome so boggy that there was no prospect of flying, the atmosphere in the mess was relaxed and cheery.

"O'Neill sent me a postcard," the doctor said. "Packs of wolves are roaming in Westminster. They ate the Home Secretary."

"O'Neill couldn't tell a wolf from a white elephant," Gerrish said. "He's blind as a bat."

"I've often wondered about bats," McWatters said. "Clever little creatures. Fly like the devil and never hit anything. Your churches are full of them, padre. How's it done? What's the trick?"

The padre took some more roast potatoes. "God moves in a mysterious way," he said.

"Chap called Mannock in 40 Squadron," Lynch said. "Only got one good eye. The other's not worth a damn."

"That's nothing," Simms said. "The whole of 56 Squadron's only got one ball." It was an old joke, and it produced a few tired groans. A new man, called Griffiths, looked puzzled. "Albert Ball," Simms told him.

"Oh, yes! Captain Ball," Griffiths said. He was glad to be part of the conversation at last. "People were talking about him at the depot. What's his score?" It seemed a perfectly natural question, but as soon as he'd asked it, Griffiths knew it was wrong. Bad form to discuss scores during dinner. "Doesn't matter, really," he mumbled. His face was hot.

Lynch took pity on him. "A couple of dozen," he said. "The answer to your question is a couple of dozen, which puts Captain Ball far out in front."

"And all done in a Nieuport," Ogilvy said. "Ball prefers the Nieuport."

"I want Nieuport," the duke said abruptly.

"Get me Nieuport too," the count said.

Everyone looked. They were serious. They sat straight-backed, heads high, and looked down their beautiful noses at them. "This is not the time or the place," Ogilvy said. They spoke to each other in Russian. "Two Nieuports," the duke said. "Quick. Tickety-boo."

"You mean lickety-split," Munday said. "Tickety-boo means all-serene."

"Tickety-boo *and* lickety-split," the duke said.

"We'll discuss it later," Ogilvy said.

"Please, sir, can I have a new bicycle?" McWatters said.

"Tell me, Uncle," the doctor said, speaking slowly and clearly so as to distract attention from the Russians, "tell me, why is the British Army so fascinated by Ypres? It's a smelly bog. I should have thought the Allies had all the bog they needed. Yet every time I pick up the paper, there's another thumping great Battle of Ypres going on."

"Only two battles," the adjutant said. "Strategic necessity."

"Oh. I see. Well, that's alright then."

"Russia got biggest bog," the count said with a gloomy pride.

"Pinsk Marshes. Big as Switzerland."

The duke said: "German Army invades Pinsk Marshes. Russian Army attacks German Army." He knocked his knuckles together. "All lost in marshes. All." That silenced the rest of the squadron. "Great victory for Tsar," he added.

"Plenty more armies in Russia," the count said.

"My goodness!" the padre exclaimed. "Rice pudding. With currants in it. What a treat."

The wind howled suddenly in the chimney, and the stove roared. The doctor glanced at the adjutant. "How are our coal stocks?"

"Excellent. All thanks to Lieutenant Dash and his cousin, the pork sausage maker."

"Ah. Well done, lad." A dozen fists briefly pounded the table in applause, and Dash nodded. For the first time, he felt accepted by the squadron.

* * *

As he walked to his hut, Captain Brazier heard music coming from the orderly room. He found Sergeant Lacey playing the gramophone as he worked at his desk.

"Sounds like a fight in a fireworks factory," the adjutant said.

"Stravinsky. His music for the new Diaghilev ballet, *Les Abeilles*. It's on in Paris. You'd love it. Pure joy."

"Stravinsky," said the adjutant. "Isn't he that anarchist-musician johnny? Caused a riot?"

"And a very splendid riot it was," Lacey said. "At the *première* of *The Rite of Spring*."

"I suppressed a riot once. At the market place in Peshawar. And a very splendid suppression it was." Lacey rolled his eyes. "I assure you, sergeant. I had the ringleaders tied to the mouths of our cannons and I blew their little Indian lights out. Blew them clean out!"

"Rather like a birthday cake," Lacey said. He was flicking through a batch of signals. He held up a pink form. "Plum jam. Brigade are still unhappy. The quartermaster insists that we have two hundred pounds more than our entitlement." Lacey polished his glasses with the flimsy paper.

"We explained all that. Didn't we?"

"We said that he sent us strawberry jam in error and that we returned it."

"Well, tell him again."

"No, no. The man is a halfwit. He needs guidance." Lacey rolled a form into his typewriter and rattled out a reply:

Plum jam, squadron entitlement for, mislabelled as supplied, local transfer of. Your PNT/14Q dated 06.03.17. Can confirm manufacturer's error resulted 200 lbs jam labelled plum in fact contents half strawberry half raspberry therefore transferred to 40 Squadron on authority Duty Officer that Squadron.

The adjutant read this. "Blame it on the manufacturer. Quite right. I suppose you had a reason for picking 40 Squadron."

"They moved to England last week."

"Ah." He signed the paper. "Duty officer, eh? Could be anybody. Poor chap's probably gone west by now."

Lacey leaned against the doorframe, his thumbs hooked in his pockets. "Probably," he said. Brazier sat squarely, and cleaned the nib of his pen with a bit of blotting paper. Eventually Lacey looked at him and said: "Strawberry jam." Brazier raised a bushy eyebrow just a fraction. "Isn't there something horribly symbolic here?" Lacey asked. "The army can afford to lose millions of men, year after year. But not a few cases of strawberry jam. Jam *matters*."

"Civilian talk," Brazier said briskly.

"Jam matters more than men?"

"Regulations matter more than anything."

"War isn't regulated. War is confusion and disorder and luck and waste, especially waste. Every week – even now, when nothing is happening – hundreds of men, wasted. Thousands of tons of shells, wasted. So why this obsession about jam? I apologize for interrupting you."

"Not a bit of it. I'm pleased to see you developing the Fighting Spirit, Lacey."

"Mere bile, sir."

"You should apply for a commission."

"I should take one of Beecham's Pills."

"We need keen young subalterns at the Front."

"Only because you keep losing them. Which reminds me. Your ammunition has arrived."

He fetched a wooden box stencilled Signal Flares (Very Pistol) Handle With Care, and placed it on the adjutant's desk. "A posthumous token of respect from the late Lieutenant Morkel."

Brazier prised open the lid and eased a few records from their straw packing. "Band of the Grenadier Guards . . . 'Blaze Away' . . . 'Colonel Bogey' . . . 'Sussex by the Sea' . . . Good. Real music, this." He dug deeper. "Hullo . . . Orlando Benedict and his Savoy Orchestra?" He peered at the labels. "'I'm Lonesome for You' . . . 'Here Comes Tootsie' . . . 'If You Could Care for Me' . . . 'Poor Butterfly' . . ." One nostril flared. "Tosh. Utter tosh."

"I think Captain Lynch hoped it might soften your stony soul, sir." Lacey pointed at a label. "Novelty foxtrot. Splendid exercise for the deskbound office worker."

Brazier grunted, and put "Blaze Away" on the gramophone. "Keep your jazz," he said. "This is real music."

* * *

The day after he left France, Cleve-Cutler was eating breakfast at Taggart's hotel, near Piccadilly. Taggart was a gloomy Irishman with an eyepatch and a bad limp. He had been invalided out of the R.F.C. early in 1915 when a friendly shell had rushed through the gap between his wings and removed several vital struts, forcing him to make a messy landing in a wood. Now he sat at Cleve-Cutler's table and helped himself to toast. "My advice," he said. "Wear mufti. Otherwise wherever you go, the bloody civilians will buy drinks for you, and then they'll ask you how many Fritzes you've shot down."

"Fritzes? They really say Fritzes?"

"They know nothing. All they know they read in the bloody silly newspapers, and that's lies dreamed up by the bloody silly War Office. Cavalry of the clouds, that's you. Take their drinks, tell them any old lies, fuck their women if you want to, they'll consider it a privilege, with those wings on you and all, like being fucked by an angel. Just don't take anything they say seriously. They know nothing." He limped away, dropping crumbs.

Cleve-Cutler wondered what to do with his week. If he moved fast, he could catch an express and be in Cornwall by tea-time. Grey seas, grey granite, soggy moorland. His parents would ask a lot of questions. Then their friends would visit and ask the same bloody silly questions: what's it really like? When are we going to win? And, no doubt: how many Fritzes have you shot down? Resentment gripped like indigestion. If he told them what France was really like, they'd never believe him. Bugger Cornwall.

So he stayed at Taggart's and went to a different show every night; often two shows, with supper in-between or after or both. The West End of London was bustling with young officers. He quickly fell in with a bunch hellbent on squeezing the most out of their leave. They called him the Mad Major – to the infantry, any R.F.C. major was mad – and when they ended up at Taggart's, he made jugs of Hornet's Sting for them. They thought he was a hell of a fellow. He relaxed in the luxury of not being a commanding officer. For the first time in a year, he did what he damn well pleased. It was a strange experience, like taking his clothes off in a crowded room, and he soon grew sick of it, but for a few galvanic days he thought he was happy.

He went to a dance. It was a tea-dance, held at Malplacket House. The young Lord Malplacket had gone to France with his regiment in 1914 and soon was Mentioned in Despatches for conspicuous gallantry, too conspicuous for his own good: a German sharp-shooter picked him out and picked him off. Nobody in the British Army wore a steel helmet in those dashing, innocent days. Eventually the remains got shipped home and placed in the family vaults while a cannon left over from the Civil War boomed out the dead man's years. His widow wondered what to do with herself. Belgian refugees needed help. She found them dull. The Red Cross wanted people to roll bandages: not a thrilling prospect. She decided that her war-work was to give tea-dances at Malplacket House for officers on leave. Every afternoon, the ballroom was brisk with the foxtrotting of subalterns and widows. Cleve-Cutler went, and found it the most enormous fun.

The second time he went, he saw a girl sitting in the gallery that overlooked the ballroom. Emerald dress, dark red hair. Quite alone. He danced a waltz and got some lemonade for his partner and looked up. Still there. Still alone. He excused himself and found the stairs to the gallery.

"Hullo," she said, as if they had known each other for years. "You're wasting your time with me."

"Well, I've got plenty of time, and I can't think of a better way to waste it . . . May I sit and talk?" He really wanted to sit and look.

She was unfashionably slim and her face had a delicacy that made him feel powerful and protective, until she looked him in the eyes. Fear did strange, apparently useless things to a man, as he knew; it dried the mouth, it tightened the lungs, it made the heart hammer and the palate detect strange metallic tastes. Now he discovered what sudden love could do. It knocked the stuffing out of a chap. Fear multiplied; love subtracted. This was all new to him. Cleve-Cutler had confronted fear and overcome it. He wasn't going to submit tamely to love. "You know, you remind me of someone," he lied.

"Oh, come on," she said. "You can do better than that."

"Um," he said. He looked away, but looking away was pain. "What I meant was . . ." He looked back, and was ruined again. "Look here, you're being jolly unfair."

"Am I? Well, do something about it." She was infuriatingly calm. He was in a fever; what right had she to be so calm? "For a start," she said, "you can tell me who you are."

You crass ass, he told himself. "Hugh Cleve-Cutler," he said.

"Ah." She was looking down at the dancers, which he resented. "I used to know a Stanley Cleve-Cutler."

"Very remote cousin. Went into the Foreign Office. Never seen again."

"There you are. I knew you could do better if you tried." Hope surged in him. "I'm Dorothy Jaspers, which makes me a remote cousin of our hostess."

"Splendid. May I ask for the honour of a dance?"

"You may ask, but the answer's no."

He felt as if he'd swallowed a stone. A sane man would get up and leave. He wasn't quite sane at that moment. "Look," he said, "I'm somewhat confused about exactly what's going on here."

She turned to him and took hold of his face with both hands and looked into his eyes. "Tell me true," she said. "Do you know where we can get a drink at this hour of day?"

"Yes, I think so."

She let go. "Get your hat and find a cab. I'll meet you downstairs."

He helped her into the cab. She was smaller than he had thought. The emerald silk dress brushed the ground. Tricky dancing the foxtrot in that, he thought. They went to Taggart's Hotel. On the way, she said nothing. Cleve-Cutler watched her, secretly, and marvelled that no man had captured her. Were they all blind? Was he massively lucky?

Taggart opened the bar for them.

They all drank brandy-sodas and talked about the new shows and the best songs in them, until Taggart went off to organize dinner and left them in charge.

"Decent chap, old Taggart."

"Yes," she said, crisply.

"That show he mentioned. We might—"

"Yes."

"Perhaps some supper? There's a place—"

"Yes."

"Splendid." But this was all moving too fast for Cleve-Cutler. "Fancy you knowing Stanley," he said. "Not that I knew him well."

"Forget Stanley. This face of yours: it's not your real face, is it?"

"Good God, no." He'd explained his jaunty looks to so many people – family, army doctors, medical boards – that he was ready with the answer. "Dodged an idiot in a Gunbus, flew into a barn. The quacks stitched me together again. Improvement on the original, some say."

She freshened his drink with brandy. "Well, damn it all to bloody blazes," she said, and freshened her own drink. "There are three things I wish I could do. I wish I could dance, and run, and go swimming at the seaside, but I never shall because I have a wooden leg, and it's definitely not an improvement on the original. If you want to see it I charge nothing for public displays but from the funny look on your funny face I suggest you take a big drink first."

Cleve-Cutler was too shocked to move or speak.

"Take a drink and have a look," she advised. "Otherwise you'll never believe me."

"But you're wearing shoes." His voice was husky; he drank to strengthen it. He watched, fascinated, as she raised the hem of her long green silk ball-gown, and he saw a wooden leg fitted into the right shoe. The hem kept rising. The wooden leg ended just below the knee. Leather straps secured it.

She let the dress fall. He finished his drink in one gulp. "Told you so," she said.

* * *

It had happened when she was six. Her father was a banker. Liked horses, liked hunting, had an estate in Berkshire. He gave young Dorothy a pony-and-trap, a miniature of the real thing. She wasn't allowed to drive it alone, but one day all the grooms were busy, so she took it. And for fun, she rode the little pony bareback, and they were trotting along a farm track, all going as fine as ninepence, when the pony shied. She was thrown. The trap ran over her leg. Very bad fracture. Lots of operations, but in the end it had to come off.

"That's so dreadfully unfair," Cleve-Cutler said.

She took his face in her hands, as she had done in the gallery, and looked into his eyes. "Tell me true," she said. "If your washer-woman's husband had a wooden leg, would you think it dreadfully unfair?"

"Um . . . no. Possibly not."

She released him. "Well, then. It's just people of our class who are supposed to be unblemished."

"I suppose that's so."

"I know shops that sell artificial hands and fingers. Even artificial noses. Factory work is dangerous. So is farm work."

"Excuse me."

He went to the lavatory and washed his face in cold water. He had seen many violent deaths and mutilations in France. He had seen a pilot walk into a spinning propeller. He had seen men blinded, and men gutted, and men incinerated in the gush of petrol from bullet-holed tanks. But that was war, and they were only men, and they were fighting for decency and purity and all that was best in the world, as symbolized by this wonderful creature he had found in the gallery. Who turned out to be a fraud, a swindle. So maybe the war was a fraud and a swindle too. He leaned on the wash basin and looked at his reflection "We make a fine pair," he said. He dried his face and went back.

"I know the best place for oysters," she said.

"I never doubted it for a moment," he told her. He still loved her. From the knees up, anyway.

*   *   *

Taggart gave them a large room with a large bed.

Dorothy had been staying at Lady Malplacket's place. She telephoned from the hotel and had someone pack a bag and bring it over.

Cleve-Cutler said: "Won't your cousin think it strange? Moving out like this?"

"Do you care what she thinks?"

They had each undressed separately, in the bathroom. Now she was sitting on the bed, brushing her hair. It caught the light as she moved, black chasing red chasing black.

"I don't want to ruin your reputation," he said.

"Do you care about my reputation?" She spoke easily, lazily. It had been a long and happy evening. "Now? At this very moment?"

"No." He sat beside her.

"Good. Because I certainly don't care about yours." She used the tip of the hairbrush to comb his moustache. "What *do* you care about?"

"You. I care about you. Absolutely."

"Including the woodwork?" Her arms slipped around his body.

"To be perfectly frank," he said, "no, I don't feel any affection for the woodwork."

"Then suppose," she said. "Suppose I take it off, and you remove your pyjamas."

"Excellent suggestion." He stood up. "Long overdue. Warmly welcomed and strongly endorsed by all right-thinking men. Put to the vote and passed nem con." He threw the pyjamas into a corner and turned around. She was lying on the bed, equally naked.

"My goodness," she said. "Rather less of me, but a good deal more of you. Isn't that a lucky coincidence?"

"Reminds me of a jigsaw puzzle I got for Christmas," he said. "Hours of innocent fun." It made her smile, which was worth more to him than winning his M.C.

* * *

They slept for an hour, and then he awoke, wondering where the hell he was, not France, it didn't feel or smell like France, so what the devil . . . And then he remembered, and relaxed. Sharing a bed was a strange experience.

He was afraid of disturbing her; on the other hand the lush warmth of her presence was exciting and before he could stop himself his hand had stroked her body; and as if he had touched a trigger she was awake and sitting up, propped on one arm, reaching for his face and kissing it. Soon she was straddling him. Now there's a surprise, he thought. No complaints, though. He worried, briefly, about hurting her damaged leg, before he realized that she was twice as lithe as he was; and in the tangle of limbs, who was counting feet?

After that he slept deeply and awoke grudgingly, he knew not why. The room was black. She was mumbling. Or was she crying? He put his hand on her shoulder. The noise stopped.

"Oh, oh, oh," she said.

"What's the matter?"

"Poor butterfly."

That made no sense to him.

"'Poor butterfly,'" she said. "Do you remember? They were dancing to the tune, this afternoon. *Yesterday* afternoon. 'Poor Butterfly' . . ." She sang a couple of bars. "Isn't it a lovely tune? Just perfect for dancing."

There was nothing he could say to that. He held her and she quickly fell asleep. He was glad of that. He was very tired.

* * *

By dawn she was out of bed and dressing. He allowed himself the luxury of watching, without feeling that he had to abandon the warm sheets. The cold air made him sneeze, and she glanced sideways.

"You're very nimble," he said.

"Well, I've done it before."

"Do I mean nimble?" He yawned. "Makes you sound like an acrobat."

"Do you like racing?" She was as blithe as a blackbird. "Do you like Scotland?"

"Let's see . . . Where the whisky comes from?"

"They're racing at Edinburgh this afternoon, Hugh. There's a fast train,

Monarch of the Glen, first stop Edinburgh, gets us there in time for the second race."

"Edinburgh. That's—"

"Four hundred miles. It's a *very* fast train."

"You're quite mad. We'd never get seats. Not a hope."

"What a shame." She put her hat on. "Perhaps I'll send you a picture postcard."

"Wait! Look, I haven't shaved."

They went by cab to King's Cross. She called on the stationmaster, and they travelled first class on the *Monarch of the Glen*. Cleve-Cutler shaved. They had a long, lazy breakfast in the dining car as the fields and woods of Hertfordshire rushed past. The ticket collector came by. Dorothy showed him a dull gold medallion, slightly larger than a sovereign, and he saluted and moved on. "Ahah," Cleve-Cutler said. "Now I know. You're head of the Secret Service."

"What a wonderful idea." The sun had come out and she was drowsy in its warmth. "Then I could be invisible. I've always wanted to be invisible."

"I don't think it works quite like that."

"Well, I'll be tremendously secret, then. So secret that nobody knows who I am except you, because nobody else knows the password . . ." It was a highly satisfying fantasy. She could never be a total part of this world, so she would invent her own world and vanish into it. "What is the password?" she asked.

The words *poor butterfly* came to his mind. He decided not to take the risk. "The password is *Poppycock*," he told her. "Because I say so . . . Now, explain that medal-thing."

She explained. Father was a director, past chairman, of the railway company, and so travelled free; the medallion was a perpetual ticket for two, anywhere, first class. "He lets me borrow it," she said. "I'm afraid it doesn't pay for breakfast."

He rested his head against the cushioned seat. The train strummed through a length of meadows, cattle standing as steam rose from their backs. Suddenly the train hammered into a cutting and made him blink.

Now he could see her face reflected in the window. This time yesterday we were strangers, he thought. Lucky, lucky, lucky. And she thought: We could keep travelling for ever, just him and me. On Father's medallion. Together for ever. Then the cutting ended and the dark battering fell away, and the train went back to its tidy racy strum.

"Do you remember singing 'Poor Butterfly' last night?" he asked.

She nodded, and hummed a few bars. "Why do you ask?"

"Oh . . . just feeling brave, I suppose."

"You are braver than you know. So many men, when they discover my leg – or rather when they discover no leg – they panic. They decide that the rest of me is . . . oh . . ."

"Not in full working order?"

"I frighten them. They wonder what other terrors await them if they take me to bed. Men are so nervous."

"Well, nanny told them if they kept on playing with it, then it would fall off."

"Did your nanny say that?"

"No. My nanny said if I told her where father kept the whisky hidden, I could do what I damn well liked. So I did and she got the sack, father being nobody's fool."

"Well, I think you were jolly brave with me." She looked thoroughly happy. Cleve-Cutler had never made anyone happy before. He was pleased with himself.

* * *

A taxi got them to Edinburgh races. Hugh, betting by instinct, lost a fiver. Dorothy, going always for the second favourite, won thirty pounds. They dined at the Waverley and went back to London by sleeper, thanks to her father's medallion. Hugh took a large fresh salmon with him for Taggart.

"Edinburgh?" Taggart said. "You must be exhausted, so you must."

"We came by sleeper," Hugh told him.

"I can never get any rest in those things."

"No. Ours was a bit rackety."

They went to their room. "Rackety," she said. "I've never heard it called that before. Rumpty-tumpty. Hanky-panky. Jig-a-jig. Lots of things. But never rackety."

"Well, that's our word. Our password."

"Oh." For the first time, she seemed unsure of herself. "You mean . . . whenever . . ."

"Just say rackety."

"Heavens above. And to think that Father keeps complaining that the art of conversation is lost."

"Does he? Well, next time you see him you can tell him we found it again. Tell him it was in the bed. The maid must have left it there."

She glowed with pleasure, and this gave him some idea of a stern but loving father whom he had no wish to meet. "Is it too early for me to say rackety?" she asked.

"It's odd . . . In an aeroplane, at fifteen thousand feet, I feel okay. But when you look at me like that, I get a sinking feeling in the pit of my stomach."

"I don't know much about men's anatomy." She loosened his tie. "But I don't *think* the pit of your stomach comes into it, actually."

Cleve-Cutler tried to grin, and failed, and realized it was a wasted effort because his face was hooked into a grin anyway. He was trapped by his own desires. Part of him itched to peel off her clothes, and his, and to carry on where they had left off in the sleeper. Another part cringed away from the prospect, scared of failure. His balls ached while lust sent his heart pounding. Make up your bloody mind! he told his body. "Oysters," he said. "Let's go out and eat a bucket of oysters."

Taggart saw them leave hand-in-hand. "I thought you two were going to have a nice lie-down," he said.

"Oysters," she told him, smiling like a bride.

Taggart went into his office and spat on the fire. He really disliked loving couples. They peacocked around as if they knew the answer when they didn't even know the bloody question.

* * *

All across the Atlantic, masses of air jostled and spun and drove east. What began as a warm front off New England dropped its rain into the ocean and matured into a sequence of brisk westerlies that swept across Europe and gave the fields a chance to drain and dry. Thanks to the Chinese labourers' ditches, the aerodrome at Pepriac dried quickly. Soon Hornet Squadron was flying again. As usual, Wing wanted Deep Offensive Patrols.

* * *

For three more days they were never apart, and then he had to go back to France.

He wanted to say goodbye in London. "Dover is dreary. Nothing but troops. Worse than a garrison town. You'll hate it."

"I've never been to Dover," she said, and put the medallion in her eye like a monocle. "This is Field Marshal Haig speaking. Don't sulk, or I'll get Taggart to kick you."

"I'm not sulking, I'm furious."

"Well, you're a soldier. You're paid to be furious."

"Why aren't you furious?"

"Oh, Hugh, just look at me." She let the medallion drop into her hand. "Poor butterfly. Can you imagine a furious butterfly? People would think I was drunk."

On the way to Victoria, he stopped the cab at a music shop and bought a record of "Poor Butterfly".

"This is for you. A keepsake."

But she wouldn't take it. "Being a butterfly is bad enough." She was pleasant but firm. "I'd rather not be reminded." Which left him feeling foolish, carrying a gramophone record that neither of them wanted. Why the devil couldn't she just take the thing and throw it away later? Why did she have to be so damned honest?

They had little to say on the boat train, and not much to see through windows streaked with rain. They travelled with a bunch of cavalry officers who spoke gruffly among themselves about polo.

At Dover the showers had all blown away, the sun was out, and it was a lovely day for anything except what they were there to do.

They stood on the platform while a porter got his bags out. "There's no point in your coming down to the harbour," he said. "You'd just have to come back here again." His voice was hard. Almost accusing. He wondered why, and he made himself laugh. "Why are we so gloomy? I don't understand."

"Look at that," she said, and pointed high behind him. "What is it? You must know."

He turned and squinted at the bright blue sky. "Sopwith Camel." He had heard the rasping buzz of its engine and he had resisted looking; now he could get his fill. "First-rate machine. They get ferried to France from here. Wish I had them on my squadron. Climbs like a rocket, turns on a sixpence, twin Vickers to blow the Boche to bits. Beautiful."

"I can't compete with that," she said, without bitterness. "No woman can." She kissed him on the lips: one quick kiss. "Off you go and enjoy your war. It won't last for ever."

"Of course it won't. Anyway, I'll be back soon."

"No, you won't."

She was calm; he was baffled. He said, "I will, I tell you. I'll write. We'll meet."

"No, we shan't."

The porter was waiting.

"Don't take it so badly," she said. "You haven't done anything wrong."

"But this is absurd."

"Yes, it's absurd." And she limped away.

On the boat, he brooded over the bloody silly mystery of women. In mid-Channel he took the record of "Poor Butterfly" and sent it skimming into the waves. By the time they landed in France he was actually, and to his great surprise, looking forward enormously to getting back to the war, back to Pepriac and the men he commanded. It was a relief to be out of England. Taggart was right: England knew nothing.

* * *

Dusk came early to Pepriac. Grimy clouds drifted out of the west and built a barricade too strong for the setting sun. Electric lights burned in the orderly room and the kettle sang on the cast-iron stove, which glowed a soft mauve in places. Occasionally rain rattled on the roof and the odd drop plunged down the chimney and died a martyr's death.

Sergeant Lacey was listening to the gramophone playing Ravel's string quartet, while he practised the signature of Daniel T. Latham. It was difficult because *Daniel* was much bigger and bolder than *T. Latham*. Usually there was a final flourish to a signature, but this one ended in a weak dribble of ink. Perhaps, Lacey thought, Lieutenant Latham hadn't liked his name. Perhaps he hadn't respected his father or his family.

He made ten more attempts and then reached for Latham's cheque book and dashed off the signature. The cheque was payable to the Polperro Home for Distressed Mariners, in the amount of twenty-five guineas. It was dated six weeks earlier. Lacey slid it into an envelope and addressed the envelope to Polperro. He threw the experimental signatures into the stove just as Ravel reached his closing chord and Cleve-Cutler came through the door, grinning like a shark. "God's teeth!" he cried, and went straight to the adjutant's room.

"I trust you enjoyed a good leave, sir," Lacey said.

"None of your damned business." He kicked the adjutant's desk and came out. "What's the score? Nobody in the mess, nobody at the Flights, nobody here. Where's Brazier?"

"At the churchyard, sir. Would you like some tea?"

"Oh." The C.O. came to an abrupt halt. "Churchyard, eh?" He found himself looking at the gramophone and he twisted his head to read the record label. "Churchyard. Well I'm damned. The usual?"

"Mr Cooper and Mr Radley, sir."

"Good Christ." All the way from Boulogne, Cleve-Cutler had been enjoying a mounting gusto for the war. Dorothy was a dear sweet woman, but his memory of her faded with every mile until now it was almost erased. He was impressed by his own callousness. Still, he hadn't bargained on coming back to *this*. "Accident or . . . or what?"

"Archie, sir."

The C.O. grunted. "Rotten luck." Yet he was relieved: at least they were killed in action. And probably quickly. Archie was all or nothing. Either Archie missed, or he blew you to bits. But invariably the bits came down in Hunland. "Sure it was Archie?"

"No lack of witnesses, sir." Lacey was making tea. "It was British Archie."

"Sodding bastards," the C.O. said. "Blind murdering sodding bastards."

"The battery commander sent his apologies."

"Stuff 'em up his arse."

"Also a pair of wreaths."

"Ten francs each. Twenty francs, two pilots. What a rotten waste." All his gusto had gone, and bitter rage had taken its place. The military part of his brain reacted quickly. Losses, it told him, just losses, that's all, you've had 'em before, don't stand there mumbling, do something! "Where are the replacements?" he demanded. "And where's the bloody adjutant, for God's sake?"

"Still at the churchyard, sir." Lacey was pouring the tea.

"Churchyard? That's not his job, it's the flight commander's job. Tim Lynch's job."

"Mr Lynch died a week ago, sir. We buried him the following day."

Cleve-Cutler took a mug of tea and sat on the nearest desk. "God speed the plough," he muttered.

Lacey took the record off the turntable and slipped it into its brown-paper sleeve. "Perhaps I should tell you everything, sir."

"More deaths, you mean?" Lacey nodded. "Telephone the mess," the C.O. said. "Tell them I want a bottle of whisky sent over." Lacey went into the adjutant's office and came back with whisky. "Totally irregular," the C.O. said. "Someone will pay for this." Lacey poured whisky into his tea. "Is Brazier a secret drinker?" the C.O. asked. Lacey shook his head. "The adjutant before him was an awful soak," the C.O. said. "Applegate, Appleford, something like that. I had to send him packing. Bit of a crook, too." He drank his tea-and-whisky. "Hell of a crook, in fact. Applecart? Appletart?"

"Appleyard, sir."

Lacey leaned against a wall, arms folded. He watched and waited, and wondered why the C.O. was being so evasive. Casualties had never upset him before. They had caused regret, but not distress. Death struck and life went on, that was Cleve-Cutler's style. Brisk. Positive.

"Well, I suppose you'd better tell me," the C.O. said.

"Mr Lloyd-Perkins in 'A' Flight was a landing accident, fractured skull and internal injuries. Died in hospital. Mr Lynch was shot in combat, it seems. He managed to return, but by then he had lost too much blood and there was no time to take him to hospital. Wing has sent us Captain Crabtree to take command of 'B' Flight, but as yet we have no replacements for Mr Cooper and Mr Radley. In 'C' Flight Mr Shanahan has a touch of pneumonia and a broken nose."

"From flying?"

"Only a very short distance. His motorcycle hit a cow and he flew into a ditch."

"A *cow?* Was he drunk?"

"The night was dark, sir. And the cow was black."

"And Shanahan's an idiot."

"The mess bought the cow, sir, at a very fair price."

Cleve-Cutler stared. "Well, that's alright, then, isn't it? As long as we get our steak-and-kidney pie, the squadron can go to hell, can't it? What? Straight to hell!" he banged his mug on the desk. Tea slopped. "Dammit," he said.

"We also lost a rigger," Lacey said gently. The C.O. took a deep breath and held it, while he looked at the roof. Then he let it out. "He obtained a small German bomb as a souvenir," Lacey said. "He attempted to defuse it and blew the fingers off his right hand. Corporal Blunt. The obvious jokes have been made, sir."

"Oh?" The C.O. thought about that. "Jokes, you say. Some people think it's funny, do they?"

"I believe I see the adjutant coming, sir."

Brazier shouldered the door open. He was carrying a wreath in each hand. "Hullo, sir," he said. "Good leave?"

"What the blazes have you got there?" Cleve-Cutler snarled. "You look like a two-handled teapot."

"If I'd left them in the churchyard, the goats would have eaten them."

"Best thing could have happened. Get 'em out of my sight. Where are the flight commanders?"

Brazier frowned. "Now let me see . . ."

The flight commanders were quickly rounded up and sent to the C.O.'s office. He shook hands with the new man, Captain Crabtree, and welcomed him to the squadron. He thought Crabtree was the most unpleasant officer he had ever seen. A thin face, slightly twisted so that one corner of his mouth sagged; a chin raddled with acne scars; hostile eyes; ears like rudders; and hair that was uniformly white. God dealt you a bloody awful hand, the C.O. thought. If there is a God. If He plays cards.

"I'm sorry you couldn't join us at a happier time," he said bleakly. "For this unhappy state of affairs I blame myself entirely. I go away for ten days and when I get back I find my squadron in tatters. It won't happen again, I assure you."

"That's a bit hard, sir," Plug Gerrish said. "Lynch was leading his flight when he met a flock of Fokkers, and he copped a bullet. That's no disgrace. He did his best."

"No doubt. Did Lloyd-Perkins also do his best?"

"He was out of petrol, he had to land, there was a rainstorm. He made a pig's ear of it. I might have done the same thing."

Ogilvy said, "And if you're going to ask about Cooper and Radley, sir, nobody's to blame for Archie, especially when it's British Archie. A shell hit Radley, and it blew Radley into Cooper."

"And Shanahan?"

"Well, Shanahan's a bloody idiot, sir."

"He's another pilot I haven't got. Five pilots in ten days. At that rate the whole squadron will have gone west in a month! Well, I have news for you." Cleve-Cutler's artificial grin was frozen. "I am going to revive a quaint, old-fashioned notion called *discipline*. We are going to tighten up this squadron until every man squeaks when he salutes! You will *train* your flights to fly together, fight together, kill together and land back here together, in one piece, ready for orders from Wing to go off and do it again! Do I make myself clear?"

They left. Cleve-Cutler looked around him and saw framed photographs of people he did not wish to remember. He turned off the light and sat in the darkness, waiting for his anger to fade. Tim Lynch had been a decent chap, a competent flight commander, deserved a posthumous medal, wouldn't get one. He imagined Lynch's last fight, a dozen machines all whirling around the sky like leaves in a squall, until suddenly Lynch got a bullet in the leg. Must have been a long slog home, against the wind, against the Huns, and all the time blood getting pumped into his boot. There was a clever act that Lynch had performed on guest nights in the mess: he rode a bicycle, facing backwards, and blindfold, while he sang "The Skye Boat Song". Not any more. Cleve-Cutler would miss seeing him do that trick. Rode all around the mess and never missed a note. Oh, well.

Cooper and Radley had been new boys, keen and cheerful and totally interchangeable. He would have to write to their parents. The same wording would serve for each. Brazier would know what to say without actually lying. Ditto *re* Lloyd-Perkins.

Writing letters was a frightful chore. There was that woman in London. He had promised to write to her. He knew now that he would never write, just as she had told him he wouldn't. Was he so transparently selfish?

The question left him feeling shabby and unworthy, which was infuriating, so he thought instead of Lieutenant Shanahan and the dead cow. Bloody idiot. Men like Shanahan let the squadron down. Not good enough! He'd make them jump through hoops of blazing fire. Discipline!

* * *

Late next afternoon, when the patrols had returned and the air in the anteroom was grey with the lazy writhings of tobacco smoke, a staff car approached the camp. The duty N.C.O. in the guardroom was alert, which was just as well. The car was a Rolls-Royce. In it was General Trenchard. He commanded the Corps.

"Unexpected pleasure, sir," Lieutenant Heeley said. He was duty officer; he had run from the mess; one epaulette was flapping.

"Assemble your mechanics."

"Yes, sir. Where, sir?"

Trenchard looked down. He was six feet four. In his greatcoat he seemed massive. His face was as gaunt as a Highland shepherd. Heeley felt his guts churn, and he tasted the last of his lunch, and he said, "Number one hangar, sir!" in a curiously reedy voice. He turned and ran.

Trenchard was known throughout the corps as "Boom". He was not comfortable with the English language; he boomed words as if they were shells to be discharged, in case they blew up in his face. Now he stood on a box and did his gruff and gloomy best. Behind him stood Cleve-Cutler and Baring, Trenchard's private secretary.

"You fellows," Trenchard told the mechanics, "are. The backbone. The backbone of. The Corps. Without you. And. Your skills. We are nowhere. At all. You have toiled. Wonderfully. I can promise. You. Even greater toil. Before. Victory."

Cleve-Cutler glanced sideways. Baring shook his head.

"Arrives," Trenchard boomed.

Baring nodded.

"Three cheers for the general!" the C.O. cried.

The Rolls-Royce carried them to the mess. On the way, Trenchard said, "How is morale?"

"A few kills will buck it up, sir."

Trenchard grunted. "You've had losses."

"Yes. We need the rub of the green, sir."

Trenchard grunted again.

All the officers were gathered in the anteroom. Most had never met the Corps commander before, and they were surprised to see wings on his tunic. "Pontius Pilot," McWatters whispered. Ogilvy frowned. It was an old joke.

"Don't complain," Trenchard boomed, "about your aeroplanes." He let that soak in. "Do your best. With what you've got. Next point. The aeroplane is good for only one thing and that is attack." He breathed deeply after this rush of words. "Your motto. Attack! Search. Find. Attack the enemy. Conquer his sky. Give the Hun. No peace until. One day. The Hun will. Beg. For peace."

Cleve-Cutler glanced at Baring. Baring shrugged. The C.O. took a chance and stepped forward. "Thank you, general. I'm sure we are all in total agreement with your every word."

"Hear, hear," the adjutant said.

"Not total," Crabtree said softly.

There was a moment of frozen time, and then a shuffling of feet as men tried to get a better view.

"What, then?" Trenchard said.

"I don't agree, sir. Not totally."

By now Trenchard had picked him out. Crabtree was of medium height, thin, his face deeply lined, eyes almost haggard.

"Captain Crabtree," the C.O. murmured. "Commands 'B' Flight."

"Why not totally?" Trenchard asked.

"Well, it's not a fair fight, sir, is it?" Crabtree said. His tone was mild; he sounded a little regretful. "The Hun has the advantages. We fight over there. If he doesn't like it he runs away. If we don't like it, we've got a head-wind against us. You say: conquer the enemy sky and make him beg for peace. Up there, performance counts and the new Hun machines are better than ours. Always attack, you say. And fighting spirit is a fine thing. But on its own it won't conquer the sky, sir."

Trenchard leaned his great shaggy head forward and examined the medal ribbons below Crabtree's wings. "You're a brave man, captain," he said. "You have told me. What not to do. Now give me. Your alternative."

Crabtree sighed, and glanced around the room. "Get hold of a few squadrons of the new Albatros, sir," he said gently; and the shout of laughter seemed to startle him.

Trenchard did not smile. He let the laughter fade to an expectant silence. "Not a fair fight. You said. War is not. About fairness. It's about. Winning. Stop fighting and. The battle's lost. We learn to win. By fighting. Don't complain. Fight hard. With what weapons. You've got. When a better. Weapon arrives. You'll know. How best to use it. War is hard. But it makes. Victory. All the more. Sweet."

Cleve-Cutler did not need to call for three cheers; the applause broke out spontaneously. Baring murmured into Cleve-Cutler's ear: "D'you know, I've never heard him so eloquent."

As they went in to dinner, the adjutant sought out Crabtree and took him aside. "What the blazes possessed you?" he demanded. "He'll think we're all pansies."

"I don't care," Crabtree said. He was still calm and untroubled. "I just don't care."

"Well . . . For God's sake, pull yourself together. You volunteered to join the Corps, didn't you?"

"That was a long, long time ago, Uncle. I've flown five hundred hours. More than a lifetime. Now I don't care."

Brazier's temper ran out. "You ought to be shot," he growled.

"I certainly shall be," Crabtree said. "Beyond a doubt." His nose twitched. "Pork. I like pork."

* * *

Baring sat between Spud Ogilvy and Duke Nikolai.

"Is America really in the war?" Ogilvy asked him.

"Yes. President Wilson finally took the plunge," Baring said. "The U-boats, you know. The Kaiser let them off the leash and so they sank the *Housatonic*, which was American, and the *Sussex*, which was American, and the *California*, which was very American, a big liner, nine thousand tons. No warning. Straight to the bottom. Oh, I say: celery soup, how wonderful. I haven't eaten since breakfast."

"My Uncle George is in Alberta," Munday said. "Everything's awfully big and everyone's tremendously tough. They all carry guns and chew tobacco and eat steak for breakfast. Quite terrifying, he said."

"Russian Cossacks more terrifying," the duke said. The others nodded.

"I think you'll find that Alberta is in Canada," Baring said. McWatters smirked.

"Medicine Hat isn't in America?" Munday asked.

"Scarcely at all."

"Oh. Well, it doesn't matter. Uncle George hated Medicine Hat. Rotten whisky, and he couldn't get the county cricket scores. He's probably in Arizona or Texas by now, and sucks to you," Munday told McWatters.

"What news from Petersburg?" the duke asked Baring.

"Let me see . . . The Tsar has appealed for unity. All must work for victory, that sort of thing."

"Of course. All will work! Russians devoted to Tsar."

Simms, sitting nearby, heard this. "Then it's all a bit pointless, isn't it?" he said. "If everyone loves him, why does he need to appeal for unity?"

The duke stiffened. He frowned at his plate.

"Oh, there's some story about a minister called Protopopoff," Baring said. "He claims to be in contact with the spirit of the late Mr Rasputin, who tells him how to fight the war."

"Protopopoff is cockroach," the duke said, more loudly than necessary.

"Obvious nonsense," Ogilvy said.

"But if it's nonsense," Simms said, "the Tsar wouldn't pay it any attention, would he?" Simms rarely had an idea, but when he did he clung to it. "Surely he's got advisers? Isn't there a sort of House of Commons?"

"He means the Duma," Baring said.

"Duma is cockroach." By now the duke was staring at nothing. He clutched his soup-spoon, rigidly, as if someone might steal it from him.

"I'm beginning to be sorry I asked." Simms tried a warm chuckle but nobody joined in.

"When do you think the Americans will be here?" Ogilvy asked Baring.

Duke Nikolai spoke a few harsh words in Russian. He stood up so abruptly that a mess servant had to grab his chair. He turned towards Trenchard and Cleve-Cutler. "With permission," he said, and marched out, still holding the soup-spoon. Ogilvy got to his feet but when he saw the adjutant hurrying after the duke he sat down.

"If you mean the American Army," Baring said, "it barely exists at present. When they have one, no doubt we shall see it, brandishing its revolvers and eating steak for its breakfast."

The duke was outside, arms folded, looking at the stars. After the noise of the mess, the night was so silent that his ears heard the tiny whistle of his blood.

"What's wrong, lad?" Brazier asked. No answer. "Pay no attention to those clowns in there," he said. "They've got trench foot in the brain. Ever seen trench foot? Yes, of course you have. Nasty-looking stuff, isn't it? Doesn't smell very nice, either." Brazier was surprised to hear himself sounding so friendly, even protective. Well, damn it, he might be a duke but he was a good ten inches shorter than the adjutant, and too slim to be a proper soldier, and a very long way from home. "Getting chilly, isn't it?" Brazier said. "How about a hot toddy? We might play some chess."

The duke made a fierce kick at the snow and sent it whirling. A door slammed and Count Andrei came towards them. He and the duke had a short, subdued conversation in Russian.

"I am in the dark," Brazier said. "In every sense."

"Treachery," the count said. "Tsar is stabbed in back. Russia bleeds. Duke bleeds."

"My goodness. That wasn't in the newspapers, was it?"

Duke Nikolai flung his arms out wide. "I love Tsar! I give my life for Tsar! If I die Tsar will live!"

"Full marks for loyalty," the adjutant said.

They went back to the mess. They were just in time for the pudding: plum cobbler. "Give me a big helping," Brazier told the servant, "and don't stint on the cream."

* * *

After dinner there was to be a smoking concert. While the anteroom was being prepared, Cleve-Cutler took Trenchard and Baring to his room for coffee.

"That captain," Trenchard said. "Ugly fellow."

"Crabtree, sir. He's crashed rather a lot. 'Crash' Crabtree, they call him."

"No fool. Brave, too. Dangerous combination, that." Trenchard looked at Baring.

"On the other hand, sir," Baring said, "if Crabtree were to be . . . um . . . sacked, or sent home, the rest of the squadron might think that perhaps . . ."

"He was right all along," the C.O. said.

"Of course he was right," Trenchard said. "Only a lunatic would fly Deep Offensive Patrols if there was any alternative. Worst possible way to fight."

"Except for all the others," Baring said.

"Show Cleve-Cutler the memorandum."

Baring gave him a sheet of paper, headed VIGOROUS OFFENSIVE.

An aeroplane is an offensive weapon.

An aeroplane is not a defensive weapon. Hostile aircraft can always cross the enemy's Lines.

The policy of British air fighting is one of relentless offensive.

This gives the enemy no opportunity to make hostile raids.

Thus superiority in the air is achieved.

An aeroplane is an offensive weapon. An aeroplane is not a defensive weapon.

"Most interesting," Cleve-Cutler said. He returned the paper to Baring, handling it carefully, as if it were part of a rare and valuable archive.

"Attack!" Trenchard boomed. "Take the battle to the enemy! Fight the Hun on your terms. Not on his."

"Oh, absolutely." There was much more to the air war than Trenchard's plan allowed for. There was the little matter of sending undertrained pilots in outclassed aeroplanes so deep into enemy territory that British losses were four times greater than German losses. How did that achieve superiority in the air? But the C.O. looked at the general's craggy face, granitic with certainty, and decided not to debate the point. "D'you know, I think they might just be ready for us," he said. "Shall we toddle back?"

* * *

The smoker began with a song-and-dance chorus. Four of the youngest pilots, lavishly made-up and dressed in split skirts, overstuffed blouses and flaxen pigtailed wigs, danced onto the makeshift stage with such enthusiasm that one stepped off the end and fell over the piano. Loud laughter surprised the other three and they stopped. Spud Ogilvy was master of ceremonies. He stepped forward. "Silly girl crashed on take-off," he announced. "The patrol is cancelled." For that he got thoroughly booed. "Well, alright, then," he said. "Postponed, slightly."

The second time they got it right. Briskly they sang:

> *"We're four plucky maidens*
> *All out on the spree!*
> *We've got the keyhole*
> *If you've got the key!*
> *Now Major Cleve-Cutler, don't make us be subtler,*
> *Can Hornets please come out and play?*
> *We're four plucky maidens*
> *All out on the spree!*
> *We've got the keyhole*
> *If you've got the key!"*

It brought a storm of applause. They performed a high-stepping dance routine that was clearly under-rehearsed. One dancer turned right when the others turned left, and had his legs kicked from under him. This was very popular. He was trampled as the remaining three doggedly finished their routine, and he crawled off while they took several bows.

"What you might call the offensive spirit," Cleve-Cutler said.

"Catchy tune," Trenchard said.

A corporal from the orderly room came on and did card tricks. Then Count Andrei sang a Russian ballad. It lasted too long and got only polite applause.

"Not a catchy tune," Trenchard said.

Ogilvy appeared and announced, "At huge expense, we now bring you an unforgettable dramatic performance. The padre will recite that unrivalled masterpiece, 'The Green Eye of the Little Yellow God'."

The padre was in tropical kit. His shorts had been lightly starched so that they stood out like wings. He wore a pith helmet, a cummerbund and a clerical collar. He got a standing ovation. He waited for absolute silence.

"The Green Eye," he declaimed, "of the Little Yellow God." He struck a pose: right arm raised, fingers extended.

"There's a one-eyed yellow idol to the north of Khatmandu;
There's a little marble cross below the town;
And a brokenhearted woman tends the grave of Mad Carew . . ."

Sudden hubbub at the back of the hall stopped him dead. All heads turned. Simms and McWatters strode to the front, talking loudly. Simms wore his flying helmet and flying boots. McWatters wore a false nose, plum-red, and a false moustache, grey turning white. "I say, I say!" McWatters brayed as they stamped onto the stage. "Twenty years on – and look! Nothing's changed. God, what memories!"

"Do you mind?" the padre said. "I'm trying to—"

Simms ignored him. "This was your squadron?" he asked.

"Dear old Hornet!" McWatters brayed. "1917, I was here, you know. Of course, the war hadn't got into its stride then."

"No?"

"1924, that was when things got serious. Then came '28 and '31, cracking good years, they were. Especially '31. Nineteenth Battle of the Somme. What a spiffing show!" By now the laughs were coming thick and fast.

"There's a one-eyed yellow idol—"

"Be a good chap," Simms told the padre. "Put it in the mess suggestions book."

"And here we are in 1937," McWatters said. "D'you know . . . we on the staff reckon we're really beginning to get the hang of the war." Ironic cheers greeted this.

Simms asked, "You think we'll soon have the Hun on the run?"

"By 1941. Well . . . let's say, 1943 at the very latest."

"He was known as 'Mad' Carew by the subs at Khatmandu . . . He was hotter than they felt inclined to tell," the padre said in a rush.

"Hot?" McWatters exclaimed. "I remember a dogfight in 1917. There I was, outnumbered fifty to one."

"Good Lord," Simms said. "What did you do?"

"The only thing I could. I roared defiance!" McWatters let out a long, hoarse bellow: *"Aaaaarrrr!"* He flexed his knees and shook his head. "I don't mind telling you, I fouled my breeches."

"Not surprising, sir. Fifty to one against you."

"No, no. Not *then*. Just now. When I went *Aaaaarrrrl* Damn . . ." More knee-flexing. "Done it again."

Huge laughter. The padre waited for his chance.

"There's a one-eyed yellow idol—"

"Tradition! That's a wonderful thing," McWatters said. "Here you are, Hornet Squadron, 1937, twenty years on, still biffing the Boche. What machine are you flying?"

"Sopwith Pup," Simms said.

"Ah – you know where you are with the Pup . . ." But McWatters' voice was drowned in a wave of laughter.

After the smoker, when the general had been escorted to his bedroom, Baring and the C.O. had a nightcap in the mess. "The 1937 sketch," Baring said. "Is that a running joke in this squadron?"

"No. Written specially."

"It didn't make the general laugh."

"Perhaps because it's not such a funny joke."

"Do you really think all this will just go on and on?"

"What's to stop it?" Cleve-Cutler said. "America? Can you really see American troops going over the top? Like the Somme? For our sake?"

"But it's such a waste. Not for me, I was middle-aged when it started, but for chaps like you—"

Cleve-Cutler laughed. "Chaps like me are having a whale of a time. I can't imagine any other life. I hope this war lasts for ever. Or until we get a replacement for the Pup. Whichever is sooner."

"I've made a note," Baring said.

* * *

"Gross impertinence?" Bliss said. "And Crabtree reckons it doesn't matter?"

Cleve-Cutler thought for a moment. "Actually, what Crabtree said wasn't impertinent. It was all very pertinent."

"That's not the blasted point," Colonel Bliss said, in a voice that silenced the rats under the floorboards. He had arrived from Wing H.Q. without warning, less than an hour after Trenchard and Baring departed. "You've given him a good kick in the goolies, I hope."

"Oh yes. Asked him what the hell he thought he was doing, putting damnfool ideas into the minds of the others."

"And he said what?"

"Said he couldn't resist telling the general the truth, because he might never get another chance, but it didn't matter."

"God's teeth," Bliss said. "It's not for every mouthy flight commander to have his say-so about the strategy of the Corps. What next? Shall we have a vote before every patrol? Elect the generals? Shall we do that? What's wrong with this Crabapple? Communist, is he?"

"Crabtree," the C.O. said. "Not Communist. Damn good flight commander, very experienced. Perhaps we should hear what the doctor has to say, sir."

Captain Dando brought a fat file with him. He rattled through Crabtree's medical record: "On a troopship that got torpedoed . . . rescued by destroyer, sent to France by ferry which hit a mine; broke two ribs and an arm . . . joined his regiment at the Front, shrapnel wound to the head . . . Military Cross . . . joined R.F.C., crashed, broke collarbone . . . taxying accident, gashed head . . . hit by Archie, crashed, concussion . . . ditto, burns to legs . . . ditto, dislocated shoulder . . . damaged by enemy scouts, hit tree, concussion . . ."

"And so on and so on," Cleve-Cutler said. "He crashed five times in 1916 without doing himself any permanent damage. Then he got knocked down in the middle of the battle of the Somme. Missing for a week."

"Probably spent it getting chased from shell-hole to shell-hole by the whizzbangs," Dando said.

"He couldn't remember the battle," the C.O. said.

"Not unusual with concussion," Dando said. "He got packed off to a convalescent home outside Paris. Told to rest. Eat lots of cheese."

"*Cheese?*" Bliss said.

"There was a medical theory . . ." Dando began; but Bliss raised his hands. "Spare me," he said. "I suppose I'd better see him."

Dando telephoned. The C.O.'s servant brought coffee. Bliss sipped it and frowned. "Much better than the muck they give us at Wing," he grumbled. "No point in asking where you get it?"

"No, sir."

Crabtree came in and saluted. The C.O. introduced the colonel. "Sit down," Bliss said. "How's the war going? Speak freely."

"Well, it's going splendidly, sir." Crabtree's voice was dull, and his gaunt, lined face was blank. "We're hammering the Hun on every Front," he said bleakly. "One more big push and Germany will crack like a rotten egg."

"Will it really?" Bliss pretended to be impressed. "The Somme didn't do the trick, did it?"

"The Somme was a splendid test of British guts and gallantry." The words came out as flat as slate, as if Crabtree were dictating them. "We slogged it out. The Boche took a pasting."

"Slogged it out. Is that how you saw the battle?"

"Well, now." Crabtree relaxed a little. "Actually there wasn't much to see, sir. Far too loud. Frightfully noisy." Gradually, life was creeping into his voice. "Awfully nice Gordon Highlander gave me a sandwich, bully-beef, thick as a book. Delicious. I couldn't make head nor tail of him, either. Scots, you see. *Awfully* nice chap." Crabtree shook his head, touched by the memory of human kindness.

"Anything else?" Bliss asked.

"I see General Haig's been made a field marshal," Crabtree said. "So the Somme must have been a victory, mustn't it? But I don't care, sir. I've heard it all before."

When he had left, Cleve-Cutler said: "Sack him if you like, sir, but I want someone just as experienced to replace him. He may be odd on the ground, but he's damn good upstairs."

"A week in the Somme, and all he can remember is a Scotch bully-beef sandwich," Bliss said.

"Shaky memory proves nothing, sir," Dando said. "I've known pilots to land after they had two scraps and bagged a flamer, and can't remember a damn thing."

"Anyone who argues with Boom Trenchard is off his rocker," Bliss declared. "Do something to this lunatic, give him some pills, get him drunk as a skunk, it might straighten out his head. God speed the plough! If the Somme was a victory, we'll never win."

"Ah!" Cleve-Cutler said. "We're going to win, are we, sir? I mean, is that official?"

"Don't you start," Bliss said.

* * *

"A brace of frogs," Crabtree said. "Lost, probably."

"Ask them to lunch," Ogilvy said. "Then we can have frogs' legs for starters."

They were stretched out in deck chairs, wrapped in blankets and enjoying the rare warmth of the weak and watery sun. Ogilvy's eyes were shut. Crabtree was looking through binoculars at a pair of biplanes, gauzy in the sunlight, circling high above the aerodrome.

"Very small frogs," he said.

"Not so loud. The others will want some."

"Here they come," Crabtree said.

"That's the trouble with this war," Ogilvy said lazily. "Everyone's in such a blasted *hurry.*" He opened his eyes.

The two biplanes were descending in opposing spirals. Each spiral turned around the same invisible central column, and the machines were so close to each other that they seemed to be on a permanent collision course. The reality was that, as the spirals crossed, one machine cleared the tail of the other by a length. It was a tiny margin. A bump in the air, a surge of power, a wobble in the controls would be enough to turn a display into a disaster.

"They may be frogs, but they can fly," Ogilvy said.

At three or four hundred feet the biplanes peeled away from each other, came together in line abreast, sideslipped in unison, and landed simultaneously. Cleve-Cutler was there to watch and admire.

The pilots were, as Crabtree had guessed, French. *"Félicitations,"* Cleve-Cutler said. *"Qu'est-ce que vous cherchez?"* What they were looking for was his signature on the delivery documents for two Nieuport 17s, factory-fresh.

"Nobody ordered Nieuport 17s" he said. They shrugged. They were test pilots from the Nieuport company, and they wanted transport to the nearest railhead so they could go home. They gave him a pencil. He hesitated. In the British Army, once you signed for something you were stuck with it. He had once signed – hastily – for twenty mules, which had turned out to be lame. He never forgot that. He walked around the nearer aeroplane, looking for faults. When he got back, the test pilots were waving the documents to dry the ink and Duke Nikolai was screwing the cap on his fountain pen. "What the dickens?" the C.O. demanded.

"Is mine," the duke said. He nodded at the Nieuports. "Is part of Imperial Russian Air Force."

Cleve-Cutler stared. "Are you drunk?"

"Is part of Imperial Russian Air Force."

"Not in my squadron."

"Is part of Imperial Russian Air Force."

"It'll take more than your say-so."

"Is part of Imperial Russian Air Force." The duke's face, grave and beautiful, showed all the confidence of a second cousin of God's appointed Tsar.

"Ah . . ." Cleve-Cutler groaned. "Christ Allbloodymighty." He went to his office and telephoned Colonel Bliss at Wing.

"Do nothing," Bliss said. "One false move might bring the whole house of cards tumbling down."

"What house of cards?"

"Do nothing."

Thirty minutes later, Bliss called back. "Have you done anything?"

"No. The Russians are out there, trying to read the pilot's manual. It's in French. What's going on, colonel?"

"For a start, they've bought those Nieuports." Bliss let that sink in. "I called the factory. They said the Russian embassy ordered the machines. I called Brigade, and Brigade called Corps, and Corps called Army H.Q., and finally somebody who went to Oxford with the Russian ambassador's first secretary got the truth out of him. Last week your Duke Nikolai bought two Nieuport 17s for cash."

"I'll be damned. How much?"

"Five thousand pounds. He has a bank in Paris."

"You mean a bank account."

"No, the family owns a bank. A small bank."

"Well, I should hope so. Nothing ostentatious."

"Don't get huffy, old boy. And for God's sake don't get snotty with those two. Strange sounds are coming out of St Petersburg, so I'm told. It's crucial that you don't rock the boat."

"Suppose my Russians want to play with their toys." Cleve-Cutler suddenly felt reckless. "If I say no, that'll rock the boat and it might bring down the whole house of cards. Then the cat will be out of the bag and the fat will be in the fire."

Bliss was not amused. "Do nothing," he said. "Wait for my call." He hung up. A minute later he called again. "It really is no joke," he said. "The fate of nations may be in your hands." The phone went dead.

Cleve-Cutler stared at the ink-stains on his desk. There was one that looked like a squashed rat with a stupid grin. "Idiot," he said, and banged it with his fist. The real rats under the floorboards started squeaking. "Nobody asked your opinion," he said. He sent for Captain Ogilvy. "Keep your Russians on the ground, Spud. Invent a reason. What are they doing?"

"Still trying to read the pilot's manual. And there's a nice yellow fog coming down."

"Good."

The fog did not keep Colonel Bliss away from Pepriac. "Couldn't call you," he told Cleve-Cutler. "This business has become too hot for the telephone." He made sure that the C.O.'s office door was shut. "It seems that a potential heir to the Russian throne may be on your squadron."

"Good Lord . . . And you're taking him away? I'll tell his servant to pack."

"The devil you will. He's staying here."

"But the risk—"

"The risk is just as great in Russia. Maybe greater. A month ago your Duke Nikolai was twenty-seventh in line for the throne. Since then, princes and grand dukes have been dropping like flies. Two had heart attacks and one drowned when he fell off his horse. Diphtheria has killed a couple more and influenza took five. The rest got eaten by wolves or mammoths or Cossacks or something, I don't know and it doesn't matter. The point is, Duke Nikolai is now only thirteenth in line."

Cleve-Cutler made a couple of whisky-sodas and thought about this astonishing development.

"Only twelve to go," he said. "Still, the Tsar has a big family, hasn't he?"

"Four daughters, unfortunately. One son, with haemophilia. If he takes a toss from his rocking-horse he'll bleed to death."

"Crikey. What a gloomy crew." When Colonel Bliss gave him a sharp, sideways look, Cleve-Cutler added: "Or, to put it another way, sir, our staunch and gallant allies in the east."

"Who need a hero. Now, more than ever, they need a thumping great hero."

"He's a lousy pilot, sir. Just because he's got a Nieuport he believes he's Albert Ball. He thinks Hun pilots are going to drop dead out of sheer humiliation."

Bliss wasn't listening. "Look what Ball's done for morale in England. Bucked it up wonderfully. Russians are a melancholy lot. Bad losers. They need a Ball of their own to buck them up."

"He can't shoot, sir."

"Thirteenth in line for the throne! An ace, and close to the Tsar! They'll cheer their gloomy heads off!"

"Sir, he couldn't hit a Zeppelin if you tied it to a tree."

"Oh yes he could. And will." Bliss slowly waved his hat. "Huzzah," he said softly. "Huzzah."

"I see." Cleve-Cutler dipped his little finger in the ink bottle and made the blot of the squashed rat even uglier. "You want me to send the Russians on D.O.P.s."

"Far more important, I want you to bring 'em back."

"Which means . . . large escorts."

"Use the whole damn squadron, if you have to. Just give me a Russian hero. Preferably two."

That was that. The decision was made. "You'll stay to dinner, colonel?"

"Another time. We've got lamb cutlets tonight, at Wing. Also a Stilton which is at its peak."

They walked to his car. "I might as well say what I think, sir," Cleve-Cutler said. "This is a bloody silly way to fight a war. I mean, why don't you simply lie? Give Duke Nikolai an M.C. and a D.F.C with bar, and say in the citation that he shot down six Albatroses and four Halberstadts and a Hun carrier pigeon, and ship him home to Russia?"

"He wouldn't wear it, old chap. Nikolai is an honourable duke. He won't lie, and he won't let us lie about him. I don't pretend to understand it, but I believe it's called breeding."

"It works for pigs and horses," Cleve-Cutler said, "but it'll be the death of us out here."

* * *

Nikolai and Andrei celebrated the arrival of the Nieuports by taking a couple of bottles of pepper vodka – a gift from their Paris embassy – down to Rosie's Bar. The place was busy. Cavalry officers were celebrating somebody's birthday. A bunch of gunners were celebrating an M.C. Two lots of sappers were trying to out-sing each other. When a crowd of Hornet Squadron pilots arrived, the atmosphere became highly charged.

McWatters was in the party; so were Crabtree, Simms, Dash and an Australian called Maddegan, just arrived in France, almost nineteen years old, straight from flying training in Kent, and so pleased to be on a fighting squadron that he couldn't keep still. He wasn't especially tall, but he was broad and heavy: the floorboards groaned as he shifted from foot to foot, anxious not to miss any casual remark. Crabtree watched him. "You're jolly hefty, aren't you?" he said.

"Comes from heaving barrels around, sir. My father owns the biggest brewery in New South Wales, sir."

Despite his menacing bulk, Maddegan had an innocent face and an eager smile. Only his crooked nose spoiled his looks. "You box?" Crabtree said. Maddegan nodded. "Dad taught me not to hurt the other fellow unnecessarily. I smack him hard in round one, sir."

Crabtree was impressed. "Goodness," he said. "A philanthropic bruiser."

Count Andrei was glad to see the pilots arrive. Success and vodka had made Duke Nikolai very Russian. He had harangued Andrei about the divinely-appointed genius of the tsars, of Ivan the Terrible, of Boris Godounov, of Peter the Great, of the magnificent Catherine, of the bravest of the brave, Tsar Alexander, who had flung Napoleon out of Russia . . . Andrei occasionally put in one or two words of support. But not three words, or four. Nikolai was not a good listener. On the other hand, he was not a great speaker, either, especially when the vodka led him to try to quote heroic Russian poetry and he mangled the words and crippled the lines and choked a little at the tragic beauty of it all. Andrei sat quietly and knocked his fists together under the table. He was relieved when Crabtree came over.

"You fly tomorrow," Crabtree told them. "Orders from Wing. In fact we all fly tomorrow." The duke stood and embraced him. "I say, old chap," Crabtree said. "Not in front of the children."

"Big killings tomorrow," Nikolai said happily. "Big Hun massacre."

"Well . . . That's as maybe." Crabtree was uncomfortable: boasting and bragging wasn't done in the R.F.C. "We've got a new boy. He's from Australia. Maddegan, meet our Russian bigwigs."

They shook hands. Crabtree drifted away.

"Magellan," Duke Nikolai said. He turned to Count Andrei. "Discovered Pacific Ocean. Here is relative! We drink toast."

"It's Maddegan," the Australian said. "But most people call me Dingbat, because that's the way I box."

"Dingbat." Nikolai liked the sound. He turned it into a toast. "Dingbat!"

"Sorry, but I never drink . . ." Maddegan began. Count Andrei pressed a tiny glass into his hand. Its contents were clear as water. "Well, I reckon one little sip won't harm," he said.

Nearby, Charles Dash and Harry Simms found a table and ordered a bottle of wine. "Pepriac's a rotten dump, isn't it?" Simms said. "I haven't seen a girl in weeks. And just look at this mob."

Dash poured the wine. "On the subject of girls, I need some advice," he said, "but only if you promise to keep it secret."

"You're speaking to the tomb, old man."

"Thing is . . . I seem to have struck it rich with a rather . . . um . . . generous girl." Simms' eyes opened wide. "Or girls," Dash said.

"You mean you can't remember how many? You must have been well ginned that night."

"No gin. And it was more than one night. The circumstances were somewhat . . . strange."

McWatters arrived with a glass and helped himself to wine.

"Go away," Dash said. "This is a personal matter."

"Women keep raping him," Simms explained.

"Shocking business," McWatters said. "Eat lots of anchovies, that's what I do. Anchovies put starch in your dicky."

110

"Anyway, where's the problem?" Simms said. "Popsies falling over themselves to oblige, doesn't sound like a problem. More like a solution."

"I'm not going to discuss it," Dash muttered.

"You've got the pox, is that it?" McWatters asked.

"Don't be disgusting."

"Doc Dando is your man. Sorted out my athlete's foot in no time." He signalled for more wine.

"It's not the pox. I just wonder if I've overdone it, that's all."

"Ah ha!" Simms said. "Now I understand. It's a question of quantity, not quality."

"At the time, it was a question of sheer bloody survival," Dash said. "I mean to say, is there a limit?"

"A chap can pump himself dry, I suppose," McWatters said. "It's just spinal fluid, after all. You can't have much of a reserve tank in your spine, can you?"

"I don't want to rupture myself."

"My father has a stallion on stud," Simms said. "Won the Cesarewitch. Earns his corn twice a day, seven days a week. Fifty guineas a poke."

Dash said curtly: "I wasn't in a position to ask for payment."

"Maybe all you're suffering from is cramp," McWatters said. "Try anchovies. Very good for cramp." He saw the Russians and their bottles and moved to their table.

"It's supposed to be perfectly natural," Dash said, "so why did it give me such a headache?"

Maddegan, sitting between the Russians, was explaining that his family was teetotal. "After working all day in a brewery the last thing you want is beer. I never touched the hard stuff because I was always in training." He took another sip. "Hot, isn't it?" This was his third glass. The first two had gone down easily.

McWatters slid into a chair. "You're a lucky chap, Dingbat. This stuff is like Holy Water in Russia. Turns your blood to fire. You'll soar like an eagle tomorrow."

Nikolai gave everyone half an inch of vodka.

111

"I suppose the pepper makes it so hot," Maddegan said.

"Dingbat is the heavyweight boxing champion of all Australia," McWatters told them.

"Hey, steady on. I won a few fights, but—"

"A toast," Nikolai announced. "Victory to Tsar and champion Dingbat!" Maddegan saw the others knock their vodka back, and he did the same. He sat quietly until his eyes stopped watering. The amazing thing was McWatters was right: the stuff did turn his blood to fire. With enough of it inside him, he could easily be heavyweight champion of anywhere.

"Confusion to the Tsar's enemies!" McWatters declared. "Let battle commence! The Hun is doomed."

"And we're here to doom him," Maddegan said.

It seemed like an obvious toast, but Nikolai failed to pick up his glass.

"Hun is not real enemy," he said. Hunched shoulders made him look even smaller. He was staring into the smoky, noisy room as if it were a battlefield. "Real enemy is Socialists."

"Absolutely correct," McWatters said. "D'you know, I can see one of the bastards from here. That ginger-haired chap over there. Notorious Socialist. See him, Dingbat?" Maddegan stood and stared. "Hates Australians too," McWatters said. "Dingbat, why don't you go and knock him into the middle of next week?" He gave Maddegan a shove, just enough to get him going.

Maddegan vanished into the crowd. Quite soon, there was uproar at the other end of the room as a table crashed and glasses shattered. "Damned Etonians," Simms said. "You can't take them anywhere."

"I'm still not sure what to do next," Dash said.

"Reinforce success," Simms said. "That's the army's motto, isn't it?"

Maddegan found people side-stepping out of his way. Or maybe he was side-stepping out of their way, it was hard to tell, because sometimes he saw two of everybody. But a path always opened up and he found the Russians' table and dropped into his chair far more heavily than he intended. "Blocked his knock off," he said. They drank to that.

"I doomed the bastard," Maddegan said. "Doomed him."

"Medal for Dingbat," Nikolai told Andrei.

"I say," McWatters said. "I'll be damned if there isn't another bloody great Socialist!" He pointed at a sapper captain. "That bald fellow."

"Watch me doom the bastard," Maddegan said.

"Please," Andrei said to McWatters. "Is this wise?" But he was too late. Maddegan was already up and weaving his way towards the sapper. "The duke should leave now," Andrei said. "We must not risk a diplomatic incident."

"*Sacré bleu*," McWatters said. "Your English got better very fast, didn't it?" Shouts of rage, and the sound of breaking furniture, reached them.

Simms and Dash went over to the Russians' table. "What's all the racket about?" Simms asked.

"Diplomatic incident," McWatters said.

Maddegan came back, jumping from table to table, leaving a trail of curses and spilled drinks. He was dirty and his face was bleeding and he was gasping for breath. "Doomed the bastard," he said. "Doomed him!"

"I had nothing to do with this," McWatters said. He was speaking to several officers who had come barging through the crowd. They had been in a fight and were very ready for another. "Just arrived," McWatters told them. "Just leaving."

"Fucking Flying fucking Corps!" roared a young gunner. Both his lips were split and, in his fury, he spat blood. "I say we chuck the fuckers out of the window! See how they fly!" That got a harsh cheer. Dash felt his guts shrivel as if trying to hide inside him. These lunatics were going to break his neck. It was a twenty-foot drop. He wasn't going to die fighting the Hun. He was going to die on a filthy stretch of French cobblestones. Dead at nineteen, and now he'd never know her name. And then all the lights went out. The blackness was blinding. He held up his arms to guard his face and ran for his life, bouncing off men, cracking his shins on stools, ignoring the pain.

* * *

"We shall be like an umbrella," Cleve-Cutler said. He wanted his breakfast. His voice had an edge like a rusty knife. The duke stood erect, his head tilted back so that he could look under the steep peak of his cap. His calf-length boots made a liquid gleam, and his buttons shone like gold. Maybe they are gold, the C.O. thought. Maybe his blood is blue. Maybe his nerves are steel and his balls are brass and his brains are pure cauliflower. "I suppose you have umbrellas where you come from," he said.

Duke Nikolai and Count Andrei spoke briefly in Russian. Nikolai cleared his throat but Cleve-Cutler got in first: "Not in Imperial Russian Air Force," he said.

Nikolai frowned until he was looking through slits. He seemed confused, as if the C.O. had suddenly barked like a dog.

Andrei said, "His Highness is a little low this morning."

"Not in Royal Flying Corps, chum. Nobody in this Corps is allowed to be low. He wasn't low last night, was he? High as a kite, so I'm told. And now His Highness is going to be high again. As soon as you've discovered how to fly these buses, tell me. Big offensive patrol today. You'll be at ten thousand. The rest of the squadron will be at twelve and fifteen thousand. Like an umbrella. Because the sky is going to be raining Huns over there."

They were standing at the edge of the airfield. The sky was all bare blue, made lovely by a sun that promised warmth and wellbeing to all. It lied. Early spring was full of such lies. The wind would bring cloud and veils of rain and sudden, black squalls.

"Why ten thousand?" Nikolai asked.

"High enough to be above the worst Archie, low enough for you to find the enemy. Find some nice fat slow two-seaters doing reconnaissance. Good targets. Easy meat."

"Albatros is better."

"Not for you. Murdering bastards are Albatroses. You go and knock down some rabbits first and—"

"Albatros is better."

"A kill is a kill. Learn your trade. Now – breakfast."

Already the fitters were testing the engines, the riggers were checking the tension of the control cables, the armourers were cleaning the guns, oiling the interrupter gear, fingering the belted ammunition in search of an irregular round that might jam the breech and leave the pilot defenceless.

The Pups were not in the best condition. Most had spent the winter in the open, rocking and shuddering in the wind and the wet. They were made of wood and canvas, stressed by wires. Sometimes the weeks and months of rain and fog and snow made small but significant warps in the structure. A one-inch distortion in a wing was enough to alter the airflow and spoil the performance: lift was lost, speed was lost, perhaps – in a fight – everything was lost. Dope never made canvas totally waterproof. Moisture might gather inside the aeroplane. In time, it secretly rotted corners of the fabric. How could anyone tell, except by stripping off the canvas? There was another method of discovery, and that was the violent manoeuvre of combat. Sometimes a Pup fell out of battle with ragged flags flailing from its wings. Perhaps the canvas was unstitched by enemy bullets, perhaps by French mildew. There was rarely a chance to know.

Cleve-Cutler was eating bacon when he heard a dull drum-roll of thunder. He stopped chewing. The thunder exhausted itself. "Nasty frog weather," Crabtree said.

"Come with me," the C.O. said to Crabtree.

Cloud was building up on the western horizon.

"Doesn't smell like thunder," Cleve-Cutler said.

Gerrish joined them. "Probably an ammo dump went up. I remember hearing one that was fifty miles away."

But there was more thunder, dotted with the gloomy thud of individual explosions. It came from the east. This was an artillery barrage. "Damn," Crabtree said. "They're at it again." He sounded like a tired schoolmaster at the end of a long term.

"Us or them?" Cleve-Cutler wondered.

The adjutant had appeared and was lighting his pipe. "Not us," he said. "No build-up. No reserves."

"Can't be a Hun offensive," Gerrish said. "No-man's-land is still a bog."

"That leaves the French," Crabtree said. "They're probably shelling the

Portuguese." The others ignored him. "Not an easy target," he said. "Small and elusive."

The C.O. telephoned Wing H.Q. "It's the Boche," Colonel Bliss told him. "God knows what they're up to. Maybe it's a decoy, maybe it's a Teutonic blunder. Intelligence were taken completely by surprise. How are your Russians getting on?"

"No complaints, sir." Almost true, he thought.

"Good. One thing about this barrage, there should be lots of trade for you upstairs. Huns directing guns and so on. You'll be spoiled for choice."

By mid-morning, every pilot had flight-tested his Pup and the mechanics were making final adjustments. The Russians were an exception. They taxied their Nieuports up and down the field, then got out and reread the manufacturer's manual. Finally, Spud Ogilvy went over to them.

"What is *mitraillette?*" Nikolai asked.

"Machine gun."

Nikolai nodded. "*Naturellement,*" he said. He made it sound like a test of Ogilvy's knowledge. He tossed the manual to Andrei and walked away.

"What's his problem?" Ogilvy said.

"Pepper vodka. Afterwards he is depressed."

They looked at Nikolai, who was kicking a wheel of his Nieuport. "He's not stupid," Andrei said. "But when you grow up knowing that everyone will always do exactly what you say, there is no incentive to think."

"What about you? Can't you get your machine off the ground?"

"He must fly first. For me to fly before the duke would be bad manners."

"I don't suppose we could forget manners and just concentrate on the war?"

"Not in Imperial Russian Air Force," Andrei said lightly.

Cleve-Cutler briefed the flight commanders. He would lead the squadron a mile or two inside enemy territory and prowl up and down until the Russians found something slow and stupid to knock down. If any Hun scouts tried to interfere, then it was all hands to the pumps. Above all, the Russians must get home intact.

116

"That's assuming they can fly," Ogilvy said. "The duke's got a royal hangover."

"Everyone flies. Which reminds me: what the hell happened to the new boy? Maddegan? He looks as if he fell downstairs."

"He fell downstairs, sir," Crabtree said. "The lights went out at Rosie's and he fell downstairs."

Ogilvy said, "Didn't he go slightly berserk, first?"

"Not berserk," Crabtree said. "Amok, perhaps. He was running amok, so the lights went out. I did it. I went outside and smashed the generator."

"No more parties," Cleve-Cutler ordered. "Rosie's is now out of bounds. For God's sake try and fight one war at a time. Can Maddegan fly?"

"He flies like he fights," Gerrish said. "He's all over the place."

"Make sure he gets the worst Pup. Right, we'll take an early lunch."

As they walked to the mess, a Nieuport flew low overhead, roaring lustily. The other soon followed. "Progress," Cleve-Cutler said. "You'll have to pay for that generator, you know."

"I don't care," Crabtree said placidly.

"Is there anything you *do* care about?"

The crevices in Crabtree's face deepened as he made himself think. "Does *Wiener schnitzel* count? I used to be passionately fond of a good *schnitzel*." He spoke without passion. "But we can't get it now, can we?"

"If it's any consolation, neither can they. Or so the newspapers say."

"Dear me," Crabtree said. "Everybody's fighting for it and nobody's got it. Someone's made an awful jorrocks of this war."

They were halfway through their soup when a waiter told Ogilvy that a sergeant-fitter wanted to see him. It was about the Russian gentlemen. "Crashed," Gerrish guessed.

But Ogilvy came back with a different report. "They've gone. They refuelled the Nieuports and told the sergeant they were going to get an Albatros. Then . . . cheerio."

The soup plates were cleared. Curried sausages and rice were served. The flight commanders waited for Cleve-Cutler to speak. He said nothing.

He ate unhurriedly and enjoyed the illicit pleasure of allowing time to slip by when he might have been hurrying the squadron into the air. He thought: Sod 'em. Let 'em go. They're so keen on getting killed, I can't stop them. But the correct course of action was to abandon lunch and lead a search . . . Search where? Nobody knows where the silly sods have gone. But inaction was a dereliction of duty. Too late. Never find 'em now. If it was too late, that was caused by delay . . . Sod it, he thought. Let them play silly buggers, I'm having my lunch. And so more time slipped by; until steamed treacle duff was served and by then it really was far, far too late.

*   *   *

Plans were changed. The squadron would still fly, but now it would carry out a Deep Offensive Patrol.

There was a sense of muffled regret among the pilots as they ambled over to the flights. So much time had passed since the last man was lost in action – two weeks? three? – that nobody was sure who it had been. Crabtree had replaced Tim Lynch, yes, but when did Cooper and Radley catch a packet? The discussion was half-hearted. Anyway, Nikolai and Andrei were a special case. They had *chosen* to fly into oblivion. Eccentric in life and dotty in death. Ogilvy summed it up when he said, "They've gone looking for trouble in a sky lousy with Huns. They can't shoot straight, they can't fly crooked, and they're actually trying to find a bright, shiny Albatros. Or two. Or ten."

"A" Flight taxied to the far end of the field and ruddered around to face into the wind. Cleve-Cutler was leading; Gerrish would fly beside him. The C.O. raised his arm and glanced left and right. The other five Pups were waiting, trembling in the prop-wash, smoke pumping from their exhaust stubs. "B" and "C" Flights were bumping and swaying around the perimeter. He felt enormous pride in his command. Women were pretty, sex was fireworks, but to be leading a squadron of scouts into battle – that was bliss. Two black shapes wandered into his vision. He looked up. A pair of Nieuports drifted ahead of him, losing height, reaching for the grass, bouncing and then running safely. "Fuck," said Cleve-Cutler.

The Pups could not wait: the engines would soon overheat. This was turning into a rotten day. He unclipped the Very pistol and fired a red flare, straight up. It was the wash-out signal. Within a minute, all eighteen Pups were taxiing back to where they had come from.

Duke Nikolai had his helmet off and he was brushing his hair. "Waste of time," he said. "No Huns."

"You disobeyed orders." Anger made Cleve-Cutler hot. "You took off without permission." Nikolai shrugged. "No Huns," he said. "Waste of time." Oil fumes had coated his face, leaving white circles where the goggles had been. "Could that be," Cleve-Cutler said, "because you failed to cross the Lines?"

Nikolai looked at him as if he had tried to borrow money. He picked up his helmet and said: "What is lunch?"

"Bugger lunch."

Count Andrei was approaching. "He knows," Nikolai said, and headed for the mess.

"The guns have stopped," Andrei said. The last Pup engine had been switched off and the silence was total.

"Bugger the guns. You took off without permission. Where did you go?"

"We flew east. Crossed the Lines, a little Archie, not much. No Hun balloons. No Hun aeroplanes. We flew on, ten miles, fifteen. Still no Huns. Some English types, FEs I think, they waved, we waved. But still no Huns. So we went down low and looked around. Nothing. Empty. No Huns in the sky, no Huns on the ground."

"Impossible. They're hiding."

"The trenches are empty, major."

"But that's ridiculous." Cleve-Cutler saw his squadron all around him, fuelled and armed and ready to fight. Five minutes earlier he had been about to lead it in combat; he still had a trace of the metallic taste of adventure in his mouth; and now these Russian jokers strolled home and said there was no enemy to fight . . . "I don't believe it," he said. "Empty trenches? No Huns anywhere?" The bottom had dropped out of his world.

The flight commanders were standing nearby, waiting for fresh orders.

"Didn't you see anything at all?" Ogilvy asked Andrei. "Cars, horses, trains, tents, fires?"

"Burning buildings we saw. But nothing that lived."

"For fifteen *miles*?" Cleve-Cutler said. "That's absurd."

"Jerry's done a bunk," Crabtree said. "He's a treacherous customer. A slithy tove."

"Shut up!" Cleve-Cutler said. "If you can't talk sense, don't talk tosh." That left everyone silent. "Oh, sod it," he said. "I'd better go and speak to Wing. If anyone tries to take off," he told Gerrish, "shoot him. Shoot him somewhere painful." He strode away.

Bliss and all the senior officers had been summoned to a meeting at Brigade. Eventually a middle-aged lieutenant came to the phone. "To be honest sir, there's a bit of a panic here," he said. Cleve-Cutler banged the receiver on its rest. As usual, loud noises made the rats squeak. "At least you vermin are loyal," he said.

*   *   *

One Pup refused to start. Another threw a cylinder while it was taxiing. The C.O. took a sixteen-strong squadron across the Front at six thousand feet: well within range of light Archie and heavy machine guns. He skirted a cloudbank, ready to duck into its cover. Nothing fired. A few shells burst in the fields behind the German lines: probably British batteries still searching for enemy guns. Far below, two RE8s were trying to help. He pushed up his goggles and used his binoculars to search the ground. The image jumped and blurred with every bounce and twitch of the Pup, but he got one good look at a long stretch of German trench and it was empty.

They flew east for five or six miles, climbing steadily and always looking up, past the towering hills of cloud, at the high spaces where packs of Albatros and Pfalz and Fokker liked to lurk. A flight of SE5s went by, returning home; that was all.

Cleve-Cutler took the squadron up to fifteen thousand feet, half a mile above the clouds. It was a glorious afternoon and they owned it. For the next fifteen minutes, his sixteen Pups sat high in the sky, their chocolate-brown skins gleaming in the sunlight. And still nobody came up to argue.

When they were at least fifteen miles beyond the enemy Lines, he put the flights into line astern and led them in a shallow dive, picking out the canyons and tunnels through the clouds. He flattened out at two thousand feet and waved "B" and "C" Flights away to left and right. In this wide formation they cruised home. Nobody fired a shot at them. Nothing down there moved, nothing lived. Crabtree was right: Jerry had done a bunk. "Bastards," Cleve-Cutler said.

EARTHQUAKE STRENGTH 4:

Windows and dishes rattle. Glasses clink. Crockery clashes.

Next morning at ten, Sergeant Lacey filled Captain Lynch's fountain pen from a bottle of Oxford-blue ink that had been in Lynch's room. A Janáček piano sonata was playing on the gramophone. As he wiped the nib with an Old Harrovian tie which he kept for that purpose, he looked out of the window and saw Colonel Bliss approaching. He opened Lynch's cheque-book, made a couple of gentle flourishes with the pen and then wrote, quickly and confidently: *Scottish Fund for Distressed Gentlefolk. Twenty guineas.* He signed *Timothy Lynch* and dated it five weeks ago. He stood and lifted the needle from the record as Bliss came in. "Good morning, sir. The adjutant is at the churchyard, in charge of the burial party for Lieutenant Shanahan."

"Really?" Bliss was booted and spurred and he shone with the care of a devoted batman. "I didn't know you'd lost another chap."

"Mr Shanahan's motorcycle was in collision with a cow. He died in hospital, sir."

"Why couldn't Shanahan be in collision with a Hun? Anyway, I'm not here to talk about him. Look here: Great Wall of China. Built by the Chinks to keep out the Mormons. Right?"

"Probably not, sir. The Mormons are a religious sect in Utah. Perhaps you meant the Mongols."

"Did I say Mormons? I meant Mongols."

"Although the Mormons are by far the greater menace. They reject all forms of alcohol, for instance."

"That's their funeral. The Great Wall of China didn't work, did it?"

"So we are led to believe, sir. However, China is still full of Chinese.

For Mongols, you have to go to Mongolia."

"Don't quibble, sergeant. Isn't that an Old Harrovian tie?"

"It belonged to Shanahan, sir. I'm having it cleaned before I send it to his next-of-kin."

"Oh. Jolly good."

Bliss was no fool. He was a little too fastidious about his appearance, he despised foreign food without tasting it, he could be a great bore on the subject of fox-hunting. But he had seen the military value of aeroplanes long before 1914, and he had paid to learn how to fly. Soon he was promoted out of the cockpit and into a staff job, but he remembered what it was like to be a pilot: the glorious, god-like feeling of soaring away from the pettiness of Earth, and the brutal terror when you suddenly thought this frail machine might be falling apart around you; he knew the value of belonging to the most exclusive club in the world, with its buoyant, rowdy comradeship, and he knew the silent acceptance of frequent deaths from crashing on take-off or breaking up in midair or catching fire anywhere at all.

So Bliss had developed a shrewd nose for squadron morale. He reckoned that the abrupt German retreat had left Hornet Squadron puzzled and a bit discouraged.

The pilots were assembled in the anteroom.

"First, the facts," he said. "The Hun has surrendered a massive amount of territory along fifty miles of the Front, from Arras in the north to Soissons in the south. The average retreat is twenty miles but near St Quentin it's more like thirty. Yesterday's bombardment was merely cover while the Hun rearguard fell back behind their new Line, which is called the Hindenburg Line, although I doubt if Field Marshal von Hindenburg did much of the digging." A couple of pilots chuckled.

Bliss then explained just what the retreat meant.

Pepriac was now forty or fifty minutes' flying time from the Hindenburg Line. That was no good. The squadron could expect to move soon, but not to any of the aerodromes just abandoned by the Hun. They were unusable: the fields cratered, the buildings booby-trapped, the roads mined. Indeed, all the territory that the British Army was taking over was a wasteland. Every bridge was down, every house was burned, every well was poisoned. The enemy had been busy.

Finally, Bliss came to the big question.

What had the Hun got out of this massive retreat? He had got the Hindenburg Line. By all reports, it was a wall. Well, history had seen plenty of walls. Hadrian had built a wall, hadn't he, to keep the Scots out, and a fat lot of good it did him. The Chinese built their Great Wall of China to keep the Mongol hordes out, but they forgot to inform the Mongol hordes of this, and the Great Wall was a Great Flop. Now Hindenburg had his Line. Maybe he expected to win by sitting on his Prussian bum on cold concrete. Fine! "Just remember this," Bliss ended. "Nobody ever won a war by going backwards."

He stayed to have coffee with the C.O. "Glad you came, sir," Cleve-Cutler said. "Some of them need bucking up. Not the new boys so much as the old sweats who remember the Somme."

"They're precious few."

"Yes. Odd, isn't it? Months of slog and rivers of blood got us six miles nearer Berlin, at most. Now Fritz gives us thirty miles for nothing. I thought he wasn't supposed to have a sense of humour."

"Hullo!" the colonel said. The distant hiccuping blips of Pups warming up had grown to a solid roar. "They're off."

They took their coffee outside and watched "A" Flight transform itself from a bunch of wheeled vehicles, wobbling at every bump, into six flying machines, lifted strongly by the air rushing past their wings. The two Nieuports followed. Nobody stalled, nobody collided, nobody crashed. Everyone on the airfield relaxed. The doc went back into his office. "They won't score today," Bliss said. "The Hun's still settling in."

"I hope so. We need some practice. Look at Maddegan, waffling about at the tail. God knows how he got his wings."

Bliss pretended surprise. "My dear Hugh! Boom wants more squadrons. If a man doesn't kill himself in England, he's sent to France, lickety-split."

"And kills himself here."

"A" Flight droned around the sky, climbing. The Nieuports had placed themselves several lengths away from the formation.

"Some chaps survive and prosper," Bliss said. "Look at Ball. Dreadful pilot at first."

Suddenly Cleve-Cutler had had enough of Bliss's official optimism. "I bet you twenty to one that Maddegan won't last a fortnight."

"Bad taste, old chap," Bliss said. "Also poor odds." He waved at his driver to bring the car over.

* * *

The weather was rubbish.

Gerrish took his patrol up through dirty, patchy cloud that gave way to a lucky slice of clear air at four thousand feet; lucky because it gave him room to circle so that the flight could close up and the Russians could find them again. Maddegan never succeeded in closing up. He was still five or six lengths behind when Gerrish climbed into the next layer of cloud. It blew out of the southwest, as white as surf.

Maddegan winced and braced himself as his Pup smashed into it. Nobody had taught him how to fly through this stuff. It blinded him, so he shut his eyes. As long as the seat of his pants told him he was leaning back, he let the Pup fly herself. After a long time a sudden dazzle made him look, and the horizon was at a violent angle. Gerrish circled again, while Maddegan straightened himself out. They were in another slice of clear air. Above them, a wilderness of cloud hustled along as if it was late for a storm. Seen from below it was all hills and holes which changed shape as they crowded each other. Gerrish steered for the holes and hoped they weren't dead ends. Sometimes he saw the two Nieuports, far off to his left. They looked like flies in a canyon.

At sixteen thousand feet there was still no sight of the top of the wilderness. Gerrish knew he couldn't outclimb it. The wind was strengthening and scattering the Pups. He took them back down to the sanity of clear air.

By now Maddegan had no idea of their position. Gerrish was fairly sure

125

they were over the Hindenburg Line. A lot depended on the strength and direction of the wind. He found a pin-point on the eastern horizon and flew directly at it, keeping one eye on the compass. The wind shoved him hard off-course. He nudged the Pup around until he was head-on to the wind. It blew from the southeast. That was a huge swing: more than ninety degrees in less than an hour. If it stayed like that, it would help them fly back to Pepriac. Good.

They patrolled for another half an hour and saw nothing. Gerrish was stiff and cold and bored. He turned for home and within five minutes a German aeroplane dropped out of the wilderness above them, four hundred yards ahead and flying in the same direction.

"Lost!" Gerrish said. He signalled by hand for the flight to spread out wide and rewarded himself with a chunk of chocolate. Now there was nothing to do but watch the Russians make a botch of it.

The two Nieuports crept up on the machine. It was an LVG, unmistakable with its great six-cylinder engine sticking up, bang in front of the pilot's face. The observer had a gun, but he wasn't facing backwards. He was leaning forward and shouting at the pilot.

"*Very* lost," said Gerrish. "Got the wind wrong, didn't you?"

This was the first time Duke Nikolai had fired the Lewis gun in action. It was rigged on the Nieuport's upper wing so the bullet stream would clear the propeller arc. Still the idiot Huns had not seen him. He eased the stick back and the Nieuport floated up to the LVG. As he squeezed the gun-button his machine bounced in the LVG's wash and all his shots went high. One in three was tracer. The enemy observer pointed to the burning bullets streaking away; he actually *pointed*. Nikolai was so furious with himself, and with this crass Hun, that he overcorrected and missed again. Now the drum was empty. He hauled the Lewis down its slide.

The German pilot flung the LVG into a vertical bank, and dived, and saw a line of Pups waiting, and changed his mind and decided to climb for the clouds. Count Andrei was waiting above and cut him off. Nikolai had a second chance, attacking from the beam. It should have been a full-deflection shot. Ogilvy had taught him to aim well ahead. Instead he aimed at the pilot and saw all his bullets pass behind the tail. As he zoomed over the LVG he remembered that Ogilvy had also told him always to dive under a two-seater. The German gunner got in a long burst and wrecked one of the Nieuport's wingtips.

None of the Pups attacked the LVG. They put themselves between it and escape, while Nikolai again dragged the Lewis down its mounting, ripped off another empty drum, slammed on a fresh one, shunted the Lewis up into firing position and searched the whirling sky for the enemy.

With his third drum he came from below and killed the observer. He also riddled the tail unit and left the rudder flapping uselessly and the elevators smashed. Now the pilot could neither dive nor climb. Gerrish got the binoculars on him. "End of the line, laddy," he said. "All get out." The pilot took off his goggles and threw them away. He twisted his head, searching for the Nieuport, and finally found it behind and above him, turning to dive. "For fuck's sake, get it right this time," Gerrish muttered. Hot needles of tracer reached for the LVG. The Nieuport pulled out and climbed and everyone watched. Nothing happened for seven seconds. "Oh, sod it," Gerrish said. The fuel tank exploded. The LVG blew apart. Blast gently nudged Gerrish's Pup sideways. The fireball made the sky look dingy, and then it shrivelled. A spray of bits, some burning, fell quite quickly and got swallowed by the cloudbank. The Pups were left circling a smear of smoke.

* * *

"Not exactly Queensberry Rules," Gerrish said to the C.O. "More like amateur night in the abattoir."

"It's a start."

"I don't like my lads being used as nursemaids, sir. Even if he is the next Tsar but twenty-eight."

"I'll spread the chore around, Plug."

When Cleve-Cutler next saw Duke Nikolai he congratulated him.

"Was luck. LVG was stupid. Albatros is better, I think."

"You'll have another chance this afternoon. With 'B' Flight."

Nikolai delicately wrinkled his nose. "Is better with 'A' Flight."

"Well, that's my decision."

"Is better with 'A' Flight."

Cleve-Cutler's fingertips prickled. "One day you'll play that card once too often and . . ." But he got control of himself before he could complete the threat, and he walked away. His hands were trembling with rage. That had never happened before.

* * *

The Russians flew whenever the weather allowed, and always with an escort to give cover. A spell of easterly winds helped, and several times they chased Huns that had been blown too far west and were labouring home; always the enemy escaped.

The next patrol was a morning show. "A" Flight was gasping and freezing at nineteen thousand feet when Gerrish saw a pattern of dots drifting across white cloud about two miles below.

The Pup was not built to be dived steeply for two miles. Jokers who tried that trick found that the Pup's speed built until it went off the clock and the wings shuddered feverishly and occasionally broke. And pilots were not designed to fall like a stone for ten thousand feet, either. It gave them piercing ear-aches and gushing nosebleeds and wretched pains behind the eyes. So Gerrish descended cautiously, in stages. The dots grew into a formation of Pfalz single-seaters, chunky little fighters painted bright yellow and olive green. They had seen the Pups long ago. They were cruising around in a wide circle, waiting.

There was no pattern to the fight. Gerrish gave a signal and the Pups tipped over and went down in a rush. Red and yellow tracer flickered and bent as pilots tried to track their targets, the formations sliced through each other, and now there were no formations. The sky was a tangle of aircraft, all searching and escaping, all hunting and being hunted.

Duke Nikolai followed the flight and fired off half a drum in four very brief bursts. Every Pfalz that came within range swerved as he squeezed the trigger-grip and his tracer went racing wide. It was like trying to nail a butterfly. He hauled back the stick and the horizon fell away and the little Nieuport soared easily into a loop. His ears popped as he went over the top. The opposite horizon swung into view, and then the air battle was spread below him and he was diving again. He knew he was safe; Count Andrei was always close behind him. He picked out a sluggish-looking Pfalz, trailing smoke. It rapidly expanded into a juicy target and as he fired, something ripped the joystick from his hand and at once his Nieuport was rolling like a barrel down a rocky hill. His fingers burned as if thrashed and his brain was too rattled to think. His other hand took charge, found the stick and centred it and stopped the roll. He was sick. While he was vomiting, his hand took the opportunity to bring the nose up and make the machine level again. His brain began working, he looked around and Andrei's Nieuport was sitting nearby. Andrei waved. The Huns had all gone, the Pups had all gone.

He followed Andrei home, flying one-handed. His right arm was as numb as cold mutton. He used his left hand to stuff his right hand into a coat pocket, but whenever they hit some lumpy air the Nieuport strenuously bounced him about until it had worked the hand out of the pocket and then his shoulder hurt. Never before had anything hurt him like this. The pain in his fingers had been hot and bright; the fingers were on fire. The pain in his shoulder was dull but immense. It possessed all that corner of his body and in its greed it sucked strength from every other part until Nikolai felt like a hunchback being punished by his aching, lopsided hump. The air cleared, the bouncing stopped. He stuffed his useless hand back in its pocket again. The Nieuport was wandering. He kicked it until it learned to behave better.

The field at Pepriac had a Pup standing on its nose in the middle, looking stupid.

Andrei led him on three long circuits, each lower than the last. At the end of the third circuit Andrei eased back until he was flying alongside Nikolai. When they crossed the hedge they were thirty feet up. Nikolai cut his engine. It was the wrong thing to do, but pain was the master and with one hand he couldn't handle the engine controls and the joystick at the same time, and he didn't need an engine now that he was home. He kept the Nieuport fairly level, so when it dropped like a brick, both wheels hit together and it bounced high. That bang was all the encouragement his pain needed to flower. The Nieuport bounced three times more. When it ran to a stop, he was slumped sideways, out cold.

Plug Gerrish was wiping whale-grease off his face with a filthy towel as he tramped into Doc Dando's office. Nikolai was lying on a bed and Dando was examining the Russian's right hand. Andrei stood nearby, pouring vodka into small medicinal glasses.

"If you must amputate, try and leave the trigger finger," Gerrish said. Nikolai looked up. "On second thoughts, cut his head off," Gerrish said. "He's never used it, he won't miss it."

"Three dislocated fingers," Dando said. "I've just put them back. Now I'm going to do the shoulder." He took off his right shoe. "No point in waiting. It won't sound any better." He put his right foot in Nikolai's armpit, grasped the wrist with both hands and jerked hard. Nikolai screamed. "Told you so," Dando said. He took Gerrish's towel and wiped his hands. "He's good as new now. That'll be ten guineas. No cheques, no credit, no refunds if he dies after twenty-four hours. Ah, thanks." Andrei was handing around the vodka.

"You're a lucky Russian," Gerrish said to Nikolai. "A bullet bent your joystick. It looks as if it's got brewer's droop."

Nikolai said a word in Russian. Dando looked inquiringly at Andrei.

"Better you don't know," Andrei said.

"In fact you're a very lucky Russian," Gerrish said. "Just before someone scuppered you, you scuppered a Hun. You can add one Pfalz to your score. He was a flamer, if it matters. Does it matter?"

Nikolai swallowed his vodka and held his glass out for more. "Not in Imperial Russian Air Force," he said faintly.

"God's teeth! A joke! A palpable joke," Gerrish said. "The peasants have permission to laugh. When will he be fit to fly?" he asked Dando.

"Tomorrow," Nikolai whispered, and drank more vodka.

"Don't ask me," Dando said, "I'm just a bloody tradesman, one step above an undertaker's mate, that's me, what do I know?" He snatched the bottle from Andrei and stamped out.

"Pay him no heed," Gerrish said. "Doctors never win a war. It makes them moody."

* * *

The Pup standing on its nose had belonged to a pilot called Avery. He had been shot through the foot, a very messy wound because the bullet was tumbling when it struck. Simply nursing the Pup home and getting it to touch down was a triumph of determination, but then he muddled the controls. He meant to throttle back; instead he made the engine race. So the tail came up and the nose went down. The propeller attacked the turf, and the next thing Avery knew was he was being loaded into an ambulance, and Charles Dash was chatting to the driver. ". . . awfully nice girls at Beauquesne," he was saying.

"Not any longer, I'm afraid," the girl driver said. "They've moved on."

"I must say, I think you F.A.N.Y. girls are absolutely splendid."

She laughed. "It's the uniform. Irresistible."

"Everyone at Beauquesne was awfully friendly."

"Well . . . that's nice."

"I can't tell you how awfully friendly everyone was. I never knew girls could be so . . . friendly. Where are they now, d'you know?"

There was a pause. Then she said, flatly: "Look. Life's too short. Honestly. Forget them. They could be anywhere."

Avery made an effort to speak, but all that came out was a croak. Dash's face appeared, only inches away and upside-down. "Don't worry about a thing, old chap. It's just your foot," he said. "Nothing serious. Besides, you've always got another foot, haven't you?" His breath smelt of peppermint. He disappeared. The engine was started, and the ambulance vibrated in a way that Avery found alarming. Dash's face reappeared. "You scored a flamer. Did you know? They've given it to Nikolai, but everyone hit it." The ambulance began to move. Avery had a sudden swamping fear: they were leaving his foot behind, someone had cut it off. Again he tried to speak, but he heard himself whimper instead. Dash said, "One-eighth of a Pfalz, that's your share. You get the wheels, the oil tank and the gunner's left elbow. Lucky boy! Cheerio."

*　*　*

Duke Nikolai declared himself fit to fly, and to prove it he was now playing bad ragtime on the mess piano.

Plug Gerrish was dozing in an armchair when McWatters came and sat next to him. "Four more kills and he's an ace," he said.

"Don't care," Gerrish mumbled. "I'm off-duty . . . *Buggering bastard shit!*" he roared. Captain Crabtree had popped a toy balloon behind his head, and Gerrish had almost fallen out of his chair.

"Sorry," Crabtree said mildly. "Loud, wasn't it?"

"You're a maniac. You're . . ." Gerrish realized that a dozen pilots were watching, and he swallowed the obscenity. "Oh, Christ," he muttered. His knee hurt.

"Spud said it would test your reflexes, didn't you, Spud?"

"No," Ogilvy said.

"You're lucky I didn't flatten you," Gerrish said. He could feel the pulse in his neck pounding like running feet.

"Spud's got some more balloons. D'you want one?"

"No I haven't," Ogilvy said. "Come on, Plug, we need to talk."

They went out. The buzz of conversation began again. "Poor old Plug," Simms said. "If he was my hunter I'd have him put down. Send the remains to the glue factory. We need lots of glue in wartime."

"What for?" Heeley asked.

"Plans of attack are constantly coming unstuck," McWatters said. "Rather like Humpty-Dumpty."

"At least Plug jumped when that balloon went bang," Munday said. "You didn't even blink. I'd sooner have a skipper who's jumpy than someone carved out of lard." After that the talk deteriorated.

The flight commanders took a stroll and talked about patrols, tactics, Huns, Russians and Cleve-Cutler.

They agreed that the C.O. had his orders from Wing and it was a waste of time to challenge them. There was no alternative to Deep Offensive Patrols. The Pup hadn't enough muscle to beat the latest Hun machines, but nothing could be done about that. Nor about the Hindenburg Line, which was lousy with Archie. The Archie was getting worse, too: more big guns, which forced the Pups up higher and higher, where the weather was usually worse and it was always a bloody sight colder. Crabtree began talking about rumours of electrically heated flying-suits in the German Air Force, when Gerrish interrupted.

"What gets on my left tit is having to drum up trade for that snotty little Russian."

"I find him rather plucky," Crabtree said. "Also astonishingly stupid."

"He's got courage coming out of both ears," Ogilvy said. "That's why he never listens."

"Never learns, either," Gerrish said. "My lads are fed up with poncing for foreigners. So am I."

They had reached the part of the airfield known as Pocock's Patch. Long ago, a blazing pond of petrol had left the earth charred black, with Pocock cremated in the middle. Now, for the first time, his Patch was blurred by bright new grass. The wind had lost its bite. Blue sky slid behind white cloud. A few more weeks of this and the generals would feel it was safe to have a really big battle.

"Can I borrow Dingbat?" Crabtree asked. His flight was due to go on patrol.

"Take him," Gerrish said. "My granny flies better than him, and she's five years dead."

Crabtree told Maddegan to stay near the Russians, and to shoot at anything Nikolai shot at. The Australian said that he found it hard to stay near anyone and as for shooting, everything whizzed about so fast . . . "Do your best," Crabtree said.

The flight had a busy afternoon.

Cloud clogged the sky. They stumbled upon a fight – Aviatik two-seaters against SE5s who were escorting a pair of RE8s, probably coming back from a photographic job – but after some long-range gunplay the Aviatiks dived into cover. They were outnumbered; very sensibly they vanished. The Pups moved on. They had a brisk scrap with five smart-looking Fokker scouts, all green and gold, all very aggressive. Maddegan soon lost sight of the Nieuport he was supposed to be shadowing. He made up for it by charging at the enemy and firing at every image that leaped across his vision. He fired too late, because his Pup was rolling and skidding and falling and his tracer was always bending the wrong way. The Fokkers quit and flew home at a speed the Pups could never match. And then, twenty minutes later, it happened all over again, except the Fokkers were silver-grey with scarlet zigzags down the fuselage, and this time Maddegan plunged into the battle without bothering about Nikolai. He fired his second burst when a Fokker turned on him, rushed at him, swamped his vision and God alone knew how they missed collision. But in a thin slice of time he saw his bullets rip across the enemy cockpit, he saw the pilot's arms thrown high, and he tasted blood. He tasted blood because, in the fear of collision, he had bitten his lip.

*   *   *

"Two Huns?" Cleve-Cutler said. "Definitely two? Not possibly, or probably?"

"Definitely two Huns," Crabtree said. "Absolutely positively utterly certainly definitely. I swear it on my mother's grave."

"And Duke Nikolai got them both?"

"Splendid shooting." Crabtree turned aside and spat. He was still in flying kit, and sweat washed whale-grease into his mouth. "The whole flight is full of admiration, sir." He spat again.

Cleve-Cutler looked hard at Crabtree's glistening, deep-lined, empty face. It was as blank as his voice. He looked away. The last of the Pups was landing. "Two short," he said.

"Grant's engine blew. Forced landing, our side of the Lines. Hooper's gone for good. Tailplane got shot off. Fell like a brick."

"Hooper . . . Tall thin lad?"

"No, that's Cooper, 'A' Flight. Hooper had big ears. He replaced Latham."

Cleve-Cutler nodded. Latham was just a name. "Time for a squadron thrash, don't you think? Celebrate your Huns with copious quantities of Hornet's Sting? Yes. Big party tonight."

Maddegan was always the last to land. He was excited, came in too fast, needed all the field; still, he didn't break the Pup. His mechanics called out: "Any luck, sir?"

"Doomed the bastard!" That delighted them. He said it again, more loudly. "Doomed the bastard!" They cheered.

He trudged towards the flight hut, peeling off his flying gear. He was hot but happy. As his ears cleared he heard birdsong. Men waved and applauded, not because a kill was such a great achievement but because his happiness pleased them.

Snow, the Canadian, came out of the flight hut. "I doomed the bastard," Maddegan said.

"No, you didn't." Snow stopped him. "The Russian, Nikolai, he got two Huns." He spoke softly. "Nobody else got anything. Nik got two Huns, all on his own. Understand?"

"Aw, heck. This isn't *fair*," Maddegan grumbled.

"Sure. Now be a brave boy, and smile for mommy, and go in there and congratulate the son of a bitch. Skipper's orders."

Maddegan went in. Count Andrei was pouring vodka into chipped mugs. The pilots were standing around with bribed smiles on their faces. Duke Nikolai was carefully wiping grease from his face. "Hey!" Maddegan said. Nikolai hid behind the towel and peeped over the top. "How about *you?*" Maddegan cried. "Two Huns!" He hugged him. Nikolai was a good head shorter, and Maddegan found himself looking at Crabtree. "That'll do, Dingbat," Crabtree murmured. "You're in England, remember."

Vodka for everyone.

"A toast," Crabtree said. "The duke's two Fokkers!"

"Albatros is better," Nikolai said. But he drank.

Cleve-Cutler was walking to the mess when he changed his mind and went to the orderly room instead. "Sergeant Lacey," he said. "Kindly ask the adjutant to put Duke Nikolai in for the M.C."

"The citation has already been drafted, sir."

Cleve-Cutler leaned over the desk and swivelled his head. Lacey had been making out a cheque to Selfridge's for fifteen guineas. The bank was Coutts. "What's this all about?"

"For a new piano, sir. The late Lieutenant the Honourable Jeremy Lloyd-Perkins has kindly donated one to the mess."

"We already have a piano."

"True, sir. But for how long?"

* * *

Hornet's Sting was invented by Cleve-Cutler to be drunk by the squadron on special occasions: some sad, some not. There was no fixed formula. He let whim and inspiration guide him as he emptied bottles into a galvanized hipbath. Brandy and champagne made a good base, followed by port, gin, apple juice, fresh ground pepper, more champagne, a couple of bottles of Guinness, some rum, a blast of soda water for fizz, a splash of Benedictine for good luck. Count Andrei donated two bottles of vodka. "Just what we need to encourage the brandy," Cleve-Cutler said. He tipped them both in. "What's that green stuff?" he said. "Never mind, I like green, let's have some." He tasted the mix. "Needs aniseed," he declared. "And claret! Lots of claret."

It was a typical mess-night party. There were guests: pilots from a nearby Pup squadron; some Cameron Highlanders, in camp at Pepriac; and a passing major-general whose car had hit a pothole, broken an axle and stopped passing. By a tradition dating back several months, dinner was served at tables arranged in a circle and each man ate from his neighbour's plate. By the same tradition, roast potatoes were always thrown, never eaten. "You can always tell the cricketers," Ogilvy said to a Cameron Highlander. "They eat with one hand and field with the other." He forked a carrot and, at the same time, caught a roast potato as it whizzed by. "See?"

"I detest cricket," the Scot said amiably.

"Well, I don't care for potatoes." Ogilvy flung it at Munday and hit Dash instead.

"In fact, all games are a waste of time," the Scot said.

"No, no, no. Take footer," Simms said. "Christmas 1914. British troops and Huns playing footer in no-man's-land. Damned sporting!"

"Bunkum," McWatters said. "Bloke I knew was there. He said they cheated disgracefully." He threw his potato and winged a waiter.

"That's your Prussians for you," Ogilvy said. "I wouldn't trust them at ping-pong."

"Not *them*," McWatters said. "Our lot. Downright cheats, every one. Permanently off-side. Especially the Welsh regiments."

Cleve-Cutler pounded on the table. "We shall now take to the air," he announced, "and drink the squadron toast." This was another tradition: nobody's feet must touch the floor. Everyone climbed onto chairs. "Hornet's Sting!" they roared, and drank. Heeley, the youngest pilot on the squadron, had already put down a base of whisky-sodas. He was a slim lad who shaved only twice a week, more to encourage growth than to remove it. He dropped his glass. His knees folded outwards and he toppled from his chair. The adjutant caught him, one-handed, by the collar, and gave him to a waiter. "The mixture isn't right," Cleve-Cutler said. "Add more champagne! At ten francs a bottle," he told the general, "these chaps can afford it."

"I'd like to make a speech, if it's alright by you," the general said. He managed the supply of disinfectant to the army: essential work but not thrilling. Meeting a fighting squadron was an exciting stroke of luck.

"My stars!" the adjutant said. "You're a brave man, general."

"I wouldn't advise a speech unless you know a lot of good jokes, sir," Cleve-Cutler said. "The chaps are a bit inflammable tonight."

"I know a joke about disinfectant." The general was on his third tankard of Hornet's Sting. Comradeship had kidnapped his wits. "Chap goes into a pub, sees a dog lying in front of the fire. What's happening is, this dog is licking its balls. Chap says, 'My goodness!' he says, 'I wish I could do that!' So the pub landlord says, 'Toss him a biscuit and maybe he'll let you.' What?" The general pounded and guffawed. "What?"

"Where does the disinfectant come in?" the adjutant asked.

"Through the tradesman's entrance."

"I say, that's jolly clever," the C.O. said. "Far too clever for my ruffians."

"It would go straight over their heads," the adjutant said. "Might get a bit shirty."

"I know a joke about shirts, too. Chap goes into a shop. Shirt shop. Chap says, 'What's the difference between a striped shirt and a pound of sausages?' Shop assistant says, 'I don't know, sir. What *is* the difference between a striped shirt and a pound of sausages?' Chap says, 'Well, if you don't know the difference, I'm damned if I'll buy my shirts here!' What?" He drank deeply. "What?"

"Does disinfectant come into this one, sir?" the adjutant asked cautiously.

"I'll say this." The general was suddenly wide-eyed and serious. "You can't have a modern war without good disinfectant. Stuff's crucial. Your chaps . . ." He made a sweeping gesture. "Fine boys. Cavalry of the clouds! But take your disinfectant out of your latrines and, believe me, plague would cut them down like the Four Horsemen of the whatsisname."

"Acropolis."

"Exactly. Thank you, major."

Captain Crabtree had been listening. "These Four Horsemen," he said. "I suppose they're stabled in heaven, alongside the angels." Nobody argued. "Is there disinfectant in heaven, padre?"

"Angels don't need latrines," the chaplain said. "They don't eat or drink."

"Well, I'm not going," Crabtree said. "If you can't get draught Bass and pickled eggs, then what's the point?"

"We shall all find out, one day," the chaplain said comfortably. It was the ace of trumps and he played it easily.

After dinner everyone went into the anteroom and played indoor rugby with a cushion as ball. The tackling was ferocious. Munday was caught by the ankle and fell hard on his left ear. Dando took him behind the piano and put five stitches in the ear and emerged to see Heeley standing, dazed, his nose running blood like a tap. Dando steered him out into the night and made him lie on his back. Within a minute, Heeley was asleep and snoring.

Inside, all the cushions had burst. One of the Cameron Highlanders was fighting Plug Gerrish; they used cane chairs as weapons. It made fine, furious sport, and it inspired others to duel with chairs and small tables. Soon the floor was littered with debris. There was a pause for drink as the mess servants carried in a fresh tub of Hornet's Sting. All the glasses were flung into the fireplace. And suddenly the mood changed. Everyone must sing.

Duke Nikolai played the piano. A lot of drink had been spilt on it and the keys were sticky. McWatters emptied a fire bucket into the piano and a greenish fluid began to seep out of the holes for the pedals. Nobody cared. They all linked arms and bawled the happy ballads from the best London shows, and the relentlessly morbid songs of the Corps: "Who killed Cock Robin? 'I,' said the Hun, 'with my Spandau gun . . .'" and "You Haven't got a Hope in the Morning" and, best of all, the chorus to "The Young Aviator Lay Dying", sung to the tune of "Wrap Me up in My Tarpaulin Jacket":

Take the cylinder out of my kidneys,
The connecting rod out of my brain, my brain,
From the small of my back take the camshaft,
And assemble the engine again!

They liked that. They sang it twice.

Then a Scottish sergeant was summoned to play his bagpipes, and eightsome reels were danced with clumsy gusto. The general lost his grip and was spun into a wall with such force that the lights flickered, or so he thought. He slid down onto his rump. "Bloody piper," he told Dando huskily. "Piping in waltz time." Dando nodded. He knew a broken arm when he saw one. Someone offered the general a glass of Hornet's Sting. "Disinfectant," he whispered. "That's the stuff to give the troops."

Outside, the adjutant was signing for a large envelope. The despatch rider saluted and roared away. His headlamp caught and lost Sergeant Lacey. "What the deuce do you want?" Brazier asked, without anger.

"The same as you, captain. The same as everyone. A warm bed, a clear conscience, and friendly bowels."

"Wrong. I can sleep on a plank, I left my conscience on the battlefield, and my bowels do what I damn well tell them to."

"Goodness. How Shakespearean . . ." Lacey shone his flashlight and Brazier broke the seal on the envelope. Together, they read the messages.

"You're an educated feller," the adjutant said. "What d'you reckon history will make of this little lot?"

"That's easy. History will make it a footnote to an afterword to an appendix."

"Well, history is an imbecile."

"Yes. The footnote will say that too. But alas, no one will read it."

Someone had stumbled over Heeley in the darkness and carried him inside, and now the pilots were tossing him in a blanket. They roared as they tried to toss him over a beam in the rafters. Heeley was too drunk to protest, but not too drunk to be terrified as he got flung up and the beam clipped his head and he dropped, utterly out of control. "Don't be so bloody flabby, Heeley!" Simms told him. "Make a bit of an effort, man, for God's sake."

Maddegan watched them until he got bored. He wandered over to the piano, and looked inside at the dance of the felt hammers. He was holding a tankard. It tipped as he leaned to see more. Hornet's Sting poured over the workings. Duke Nikolai stopped playing. Maddegan looked at him. "Go on," he said. "You're doing fine."

"Stuck," Nikolai said. "Won't work." He hammered on the keys, but they made no sound.

Maddegan prised one of the keys up. It snapped, so he gave it to Nikolai. "Keep that," he said, "we'll put it back later." He thrust his fingers into the hole and ripped out five more keys, three white and two black.

Heeley fell and the blanket split, and the pilots holding it collapsed.

"Doomed the bastard!" Maddegan said, and waved the five keys. The pilots cheered.

That was when Cleve-Cutler came in, with the adjutant behind him. Brazier had a soda-syphon. He sprayed the pilots until they were quiet. "Gather round and listen," he ordered.

"I have important news for you." The C.O. waved some signals. That silenced them completely. They dripped as they stared. "First. . . the squadron is moving. Tomorrow. To a field near . . . Arras."

A whoop of surprise and approval. Pepriac was a scruffy crossroads; Arras was a city.

"Second . . . the squadron will re-equip with . . ." A long pause tortured them. ". . . with Bristol Fighters."

That brought a roar of delight. Several pilots danced. They were drunk with joy.

"And third . . ." They laughed in anticipation of another celebration. ". . . the Tsar has abdicated." And of course they cheered. The noise was waiting in their throats; it had to come out. "Good old Tsar!" they shouted.

Cleve-Cutler walked over to the piano. Duke Nikolai was staring at the ruined keyboard. "I really am awfully sorry," the C.O. said. "I'm told that power has gone to his brother." He checked the message form. "That's the Grand Duke Michael Alexandrovitch." Behind them, the pilots had formed a circle, arms on shoulders, and were singing "When this bloody war is over, Oh how happy we shall be . . ." He moved closer to Nikolai and said, "I expect you know him."

"Is pig."

Cleve-Cutler could think of nothing to add. He left the adjutant to break up the party and send everyone off to bed.

McWatters strolled across to Nikolai, who had not moved. "All of a sudden you're nobody's cousin," he said. "Funny feeling, isn't it?"

* * *

By noon next day, all the Pups were lined up in order of flights, waiting to take off. Cleve-Cutler sat in his office, signing a pile of papers which

141

relieved him of responsibility for the aerodrome, its buildings and their contents. Each signature took him a step nearer Arras and Gazeran field and the superlative Bristol Fighters. "What's this?" he asked.

"Jam, sir," Lacey said. "Two hundred pounds of strawberry, mislabelled plum. Written off."

The CO read further. "Destroyed by accidental explosion? I don't remember that."

"You were on patrol, sir."

"Still, two hundred pounds . . ." Cleve-Cutler looked at the general, who was in a chair by the stove with his arm in a sling. He was waiting for his car to be repaired.

"I know a joke about jam," the general said.

"The quartermaster at Brigade is being a bit officious, sir," Lacey explained.

"You can turn a raspberry patch into a pot of jam," the general said. "But it's not so easy the other way around."

"How very true, sir," Lacey said. The C.O. signed, and Lacey slid the form away from his fingers, to uncover the next.

"Sounded a lot funnier when I heard it. Mind you, we were all a bit squiffy at the time."

Cleve-Cutler scribbled his name on the rest of the forms, threw them all at Lacey, and threw the pen at the door. "Come on, general," he said. "You can wave us goodbye."

"I nearly got a bit squiffy last night," the general said. "That vodka creeps up on a chap."

After a mild night and a sunny morning, the grass was dry and the air was sweet. The adjutant bicycled about, searching for the two Russians, and found them in one of the flight huts, playing poker with a mixed bunch of pilots. They were all drinking a hangover cure devised by the doctor. It consisted of raw eggs beaten up with cayenne pepper, Worcestershire sauce and toothpaste, and it wasn't doing much good. When Brazier opened the door, most flinched as from a blinding light.

"Signal from Brigade H.Q.," Brazier said. "Your Paris embassy says you've got to swear an oath to the Grand Duke Michael Alexandrovitch."

"Yes," Nikolai said. "Is stinking lousy smelling fucking shitting pig."

"A very decent oath," McWatters said.

"More than you deserve, Uncle," Simms said. "Bursting in here, shouting and stamping and frightening the children, you should be ashamed."

"I brought this," the adjutant said to Count Andrei. It was a Bible, large and leatherbound. "Not in Russian, I'm afraid. Any use?"

"I don't swear," Nikolai said firmly.

"Yes, you do swear." Andrei took the Bible and whacked him on the side of his head, and then swung backhand and whacked the other side. Nikolai rocked and gaped. A string of saliva swayed from his upper lip.

"Golly," Heeley whispered. Nobody moved. This was better than poker.

Andrei slammed the Bible on the table and pointed. Nikolai placed his hand on it. So did Andrei. He said: "We swear allegiance to Grand Duke Michael Alexandrovitch, by the grace of God, sole ruler of all the Russias." He kicked Nikolai on the leg. "I swear," Nikolai said. He sounded twelve years old.

Brazier took the Bible and left.

"I now pronounce you Mappin and Webb," McWatters said. "You may shoot the bride."

Nikolai stood up. His face was working hard to seem adult and strong, but the high cheekbones were wet with tears. He went out.

His cards lay face-down. McWatters turned them over. "Queens on tens," he said. "Fancy that."

Munday began collecting the cards. "Little Nicky is a pest," he said. "At my school we'd have toasted his tiny bottom over a hot fire. All the same . . . was it wise to box his ears? He just *might* be Tsar one day."

"Nicky is finished. The Romanovs are finished. There will never be another Tsar." Andrei stirred his cards with his forefinger, but he left them lying. "It's all up to the Socialists now."

"If Nicky's done for," Simms said, "what about you? Suppose there's a revolution. You might . . ." He shrugged.

"Count for nothing," Heeley said.

"Heaven help us!" Munday said. "The boy Heeley has made a joke! *Count for nothing*. Did you hear?"

"It was an accident," Heeley mumbled, blushing.

"I count for nothing because I am not a count," Andrei said. "I hold no rank in Russian nobility. My father is an engineer. I studied chemistry at London University. When Duke Nikolai was sent here, he must have an aide who could fly and speak English. Nothing less than a count would do. Unfortunately the Tsar was feeling a little low that week. He went to bed and refused to see his ministers or his generals. So I was not elevated. I am a counterfeit count."

The poker had come to a halt.

"I still don't think you should have hit him," McWatters said. "I mean, what if the Cossacks put the Tsar back on the throne? He might turn very shirty about blokes like you clouting his cousin."

Andrei said, "There were riots in Petersburg, and the Cossacks refused to fire. So the Tsar had to go."

"Politics is a squalid business," McWatters said.

"The riots were about bread," Andrei said. "Hunger beats politics. Hunger beats anything."

"I never heard about any riots," Simms said. "I suppose you've got some secret supply of intelligence."

"I read it in *The Times*."

"Really? Damned heavy going, *The Times*. I stick to the racing page."

Outside, a klaxon blared. They got up and collected bits of flying kit.

"What I don't understand," Maddegan said, "is why you swore your great steaming oath to the Grand Duke Thingummy, when you reckon the whole royal kit and caboodle has gone down the drain." He yawned and stretched, and accidentally hit Heeley in the face. "Sorry, chum," he said.

"It was a small courtesy to the adjutant," Andrei said. "And it will keep the Paris embassy quiet."

They left the cards on the table for the next squadron, and shut the door and walked to the aircraft. Dash edged alongside McWatters. "Remember that night at Rosie's?" he said quietly. "The business with the deserter. You made him stand on the table."

"Oh, *that*. That was years ago. What of it?"

"Well . . . what happened? What did you . . . What became of him?"

"As a matter of fact, we killed him. A deserter, you see. We court-martialled him, on the spot, and he confessed. Only one sentence. Little chap. Didn't take much killing. Threw the remains in the midden. Wet as a bog. Sank like a stone." They had reached the Pups. They stopped and looked at each other. McWatters was wearing sunglasses and Dash wanted to knock them off, but he wasn't brave enough.

"I don't believe you," he said.

"Of course you don't." McWatters moved to his machine. "You could always look in the midden," he said. "I expect he's still there."

The squadron took off in order of flights, with the Russian Nieuports the last to leave. The general stood on a tender and waved them goodbye. A sergeant-fitter helped him down. "Cavalry of the clouds," the general said. There were tears in his eyes, and he stumbled as he walked to his car. What's he got to cry about? the sergeant wondered. He's not likely to get a burst of tracer up his arse. Silly old sod.

EARTHQUAKE STRENGTH 5:

Sleepers wakened. Small objects upset. Doors swing open or closed.

"It's the poor bloody aeroplane I feel sorry for," Paxton said.

"Then you're a twat," Woolley told him. "It's just a Pup, for Christ's sake."

"It did its duty in France. It deserves a decent end in England, not to get bashed to bits by silly buggers like Mackenzie."

"Stay off the gin, Pax. Gin makes you come over all weepy."

They watched the Pup come in to land. The engine made brief belching sounds as its magneto was switched off to lose power. A small gust of wind shook the wings and slewed the machine, and the pilot lost confidence in his approach. The engine roared as he tried to make the Pup climb. It was too late. The Pup dropped ten feet and bounced. Then it stayed up and cruised across the field, head high, gaining speed, and wobbled over a hedge.

"I wish he'd break his bloody neck and get it done with," Woolley said. "Then we can all have a beer."

"Is that true, what you said about gin?" Paxton asked. "When I was at Sherborne, the chaplain was always droning on about the evils of liquor. He said gin attacked a chap's manhood. I must say mine seems to be standing up to the challenge."

"I went to Bog Street Elementary School," Woolley said. "Couldn't afford gin. We drank the ink."

"That was a joke," Paxton said. "Standing up to the challenge. Very clever joke."

"Couldn't afford jokes in Bog Street. We had to make do with rickets." A different Pup made its approach, coughing and wavering, and it landed.

"That's one of my blokes," Woolley said, and walked towards it.

"Anyway, if I'm a twat, so are you," Paxton shouted after him. "We're all twats. Only a twat would do this twattish job." Woolley tossed his hat high in the air, and the breeze caught it and sent it bowling along the grass.

* * *

The aerodrome took the name of the nearest village, Coney Garth. A branch line to Bury St Edmunds passed through the village, so travel to and from London was easy. This made Coney Garth a far more attractive posting than the many training fields which were stuck in the wilds of the Yorkshire moors or the Lowlands of Scotland. Coney Garth had half-a-dozen flying instructors and they all got out of the place as fast and as often as possible. They were experienced pilots being rested after a spell at the Western Front. Paxton and Woolley had been at Coney Garth for five months. After France, five months was a lifetime: five lifetimes. Paxton spoke of getting married, if only he could find the right girl. Woolley was learning to play the saxophone. They had plenty of time.

For the pupils, it was different.

In less than three years the war had killed about half a million men from Britain and Ireland, plus a couple of hundred thousand from the Empire. A million more had been wounded and might as well be dead for all the use they were to the generals. The Royal Flying Corps was one of the smaller departments of the army. In 1917 the Corps accounted for only 2 per cent of its manpower in France; and of these, only a few thousand made up the pilots and observers who actually flew against the enemy. On the other hand, the R.F.C lost its fighting men far more rapidly than any other unit. By the spring of 1917 it was rushing its pupils through their basic training, and then giving them little time to learn how to fly and fight. Some instructors despised their jobs, some were impatient, some just didn't care. There was no room for an instructor in the Sopwith Pup, so the pupils mainly taught themselves. Many did not reach France. For every airman killed by the German Air Force, two died in training in England.

Coney Garth was a fairly typical training field. On average there were four crashes a week and a dozen deaths a month. Paxton and Woolley had been sent home to be rested from the war, only to find it waiting for them, hungrier than ever.

* * *

"I think I'm getting the hang of it, sir," Mackenzie said. He had got the Pup down at the third attempt. One undercarriage leg was cracked. A mechanic squatted to examine it, looked up at Paxton, shook his head.

"Come with me, Mackenzie," Paxton said, "and we shall find a quiet corner where I can shoot you without disturbing your friends and colleagues stumbling around the firmament."

Mackenzie followed, unbuttoning his Sidcot suit. "Why would you wish to shoot me, sir?" he asked.

"Economy, old fruit. Think what the War Office will save. The cost of shipping you to France. Meals. Toilet paper. Sheets and pyjamas. You'll want a bed, I suppose? And then an aeroplane all to yourself, guns loaded, tanks full of petrol – have you any idea of the price of petrol? – so you can fly over the Front and get yourself blown to blazes. Just add it all up. Britain can't afford it, you know. You're bleeding the old country white, Mackenzie. That way lies defeat. Whereas if I shoot you now, the cost is trifling, a few pence only, which includes cleaning the weapon afterwards. So you see where my patriotic duty lies."

"Yes, sir."

They reached a heavy roller and sat on it.

Paxton looked long and hard at Mackenzie, who blinked occasionally. Mackenzie had boyish features and hair that curled enthusiastically. Only his eyes seemed fully adult: they were grey and watchful. "It's a funny thing," Paxton said. He found his pipe and his pouch, and took his time over shredding a slice of tobacco. "You look rather like a girl I used to know." As soon as he heard the words he regretted them: that wasn't what a chap said to another chap, especially to a chap of lower rank. But another part of him said: Who gives a fuck?

"What did she look like?"

"Delicate," Paxton said. "Very slim, she was a dancer. Turned out to be something of a bitch."

"Sir," Mackenzie said. "Shouldn't you be teaching me how to beat the Boche?"

"Oh, bugger the Boche. You'll never be a fighter pilot." Paxton stood up. "Get your things packed, report to the C.O. You're sacked."

"Why, sir?"

"Oh . . ." Paxton was suddenly tired of Mackenzie. He regretted mentioning the elfin-bitch. "You're too young. Too small. Not strong enough. Try again next year." He strolled away. He was thinking of lunch when he heard a squeaking and clanking behind him. The noise grew louder and he turned and saw the roller coming at him. Mackenzie was pushing it by its handle, his body so low that all Paxton saw was the head and shoulders. He jumped aside. Mackenzie let go. The roller rumbled past, and Paxton felt the turf tremble. The roller stopped. Its handle wagged.

Mackenzie, ten feet away, cocked his head and waited.

Paxton got hold of the handle and heaved. The roller moved, but not much.

"Alright," Paxton said. "You are strong enough. But you're still sacked. Your gunnery's rotten. Flying's no good if you can't shoot. Your scores are pathetic."

Mackenzie put his forefinger to his head. "Bang," he said.

"Missed. See what I mean? Now put this thing back where you found it."

*　*　*

When flying finished for the day, Woolley and Paxton and another instructor called Slattery got cleaned up, put on their walking-out uniforms and drove in Slattery's car to St Quentin's School for Boys.

Paxton had not wanted to go. The C.O. at Coney Garth, Major Venables, was normally a mild man. He had crashed a two-seater in 1915 and been somersaulted out of his cockpit. Onlookers said that he travelled fifty feet before he hit the ground, but onlookers always exaggerated. He never flew again. Now he was content to leave the instructing to the instructors, while he took care of the paperwork. That avoided headaches. Headaches made Venables angry, and anger made his headache worse, so when Lieutenant Paxton groaned and said he felt sure there were better people to go and lecture a bunch of schoolboys on the war, sir, people with more time . . . Major Venables felt a hot throb bite at the side of his brain. "Do as you're bloody well told!" he shouted.

"What I meant, sir, was perhaps it might be better if a couple of other chaps went with me. We could—"

"Take whoever you like!" Red and green zigzags began to drift into Venables' vision. "Get out!"

Paxton took Slattery because he had a car and Woolley because St Quentin's was a public school and he thought Woolley would hate it. "You may find this place rather strange," Paxton said as the hedgerows rushed by. "I'll gladly answer any questions."

"Oh, I went to public school," Woolley said.

"We're lost," Slattery said.

"I don't believe you," Paxton said. Slattery threw the road map at him. "Not you," Paxton said. "Him."

"Well, we're still lost."

"I went to St Bert's. It's in Wigan."

"I don't believe there ever was a saint called Bert," Paxton said.

Slattery slowed to look at a signpost. "Damn," he said, and accelerated.

"You get snotty about St Bert in Wigan," Woolley said, "and the lads will kick your face in."

"Ah," Paxton said. "A sporting school, is it?"

"We beat Eton at shoplifting," Woolley said. "National champions ten years running."

"Where are we supposed to be going?" Slattery asked. "I forget."

"You really are a bloody awful driver," Paxton said.

"Bet you don't know who the patron saint of bloody awful drivers is," Woolley said to Paxton.

"Who?"

"Saint Bert. Coincidence, isn't it?"

St Quentin's School was a stately mansion entirely surrounded by playing fields. The headmaster was burly and bearded. He gave them tea, and then took them to the assembly hall. About six hundred boys and masters were waiting. When they saw the wings on the tunics there was a gentle hum. One click of the headmaster's fingers silenced that.

"The poet Browning wrote, 'Ah, but a man's reach should exceed his grasp, or what's a heaven for?' I think we may on this occasion forgive Browning for ending his sentence with a preposition . . ." The headmaster smiled, and the older boys laughed dutifully. "The pity is that Browning is not alive to immortalize in verse those whose reach *does* exceed their grasp, those who do, literally, discover what a heaven's for – the men of the Royal Flying Corps. Lieutenant Paxton is here to tell us something of the work of this gallant band."

Applause.

Paxton stepped forward, carrying a chair in one hand. He placed it at the front of the stage and put his left foot on it.

"Fighting in the sky," he said, using the clear, firm voice he had developed in the Sherborne school debating society, "is rather like a boxing match. In order to hit the other fellow you have to get close to him. So close, in fact, that *he* can hit *you*. Which makes it a straight, clean, man-to man contest. And this may surprise you no ill feeling. Plenty of excitement! When you're throwing your machine all over the sky, dodging hot lead that's spewing from some Hun's machine guns, with nothing beneath you but eight or ten thousand feet of thin air – well, the old heart pumps a bit, believe me. And when the scrap's over, and it's goodbye to another Boche aviator . . ." Paxton's mouth twitched in a generous smile. ". . . I'm not ashamed to salute the passing of a foe who fought his best. Now, you all know there's a lot of mud and blood in France. That doesn't mean there's no room for chivalry. We in the Royal Flying Corps like to think of ourselves as a sort of cavalry of the clouds. Of course, chivalry alone isn't going to win this war. That's where you chaps come in. Why are you here? I'll tell you. A couple of years ago I was at a school very much like yours, and what I learned – apart from how to decline the subjunctive and solve quadratic equations and . . ." here he turned to the headmaster ". . . not to end my sentences with a preposition . . ." The boys laughed. "What I learned was that *cream rises to the top.*" Paxton paused and flexed the leg that was propped on the chair. "Spot of Archie in the knee," he explained. "You've heard of Archie? He goes woof-woof and if you get too close he bites you . . ." They enjoyed that. "What was I saying?" He looked at Slattery.

"Cream?"

"Ah, yes. *That's* why you're here. This is a topping school, and you chaps are the cream. No matter how hard the Hun tries – and believe me, nobody tries harder – he suffers from one awful disadvantage, which is: he's a Hun! And that's why he's bound to lose!" Applause, and some cheering. "You see, what the Kaiser didn't take into account is, there's no substitute for breeding. The Hun doesn't understand that; it's not in his blood. He doesn't know how to make a tackle in a rugger match. He doesn't know how to face fast bowling on a bumpy wicket and smack it for six. He doesn't know how to deliver a straight left to the jaw. You do; it's in your blood. Chaps like you made the Empire, and the Empire covers half the earth. That just leaves the sky to be conquered, and you're the very chaps to do it." He stepped back. The applause was warm, and he waved his chair in acknowledgement.

"Splendid, splendid," the headmaster said. "Is there anything your fellow officers wish to add?"

"I could do with a Guinness," Woolley said.

"The chaplain will propose a vote of thanks," the headmaster said.

"The words of the Prayer Book are not unfitting," said the chaplain. "'He rode upon the cherubims, and did fly; he came flying upon the wings of the wind.' We have all heard, have we not, a most stimulating account . . ."

*　*　*

They dined with the headmaster, his wife and the chaplain.

"It's good to know that the Public School Spirit is alive and well in

France," the headmaster said. He made it sound like an examination: *Discuss the following . . .*

"One does one's best to live up to tradition," Paxton said.

"Ah, tradition!" the chaplain said. He was short, dark and bald, and his right arm was limp: he used his left hand to lift it onto the table. "Great stuff, tradition. How did we ever manage without it?"

The question was aimed at Slattery. "Um . . ." he said.

"Pay no attention," the headmaster's wife said. "He only does it to annoy, he should have been a politician." She was middle-aged and pretty and lively. The chaplain smirked.

A maid was going around the table, filling glasses with water. "No Guinness at all?" Woolley asked.

"We took a pledge to abstain from alcohol," the headmaster said, "until the cessation of hostilities."

"We could send out for some. There must be a pub . . ."

"Alas, no."

His wife added: "We like to think that this small act of self-denial brings us a little closer to the men in the trenches."

Paxton nodded. "We're all in this thing together, aren't we?"

"No," the chaplain said. "Italy's in, Holland's neutral and—"

"Ah, soup," the headmaster said. "I hope you like tomato."

"Anyway, the Guinness wasn't for me," Woolley said. "Lieutenant Paxton needs it for his leg. Nothing else soothes the pain, the biting, burning pain."

"Oh, I say. Steady on." Paxton ripped a bread roll in half.

"Matron has a wonderful liniment," the headmaster's wife offered. "It cures rugger sprains in no time. Perhaps . . ."

"What sort of cricket team have you got this year, sir?" Paxton asked, which kept the headmaster going right through the soup and into the fish pie. "So, despite everything, we beat St Stephen's by two wickets," he said. "And it was only afterwards that I discovered young Lumley had been batting with a broken nose. Of course, I awarded him his school colours on the spot."

"Commissioned in the field, so to speak," Slattery said.

"He looked better for it," the chaplain said. "Very ugly boy."

"I went to public school," Woolley said. "St Oscar's, in Brighton."

"St Oscar's," the headmaster said. "Brighton, you say?"

"I didn't know there *was* a saint called Oscar," his wife said.

"Spent his life saving virgins," Woolley told them. "Martyred for the cause."

"Not much good at it, then," Slattery said.

"You can't get sanctified nowadays unless you've been martyred," the chaplain said. "It's a very difficult choice." He winked at Slattery.

"Hullo!" Woolley said. "Somebody's up."

It was a mild evening; the windows were open. A faint, lazy buzz came to them, and faded, and came again. "Excuse me," Woolley said. He went out by the French windows and stood on the terrace. "It's a Gotha," he said.

That ended dinner. "A damned Hun?" the headmaster said. Everyone hurried out, and looked where Woolley pointed, and saw a speck like a pinprick in the sky.

The English were a phlegmatic people. They had accepted casualty lists of tens of thousands, hundreds of thousands, growing to a million and more; but that was in France, abroad, invisible and glorious; even the battle of the Somme had been a triumph, all the newspapers said so. But when Zeppelins and bombers attacked England, all stoicism suddenly dissolved in a howl of fear and fury. Death was prowling the skies. This wasn't the war the civilians had agreed to fight. This wasn't *fair*.

"Are you sure?" the headmaster asked.

"It might not be a Gotha," Woolley said. The headmaster relaxed slightly. "It looks more like a Giant," Woolley said. "That's twice as big as a Gotha."

"Swine. How dare they . . ." The headmaster hurried off to get all the boys indoors. His wife left to see to the servants. The chaplain escorted the pilots to their car.

"I enjoyed your visit," he said. "You mustn't be too hard on them. They haven't the faintest idea what it's like in France."

Suddenly Slattery understood. "But you do."

"I went over with the Duke of Wellington's Regiment in 1914. We got rather knocked about. The army likes its padres to be able to act as stretcher-bearers, so . . . I was lucky to get this job."

"Don't be too hard on us," Paxton said. "We've all fallen out of too many aeroplanes." They shook his good hand and drove away.

* * *

Slattery got lost again. Suffolk was a pleasant county to be lost in. The slanting sunlight of evening burnished the fields of early wheat and barley, and brightened the greens of woodland and pasture. Enormous farm-horses looked over gates and watched the car go by and flattened their ears at the noise. Children left their games and ran and cheered, and flung old potatoes, and missed. "No idea of deflection shooting," Paxton said.

At dusk they stopped at a pub to find out where they were. Slattery glanced into the public bar. "Full of gnarled Shakespearean types wearing corduroy trousers secured with twine below the knees," he reported. The saloon bar was empty. The landlord brought them bottled Guinness and went away.

"We of the Royal Flying Corps," Woolley said, "like to think of ourselves as a sort of cavalry of the clouds. Show us your roses and we shall shit on them."

"That was you, was it?" Slattery said. "I thought it was hot lead spewing from a Hun's machine guns."

"Archie goes woof-woof," Woolley said. "Stanley went puke-puke."

Paxton dipped a finger into his stout and licked the cream. He was unmoved by their comments. "The boys seemed to enjoy it," he said.

"Ask them again in a year," Woolley said. "When the oldest ones meet an Albatros and try to kill it with breeding."

"Something you'll never die of, Woolley."

"You did lay it on a bit thick, Pax," Slattery said.

"Did I?" Paxton tipped his chair and balanced on its back legs. "Woolley takes the biscuit for talking tosh. That wasn't a bomber we saw."

"What was it?" Woolley asked.

"Don't know, but—"

"So it *might* have been." They stared at each other.

"Anyway," Slattery said, "it got us out of that perfectly bloody dinner. More drink, landlord!" The man appeared. "Same again, if you will."

"I won't. I called time five minutes ago." He was not impressed by their uniforms. "Act of Parliament."

"I sometimes wonder what we're fighting for," Paxton said.

"Free speech, isn't it? So now you're free to say goodnight."

In the car, Slattery said. "I suppose he had the law on his side."

"He's a Hun," Paxton said. "When we win the war I shall have him shot."

*   *   *

Andrew Mackenzie's mother dressed him in skirts and blouses until he was six, and let his fair and curly hair grow to his collar. That was not uncommon in the nineties, especially in well-to-do Kensington. Then her husband came back from South Africa.

He had never been poor; now he was rich. He had made a small fortune in diamond mining, risked it all on gold mines and won hugely. He returned to his roots: the Scottish Highlands. Land was cheap. He bought a shooting lodge, bristling with turrets, which sat on a headland overlooking a loch. He bought the loch. Behind it reared a range of mountains. He bought the mountains too.

He got Andrew out of a skirt and into a kilt. He scissored off the curls. While his wife sobbed, he put the boy on a pony and he climbed on a horse. Father and son began to explore the estate. After Kensington, this was a howling wilderness. The pony's saddle bruised Andrew's little backside. He didn't understand a word the local people said. But excitement conquers all. The mountains held deer, eagles, sheep, buzzards, hare, wildcat. In the rivers were trout and salmon, otter and heron. There was sailing on the loch. London couldn't compete with such adventure.

By the time he was twelve, Andrew was strong enough and smart enough to do most jobs on the estate, from sheering sheep to felling timber. He was a better shot than his father: farmers down in the glens invited him to shoot the crows that threatened their lambs; he rarely wasted a cartridge. Sometimes, to make it more challenging, he shouted at the crows and sent them clattering and climbing away. Sometimes he chased them on horseback and shot them from the saddle.

None of this could change his face. His eyes were large and strong, but that only confirmed how demure the rest of his face was; how charming. He went off to boarding school, and a procession of older boys became besotted with it. Nothing bothered Mackenzie. If anyone grew too affectionate he kicked him in the balls.

Then something horrible happened. His father died. Andrew was fifteen. He grieved longer than his mother did; she had two small daughters to fuss over. When he left school he was nearly eighteen. He was a man, all set to take over the estate; and to his great surprise she began urging him to join the army. "Your father would have gone," she said, grimly. "Gone like a flash."

"Nonsense. He would have been forty-eight by now."

"All your friends are in uniform."

"D'you want to get rid of me?"

"I want you to do your duty."

"So that you can boast about me to *your* friends?"

She turned away; he was too much like the man who had died. Also too little like him. Everything was unsatisfactory. "Surely you're not afraid?" she said.

"Mother, you are a brilliant blackmailer, but you don't know when to stop. Of course I'm afraid. Having your head blown off is a frightening affair." All the same, the following month he lied about his age and joined the Royal Flying Corps. She cried a little when he left.

* * *

Paxton had started with six pupil-pilots. One was dead, one was in hospital, one had been sacked. He met the remaining three after breakfast.

The morning was bright. "Go up and try to kill each other," he said. "One against two. The two can fly off somewhere, anywhere, I don't care.

The other chap climbs up and hides in the sun. Nasty Hun habit. You two come back, he falls on you like the wolf on the fold. Understood?" They nodded. "I may join in the fun. Who knows? Life is full of surprises. So is death. If I surprise any of you, please keep flying until you crash in the North Sea and drown yourself, because otherwise you will only become a burning wreck in France, which is unfair on the Poor Bloody Infantry who have enough scrap metal landing on their heads already. Be off with you." He turned and saw Mackenzie, standing waiting. "I sacked you yesterday," he said. "Get off the damned aerodrome."

"I couldn't report to the C.O., sir. He's gone to attend a crash inquiry. Tony Yabsley."

"Yabsley?" Paxton squinted at the sun until his eyes closed and all he could see was a pulsing yellow glow. "Yabsley." Then he remembered. Yabsley had (presumably) got lost, tried to land at another airfield, made a nonsense of it and charged straight into a busy hangar. Killed three airmen. And himself. Destroyed two machines. And his own. Yes, young Yabsley deserved a Court of Inquiry. He opened his eyes. "I knew a chap," he said, "flew into a hangar. German hangar. Flew straight through, came out the other side. There were witnesses," he told Mackenzie, "so don't stand there with that sceptical Scottish look on your face. Why are you carrying a flying helmet?"

"You said I couldn't shoot, sir."

"You couldn't hit a hangar if we locked you inside it, chum."

"I can shoot grouse, sir. From a Pup, I mean. I can fly a Pup and shoot grouse with the Vickers."

Paxton took off his cap and read the name inside and put it back on. He looked at Mackenzie's calm and delicate face. "Am I mad?" he said. "Or is this a training squadron without a grouse in the sky?"

"I know a grouse moor about twenty miles away. It belongs to Lord Delancey. We could shoot there."

"We?"

"You won't believe me unless you see it done, sir." Mackenzie kicked the head off a young thistle. "Bet you a fiver I get ten birds, sir." A fiver was a week's pay for Paxton.

"If you lose and you can't pay," Paxton said, "I'll have you cashiered for fraud."

"If I win?"

"You'll be flogged for insolence."

* * *

From five hundred feet the moors looked like velvet, slightly ruckled in places, stretching on all sides to the distance. From a hundred feet the ruckled places turned out to be streambeds and outcrops of rock. From fifty feet the heather was pitted with pot-holes. Paxton, flying alongside Mackenzie, tried not to think what would happen if his engine failed. The stretcher-party would take half a day to find him. Mackenzie was not thinking of failure. His head was half out of the cockpit and he was searching the moor. He banked gently, straightened up, throttled back until the Pup was down to twenty feet and dawdling just above its stalling speed of fifty miles an hour.

This was good grouse country, and yet no birds appeared. He glanced behind him: birds were rocketing up, scattering, raised by the racket of his engine. By the time he turned they would be gone. He needed a beater, ahead of him. For a second he despaired; then he touched his gun-button, just to see what happened. A dozen bullets lashed the heather, far ahead; and far ahead the grouse leapt into the air. Mackenzie nudged the rudder and his thumb released brief rattles of fire. He eased the stick back and chased the dark blurs. The Pup trembled as something hit the wires that braced the wings. Well, at least I got one, Mackenzie thought.

* * *

A rigger used a long-handled screwdriver to prise a bundle of black and red feathers from the wire, and let it drop to the hangar floor. "Three," he said. "Plus some bloody guts on the right wheel, sir."

"Plus seven I shot but didn't catch," Mackenzie said. "Ten."

"You hit four," Paxton said. "I counted four."

"I was closer than you." Mackenzie stooped and plucked a tail feather and tucked it behind his ear. "With respect. Sir."

"Send these over to the mess," Paxton told the rigger. "If they find any bullets, I want them. Now . . ." He removed the feather and tickled Mackenzie's nose. "Let us get out of earshot of these skilled tradesmen before I tell you what a fucking maniac you are."

They walked across the field to the roller.

"Bring it," Paxton said and walked away.

Mackenzie rocked the roller, gave it a heave, got it moving, and followed him.

"Benefit of the doubt," Paxton said. "Ten birds. You win."

"Thank you, sir." Mackenzie was leaning hard.

"Proves nothing, of course. Grouse can't fire back. Toddle over the Lines as low and slow as you did and the Hun machine gunners will toss for the privilege of shooting you down and still have time for a plate of sauerkraut before you arrive. Is that device heavy?"

"No, sir." Mackenzie's lungs were toiling.

"Pity. I need some enormous weight to flatten the restless soul of a cove called Milner. Not a *bad* pilot, Milner – better than you, for instance – but not good enough, either. He was directly above us." Paxton halted, so Mackenzie stopped too. Sweat trickled into his eyes. "A thousand feet?" Paxton suggested. "Quite high, anyway. Flew into a bird, smashed his prop, panicked, lost speed, panicked some more, tried to turn, spun like a top, and I expect he was still panicking like the devil when he met his Maker precisely *here*." Paxton stuck the feather in the top of a mound of earth. "We keep flattening it but it keeps bulging up. A restless soul, Mr Milner. Squash him."

Mackenzie dragged the roller back and forth. Paxton sat on the grass and watched.

"Squashed," Mackenzie said.

"Milner was unfortunate," Paxton said. "*You*, on the other hand, went looking for bad luck. If one grouse had clipped your prop you would have crashed."

"Chaps forced-land all the time."

"Not on hillsides. Not on heather. Wheels can't run on heather. You'd go arse-over-teakettle, sonnyboy."

Mackenzie looked at him. He thought of pointing out that Paxton had known he was going to shoot grouse, and he decided it would do no good. Instead he walked onto the flat circle of earth and jumped up and down. "I thought I saw it move," he explained.

Paxton helped him tow the roller back where it came from. "Now go and write Lord Delancey a note of thanks," he said.

"Why? He doesn't know anything about it."

"You didn't get his permission?"

"No fear. He'd have had his keepers out shooting at us, if he'd known. It's the close season for grouse."

"Sweet Jesus Christ." Paxton had been in the R.F.C. for over a year; he was a veteran; he had learned how to survive. "We've been to the seaside," he said. "Those were seagulls you shot."

"Of course, sir. What was my score?"

"Go to hell," Paxton said. "Go to blazes. Go to France. Go up and get yourself killed. Nobody stopped me. Why should I stop you?"

*　*　*

Thunderclouds blew in from the west. The wind gusted so hard that the aeroplanes had to be lashed down at wingtips and tail. The instructors retired to the anteroom – half of a long hut, the other half being the mess – and played poker. A tall Canadian called Quarry skinned them. By the time they went in to dinner, his cap was bulging with the weight of coins. "What's your secret?" Slattery asked him.

"Never draw to fill an inside straight," Quarry said.

"Oh. Thanks awfully." Slattery turned to Paxton. "What does that mean?"

"Don't come blubbing to me. You should have done your prep, like everyone else."

"We didn't have prep at Bog Street Elementary," Woolley said. "We were lucky to have a lump of coal to suck on."

"Also it helps if you have endless funds," Quarry said. "Which I now have."

"That's how we're going to win the war," Slattery said. "We've got deeper pockets than the Germans. When they've all been killed, we shall still have chaps left over. You wait and see. I read it in the *Daily Mail*"

"How long will all this take?" Paxton asked. "Only I've got a dental appointment in 1928."

It rained all night and all next morning. Players dropped into the game and dropped out again. Quarry kept winning; now he was taking IOUs.

"At this rate, England's going to be a colony of Canada, not vice versa," Paxton said.

"Canada is a *dominion*," Quarry said.

"Don't upset him, for God's sake," Slattery said. "He'll start charging interest."

"And we wouldn't take England at any price." Quarry dealt. "Too wet. Too small. Too old."

"So what are you doing here?"

"Oh . . . just saving your bacon. Cards?"

"This isn't a hand," Woolley said. "This isn't even a thumb." He threw in four cards. The door opened, and the wind made the fire howl. Major Venables kicked the door shut. They all stood, out of respect for his temper. "Who's been doing what to Lord Delancey?" Venables said. His voice had been overworked lately and now it cracked a little.

The silence became uncomfortable. Paxton sniffed, hard, and Woolley glanced at him. Paxton's face was pale and his neck was bright red. Someone asked: "Is he a pupil, sir?"

"Is he a pupil?" Venables threw his hat at a mess servant. "No, he's not a bloody pupil. He's a peer of the realm and he lives in a damn great castle and he wants my head with an apple in the mouth. Now, *why*?"

Paxton cleared his throat. "Did . . . um . . . did he give you any, you know, sort of indication, sir?"

"Lord Delancey doesn't speak to the likes of me, you idiot. His butler telephoned. A grave incident, he said. So who's been playing silly buggers?"

A gurgle from Slattery's stomach broke the silence. Nothing else did. "Beg pardon, sir," he murmured.

"Senior instructor," Venables said. Woolley raised a finger. "Get into your Number Ones lickety-split," Venables said. "If I'm going over the top, you're going too." His head kept wobbling, as if loose on its bearings. "Where's my bloody hat?"

* * *

They went in the C.O.'s car. The lanes were slick with mud and the driver kept his speed down; still, the wheels enjoyed an occasional skid. Every time the car wandered crabwise, Major Venables whispered the same fierce profanity. Woolley put up his collar. The car windows did not fit properly and rain kept spitting at him.

There was no castle. Lord Delancey lived in a palace surrounded by a deer park. The driver had to stop to let a stag amble across the drive. Woolley wiped a window and they looked at the place, but saw only half. Woolley opened the window and they looked out and saw the other half. "God Almighty," he said.

"God couldn't afford the rent," Venables said. "Go to those pillars," he told the driver. "That's probably the front door."

The pillars turned out to be as tall as beech trees. Two servants were waiting with umbrellas. They escorted the officers up some steps and under a portico and through a huge doorway. A silver-haired man in a tailcoat met them and took their coats and hats. "Are you the butler?" Venables asked.

"That is not my privilege, sir. If you will follow me?"

Everything echoed. Rain pattered on a glass dome, fifty feet above. The corridor was wide enough to take a horse team with an eight-pounder gun at the gallop. The floor was marble and the tramp of leather-soled boots sounded like a parade. The butler met them in a room lined with oil paintings of large men in rich clothes who could see nothing to smile at. He apologized for not being present when they arrived. Circumstances had unavoidably detained him elsewhere. His Lordship hoped to be able to receive them soon. He left.

They sat on opposite sides of the room. "The old bugger's polishing his ear-trumpet," Venables said. "Cursing his gout." Woolley nodded. He wondered if he had ever met a lord. There had been a baronet in his regiment when they were in the Lines in 1915, Captain Sir Gerald Somebody. Got mortared. Nothing left. It was unusual to vanish like that. Bits hanging on the wire, maybe, but nobody was going to go out and collect those. There had been a Polish count, too, thin chap with a bad cough. You never met a Pole who wasn't a count, so forget him. But no lords in the Lines. Trench-fighting was a young man's game. You got trench foot, and trench foot was bad for the gout. And all those loud bangs, too. Bad for the ear-trumpet.

The butler returned. He was sleek as a cabinet minister.

They marched down another corridor. Double doors were opened. "Major Venables and Captain Woolley, my lord," the butler said.

Plaster swans stretched their delicate necks as they flew across the high ceiling. Tall windows overlooked a paved courtyard where the rain was faithfully washing the stones until given orders otherwise. The room had a floor and walls of light oak: a very large tree had died for this room. Two men in dark suits stood at a desk, also of oak, about the shape and size of a family tomb. One man was old, one was not. They were looking at documents. After a while the older man murmured something and moved towards the officers. "Good afternoon, gentlemen," he said. "I am Sir Frederick Parfitt."

"That's as may be," Venables said. "My appointment is with Lord Delancey." The cracks in his voice were wider.

"Lord Delancey has urgent business to settle." Parfitt made the smallest gesture towards the other man. "As his legal adviser, I can outline to you the salient features of the problem. In a nutshell, it concerns aerial poaching of grouse on the estate . . ."

Woolley was only half listening. He was watching Lord Delancey sign letters and documents. The man looked no more than twenty-five. His hair was straw-coloured; it had been barbered to perfection. He looked very alert. He sat upright and only his head and his hand moved: he scanned a page, signed it, turned it, scanned the next. Sometimes the tightening of the jaw muscles betrayed a little tension.

"Potential suffering cannot be discounted," Sir Frederick was saying. "The breeding of game birds is a highly sensitive affair. The financial loss is arguably very considerable."

"I'll make enquiries, dammit," Venables said. "I've told you I will make enquiries, and I will. There's no evidence my squadron did this."

"Pheasant, in particular, are susceptible to shock."

"You can't train pilots without letting them fly low. Even if my squadron is involved, and as I said, there's no evidence—"

"Low flying, you say?" The lawyer made a note. "No doubt the War Office has issued regulations—"

"Alright, Freddy," Lord Delancey called. "That's enough. Come and sit down, everyone." There were chairs ranged around the desk. As they sat, he stood. He was not tall; slim; with neat and regular features except for his left ear. The sight of that ear startled Woolley: it had been ripped and mangled as if a wild dog had attacked it. The contrast between the young face and the ruined ear was unnerving.

"Let's forget my grouse and their shattered nerves," Delancey said. His lawyer began to speak and was waved away. "I'm on the boat train tonight. There's time only for urgent business."

"That's a Guards tie," Venables said. "You're a Guardsman."

"Yes. I'm Captain the Lord Delancey, and strictly speaking you outrank me, but as this is the last day of my leave I hope you will allow me to lead this show? Thank you. Now: I come from a large family. Scattered about this house are aunts, great aunts, cousins, both my maternal grandparents, I won't bore you with the list. My wife is here, of course. Pregnant. Our first child. And so to aeroplanes. I dare say you fellows in the Flying Corps take aeroplanes in your stride."

"We do."

"This household does not. Aeroplanes frighten them. In particular my wife. The sound of a flying machine terrifies her. She fears it is German and it will drop its bomb on us."

"Highly unlikely."

"You think so? For the last two years Zeppelins have wandered all over England, even as far as Cheshire and Lancashire, bombing as they wished. One Zeppelin bombed Piccadilly Circus! How long before German aeroplanes do the same? How long before Liverpool Street Station looks like Ypres? Or Arras? If my wife cannot take the train to town in safety, how can I assure her that she is safe in her own home?"

"I honestly can't see the Germans coming all the way here, just to throw out a few bombs. What would be the point?"

"What was the point of bombing a children's playground in south London? But they did it."

"Fortunes of war."

"Which exist, I agree. However, I have never believed in meekly accepting one's luck when the odds can be improved. Here, for instance, we have your squadron of well-armed Sopwith Pups on the doorstep, so to speak, and, I'm sure, itching for battle."

Venables' head was wobbling again. "Look: I take my orders from—"

"I know. I know precisely who gives you your orders. Know them personally. Many have been guests in this house."

"You're suggesting that my squadron gives your family special protection."

"Not a bit. The fact that this year I paid in taxes more than enough to buy several squadrons of aircraft is neither here nor there." Delancey smiled. He had a pleasant smile, slightly wistful. "Although some might think we *deserve* special protection, if only to guarantee that you can go on buying more squadrons."

"I don't believe you understand. I command a *training* squadron."

"What better training than to attack any German aeroplanes that intrude? Shoo them away. Send them packing."

"It's a spiffing idea, sir," Woolley said brightly. Venables glared. "Come on, major," Woolley said. "You know the chaps are keen as mustard to take a crack at the Boche."

"The first pilot to bag a Hun gets fifty guineas," Delancey said. "I'll tell my wife."

"She might not see us. We fly extremely high, to get a better view." Woolley snapped his fingers. "Here's a thought. Why don't you give her our phone number? If she's the slightest bit worried, we'll pop upstairs and wipe the sky clean."

"Splendid, splendid."

Delancey walked with them along the echoing corridors to the porticoed entrance. Sir Frederick had stayed in the study. "Never mind old Freddy," Delancey said. "He thinks that shooting grouse out of season is worse than fighting in church."

"I've fought in a church," Venables said. "What was left of it."

Their driver was at the door, weighed down with haunches of venison. "Your flying poacher strafed a deer," Delancey said. "May you have as much success against the Hun."

*   *   *

"Damn fool," Venables said. "Bloody lunatic." The driver half-turned his head. "Not you," Venables said wearily.

"His lordship's happy, sir," Woolley said. "He thinks he's had his wicked way with us, which proves that a gallon of blue blood is worth more than two pints of peasant piss like us. Did you see him smile?"

"Did you see me smile? While you were treating *my* squadron like a lucky dip? Roll up! Anybody want a dozen Sopwith Pups? *Jesus.*" The car had stopped so abruptly that it skidded a little on the gravel.

"Stag, sir," the driver said. It stood in the middle of the driveway, its great head swaying, apparently dozing in the rain.

"That's the same bloody beast," Venables growled. The driver nodded. It was a different beast, but he was only a corporal. "Even Delancey's bloody animals think they own us."

"I don't give a twopenny toss what Delancey thinks," Woolley said. "Do you, sir? As soon as I heard him say 'Shoo them away' I knew he was talking out of his arse. He thinks Huns are like trespassers and we're the village bobby. I could have told him it takes our clapped-out Pups half an hour to reach ten thousand, and by then the Boche has cheated and gone somewhere else, not that we could catch him if he played the white man and waited to be killed. But Delancey wouldn't have liked that, sir. Not what he wanted to hear."

Venables sighed. "No, I suppose not."

"Whereas now he thinks we'll be flying high-level patrols over his lovely wife, dawn to dusk, and it was all his idea, clever sod."

"If word gets out—"

"He won't tell anyone. It's our little secret."

"He'll tell his wife. She'll telephone—"

"And I'll tell her we're on patrol. I'll tell her she's perfectly safe. I'll lie."

"Yes. You're good at that, aren't you, Woolley? I'm not. I was taught soldiering. Find the enemy, bash him, take his territory." Venables threw open the car door, strode over to the stag and booted it in the rump. It bounded away. He got back in. The car moved off. "Did you see the man's ear? Looked more like a bayonet than a bullet."

"Cut himself shaving," Woolley said. "The butler told me so."

"Is that a joke?" Venables said. "Bloody stupid one, if it is." That ended all conversation.

* * *

They were still playing poker.

"Back already?" Slattery said. "I just had four kings."

"That's nothing," Woolley said. "I just had fifty lashes. From Lord Delancey's butler. Proper toff, his lordship. Watched it all and never flinched once." He sat at the table. Quarry dealt. "Don't you want to know what it was about?" Woolley asked Paxton.

"No," Paxton said. "'Cos it doesn't matter. We're off to France tomorrow. Postings just came through."

"France, eh?" Woolley said brightly. "What's going on there?"

"Tossing the beanbag," Quarry said. "We're in the finals. How many cards d'you want?"

EARTHQUAKE STRENGTH 6:

Persons walk unsteadily. Small bells ring.

The sky above Gazeran had been washed clean by the rainstorms of winter and blown dry by the gales of spring, and now Cleve-Cutler thought he had never seen a more delicate blue. Of course he knew this was nonsense. He had often flown above the weather, and he knew the sky was always blue, come rain or shine or thick grey fog. But a C.O.'s job left precious little time to enjoy beauty, it was mostly a matter of kicking junior officers up the arse before Wing H.Q. discovered their mistakes, and so when he found himself standing at the window of the anteroom he chose to look at the serenity of the sky rather than at the oily chimney of smoke that was boiling up and spoiling it all.

"Who's in camp over there?" he asked.

"Australian infantry," Plug Gerrish said. "I expect they saw it coming and got out of the way."

"I was on the phone at the time. Lousy line, bloody idiot at Brigade bawling and shouting, I never heard the klaxon."

A waiter brought two whisky-sodas.

"Heard the bang, though," Cleve Cutler said. "Come on, Plug, speak up."

"Well, it's either Maddegan or the new boy, Stamp. They went up to have a practice scrap. One got in a spin. Quite a slow spin. Don't suppose *he* thought it was slow, poor devil."

"Don't suppose he thought anything. Too giddy for that."

The smoke was thinning. Not much petrol in a Pup. This one probably had about ten gallons in its tank when it hit, enough for a short, hot fire. The rescuers would be there by now. The squadron had a well-drilled rescue team. No point in rushing over and getting in their way.

"It wasn't Dingbat, because here he comes," Gerrish said. "The original kangaroo." They watched the Pup make its approach and bounce four times before it ran. "He's getting better."

Cleve-Cutler finished his whisky-soda. "Keep them flying, Plug. Nobody broods. I'm off to write the bloody letter."

The orderly room at Gazeran field was in a gloomy barn that was suffering from age and war and rats. For nearly three years the place had been swept daily by the troops of whichever squadron was stationed there, but it still radiated the warm, peppery smell of horse dung. On the day he moved in, Captain Brazier had ordered that Jeyes Fluid be liberally sprinkled about the place. The disinfectant overlaid the ancient aroma, but could not defeat it. Soon the smell of horse dung reappeared like a peasant army which has fled to the hills only to creep back and reclaim its homeland. Next day the adjutant had talked of stronger measures: bleach, creosote, ammonia; even chloride of lime, used in the trenches against the stench of rotting corpses. "You are fighting history," Lacey had warned him.

"History and flies, sergeant."

It was true: squadrons of heavy French flies cruised around the barn, pilgrims at a shrine. Brazier thrashed the air with his copy of *King's Regulations*. A dozen fell dead.

"Now you are fighting history *and* natural history," Lacey said. "But I may have the answer." He got on the phone to a Royal Navy storekeeper in Boulogne and swapped a lambskin flying jacket, slightly bullet-holed, for six big tins of pungent black pipe-tobacco. Inhaled, its smoke made the adjutant's eyes water. Exhaled, it sent the flies racing to the nearest window.

Half an hour after the crash, Cleve-Cutler went into the adjutant's office. Brazier was with a couple of officers. The air was bruised blue with tobacco smoke.

"Look here, Uncle . . . I've knocked something together, but . . ." The C.O. looked chirpy, but he sounded annoyed. The officers moved away. "I mean, it's all well and good to tell his folks he made his mark on the squadron, but what did he actually *do?*"

170

"Stamp was quite keen on getting a cricket team going here, sir. You could say he never let the side down."

Cleve-Cutler grunted. "Didn't exactly cover himself with glory, either." He folded the paper and used a corner to clean his fingernails. "Covered himself with broken Pup, more like. What d'you call that, Uncle? Go on, give me an epitaph."

The adjutant blew smoke at a solitary, inquisitive fly. It whirled and tumbled to the ground. "Sorry, sir," he said, comfortably. "No can do."

The fly lay on its back and buzzed.

"See that?" Cleve-Cutler said. "Made the same mistake as young Stamp. Stalled and spun, stalled and spun. Silly boy." He trod on the fly, and immediately wished he hadn't. "Spinning is such a plague," he said. "It's worse than Archie. You can dodge Archie, but a bad spin . . ." He shook his head.

"There's an answer to it," one of the officers said.

Cleve-Cutler turned and saw an angular, black-haired pilot in a uniform that should have been pressed a week ago. His face had a grubby quality. His eyes looked old, but that was not unusual among pilots: even the best goggles could not protect eyes from the bitter gale that hammered at an open cockpit. What was unusual was his mouth. It was a wide mouth in a thin face and it curled in a way that might mean something or nothing. Either way, the C.O. disliked it.

"Captain Woolley, sir," the adjutant said. "And you remember Lieutenant Paxton, of course."

"Good Christ, Paxton," the C.O. said. "What a dreadful moustache."

"Thank you, sir." A year ago, Paxton would have burned with shame. Not now. A year ago, when he had left Sherborne School and got his wings and joined this squadron, he had been stiff and priggish, and the other officers had made his apprenticeship very sticky indeed. During the battle of the Somme he had grown up very fast. He survived a bad crash and was sent home to instruct, and now he was back with good old Hornet. The C.O. could say what he liked. Paxton was fireproof.

"Mr Woolley," Cleve-Cutler said. "A machine in a bad spin is a coffin.

The answer is not to let the machine get into the spin to start with. That's what we teach on this squadron."

"A pilot can get out of a bad spin if he knows how," Woolley said. "Sir." He wasn't arguing.

"Captain Woolley has been instructing, sir," the adjutant said.

"Ah! Instructing, has he? That explains why we get replacement pilots who never last long enough to pay their mess bills! What d'you teach them? Hopscotch?"

"They get their wings too soon," Woolley said. "That's not my fault."

"They get their *funerals* too damn soon. And I have to write these bloody letters! So don't come bragging to me about your brilliant methods, captain. We shovel the results into coffins every week." Cleve-Cutler hadn't finished. He didn't like Woolley's unreadable face or his easy stance or his grubby uniform. "Chaps like you make the Hun very happy," he said. "Mr God-Almighty-Richthofen depends on chaps like you to send him the bunnies he knocks down before breakfast."

"Richthofen depends on his skills, sir. He's a professional."

"He's a bloody butcher."

"Butchery is an honest trade."

Cleve-Cutler gave up in disgust. He turned to the adjutant. "This officer is a tradesman who has been sent, in error, to a squadron of gentlemen. Make him duty officer until further notice. Since he regards himself as no better than the municipal rat-catcher, he can get rid of the rats that plague this camp." He left. The door banged, and its shock shivered the remnants of tobacco smoke hanging in the air.

"The major's a bit touchy," Brazier said. "We've had a few losses lately."

"That's alright, Uncle. I never wanted to come here, anyway," Woolley said. "I bet there's no draught Guinness in the mess."

Brazier gave him a duty officer armband and a clipboard. "The funeral's tomorrow morning. The burial party know the drill. I trained them myself."

"See? This is a top-notch squadron," Paxton told Woolley. "Keen as mustard."

They left. Brazier strolled into the orderly room. "You fancy yourself as a scribbler," he said to Lacey. "The C.O. needs something to spice up his next-of-kin letters. Knock out a few patriotic lines."

Lacey was slightly nettled. "Certainly, sir. Do you want sentimental rhymes, or deathless prose? I should warn you that the latter may take a lifetime."

Brazier nodded. "Start now," he urged.

* * *

Only a handful of Bristol Fighters had been sent to France. Hornet Squadron was to get six. The day before they were ferried in, General Trenchard sent for Cleve-Cutler. A single Bristol Fighter, he told him, was worth two of any other type. The squadron had three weeks to learn how to use it. And the enemy must know nothing of its existence. "You," Trenchard said, "are entrusted. With a weapon. That could well turn the tide. Of battle."

Rashly, Cleve-Cutler said, "The battle of Arras, by the look of things, sir."

Trenchard gazed down at him from his great, gaunt height.

"That's pure speculation, of course," Cleve-Cutler murmured.

"Impure," Trenchard growled.

Next day, six Bristol Fighters circled Gazeran and the first sight of them was a disappointment. "It's an elephant," Spud Ogilvy said. He handed his binoculars to Crash Crabtree. "What a monster! Must weigh a ton."

"Perhaps it's a Bristol Bomber. Or a clerical error."

Nobody wanted to hear that. The R.F.C. had bomber squadrons, brave chaps who flew deep into enemy territory, bombed from beneath the clouds, and got harried all the way home. No thanks.

The Bristol Fighters landed neatly and in quick succession. Cleve-Cutler and his pilots ambled towards the aircraft, hands in pockets, out of step, exercising the privilege of airmen to be unmilitary.

"We shall need bigger hangars," the C.O. said. He walked around the nearest machine.

Plug Gerrish paced out the wingspan. "Forty feet," he said. "Half as wide again as a Pup. Nose to tail, I'd say a good six feet longer."

McWatters approached the C.O. "I don't know if you've noticed, sir," he said, "but the bottom wing seems to have come away from the fuselage."

"I'd noticed."

"You can see daylight between them, sir. The bottom wing's actually hanging from the top wing."

"So it appears."

"Sloppy workmanship, sir."

"Try not to be a greater idiot than nature created, McWatters."

"Yes, sir. They seem to have forgotten to give the pilot a Vickers, sir."

Cleve-Cutler nodded. It was true: where the Pup had a machine gun bolted on top of its nose, this had nothing – just a hand-held Lewis in the rear cockpit. He was looking at a hulking aeroplane with a vast spread of wings, a disturbingly experimental design and no weapon for the pilot. It was not the thrilling new fighter he had expected to see. He remembered other models that had disappointed: the DH2 Gunbus, soon known as the Spinning Incinerator; the BE12, which refused to dive with the engine full on, and if the engine was throttled back the interrupter gear failed and the pilot often shot his propeller off; the RE8, underpowered and a bitch to land because two fat exhaust pipes stuck up in front of the pilot . . . Then he saw a familiar figure in a flying suit: Colonel Bliss.

"Gather your chaps, Hugh," Bliss said. "I bring them tidings of great joy and bloody slaughter."

While the pilots assembled, Bliss climbed into the pilot's cockpit and stood on the seat.

"This is the F2A, popularly known as the Bristol Fighter," he announced. "No other aeroplane, in any air force, can fly as fast, *and* climb as fast, *and* fly as high, *and* stay up as long, *and* carry as many guns, as this machine. No Albatros can do it. No Fokker can do it. No Pfalz, no LVG, no Halberstadt. This machine, gentlemen, is the last word in fighters. And it is yours."

"Guns, colonel?" Cleve-Cutler said. "No sign of a Vickers."

"Absolutely none. That's because the gun is tucked away *inside*, on top of the engine, which keeps it warm. A frozen gun is therefore a thing of the past. If you care to look above the propeller hub you will see a discreet hole in the radiator. From this orifice will emerge a string of bullets." They surged to look. "Greatly to the shock and chagrin of the foe," Bliss said; and thought: No, no. That's too much. Keep it simple

"Sir, some of us were wondering," Ogilvy said. "The wings—"

"Ah yes, the wings. Now, Captain Frank Barnwell designed this bus. Barnwell's an R.F.C. man. He knows what you want when you go on patrol. Above all, you must see the enemy! If you can't see him, you can't kill him. But the wings obstruct your view. They're a damned nuisance. So Barnwell did something so simple that it's brilliant. *He moved the top wing down.* Down to the pilot's eye-level. So now you've got perfect vision forward, sideways and upwards, because you can look over the wing! If you lower the top wing, you've got to lower the bottom one. And that, Captain Ogilvy, is why the lower wing is slung six or nine inches below the fuselage. Or, to put it another way, Barnwell left the wings where they were, but he put the fuselage midway between them. Very accessible. Makes dusting so much easier, don't you know."

"Big aeroplane, sir," Gerrish said. "Big engine?"

"Rolls-Royce Falcon. One hundred and ninety horsepower. Treat it nicely and she'll stay up for three hours. Maybe more." Bliss allowed the rumble of comment to die down. "Now, Barnwell remembers the bloody awful layout of other two-seaters. The BE2c, for instance. More wires than a birdcage. Every time the observer fired his Lewis, bang went a wire." He pointed at Heeley. "You, sir. Jump up and try this one on for size."

Heeley climbed into the gunner's cockpit. Bliss slid down into the pilot's seat. They were back-to-back, their shoulders only inches apart. "Can you hear me, gunner?"

"Perfectly, sir!"

"Give that gun a spin. See what you can see."

The Lewis was mounted on a Scarff ring, which was a hoop that fitted the circular cockpit. Heeley rotated it enthusiastically through a full circle,

175

and then back the other way. "I can see everything, sir!" he cried.

"Of course you can, my dear chap." Bliss climbed onto his seat. "Notice how the fuselage tapers *downwards* towards the tail," he said. "Observe how much of the rudder is placed *below* the level of the tailplane. All this gives the gunner a wonderful field of fire. He can hit virtually everything except his own pilot. And we're working on a new design to let him do that . . ." They laughed generously. "No further questions? Good. There will be a silver collection at the door, and meanwhile I'm looking forward very much to a large drink, major."

A tender carried them to the C.O.'s office. Bliss took off his flying suit while Cleve-Cutler poured the whisky.

They toasted each other in silence, and drank in silence.

"What's wrong with it, Colonel?" Cleve-Cutler asked.

"That's for you to find out."

"So it's not perfect." He got no answer. "But if it out-flies and out-climbs and out-shoots—"

"I never said that." Bliss took his whisky to the fire. "I said no other aeroplane *combines* all the abilities you've got in this one fighter. The latest Albatros is slightly faster, but it has no rear gunner. The Fokker Triplane climbs faster, but it lacks endurance. The Halberstadt can stay up for ever, but the Bristol Fighter climbs faster. And so on and so on. Nobody else *combines* what we combine. That's what I said."

"With respect, sir, a three-hour endurance is no damn use if you can't catch the Hun."

"Well, every aeroplane is a compromise. If you want this one to go faster, jettison the wheels and you'll get an extra ten miles an hour. Probably kill yourself when you land, but . . ." Bliss kicked the coals and made sparks fly. "That's part of the compromise, isn't it?"

His bland equanimity began to annoy Cleve-Cutler. "Sir: you just told my chaps they've got the best fighter in the world. How can I—"

"No." Bliss used his little finger to clear a stray lash from his eye. "No, I never said that. What I said was the F2A is the last word in fighters, and so it is. Tomorrow, there will be a new last word. Different. Maybe better, maybe worse; we shall have to wait and see."

"With respect, sir—"

"Oh, bugger respect, Hugh. Half the battle up there is confidence. Men fight better when they believe they can win. You know that. Well, the F2A is a damn good bus, so they stand a damn good chance, provided they use the thing properly. Here."

He gave the C.O. a thick envelope, heavily sealed.

"Read it carefully," Bliss said. "Apply it faithfully. I dined with Frank Barnwell in Bristol last night. Salmon fresh from the Severn, new potatoes, mashed turnip; delicious. His fighter is built to a special design, and it works best when it's flown in a special way." He tapped the envelope. "Train your squadron until that way is second nature. Come the battle, they'll do great slaughter."

"I see."

"And now I'm off. Incidentally, how are your Russians?"

"One's suicidal, sir, and the other isn't."

"Yes. I think I saw the play. Chekhov, wasn't it? Not many jokes."

* * *

Cleve-Cutler announced that he himself would be first to fly this thundering brute. If it killed anyone, it should kill the C.O. The crews applauded.

One ferry pilot had stayed at Gazeran to help the squadron convert to the F2A. Cleve-Cutler got into the rear cockpit and looked over the man's shoulder. He was pleased to see that starting the engine was simple: a mechanic swung the prop while the pilot wound the magneto and with no reluctance at all the Falcon fired and uttered a huge, deep-throated roar. Cleve-Cutler watched the pre-take-off checks as the pilot pointed to them. Run up the revs and check oil pressure, water temperature, both magnetos. Set the tail adjustment. Test the controls. The rest was routine. They turned into wind, the throttle was eased open, the fighter bustled forward. Cleve-Cutler gripped the cockpit rim and braced himself against the torrent of air; he wanted to see what revs it took to get the tail up. Too late: the tail was already up. Now he wanted to know their take-off speed. Too late: the wheels had already unstuck. He looked down: the ground was falling away. Take-off had used less than two hundred yards. The thing was as big as a bomber and it soared like a Pup.

When it was his turn to fly it, he felt that this was the first real aeroplane he had ever known. Everything was beautifully balanced; the F2A actually felt graceful. The surge of power when he nudged the throttle was like nothing he'd ever got from a buzzing rotary. At seven thousand feet he was so happy that he felt anxious. He wondered: suppose I saw a couple of Huns down there? He eased the stick forward and the nose fell like a diver off the high board. Suddenly he remembered the sheer weight of this machine. The way the air-speed indicator was hustling around its dial was startling, and exciting, and then alarming. He got both hands on the stick and hauled, and the big elevators bit on the slipstream and sent the fighter curving into a pull-out that made the blood retreat from his eyeballs.

After that he behaved himself. The Bristol Fighter, with a little help from its pilot, returned to earth, stalled nicely in a three-point position at forty-something miles an hour, and ran to rest in no distance at all.

"Colonel Bliss was right," he told the crews. "This is what we've been waiting for." His conscience could live with those words.

*　*　*

"Teamwork kills," Cleve-Cutler said. "That is our new motto."

He had studied the tactical orders delivered by Bliss, and selected his crews. Six Bristol Fighters needed twelve men. For pilots, he chose his flight commanders plus Snow, McWatters and Simms. As gunners he chose Munday, Dash, Heeley, Maddegan and the two Russians. Since the fall of the Tsar, London seemed to have lost interest in them. Cleve-Cutler let them keep their Nieuports but he took away their extra servant. Duke Nikolai did not complain.

Cleve-Cutler assembled the crews. "This is a new kind of fighter," he said. "It's been tested in mock combat in England, and it scored best as a killing machine when it was flown in close formation. That's because, if you give the pilot freedom to manoeuvre, he can give his gunner the best shot at the enemy. Apply those tactics to a whole formation, and the gunners can provide crossfire, so they can attack the enemy from several quarters at once. Of course the pilot still has the Vickers. If he can get in a burst too, that's a bonus. But what makes the F2A so lethal is *teamwork*. The pilot concentrates on flying the bus, because he knows his gunner is protecting him. And his gunner knows he'll be perfectly positioned to hammer the Hun. Two experts are better than one. Teamwork kills."

For the next five days they practised formation flying. Every morning, weather permitting, the six fighters flew westward, away from the risk that any stray German reconnaissance machine might see them, to a disused landing ground at Braye. The C.O. came with them, in a Pup. They flew box formations, arrowheads, echelons to left or right, single file, double file, diamond, line abreast. They learned hand signals to change from one formation to the next. They got to know and like the Bristol Fighter, which was too much of a mouthful. They called it the Biff.

On the sixth day, Cleve-Cutler introduced simulated fighting. The flight commander fired a flare to signal an attack, and they altered formation so as to be broadside to the imaginary oncoming machines. The method worked well. When a colour arched across the sky, all six fighters swung into their new positions as if worked by wires. Six Scarff rings rotated and six Lewis guns ranged on the supposed Huns.

Cleve-Cutler was impressed. He watched through binoculars and wished he could see six beady lines of tracer pulsing into one cocky Boche. When the flight landed, he mentioned this to Plug Gerrish. "I keep hoping some lost Halberstadt will wander by," he said. "Give you something to blow to bits."

"We saw a French Spad yesterday."

"Certainly not."

"The bastards shoot at us." But Plug knew it was a lost cause. "Balloons," he suggested. "Not observation balloons. Small things. Five or six feet across would do. You send them up, we knock 'em down."

Amazingly, the Royal Flying Corps had a stock of balloons, aerial, disposable, size medium. "Six-foot diameter," the quartermaster told Cleve-Cutler on the telephone. "How many d'you want?"

"Can I have fifty?"

"You can have five thousand. They've been cluttering up my stores for the last two years. I suppose you'll want gas cylinders too?"

The balloons were a great success. They zoomed up to four thousand feet, by which time they had been picked up by whatever wind was going and sent bounding and spinning and still climbing. The gunnery was not a great success. The first six balloons sailed through a spray of bullets. Each time Gerrish, leading the flight, had to cut short the attack and change formation because a fresh balloon was racing towards them from a different angle. By the time the seventh balloon came blowing along, most gunners were out of ammunition.

They landed at Braye to re-arm.

"I think you may have slightly wounded a small white cloud," Cleve-Cutler said, "for which, since it was French, we shall have to pay compensation."

"The damn balloons don't fly straight," Crash Crabtree said. "They bobble about like lunatics."

"It's hard to gauge distance when the target's spherical," Spud Ogilvy said. "I think we're far too far away from it."

"Then get closer," Cleve-Cutler said, trying to be thrustful and sounding petulant. He wondered why. Perhaps he was jealous. Perhaps he was getting old, losing his grip. "Get very close. If you can't shoot it, then bite it to death."

Sandwiches and coffee, while the armourers worked.

McWatters sat on an oil drum and threw small stones at the sparrows hunting for crumbs. Duke Nikolai joined him. "I made secret army," he said quietly. "Bring back Tsar. You join my air force."

The other men were walking back to the aircraft. A bird came zigzagging at high speed, a foot above the grass, stunted around a deckchair, landed and raced away, simultaneously it seemed, with a bit of bread in its beak. "Clever little devil," McWatters said. "Makes our bus look like a rather tired slug. How much will you pay me?"

"I have million dollars."

McWatters picked up his helmet and goggles. "Why dollars? Why not sovereigns?"

"Is secret army. Secret dollars."

"Alright, I'll join your secret air force and fight in secret for the Tsar and all his inbred family. Now that I'm part of the secret, you can tell me. Where did you get the money?"

"Yankee government."

"No, no. The Yanks don't like royalty. They even revolted against George the Third, a perfectly decent king, slightly mad when there was an R in the month, but not a cruel and tyrannical brute like your chap. America won't support the Tsar. Americans don't *like* Tsars."

"Don't like Bolsheviks also," Nikolai said. "Bolsheviks give Yankees big jitters."

Crabtree was shouting at them to hurry. "A much-maligned man, the Tsar," McWatters said. "We should not be too hasty in passing judgement on him."

The second gun-practice was more successful. They destroyed five balloons out of twelve. But they missed seven. "If the Kaiser ever decides to attack us with toy balloons, we're done for," Cleve-Cutler said to the sergeant armourer.

"It's a different skill, sir, firing to the beam. Your gunners up there are used to firing forward, in the Pup. Not the same thing at all, sir."

Cleve-Cutler telephoned Wing. Next day six gunnery instructors arrived at Braye. After that, the score improved.

* * *

A high-pressure system drifted in from the Atlantic and sat over central Europe as if it had nothing better to do than spoil an elaborate and expensive war by dumping fog on it.

The officers strolled to breakfast. The air tasted both smoky and clammy. A hurricane lamp hung outside the mess, but its glow was muffled

181

and the smell of grilled bacon was a better guide. This was an excellent fog. It might well last all day.

"I shall celebrate with a fried egg," Munday told a mess servant. "No, dammit, let joy be unconfined. Two fried eggs."

"Give him some sausages too," the medical officer said. "Fry him some bread. Devil a kidney for him, hell's teeth, put some black pudding on the poor fellow's plate, throw in some bubble-and-squeak! What are you being so stingy for?"

"No, no." Munday waved the waiter away. "Just the eggs. Perhaps a slice of toast." A newcomer called Dufee watched with interest. "This fog could be gone by ten," Munday said to him. "It pays to be careful."

"Munday has a gut like a raging compost heap," Spud Ogilvy explained. "At five thousand feet his fried breakfast turns to gas and blows both his boots off."

"Well!" McWatters declared. "Did you see this?" He was reading an old copy of *The Times*.

"Knew a chap in hospital," Crash Crabtree said. "Ate nothing but fresh tomatoes for six months."

"It says here the Duke of Beaufort has suffered a nasty accident," McWatters announced. "Look." He showed the headline to Duke Nikolai. "Very worrying."

"Doesn't worry me," Snow said.

"You're just a crude Canadian," Simms remarked from behind the *Daily Mail*. "You don't appreciate the implications."

"Yeah? So implicate me."

Munday's eggs arrived. "I shall regret this," he said.

"Think how the eggs feel," Dash said.

McWatters shook *The Times*, loudly. "While hunting with the Beaufort Hounds, the duke had the misfortune to fall from his horse. His Grace was a good deal shaken and badly bruised, but luckily no bones broken."

"Next time you blighters feel like complaining," Spud Ogilvy said, "thank your lucky stars you don't live in the Cotswolds. Can't go for a walk without a fat duke falling on you."

"Russia's worse," Crabtree said. "The Tsar fell in Russia. Made a hell of a dent."

"Dando . . ." Simms, deep in his newspaper, had heard nothing. "What's the first thing you ask your patients?"

"Money. Can the patient pay the bill?"

"Wrong. The bowels. First thing the doctor always asks about is the bowels. Says so here. Are the bowels in good order? If the liver is right you will always be cheery and well. Don't wait to be bilious, take Carter's Little Liver Pills."

"Please. Not in the mess," Crabtree said.

"My liver is alright," Dando said, "and I'm buggered if I'll be cheery for anyone."

"Can we please change the damned subject?" Ogilvy said.

Silence, apart from the crunch of toast and the rustle of Simms's newspaper as he turned the pages. "How about this?" he said. "Here's a picture of a chap with a moustache who reckons unwise living weakens the kidneys. He says Doan's Backache Kidney Pills—"

"Out! Out! Out!" Ogilvy roared.

Simms retreated to the anteroom. Ogilvy's temper had been getting worse lately, and he had been known to throw things: bread rolls, plates, chairs. It was probably his liver, Simms decided. Or his kidneys. Simms wasn't sure of the difference between them, but he knew they got worse with age, and Ogilvy must be twenty-three at least.

Plug Gerrish strode into the mess, his eyebrows glistening with fog. "No flying," he said. "The C.O. wants the Biffs stripped down and cleaned up. Kippers," he told a waiter. "Three. You lot look down in the mouth."

"Duke of Beaufort fell off his horse," Snow said. "We're in a state of shock."

* * *

Duke Nikolai faced Cleve-Cutler in his office and announced that it was necessary to have Count Andrei shot. The C.O. thought about that, while noticing that most of Nikolai was rigid with anger while parts were trembling with distress. "Not in the Royal Flying Corps," he said.

"I have been hit by count. Hit with Bible."

"Not in the Royal Flying Corps."

"Is insult to Tsar. Is act of . . ." He checked his pocket dictionary. "Act of treachery."

"Not in the Royal Flying Corps."

"Is impossible. Not live in same hut. I must have different hut." Tears were dribbling over his handsome cheekbones. Cleve-Cutler glanced out of the window and counted to five.

"Not in the Royal Flying Corps," he said comfortably.

* * *

Captain Brazier liked to walk around the aerodrome after breakfast. Corps H.Q. had sent units of heavy machine guns to protect airfields near the Front, and Brazier liked to keep the crews on their toes. He examined the weapons, inspected the haircuts and shaves, moved on to the next gun-pit.

He had found a man wearing slovenly puttees, and he was telling his sergeant of an attack at Neuve Chapelle in 1915 during which a soldier had tripped over his own loose puttees and accidentally shot the company commander dead; when Sergeant Lacey came looking for him.

They walked back to the orderly room.

"A Captain Lightfoot is on his way here, sir, from the assistant provost-marshal's office," Lacey said.

"Damn. Still . . . He's only a captain. Can't be anything serious." But the adjutant was thoughtful. The A.P.M. investigated the army's crimes, and Brazier was experienced enough to know that there were always crimes, even in the best of units. What was this Lightfoot up to? Why drive forty miles through thick fog? "Did he send us a signal?" the adjutant asked.

"No. I have a friend in the A.P.M.'s department. A mere sergeant like myself. We share a passion for the cello sonatas of Saint-Saëns, although we differ on the piano concerti."

"Don't we all. I take it he's done us a small favour."

"An understatement, sir. Saint-Saëns's contribution has been enormous."

"Get a grip of yourself, Lacey. What's Lightfoot up to?"

They discussed possible crimes and criminals. Brazier went to the mess and called together Maddegan, McWatters, Crabtree and Dash.

"Go to Arras," he said. "Get a haircut. Have lunch. Get another haircut. Don't come back till dark. The A.P.M. is on his way."

"Look here," McWatters said. "If it's about some drunken old frog who got knocked down, I wasn't even driving, and I've got witnesses."

"You never said that," Brazier told him, "and I never heard it."

"Why me? I haven't done anything wrong," Dash said; but he remembered the nights in the nunnery at Beauquesne, and his ears went red.

"I haven't done anything either," Crabtree said, "so the A.P.M. can accuse me of anything he likes, can't he? That's how the system works."

"It's called *carte blanche*," the adjutant said. "The French police have been doing it for years."

* * *

Ralph Lightfoot had the body of a warrior and the eyes of a mole. He was brave, and he wanted to fight for his country, but even the British Army — which since 1916 had been taking boys who were only eighteen and a half years old and five feet tall — even the British Army drew the line at a man who could not tell a general from a gatepost if his glasses fell off. Lightfoot had a decent law degree and a bucketload of patriotism, so he got a commission and a place in the A.P.M.'s department. Without the pebble glasses he looked every inch a fighting man, but of course without the pebble glasses he might walk into the nearest wall and break his nose.

Sergeant Lacey showed Lightfoot into the adjutant's office, and then stayed to take shorthand notes.

"Lightfoot. Lightfoot?" Brazier immediately went onto the attack. "Not the M. N. T. Lightfoot who played rugby for the Harlequins in '13?"

"Alas, no."

"Well, take a pew." Brazier remained standing. "Now, I expect you've come about the duff ammo."

"No, again."

"It's damn serious. Defective rounds jam the Vickers. Looks like sabotage. Don't you investigate sabotage?"

"No," Lightfoot said, sadly. "I mean, not me personally."

"Well, Christ Allbloody Mighty, man," Brazier said. Exasperation hardened his voice. "Men are dying up there because of this." But Lightfoot was pulling files out of his briefcase, muttering as he checked the labels, shuffling the sequence until he got it right.

"Second-Lieutenant Maddegan," he said. "Let's start with him. Causing an affray, assaulting an officer – several officers – and conduct prejudicial etcetera etcetera."

Brazier took a monocle from a desk drawer and clamped it to his right eye. He reached across the desk and plucked the file. "Ah, Maddegan. Yes. A most gallant officer. Hopelessly outnumbered. Fought like the devil. His bus was shot to matchwood. Crash-landed. Still unconscious."

"I see." Lightfoot kept nodding his head, but he could think of nothing more to ask except the name of the hospital, and he felt sure no good would come of that. "Well, let's move on to Captain Crabtree. Destruction of civilian property, to wit: one electricity generator."

Again, Brazier took the file. He shut his left eye and scanned the pages through his monocle. "M.C. and Croix de Guerre," he said softly, as if to himself. "A most gallant officer. At present in Ireland. Pall-bearer for Tommy Fitzallen. Died of wounds. But of course you knew that?" He raised his eyebrows. The monocle fell. He caught it without looking.

Lightfoot searched for a handkerchief, polished his glasses, put them on again and stared at the adjutant. In a distant hangar an engine was being tested. The pitch of its thunder intensified and, abruptly, died.

"There was a Portuguese deserter at Pepriac," Lightfoot said. "Lieutenant McWatters and Second-Lieutenant Dash were in contact with him. In *close* contact. My information is—"

The adjutant's massive hand reached out and gripped the files. For a moment the papers buckled as Lightfoot refused to let go, but when they started to tear his fingers relaxed and Brazier had won again. "McWatters and Dash, you say."

"Most gallant officers, no doubt," Lightfoot said bleakly. "Let me guess. Salmon-fishing on the Spey? Sudden appendicitis?"

Brazier roared with laughter and beat the files against his desk so furiously that the draught ruffled Lightfoot's hair. "That would be fun, eh, Lacey? What? Splendid fun. No, this is a fighting squadron and those two gallant officers are at war."

"In the fog."

"Certainly, in the fog. Don't ask me where. Military secret."

Lightfoot closed his briefcase and stood up. "Two hundred pounds of plum jam went missing at Pepriac," he said. "Now the quartermaster at Brigade reports that you have indented for, and received, exactly *twice* your proper allocation of cheese."

Brazier shrugged.

"The first allocation was destroyed by bombing, sir," Lacey said.

"Bombing," Lightfoot said. "Have you evidence of this?"

Lacey led the officers into the fog. Somewhere in the area of the cook-house, he found a small hut. "The bomb fell exactly here, sir."

"But this structure is undamaged, sergeant."

"Yes, sir. This hut *replaced* the hut that was bombed."

Lightfoot walked around it. "The ground is not even scarred. There is no sign of a crater."

"It was a small bomb, sir. Enough to start a fire which, although soon extinguished, ruined the cheese."

Lightfoot opened the door, and struck a match. The hut was full of potatoes. "This is not a cheese store," he said, accusingly.

"Certainly not," the adjutant said. "We lost our cheese to the Hun once. We've made damn sure it won't happen again."

Lightfoot declined an invitation to lunch. Brazier excused himself: urgent operational business. Lacey escorted the visitor to his car. When he got back to the orderly room, he found the adjutant studying the A.P.M.'s files. "Bloody idiots," he growled. "Why do staff officers make life so difficult?"

"Probably for the same reason they make death so easy."

"Very glib. What do you know about it?"

"I know it's two sides of the same coin."

Brazier wasn't listening. "I know that sort," he said. "He'll be back. A pound of cheese is like the holy grail to him."

* * *

Arras was never big. It had been a medieval town of about fifty thousand Flemish people, famous for making tapestry, until the autumn of 1914 when the German Army settled down in the eastern suburbs. They shelled the place for the next two and a half years. By March 1917, nearly all the high, handsome, gabled houses were gutted and skeletal. The cathedral was a ruin, few shops survived, there wasn't a civilian to be seen. When the four pilots drove into Arras, the fog was thickened by drifting smoke from fires that lurked deep inside the wrecked buildings.

"This is a bloody silly place to come to," McWatters grumbled. "We should have gone the other way. Doullens. Amiens. Abbeville."

"Uncle told us to come here," Dash said.

"Grow up, laddy. He's only the bloody adjutant. Just look at this squalor. I need handkerchiefs, and there isn't a decent haberdashers anywhere."

"Look, I've got a spare snotrag you can borrow," Maddegan said.

"I'm sure you have, Dingbat. Fortunately, its use in war is banned under the Geneva Convention."

"Look," Maddegan said. "Choo-choo."

They were in a cobbled square that had a narrow-gauge railway track running across it. Trundling by was a train of trucks loaded with rocks and dirt. "Can it be," Crabtree said, "that the French have found a market for their debris?"

"*Souvenirs de la guerre,*" Dash said. "Five francs a lump."

"Hey! I see an Australian," Maddegan said. He was out of the car and striding towards a group of men, some in slouch hats. Much hand-shaking and back-slapping, and then he was back. "Trust a Digger to find the best grub in town," he reported. "It's down a hole."

The hole was a cellar as big as a ballroom, converted into a restaurant and doing a brisk business. A little old Frenchman, bandy-legged by the weight of years, brought them bread but no menu. "Leave this to me," McWatters said. *"Garçon, s'il vous plaît . . . Pour commencer . . ."*

Dash had never seen such a collection of uniforms from so many countries in one room. It thrilled him to think that all these fine chaps had rallied to the Old Country. Soon they would stand shoulder to shoulder and give the Hun one hell of a hiding. Then he saw a face that made him kick a leg of the table. He half-stood to get a better view. No doubt about it. His loins crawled with excitement. "Excuse me," he murmured.

It was Chlöe Legge-Barrington, and as he went towards her, the officer at her table got up and walked away. Dash was astonished by his luck. "Hullo!" he said. "Remember me? The chap on the white horse."

"Charles . . ." She tugged at his sleeve. "Sit down. What a relief. I've just been bored to death by a man who is going to be the next prime minister but five. You're looking well."

"And you're looking spiffing. Isn't this the most marvellous luck? Bumping into each other."

"Not really. Arras is getting ready for the next Big Push, isn't it? So F.A.N.Y. is here in strength. We go where we're needed."

"Oh." He hadn't thought of that. "Still, it's a far cry from Sainte Croix." She nodded. "D'you know," he said, "those were the happiest days of my life." He discovered that he was chewing his lower lip, so he stopped doing that. Now he felt like a sack of potatoes. "Definitely the happiest," he said. "It's an awful cheek, but d'you think you could put me in touch . . ."

She propped her chin on her hand and examined his freckled face. "My dear Charles," she said, "either you led a very dull life until we met you, or there was something special about Sainte Croix that escaped me."

"The latter." Dash felt his ears go red.

"Ah. And you want . . ." She was looking him in the eyes. He tried not to blink. "You want to repeat the happiness," she said. He nodded. "Well, tell me who it was," she said, "and I'll tell you where she is."

Now his cheeks were burning. "It's not as simple as that." She raised her eyebrows. "The lights were out. It was pitch black. I couldn't tell . . . She didn't say . . . Oh, damn and blast," he said, weighed down by a wretched pride in his experience, "it wasn't the time for conversation, was it?" He was close to tears.

"Golly, no," she whispered. "But—"

"Charles!" McWatters boomed. "Been looking all over for you! Introduce me, or I'll box your enormous ears."

"Go to hell."

"In that case, I'm Captain Ball," McWatters told her. He kissed her hand. "I hope young Charlie hasn't been bothering you. I have a car, perhaps I can take you—"

"Here comes my escort now. Where are you based?" She asked Dash.

"Gazeran."

She smiled, and left. They went back to their table. "Why can't you mind your own bloody business?" Dash demanded.

"A beauty like that *is* my business, laddy. What's her name?"

"Lady Macbeth," Dash said.

"I'll find out. A chap like you shouldn't attempt to fly *and* fornicate so much. There's only room for one joystick in the cockpit. Anyway, you've had more than your fair share of rumpty-tumpty. A decent chap would spread his good luck among his pals."

"Listen!" Maddegan said. Somewhere a locomotive hooted. "Choo-choo," he said.

"Goodness, Dingbat," Crabtree said. "What a fierce intellectual pace you set, to be sure."

* * *

The gunnery instructors soon changed Hornet Squadron's thinking about beam attacks. The whole business turned out to be very complex.

Everyone understood the need to lay off for speed: it was like shooting pheasant, you had to aim ahead of the bird. (And at two hundred yards' range, an Albatros was a target no bigger than a game bird.) With the Biff, the rear gunner had to lay off for three separate speeds, perhaps four. If his machine was flying at one hundred miles an hour and he fired at right-angles to its course, then its speed would tug the bullets forward of the target. If the target approached at right-angles, it would be drifting sideways in relation to the fighter; so allowance had to be made for that too. Then there was the wind, which – if strong enough – would nudge the stream of bullets one way or the other. Not forgetting bullet-drop. Bullets were heavy and they fell away. At long range it paid to aim high. Unless, of course, the enemy was already diving, in which case it might be better to aim low, all things being equal, which they never were.

One thing the instructors were adamant about: the need for the pilot to fly absolutely straight and level during combat. The gunner couldn't shoot straight if the machine was bucking and skidding all over the sky. "You do your job," the instructors told the pilots, "and the gunner can do his. That's your best chance."

The formula certainly worked on the balloons. They got blasted so fast that Cleve-Cutler abandoned them and sent up pairs of Pups to carry out mock attacks instead. The Biffs changed formation slickly, and their gunners had a clear view of oncoming targets that seemed generous after the hobbling balloons. Two of their Lewis guns had been replaced by cine-cameras. The films showed that the Pups would have been caught in a lethal crossfire. "We doomed you," Maddegan said, as casually as if it had been a cricket match. Next time, Cleve-Cutler doubled the number of Pups. The padre set up a cinema screen in the anteroom and the whole squadron watched the results. "We double doomed you," Maddegan said. "No hard feelings."

* * *

March had ended by the time Lieutenant Paxton and Captain Woolley arrived at Gazeran. Apart from the C.O., the doctor and the padre, only Plug Gerrish and Spud Ogilvy remembered Paxton. He was mildly surprised to find them still alive. They looked a lot older, but then he knew that he himself looked older: probably the moustache did that. Gerrish had always been a gloomy specimen but now Ogilvy seemed worried too. His head had developed a funny little jerk, like a chicken. Not always, but often enough to make Paxton wonder if Dando was giving Spud some of his magic sleeping pills. The squadron would need a new flight commander if Ogilvy got rested. Paxton felt ready for promotion. What fun it would be to have a flight commander's streamers flying from one's rudder . . .

Meanwhile, the squadron was occupied with its Biffs.

"Make yourselves useful," Gerrish told Paxton and Woolley. "The mess piano needs tuning. Forget the Biffs, they're all fully booked."

"You might get a flip in a Pup," Ogilvy said. "We do local patrols. Discourages the Boche."

"Frankly, I don't know why they sent you," Gerrish said.

"We'll go back, if you like," Woolley said. "The band at the Grosvenor Hotel wants me."

"He plays the saxophone," Paxton explained.

"No gentleman plays the saxophone," Ogilvy said woodenly.

"This piano-tuning," Woolley said. "I shall need a claw hammer and a crate of Guinness."

"A word of warning," Ogilvy said. "The major has no sense of humour."

"Oh, I don't know," Paxton said. "He made Woolley the station rat-catcher."

"Then my advice is to start catching rats."

The war had come as a pleasant surprise to the rats of the Western Front. The lice enjoyed it too. Millions of men arrived and brought food, warmth and shelter: all that the typical rat or louse asks. At the very front of the Front, conditions were more primitive but no less attractive. The first-line trenches were, of necessity, also latrines. Meals were a perpetual picnic. What the army called "ablutions" were scarce or non-existent. On the whole, the lice came off worse than the rats. Billions grew fat on soldiers at the Front, but the same billions were soon slaughtered in de-lousing stations at the rear. True, some rats got blown to bits by artillery, just as some men did, but the survivors had the benefit of a landscape littered with remains. Behind the Lines there were rich pickings, too.

Maconochie tinned stew was more than many British troops could stomach; the rats made sure none was wasted. But Maconochie was dull stuff compared with the diet at R.F.C. camps. Fliers ate well. Occasionally some of them threw up their half-digested meal in the hour before take-off, but that was no criticism of the cooking. At Gazeran airfield the food was good and plentiful, so the rats were sleek and plentiful.

* * *

Low cloud had put an end to flying for the day. Dufee, the new boy, had trodden on the last ping-pong ball and was in disgrace. The mess had run out of gramophone needles. Nobody wanted to play poker. When Woolley came in and asked if anyone felt like joining a rat hunt, half the squadron followed him. "You'll need your Service revolver and a club," he said. "Wear your flying boots."

They assembled at the cookhouse. Woolley had borrowed six dogs from nearby farms. He spread men and dogs until they ringed the area. He loaded a Very pistol, reached under the building, tucked the nozzle into the biggest rat hole he could see and fired a red signal flare into the colony. After a while, dirty red smoke leaked back. Nothing else happened.

"Cock-up," Snow said. "They don't know the Colours of the Day. Try yellow."

Woolley reloaded and fired a yellow. At once the dogs were yelping and chasing, pilots were lashing out with clubs, rats were racing and squealing, and a tattered volley of gunfire rattled the windows.

Woolley went around with a sack. "Ten," he said. "One's fat enough to be a major-general. Onwards."

The shots awoke Cleve-Cutler. For a long moment he felt kidnapped and abandoned and lost. He was in his office, but the dream that had gripped him was far more real than the dark walls. He had been at school, and failing miserably to find the room where he must sit an examination and knowing all the time that he was in the wrong building, perhaps in the wrong school, and he hadn't done nearly enough work, and then he was being plonked down in the wrong chair and discovering that this was the wrong examination, and desperately seeking help only to find he was alone at fifteen thousand feet, which was utterly the wrong height and there was no way down and the joystick came away in his hands, which meant death. Terror woke him. He was sitting at his desk and his head was resting on the blotter. When he straightened up a piece of paper was stuck to his forehead. It was the draft of his letter to Lieutenant Stamp's next-of-kin. The badge of failure.

He went in search of the padre and found him sorting out cricket equipment in a hut he used as a chapel.

"Bloody next-of-kin," Cleve-Cutler said. "Bigger pest than the Boche."

"Yes? An original viewpoint."

"I've got the answer, padre. Shoot the blighters! Shoot 'em all."

"Well, yes, I can see that shooting might be a solution of sorts. It rather depends on the problem."

"Here's your problem." Cleve-Cutler showed him the letter. It was sweat-stained and grubby. "Hate writing these things. Loathe and detest 'em. All lies, anyway."

"Funny things, lies." The padre held a cricket ball up to the light. "There's not a word against lying in the Ten Commandments. Lots of jolly stuff putting the kybosh on adultery and on coveting and on bowing down to graven images, but nothing against telling fibs." He tossed the ball from hand to hand, making it spin. "Do we really want total honesty? I've never known one of these things to be perfectly round. And I've yet to meet the bowler who'd want it."

"Shoot the bastards," Cleve-Cutler growled. He was wandering around the room, hands in pockets, kicking the wall. "Why should I apologize? *Dear sir, I regret to inform* . . . They knew the odds, didn't they? Bloody next-of-kin. Make me sick."

"Paul says something interesting in Philippians four, eight," the padre began, but Cleve-Cutler snatched the ball in mid-air and grabbed a bat and strode to the door and smashed the ball hard and high. It soared and vanished. "Look here, I say, old chap," the padre complained. "I took five for thirty-three with that ball last season."

"Well, I've just hit it for six. Gone for good. See? That's what I'm clever at. Sending chaps up there where they never come back. I'm bloody brilliant at losing chaps. Ask Bliss, he keeps score."

"Five for thirty-three." The padre peered out, but the cloud was even lower, the light even poorer. "My best before that was four for forty . . . Was that absolutely necessary, sir?" he said reproachfully.

"Essential, padre. Waste is my forte. I've wasted two perfectly good squadrons already. I'm good at waste." Another distant spattering of gunshots made him frown. "What's going on out there?"

"I heard nothing," the padre said briskly. He was willing to do his pastoral duty, but he refused to be a punchbag for angry self-pity.

"I heard shots," Cleve-Cutler said.

"Shots, eh? Always possible in wartime, I suppose."

Cleve-Cutler gripped the cricket bat so hard that his knuckles clicked. He was alone with the padre, nobody had seen him come in, he could say he found the fellow with his head smashed . . . Why not? Why should this man live when all the others were being killed? His fingers ached and he had to relax them.

"Ever been up in a 'plane, padre?"

"No, never."

"Soon put that right. Every man on my squadron should get a taste, otherwise how can he understand what we do? I'll take you up in a two-seater. That'll test your innards. Nearer my God to Thee, eh? Eh?"

He left, feeling triumphant, but in less than a minute he remembered the failed letter to Stamp's parents, and his triumph turned sour. Worse: his heart began to pound like a drunken drummer. He walked very slowly to the adjutant's office.

Brazier shut the door and got out the whisky. The C.O. shook his head. "Well, I need a mouthful," Brazier said. "You look as if you've been kicked in the crotch by a bull elephant. Is this a gift? Thank you kindly." He took the cricket bat and put it in a corner. Cleve-Cutler sat in a chair. His shoulders were hunched and his hands made fists. "I speak from experience," Brazier said. "I saw a bull elephant kick a man exactly as described." He took a sip of whisky. "In India, of course. Only a private soldier. That was before it happened. Afterwards, still a soldier but not so much of the private part." All the time, the adjutant was keeping a covert watch on the C.O. Whatever this crisis was, he was confident he could handle it provided the man didn't cry. Brazier couldn't stand tears. It disgusted him that men should weep just when a difficult situation demanded their full attention. You didn't see a lion or a buffalo break down and cry when the odds were against it. Certainly not. "I was on the elephant's side," he said. "No, I tell a lie. I was on the elephant's back."

"I just almost killed the padre," Cleve-Cutler said. "With that thing."

"Yes?" At least this was better than tears. "Well, I would have used a trench-knife, personally." He glanced at the bat. No bloodstains, no bits of skin. "Did he annoy you?"

The lower half of the C.O.'s face still had its jaunty grin, but his eyelids had slumped so heavily that he seemed about to fall asleep. "Look, Uncle," he said. "What if this bloody silly battle doesn't work? I mean to say . . ." But he had nothing more to say.

"Well, we try again, of course."

"Yes, but we did that already . . ." He was stopped by the dull banging of revolver fire. "What the deuce is going on out there?"

"Lacey!" the adjutant roared. The sergeant opened the door. "Be so good," Brazier said softly, "as to send someone to investigate that shooting. I'm infinitely obliged to you." Lacey closed the door.

"What if it doesn't work, Uncle?" Cleve-Cutler was fumbling with his smudged and grubby letter. "I can't write another twenty letters like this. I can't even write *this* one. They'll all go west, Uncle. I know, because I've taken two squadrons through two battles and where are they now? Gone west. It's easy for them. They just sod off and die. But who gets left with all the bloody silly letters to write?"

Brazier suddenly snapped his fingers. "Damnation! Why didn't I remember? My sergeant's been writing something . . ." He hurried out. The C.O. sat and, occasionally, blinked. Brazier came back with Lacey. "It's poetry," he warned.

Cleve-Cutler felt his heartbeat lurch, and then settle down to a steady thud. He drank a little of the adjutant's whisky. "Alright," he said. "Do your worst."

"For the next-of-kin, sir." Lacey handed him a sheet of paper. On it was typed:

Now God be thanked
From this day to the ending of the world!
Blow, bugle, blow! Was there a man dismayed?
Who rushed to glory, or the grave?
Land of our birth, we pledge to thee:
Dulce et decorum est pro patria mori!

The C.O. read it twice. "What d'you think, Uncle?"

"It's honest, sir. Doesn't dodge the sad event. But it's plucky, too. Not some damn dirge. Quite chipper, in fact."

"This last line," Cleve-Cutler said to Lacey. "It's in Latin."

"It is sweet and fitting to die for one's country. A widely held opinion, sir."

The C.O. grunted, and stared at the paper. "This bit in the middle . . . You can't tell me *dismayed* rhymes with *grave*." Another broken volley of gunshot made him clench his teeth. "Speak up."

"What about 'parade'?" Brazier suggested. 'Was there a man dismayed? Who rushed to glory, or the parade!' Eh?"

The C.O. wrinkled his nose. "Reminds me of Cheltenham. Clarence Parade, Cheltenham. Aunt of mine lived there. Terrible old trout. Last thing I'd want to do is rush to *that* parade."

"Suppose you made it 'Who rushed to glory or the *last* parade' . . ." Lacey said.

They tested it silently, their eyes half-shut. "That's damn clever," the C.O. said. "'*Last parade*' could mean . . ."

"Exactly," the adjutant said. "Gone, but still here. *Damn* clever. Well done, sir."

Cleve-Cutler was suddenly alert and alive again. "Can I use it on what's-his-name's parents, d'you think?"

"Certainly," Brazier said. "Use it on everyone."

"Patent elastic design," Lacey said. "One size fits all."

There was a knock on the door. A corporal came in. "That noise, sir," he said. "It's Captain Woolley, huntin' rats with a Very pistol."

Cleve-Cutler felt his heart begin another sprint. "Maniac!" he said.

The rat-warrens had been cleared under the cookhouse, and under the stores and under the billets. Now the hunt moved on, to the doctor's quarters.

The afternoon was fading fast. Woolley used a flashlight to find the biggest rat hole. "Stand by!" he called. He reached in, fired a signal flare into the hole and hurried around the hut. A ring of men and dogs waited. He was just in time to see a streak of burning yellow burst out of the ground. It ricocheted off someone's leg and raced into the dusk, a line of fizzing light, head-high. Shouts of astonishment, dogs yapping, the thud of clubs, and something else: the intermittent drone of an aeroplane engine.

Halfway across the camp, the C.O. heard it too, and stopped. "What's that?" he said. The adjutant listened, and heard only the rattle of the wind. "Not a Pup," the C.O. said. A truck clattered across the field and spoiled everything. "Lost, probably. Like the fool in a Camel who landed here the other day." They walked on and got a fine view of the runaway flare making its long horizontal streak. There was a bang of shattered glass. They began to run.

They found McWatters first.

"Christ on crutches!" Cleve-Cutler barked. "What the hell's going on?"

"We've got three sackfuls, sir. Dingbat shot a dog, and Dufee's not very well, but otherwise—"

"Get Woolley." But Woolley was already approaching. "You crass clod," Cleve-Cutler told him. "You feeble fart. You've turned my squadron into a fairground!"

"Sir, you ordered—"

"I didn't order this hooliganism." Woolley cocked his head and looked at the sky. The pilots stood in a guilty circle, except for Dufee, who was held up by two men. "What's wrong with him?" the C.O. demanded.

"That last flare knocked him down, sir," Woolley said.

"You shot one of my pilots." Cleve-Cutler's voice was harsh with rage. "Is this your idea of war, captain? Big-game hunting?" He booted a sack and it spilled dead rats. "Small-game hunting?"

"That machine may be trying to land, sir," Woolley said. "As duty officer I should—"

"As duty officer you're not fit to clean latrines! Go, before you kill someone!"

Gazeran airfield had an ambulance. The crew saw Woolley jogging towards them and they started the engine. He jumped onto the running-board and they drove along the edge of the airfield until he told them to stop. The motor died.

No sound except faraway birdsong in the holes in the wind.

The cloud was lower, or maybe it just seemed lower in the gloom of dusk. The wind made fools of everyone: it blustered and then fell silent and then rattled in their ears. Woolley walked over to the nearest gun-pit.

"He's been wandering around up there for ten minutes, sir," the sergeant said. "Wetting his breeches, I 'spect."

They listened. A soft growl came and went with the wind. "Ration wagons," the sergeant said. "Goin' up to the Lines."

The growl hardened to a flat drone. "Not wagons," Woolley said. The wind blustered. He turned and searched the sky downwind, the approach for a machine trying to land. Nothing in sight, only the specks of whirling crows. The sergeant shouted and pointed. Woolley saw the head-on outline of a biplane, its wings razor-thin. It was too low and too fast and it was coming in cross-wind. The ambulance engine started. The rescue truck arrived. Woolley blinked, lost sight of the machine and listened hard for a crash.

Then he saw the thing vault the hedge and skitter as a gust caught it, straighten out and turn towards the flights. The silhouette said Albatros exactly as its guns made their mechanical rattle. Six Pups stood in a row.

Incendiary bullets swept along them in a gracious gesture, and in quick order they began to burn. The gun-pits were hard at work, and the air was dense with their hammering and cordite. But their bullets went too high because the enemy was too low, down where the guns dared not fire. And then the Albatros slipped between two hangars and was gone. The second Pup from the right exploded. All the others were burning briskly.

Six Pups in ten seconds, Woolley thought. That'll cost him a packet. Drinks all round in the mess tonight.

He found the C.O. and the adjutant watching a bucket-chain try to put out the fires.

"Didn't you see that Hun approach?" Cleve-Cutler asked quietly.

"Yes, sir. It was too dark to identify until—"

"Too dark? *He* identified *us* without any trouble. No doubt your firework display helped him. No doubt he saw signal flares blazing and thought that's a juicy target. Eh?"

The charred Pups hissed and steamed.

"I was wrong about you, Woolley. You're not fit to be a ratcatcher. You're fit for one thing: court martial. The adjutant will prepare the papers." He walked away.

"I was court-martialled once," Brazier said to Woolley, quietly. "It's nothing to get upset about."

"My uncle Sid got hung for murder," Woolley said. "Told me he never felt a thing."

Something went bang, and blazing splinters flew. They moved to a safer spot.

"How on earth did you get a commission?" the adjutant asked, curiously.

"It's not mine. I'm looking after it for a friend."

"That's a bloody stupid answer."

"Well, it was a bloody stupid question," Woolley said. Brazier snorted. "And if you want to fight over it," Woolley said, "it's Very pistols at ten yards. I'm lethal. Ask Dufee."

*　*　*

Lieutenant James McWatters could write his name and that was about all. He wasn't ashamed of his failing; plenty of boys he had known at school either couldn't or didn't write. They came from the upper middle class of Edwardian England and they assumed that somebody would always be there to write for them, just as somebody would always be there to clean the boots and lug buckets of coal up the stairs. You didn't have to be stupid to be semi-literate. All it took was perseverance.

His father was a minor Anglican bishop and his mother was the heiress to a shipbuilding fortune. She had become very active in the women's suffrage movement, which scuppered any chance of advancement for the bishop. A man who couldn't control his wife didn't deserve a bigger diocese. At the age of six, James got packed off to prep school. He knew his father spent all day writing. He was damn sure he wasn't going to be like his father. "Bugger writing," he told the master who gave him a slate. He had learned the word from stable lads, and enjoyed its impact. He threw the slate through a window.

The master had just come down from Oxford. He did not have the same steel as young McWatters. They made a silent truce: no writing, no slate-chucking. James had cracked the code. If you were bloody-minded enough, you never had to do what they wanted you to do.

He changed schools quite often. He liked reading. Sometimes the headmaster was more interested in fees than in academic performance, and James did nothing but read and talk. And play footer or cricket. If something must be written, he paid another boy to write it.

It worked until he was sixteen. Then he came to suspect that the rest of the school was treating him as a joke. He was the tallest boy in the school and he couldn't write: what a hoot! He got nicknamed Invisible Ink. He went to his housemaster and announced that he was leaving. "Good idea," the man said. "I'll give you a lift to the station on my motorbike."

Next day, his father asked him to come into the study. "I've been wondering," he said. "What plans have you made for the rest of your life?"

The question caught James off-guard. "Motorcycling," he said. It was all he could think of.

"Ah. Forgive my ignorance – how is that likely to increase the sum of human happiness?"

"Well, sir, last year a chap rode from Land's End to John O'Groats in less than two days."

"And was there an ethical element to this journey?"

"Um . . . He didn't cheat, if that's what you mean. He used the pedals on the steep hills, but that's allowed."

He bought a motorcycle, found a mechanic, and made a small reputation in local races, scrambles, sprints. Got bored. Bought a car, raced that, got bored. Took flying lessons, got his Royal Aero Club certificate, and might have become bored with flying if Europe had not stumbled into war.

In the autumn of 1916 he was transferred to Hornet Squadron. When he arrived, the doctor examined him for venereal disease. "The old man's very hot on this," Dando explained. "He'd had to sack two pilots. You're clean. Put your bags on."

McWatters dressed slowly. "Girls, and so on. They're the very devil, aren't they?"

"Here's my professional advice. If you can get a girl, she's probably got the pox. If you can't get her, she probably hasn't. That's Dando's First Law of Motion."

"Thanks. I'll stick to poker."

Dando recognized that tone of voice, brave yet brittle. It meant McWatters was a virgin and resented the fact. Dando had heard it before, often. Most pilots had left one all-male environment – school, sometimes university – for another: an R.F.C. camp, where women were never seen and seldom spoken of, never in the mess.

This made Charles Dash's erotic adventures at the nunnery of Sainte Croix all the more fascinating. Some officers refused to believe him. "He's got a neck like celery," Snow said. "He's got more freckles than my kid sister. He thinks his dick is there to stir his tea with. That's what they teach you at your famous public schools, isn't it?"

"If he made it all up," McWatters said, "why isn't he boasting about it?"

"Because he knows it's bullshit," Maddegan said. "That's a very, very old Australian word. You can borrow it provided you promise not to get it dirty."

"Something definitely happened," McWatters said. "I mean, he went to see Dando. Something must have happened."

Charles Dash came back to his billet from the officers' bathhouse and found McWatters lying on Dash's bed, reading Dash's mail. "Perhaps you should move in here," he said, "and I'll live in your hut and read *your* letters."

"The doctor's wife died, pneumonia. And the daffodils look splendid. Otherwise, nothing special from home. However . . ." McWatters waved a letter. "Chlöe Legge-Barrington has come up trumps."

"Give it here, or I'll report you to my flight commander."

"She's found where Jane Brackenden and Laura da Silva are. It's nowhere near here. I have a car."

Dash's hatred was great, but his lust was greater. "No poaching," he said, "or I'll kill you."

After an hour of taking wrong turnings and backing up muddy lanes, they found a F.A.N.Y. unit in a field of ambulances. McWatters reluctantly stayed in the car while Dash went looking. Laura da Silva was in a tent, unpacking medical supplies. "Hullo," she said. "Come to help?"

They chatted for a while. Dash had a mouth full of words he couldn't find a way to use. Finally a thought blundered into his head. "Unusual name, da Silva. Are you Catholic, by any chance?"

"Yes."

Oh well, that's that, he thought. But he blundered on: "It's just that, when I was staying at the nunnery, someone left . . . um . . . left an earring in my . . . um . . . bed."

"Ah." She linked her hands behind her head and looked him in the face. Treacherously, it turned red. "Well," she said, "the priests would give me hell, so it wasn't me. And no-one in F.A.N.Y. wears earrings, so maybe it was something else she left in your bed."

"Maybe," Dash mumbled.

"Poor you," she said. "Men get no rest, do they?" She kissed him on the forehead. "That's all you get! Goodbye."

He went back to the car. McWatters wanted a detailed report. "Go to hell," Dash said. "I'm sick of this nonsense. I quit."

"Do you, indeed? Well, I don't."

The address given for Jane Brackenden was only twenty minutes away. It turned out to be a primary school, requisitioned by the Medical Corps. In the playground a few walking wounded played walking football. "Be frank," McWatters urged. "Be blunt. Women like that sort of thing." But Dash had already slammed the car door.

He met her coming down a corridor. "Charles! Good heavens . . . I was just thinking of you." Optimism soared like a skylark. She was stunningly beautiful: red hair, delicate features, healthy chest. "Not half as much as I have," he said. "You were awfully keen on women's suffrage, weren't you?"

"Still am."

"Equality now, that's what you said . . ." The corridor was suddenly busy. She saw the strain in his eyes and took him into a classroom where empty stretchers were stacked head-high. "The thing is," he said, "somebody at the nunnery really believed in equality between the sexes." Already his ears were hot. "And that somebody practised it in my bed." Her eyes widened and he heard her gasp. Fuck fuck fuck, he thought. Wrong again.

"It's a lovely idea," she said, "but I'm afraid I'm not nearly brave enough to . . . Dear oh dear. And you've come all this way."

"It was dark, you see. Pitch black." Dash felt that he had been saying this to everyone he knew.

"Such a shame. I wish we could go somewhere and talk, but I'm in charge here. Can't leave, not for hours."

McWatters was not discouraged by his failure. "Now it's better odds," he said. "Only three to one."

*   *   *

The six Pups destroyed by the strafing Albatros were quickly replaced: another squadron was getting Camels and its C.O. cheerfully donated his

204

ageing Pups to Cleve-Cutler. Pilots were not so easily found. Dufee's leg had been broken by the signal flare. One man was in Amiens having a wisdom tooth pulled. Another had double vision, the result of smacking his head on the gun butt in a heavy landing. Two had 'flu.

Training must go on, and more intensively. The C.O. made himself leader of the Pups that were making mock attacks on the Biffs and he ordered Paxton and Woolley to fly with him.

First, he briefed them. They came to his office and stood, while he sat at his desk and worried.

"I know you of old," he told Paxton. "Not a bad pilot, although God knows what cock-eyed ballyhoo you've picked up in England. As for you," he told Woolley, "I could be unpleasant, but I won't. You're a fart, and I hope to see the back of you soon. Meanwhile, remember this, both of you. The air war has changed while you've been away. It's not man-to-man any more. It's formation against formation. We fly and fight as a formation. That's what this training is all about. Clear?"

"Admirably so, sir," Paxton said.

"Don't talk like a butler. I don't want your damned admiration. I want your obedience."

Six Biffs and six Pups flew to Braye. Whenever the weather allowed, they practised interceptions. Cleve-Cutler made these as difficult as possible. Some threats were real and the Pups pressed home their attacks, charging at the fighters until they were the focus of all six imaginary bullet-streams. Other threats were fake, meant to tug and twist the formation until it was ragged and slow to respond.

Cleve-Cutler failed to fool them. His flight commanders were experienced air-fighters. They could read the sky at a glance; what's more they could read the C.O.'s mind. Their crews were as welldrilled as Guardsmen. Whenever the Pups made a charge, the Biffs turned as if tied together and crossed their path. If the gunners had actually fired, the Pups would have flown into a cone of bullets and been hacked down. Repeatedly, the cine-films proved this.

* * *

The adjutant handed Count Andrei the leather-bound Bible. "Jolly kind of you," he said. "Your people in Paris are a bit jumpy, so I'm told."

"Terrified of being ordered home to Petersburg, I expect. Who's in charge there now?" Brazier gave him a piece of paper. Andrei read it. "Crumbs," he said. "Whatever that means."

He found the duke in the officers' bathhouse, sitting on a reversed chair, being shaved by Private Bugler. Snow was soaking in a hot tub. Maddegan sat on the edge, playing with the soap, making it squirt between his fingers. He saw the Bible and groaned.

"Is big change in Petersburg," Andrei announced. "Is time to swear new oath."

"I don't swear," Nikolai said quietly.

"He'll hit you," Maddegan said.

"I don't swear."

Bugler was slow taking his hands away. The Bible clouted Nikolai's head and rocked it like a balloon on a stick, and the razor nicked his ear. Flecks of lather drifted and fell. Bugler retreated and hid the razor behind his back. Blood created small red rosettes on the floor.

Andrei hooked a foot around a leg of the chair and tipped Nikolai out. He trod on his stomach. He shoved the Bible into his hands. "You swear allegiance to Prince Lvov, leader of the Duma."

"I swear," Nikolai wheezed. He dropped the Bible and got up and scrambled to the door. "Prince Lvov is lousy greedy no-brain piece of pox!" Blood ran off his chin. "Tsar will chop head off!" He left.

"Bugler!" Snow roared. "Find the doctor." Bugler hurried away, grumbling hard.

"Look, I'm all for loyalty," Maddegan said, "but must you keep walloping him? That's the third time."

"Fourth," Snow said.

"The Romanovs are finished," Andrei said. "Now he is the servant. Now I give orders."

"Seems kind of pointless," Snow said. "He says no, you thump him, and he says yes. Still, I'm just a crude Canadian, what the hell do I know of your quaint old aristocratic ways."

*   *   *

Nothing memorable happened to Adam Gillespie Keith Heeley for seventeen years. Then he spent the summer holidays with his aunt, in Sidmouth. She was only twenty-six and looked twenty-two. On the other hand, he was only seventeen and looked fifteen. She liked dancing with him, teaching him the waltz, and looking into his cool grey eyes. She knew enough about the rest of him. In his bathing costume he made a good shape, and when he came out of the sea, with the costume clinging pointedly, she felt tremors of a lust that made it hard for her to speak. One dull afternoon she seduced him in her bedroom.

What surprised the boy most about his first sexual experience was the violence of it. He had not thought passion could be quite so passionate. When he got his breath back he said, "Crikey." That made her laugh. He said, "Why me?" He was bewildered by the fact that a grown-up should choose to do such a grown-up thing with him. "I suppose," she said, "I've nothing to be afraid of, with you." It was a spontaneous, honest answer, but not very flattering.

It explained Adam Heeley to himself. It explained the long-suffering glances that scores of schoolmasters had given him, and the brutal way that hundreds of schoolboys had ignored him. He was nothing special. The sober truth of that summer in Sidmouth was that his aunt craved his body but otherwise he bored her, as he bored most people. He went to an eminent school, wore its uniform, spoke the language of the English upper class, not because he was different but because his parents were rich. He had assumed he was special. Now he felt tricked. A long failure beckoned.

When the war came along, he didn't take much interest in it. He was only eighteen. War was a job for professional soldiers and hearty patriots, people who liked doing that sort of thing. Late in 1915 he was flicking

207

through the latest *Illustrated London News* when he saw the face of a boy called Taverner, now a lieutenant in the uniform of the King's Rifles, with a Military Cross, and dead.

In a spell when he had been very lonely at school, Heeley had hero-worshipped Taverner from afar. They had never spoken, but Taverner had grinned at him, once. Oh well, Heeley thought, if Taverner's gone I might as well go too. The whole page was taken up with awards, most of them posthumous. He shut his eyes and stabbed with a finger. Royal Flying Corps.

Everyone is good at something. The trick is finding it. When Heeley went up in an aeroplane, and looked down on people like insects in a world like Toytown, he felt special. This was why God had put him on Earth: to fly above it.

He did six months as an observer, spotting for guns and photographing enemy trenches; crashed twice, nothing serious; re-trained as a pilot; joined Hornet Squadron and had never been so happy as when he was flying a Pup. After three months of D.O.P.s, he was still alive. It came as a surprise. His confidence grew. Three months ago, he wouldn't have dared to go up to Captain Woolley and say there was a rumour that he knew how to get out of a bad spin; and if so, would he reveal the secret?

Woolley was outside his hut, sitting on a log. He thought for a long time before he said, "D'you like this war?"

"I like my bit of it. Damn good fun."

"Well, that's got to stop, hasn't it?" Woolley's voice was hard and square, not contorted to the drawl of the Home Counties. "If it's fun, it'll go on for ever. That's human nature. Right?"

"Look . . . if you don't want to tell me . . ."

"Got twenty-five francs? I'll tell you, for twenty-five."

Heeley was amazed. "That's very . . . mercenary."

"Your life's not worth twenty-five francs? Well, you know best."

Heeley gave him the money.

"Stop fooling around with the rudder. You can't *turn* out of a bad spin. Centre the rudder. Forget about using the ailerons. Centre the *stick*. You can't control the machine unless it's going forward, so make it go forward. Switch off the engine. Centre everything and push the stick hard forward. The elevators will start to bite. The tail goes up, the nose goes down. Now you're diving, you've got wind over the wings and past the rudder, and you can correct what's left of the spin."

"Thank you," Heeley said.

"And if it doesn't work, don't come running to me."

Heeley went away, feeling as if he had been hustled into buying a pair of rabbits from a poacher, except that he had nothing to show for his money. Was it possible that Woolley had sold him a lot of nonsense? He stopped and tried to remember exactly what the fellow had said, and he was gazing at a cloud when the great bombardment began.

It beat the air like a punishment. Heeley's documents said he was Church of England, but if he got caught in a storm, and the sky was split by thunder, all the hairs on his neck bristled like a dog's and briefly he knew no god but fear. Now a hundred thunderstorms roared in the east. Heeley knew the guns were ten miles away, probably more, but still his neck bristled.

Dando and Duke Nikolai came out of the doctor's hut. Silk thread trailed from the Russian's ear. "Bloody neighbours," Dando said. "Can't a man get a wink of sleep?"

"Battle begins now," Nikolai said.

"Not yet," Heeley said. "This is just spring cleaning. The P.B.I. are chucking out their old pots and pans." He noticed the ear. "What happened to you?"

"I stitched him up," Dando said.

"Why?" Heeley met the doctor's glittering glance. "Never mind," he muttered.

The thunder brought everyone out. Experienced men compared it with other occasions. Spud Ogilvy remembered the bombardment before the Somme as having been louder. Crabtree offered to run a sweepstake concerning the duration of the barrage. "On the Somme, the gunners kept it up for ten days," he said.

Paxton sniffed. "Didn't do much good, did it?"

The adjutant cleared his throat so forcefully that he silenced them all. "Valuable lessons were learned at the Somme," he announced.

As if to endorse his view, the barrage intensified. He cocked his head and enjoyed it. The day was strangely flat and airless, under a drab, blank sky; a forgettable day, only fit for demolition. Brazier said, "The Hun Front Line won't survive this shelling. I have friends in the infantry, and they tell me we have a little trick up our sleeves." He tapped the side of his nose. "Try as he might, the Hun won't shell our troops in Arras. He'll do his worst, but his guns won't harm a single British soldier." He rocked on his heels and looked longingly to the noisy east.

"The Boche machine guns will get them all?" Crabtree suggested.

Brazier took his arm. "A word in your ear," he said. They strolled away.

"We can shell *them*," Paxton said to Woolley, "but they can't shell *us*. Is that what Uncle said?"

"It's not Christian," McWatters said. "I wouldn't have joined up if I'd known there was cheating involved. What's going on, padre?"

"Not for me to say, old chap. Just a simple cleric, me. I leave the tricky stuff to the bishops."

"My dad was a bishop," Woolley remarked. "Very hard on the knees, he said."

"Well, prayer often involves self-denial."

"That wasn't prayer. That was rescuing fallen women in Huddersfield. When you're a bishop in Huddersfield, you can't turn a corner without tripping over a fallen woman."

"How distressing. Would anyone like to play ping-pong?"

"Weak ankles," Woolley said. "That's what causes their downfall."

Out of earshot of the group, the adjutant said gruffly, "I've nothing against an honest joke, but there's no place in war for cynicism. For God's sake, man, think what effect your remarks have on others."

"My dear chap." Crabtree plucked a grey hair from the adjutant's lapel. "I had no idea I caused you such distress. You should have spoken sooner."

"I did, damn it."

"The damage is done now, of course." He found another hair. "You must be brave, Uncle. Can you last out? It's only for a few more days." He patted Brazier on the arm and walked away. "Be not dismayed!" he called back.

"Lunatic," Brazier said.

Crabtree waved a friendly arm. "My pleasure."

EARTHQUAKE STRENGTH 7:

Difficult to stand. Furniture broken.

The Biff crews had a keener appetite for training now that the opening of the bombardment meant the Big Push was near. Cleve-Cutler felt the strain of waiting for action fall away. He had exhausted his capacity for anxiety and mistrust. Optimism flooded in. It was time for another mess-night party, time for a bathtub of Hornet's Sting.

Heeley knocked back a glass of the mixture. It rushed down his throat like friendly lava. "Christ!" he said. His voice was strangely husky and virile; he sounded ten years older. The drink hit his stomach and the happy uproar of the party faded and twisted in his ears, and then surged back. "God speed the plough!" he said, just to enjoy his new voice.

"Plough be damned. Send for the fire brigade." The other voice, strong and plummy, came from behind him. "What the deuce is in this drink? Apart from gunpowder and Brasso, that is."

Heeley turned and saw a tall man with a big face and a chest fit for an opera singer. He was over thirty, balding, and he wore the uniform of the Blues. Heeley squared his shoulders and tried to look intelligent in the presence of a staff officer. "The formula's a military secret, sir," he said. The man blinked, and twitched his nose. Heeley looked again, and saw he was only a lieutenant. Wearing wings. For the love of Mike, he thought. We're not that hard up, are we? "Sorry," he said. "This stuff turns you blind. Heeley."

"Savage." They shook hands. "Just arrived. Are we celebrating something?"

"Well, there's going to be a battle." Heeley had never met such an elderly new pilot. "You must be Dufee's replacement."

"Probably. What happened to Mr Dufee?"

Heeley thought, briefly. "Better you don't ask," he said. "Let's find the Old Man."

Cleve Cutler was impressed by Savage. Most replacements said *yes, sir* and *no, sir* and were happy to walk away. Savage enjoyed a chat. From time to time he hooked a thumb in his tunic pocket and surveyed the crowd of drinkers. He might have been in his club in Pall Mall. The C.O. asked him where he had come from.

"Westminster. I was one of the bright young men who made Lloyd George sound credible. Frightful hours. One scarcely slept."

The C.O. struggled to decipher this reply. "And before that?"

"Well, of course, I volunteered in '14 but the army turned up its nose when it found I had flat feet and couldn't ride a horse, so I made myself useful in the House, and eventually L.G. noticed me. I drafted his speeches, corrected his spelling, that sort of thing. Educated at an elementary school, did you know? Yes. Can't spell for toffee. Probably can't spell toffee, if truth be known."

"So you were an M.P."

"Still am. Left the government when Lloyd George tried to pin the blame for Gallipoli on poor old Kitchener." Savage shook his head. "Not cricket."

"But surely . . . Kitchener was War Minister at the time, wasn't he?"

"Yes. But he's dead. Went down with the *Hampshire* last year. L.G. blamed a man who couldn't answer back. Resignation same day. Your war may be a bit noisy, but it's not such a racket as politics."

"That's nice to know." The C.O. had to raise his voice, Hornet's Sting was having its usual effect. "I'll put you in 'A' Flight. Come and meet Captain Gerrish."

Heeley found himself next to McWatters. "For five francs," he said, "I'll tell you how to get out of a bad spin."

"Don't be absurd, lad. You couldn't get out of a revolving door."

"Captain Woolley told me how."

"Ah, that's different. I haven't got five francs, but I'll owe you ten. And

I'll make you a lieutenant in Nicky's Imperial Russian Air Force."

"He's already offered me a captaincy."

Andrei, drifting by, overheard this. "Only a captain? Simms is to be a colonel. Paxton won't consider anything below major-general. Woolley wants to be an admiral and fly seaplanes." He wandered on.

"Alright, how does this anti-spin idea work?" McWatters asked.

"Well, the important thing . . ." Heeley's brain was fuddled. "I'll try and remember."

Cleve-Cutler took Gerrish and the adjutant into a quiet corner and discussed the arrival of Lieutenant Savage, M.P. "He could be an asset to this squadron," Gerrish said. "He's been in Government. He knows which wires to pull."

"Exactly!" the C.O. said, "Why have we only got six Biffs? Why not twelve? Chaps like Savage can open doors."

"The squeaky wheel gets the grease." Brazier said. "By the way I can't make a case for court-martialling Captain Woolley, sir."

"What's wrong?"

"No real offence committed."

"Then invent one!" Cleve-Cutler said jovially. "Get the son of a bitch off my squadron. Buck up, Uncle. Put some grease on your squeak!" He stamped away.

The racket of the party subsided for a moment, and the rumble of the barrage filled the space. "This had better be a bloody good battle," Brazier said, "or that man is liable to take off all his clothes and dance in the moonlight."

As the squadron went in for dinner, McWatters gave Heeley five francs. "Dingbat owed it to me," he said. "Now we're all square."

"You promised me ten."

McWatters sniffed. "Gentlemen don't haggle, Heeley, especially in the mess. Do up your flies, old chap. This isn't *The Gay Hussars*." By the time Heeley had found that none of his buttons was undone, McWatters had vanished into the crowd.

Maddegan, as one of the newest pilots, sat next to Savage. During the soup, Maddegan advised him about the rituals of mess-night. "You throw the bread rolls with your left hand. See?" He demonstrated. "That was Munday I hit. Nice bloke. Now later, you throw the roast potatoes with your *right* hand. And when the skipper gives the toast, Hornet's Sting, you get both feet off the ground. Left *and* right."

"My goodness," Savage said. "Such a lot to learn."

"Tell you what. I'll write it down for you." He searched his pockets and found a piece of paper. It was covered with writing. He turned the paper one way and twisted his head the other, looking for the beginning. A bread roll bounced off his head. "Doomed you, Dingbat!" Munday shouted. Maddegan ignored him. "Bet you don't know how to get out of a spin," he said.

"My instructor recommended prayer," Savage said.

"See that chap? Face like a dead dingo? That's Woolley. He told Heeley." Maddegan waved the paper. "All down here! Yours for ten francs."

"Surely you jest."

"Cost me fifteen."

Cleve-Cutler banged the table. "Gentlemen! The squadron toast." Loud scraping and scuffling as they stood on their chairs. "Hornet's Sting!" they roared, and drank to the dregs. Getting down was harder. A few fell. Waiters hurried to refill the glasses. "Bloody good grog," Maddegan said. "What were we talking about?" His fingers were wet, and some of the ink had begun to run.

*   *   *

Next morning the day was bright, with high cloud and a frisky wind, sometimes soft, sometimes gusting. The barrage kept up its drum-roll in the east. Duke Nikolai refused to get out of bed. "Is big thunder," he told his servant. "Is bad storm."

"Is bad hangover," Andrei said. "Is little-boy-talk." Nikolai hid his head. Andrei got a fire bucket and emptied it over him. Nikolai whimpered. Andrei tipped him out of bed. Still he lay, wrapped in sodden blankets. "See this," Andrei said to the servant. "This is breeding. It breeds stupidity and vanity and greed." He ripped the blankets away and kicked the naked Nikolai until he stood up. Andrei put the upside-down bucket on Nikolai's head and prodded him through the door. "Bathhouse," he told the servant. "He shaves himself. If he cries, hit him."

Simms was strolling by. "Good Lord. What has he done to deserve this?"

"Better you don't ask," Andrei said.

The flight commanders had everyone kitted-out and ready by 9 o'clock. Six Biffs and six Pups would continue training. The spare Pups would patrol between Gazeran and the Lines. That left Simon Savage.

"Go up and fly round and round the field," Gerrish told him. "Don't go near the Lines. If you see a Hun, run away. Just practise the simple things. Get to know the landmarks. No stunts. If you get lost, find an aerodrome, *any* aerodrome. See me this afternoon."

When everyone else had gone, Savage climbed into the oldest Pup. Fifteen minutes later he was buzzing along on top of a dazzlingly white mattress of cloud in a clean and empty world topped with a dome of blue that nobody whose feet were in the mud could ever see or understand. This was sheer pleasure. Soon he lost a thousand feet and got to work with his map, identifying the woods and rivers and roads within a couple of miles of Gazeran. Far to the east, a thin fog of smoke hung over a flickering line of gun flashes. Savage turned away and felt the gusting westerly drag down the Pup's speed. The cloud was more broken now, and helped by the wind it went racing past the rocking wingtips.

Now the thrill of flight seized him and he laughed at the adventure of it all; he hadn't been so excited since he first sped downhill on a bicycle. The world was wonderful. Next moment the world was upside-down. From nowhere another machine had fallen on him. A bored Camel pilot, doing a routine air test, bounced this wandering Pup for fun and went on his way. Savage had looked up, glimpsed the Camel head-on, heard the shout of its engine, and slammed the stick one way and the rudder the other. The Pup tried to obey conflicting orders: half-rolled and skidded at the same time.

Bad luck sent an air pocket along. The propeller raced but the Pup fell. It hit the bottom of the pocket and Savage bit his tongue. The pain made him jerk the stick. The Pup stalled and fell, spinning like a child's top. Despite the whirl and the shock and the dizziness, Savage was still in control of himself He knew what to do. He did it and the Pup went on spinning, until it hit a field with a bang that stopped men talking a mile away.

*　*　*

"The impact killed him," the doctor said. "The fire was irrelevant."

"Fat bloody consolation that is," the C.O. said.

They were in his office, with the flight commanders. The hut had been hastily built in 1914 and it had suffered three years of baking summers and freezing winters. The putty had cracked and shrunk in its windows, and now the glass rattled like a child about to earn a thick ear.

"I told him not to do anything flashy," Gerrish said. "Just go round and round."

"Well, he did that," Crabtree said. "But not in the recommended manner."

Cleve-Cutler hunched over his desk and flicked a pencil so that it spun. He was still making it spin when the adjutant came in.

"I've been packing up Savage's things, sir," he said. "I found this letter, to his parents. He didn't have time to finish it, I suppose."

Cleve-Cutler read it. "Sodding buggering hell," he said. He told the flight commanders to leave. He sent for Woolley.

While he waited, he rolled the letter into a tight spill and scratched his head with it.

"Hard to believe," Brazier said.

"Fellow's a blackguard," Cleve-Cutler said After that there was silence.

Woolley arrived and saluted. Brazier gave him six out of ten for the salute.

Cleve-Cutler handed Woolley the letter. "From the late Lieutenant Savage to his parents. Read the lines I've marked. Aloud."

Woolley skimmed through the passage, and grunted in surprise. He said: *"This squadron is a jolly lot. They wouldn't do for the Blues, but the Flying Corps is very unstuffy. Lots of leg-pulling and practical-joking. The only thing taken seriously is the air war. There are expert pilots here whose brains I hope to pick. A chap called Woolley knows the secret of getting out of a spin and has very generously revealed it, for ten francs! I coughed up, and had it explained to me. Apparently the trick is to tip the aeroplane on its side so the rudder becomes the tailplane and . . ."*

The letter stopped there.

"I've known some selfish bastards in the Corps," Cleve-Cutler said, "but I've never met such a greedy piece of shit as you."

"This makes no sense," Woolley said.

"Oh, it's worse than that. It's trash. You sold a fellow pilot trashy advice, and it killed him."

"I never met Savage."

"Savage met you," Brazier said. "He says so."

"Heeley came to me. Not Savage – Heeley. He asked me how to get out of a spin and—"

"How much did you screw out of him?" the C.O. asked.

"Oh . . . twenty-five francs. It was a joke. He said I was mercenary, so I asked him what his life was worth. The twenty-five francs was a joke."

"What a comedian you are, Woolley. You shoot Dufee in the leg: most amusing. You let an Albatros wipe out five Pups: glorious fun. And now you coach a new boy on how to kill himself: utterly hilarious. You got good value for your twenty-five-franc joke, didn't you?"

Woolley looked into Cleve-Cutler's furious eyes, and knew that nothing he said would help him.

"You're confined to quarters," the C.O. said. "Don't talk to my pilots. Don't fly. Don't fire a weapon. Don't give orders. Just sit on your greedy, stupid, incompetent arse while I arrange for you to spend the rest of the war cleaning the filthiest latrines the assistant provost-marshal can find. Get out."

* * *

March had become April and spring became pleasant. Blossom foamed in the trees; cows emerged from winter quarters to graze the bright new grass. Sometimes pilots lounged in deck chairs facing the sun. There was talk of tennis, even of cricket.

The guns rumbled without pause, night and day, but now it was like living near a railway line: nobody noticed the noise any more. Troops were always on the move, flooding eastward. They could be heard singing or whistling on the march. The sound was irrelevant to the life of the squadron. Infantry were a different species. Once, when the music of a military band drifted across the aerodrome, Maddegan tried to hum the tune. "What regiment's that?" he asked.

"Worcesters," Ogilvy said. "Very saucy lot."

He was making an effort to sound bright and confident because he knew that his nervous uncertainty had become obvious. Jokes about a never-ending war had long since ceased being funny to him. Too many friends were dead. Ogilvy wasn't afraid to die, in fact he expected to die; but a good reason for dying would make life easier.

Woolley was confined to his quarters. He took his meals in the mess, but he sat separately and spoke to nobody. He went back to his hut and learned to play the accordion. Sergeant Laccy had got this for him in exchange for his saxophone, which Woolley said needed a complete re-bore and fresh plugs.

Late in the afternoon, Ogilvy went to have a bath and found Woolley already lying in the next tub. For a while they soaked in silence. Then Ogilvy said, "Wing H.Q. is very peeved at us for losing Savage. We had to send the coffin home." Ogilvy licked sweat from his upper lip. "More sandbags than Savage inside."

"There's no great mystery about getting out of a bad spin," Woolley said. "I'd be happy to tell you, now, but I'm not allowed to speak to anyone."

"Your trouble is you think you can stroll in here and tell us all our business."

Woolley ducked his head and came up gasping. "So I'm not even allowed to tell you what's wrong with your Biffs."

"Nothing's wrong. You haven't even flown one."

"I've done mock combats."

"Which the Biffs always win."

"That's true. It works alright in practice. But will it work in theory?" He sucked his teeth. "Just a hunch. I could be wrong."

"So far, your hunches have cost us one man killed, one maimed, and six Pups destroyed. Right now, I wouldn't trust you to count the spoons."

"Well, you'd be making a big mistake there." Woolley stretched, and the bathwater surged. "At my last squadron I got Mentioned in Despatches for spoon-counting. Under enemy fire, we were, but I never lost count. The colonel called out, 'How many spoons left, Woolley?' and quick as a flash—"

"Shut up," Ogilvy said. "Just . . . shut up."

* * *

Brazier strolled across to the anteroom for a long whisky-soda before dinner. He was warming his backside at a spot near the fireplace, and explaining the difference between a *Minenwerfer* and a whizzbang, when a servant approached him and said that the barrage had stopped.

Everyone went outside. For three days the guns had laboured around the clock. Now there was silence in the east. Night had fallen. Could the troops be attacking in pitch darkness? Recipe for disaster. Maybe we had run out of shells. Maybe the gunners had run out of targets. Maybe the Kaiser had surrendered.

"It's easily seen that none of you has been under a bombardment," the adjutant said. "What do you think the enemy is doing now?"

"Moving his bowels?" McWatters suggested. "He must be rather constipated after three days stuck in a funk-hole."

"Constipation is not the problem. To the contrary."

"Survival mechanism," Dando commented. "The lighter the burden, the faster the flight."

"Spill the beans, Uncle," Snow said.

"Extraordinary lingo . . . What is it: Cherokee? Never mind. What would you do, if you were Hindenburg? Mend your trenches, obviously. Get your dead and wounded out of your Lines. Rush up your reserves to plug the gaps. You can make good a lot of damage in one night."

"Jolly generous of us," Simms said.

"Everything they do tonight will be destroyed tomorrow," Brazier said. "A fresh lot of Huns arrive for our guns to kill. It grinds the enemy down, I assure you."

"No battle, then," Munday said.

"Not yet."

The novelty had worn off. They went inside, all but the C.O. and the adjutant. "We'll keep 'em guessing," Brazier said. "We'll blast 'em, and pause, and blast 'em again. Each time we stop, they'll think we're about to attack."

Cleve-Cutler heard a rare note of confidence. "You'd really like to be up there, wouldn't you, Uncle?"

"Storming a strongpoint is the greatest feeling a man can ever know. You fellows seize the air, but you can't keep it." Brazier grabbed a handful of air and opened his fist to reveal nothing. "Only the infantry can win a war."

"Let's eat," Cleve-Cutler said. Enough was enough.

After dinner, Spud Ogilvy took Crash Crabtree aside. "Uncle seems to think this show will be a walkover," he said.

"Oh Christ. Not another. I've been through three walkovers already. Each one nastier than the last." When Ogilvy made a sour face, Crabtree said, "Never mind. It doesn't matter."

"It matters to me. Listen . . . What d'you make of this joker Woolley?"

"Oh, I like him. He's even scruffier than me. He makes me look like the Prince of Wales. But can he fight? He may be repulsive, but is he offensive?"

"What a bloody awful choice to make." Ogilvy signalled to a mess servant. "Brandies," he said.

* * *

Next day, when the Biffs and the Pups came back from training, Charles Dash walked over to the orderly room. To foil McWatters, he had asked Lacey to hold his letters until he could collect them.

There was a letter for him, not from Chlöe Legge-Barrington but from Lucy Knight, the smallest of the F.A.N.Y. girls; the one with the curliest black hair; the one who had said, "Men are so slow."

> *Dearest Charles,*
>
> *Chlöe phoned me to get my new address, to give to you, so I thought why not drop you a line? While I have a minute to myself before the battle makes life impossible, as usual.*
>
> *I must say Chlöe was a trifle mysterious. She hinted that one of us might have left something precious in your bedroom at that awful old nunnery, and if we got in touch I might Hear Something To My Advantage, as the solicitors keep saying in their rather ominous little advertisements. But I was never in your bedroom. Perhaps Chlöe has been at the Madeira!*

Dash groaned. He rammed the letter into its envelope and shoved it into a pocket.

"Disappointing news?" Lacey asked. They were alone.

"Women. It's either feast or famine. I don't know which is worse." Lacey nodded. "Any suggestions?" Dash asked.

"I can recommend Corporal Llewellyn's wife." Lacey was censoring the Other Ranks' letters. "One hundred and three 'Acts of Joy', as he puts it, during his last leave. He recalls their sixty-fourth coupling with particular affection. Beef gravy played an important part."

"Gravy? How?"

"Better you don't ask." Lacey dipped a small brush into a pot of india ink and blacked-out half a page. "Mrs L is definitely the woman for you. A pity she is in Swansea."

"Come on, play the game, Lacey. You've been out here for years. What do chaps do?"

"Personally, my mistress is music. However, I can offer you a French widow. Her husband was a pilot." He found a letter in a file: square envelope, purple ink, slanting handwriting. "She keeps writing. She is *extremely* eager to give hospitality to a lonely young English aviator."

Dash took the letter. It came from Abbeville: quite near. He went to his hut and lay on his bed and thought about it, and after five minutes he knew that he didn't want a second-hand French widow wrapping her second-hand French legs around his, while she remembered how good it had been with her late, brave husband. He wanted the best. He wanted to be milked dry at midnight by that wonderful English girl whose memory could still wake him up in the small hours, streaming sweat and gasping and searching the bed for a ghost that had been so real his heart was trying to break through his ribcage.

Dash had been fucked by an angel. It wasn't Lucy Knight, which left only two: Edith Reynolds and Nancy Hicks-Potter, each stunningly beautiful. It had to be one or the other.

* * *

The barrage roared again, and fell silent again, and roared again.

Gerrish visited Woolley in his hut. He was playing his accordion. The rhythm was robust but the tune was shapeless. "Maybe I should go back to the saxophone," he said.

"Maybe you should go back to Blighty."

"Maybe you should piss in your hat." Woolley let the accordion fall. It groaned as it collapsed. "If that's too hard, you can piss in my hat. Or *I'll* piss in *your* hat. Or we'll both go and piss in Field-Marshal Haig's hat, it's very small, he takes a size four and a quarter, so that should give us a chance to compare our marksmanship, don't you think, old sport?" He lay on his bed and looked at two flies doing stunts around the naked light bulb.

"I have a simple question," Gerrish said. "Why do you keep running down our training and our tactics?"

"Beats me. Since it upsets so many people, I take it all back."

"You've had to take back a lot of things, in your chequered career, haven't you? Bad tactics? Bad decisions? Things like that don't come cheap, do they?" Woolley moved his head and watched two different flies doing the same old stunts. "I'll say one thing, and then I'll go," Gerrish told him. "This war, this battle, may be a joke to you, but it could just save our country. If we can only break through, if we can capture the Flemish ports – Ostend, Zeebrugge – then we can force the U-boats to go all around the north of Scotland instead of straight down the Channel."

"That was in the *Daily Mirror*," Woolley said. "They had a map of it and everything."

"Not everything. What the papers can't say is that if we fail, the Kaiser stands a good chance of starving us out of the war, long before the Americans even get here. Forget Hindenburg. We're getting torpedoed to death. Every fourth ship that leaves British ports gets sunk. American ships and neutral ships won't sail to Britain. You may wonder how I know all this. My uncle captained a freighter. Last week his ship was torpedoed in the Atlantic. Lost with all hands. The cargo was wheat. That's all I have to say."

Woolley listened to his fading footsteps. "Take that smile off your face," he told the flies. "It's nothing to laugh at." He was finishing his Guinness when somewhere nearby a Lewis gun made its dull, familiar sound, like a tidy giant ripping a carpet in half.

* * *

Andrei and Nikolai walked from the mess to their hut. As they reached it, two men came out of the darkness and greeted them in Russian. They introduced themselves as Shtemenko and Gordov, first and second secretaries of the Paris embassy. Duke Nikolai asked them to come inside. "Have you dined?" he inquired. Yes, they had. Andrei suggested a little pepper vodka. That would be welcome, they agreed. They wore navy-blue raincoats over dark woollen suits, and they carried large tweed caps. Each man looked to be about forty. They were clean-shaven and seemed tired. Shtemenko, the first secretary, had a lawyer's briefcase. Nikolai invited them to take their coats off, but they declined, saying they felt cold. "Unless I am mistaken," Nikolai said, "you were not at the embassy a month ago."

"Recent appointments," Shtemenko said.

Andrei poured the vodka. They all looked to Nikolai. He said, "May Russia be happy." They drank to that. "And God save the Tsar." But Shtemenko and Gordov had knocked back their vodka and turned away, so Nikolai drank alone. He made a little flutter of the fingers which developed into a gesture that invited the visitors to sit. He remained standing.

"The ambassador sent us here," Shtemenko said. "He has been ordered by the government in St Petersburg to arrange for your return to St Petersburg immediately and with all speed."

"Impossible."

"The count also," Gordov said.

"We take orders only from the Imperial Russian Air Force."

"*N'existe pas,*" Gordov said.

"I am sorry that your journey has been wasted," Nikolai said. "Count Andrei will show you how to leave." Nobody moved. "I don't know who your masters are," Nikolai said. He was trying to sound brisk and commanding, but his voice felt stretched thin. "Directors of the Petersburg Tramway Company, I shouldn't be surprised. Everybody runs Russia now. Everybody and nobody. I, however, am an officer. My orders came from the Tsar."

"*N'existe pas,*" Gordov said. He swallowed a yawn and looked down. It had obviously been a long day.

"Without royal orders to leave, it would be an act of desertion. Desertion from the Imperial Russian Air Force."

"*N'existe pas,*" Gordov mumbled.

Shtemenko began: "When you reach Paris I am sure—"

"Where are your orders?" Andrei demanded suddenly. "Where is your proof of identity?"

Shtemenko opened the briefcase and took out a sheet of typewritten paper which had the Paris embassy heading. While they read it he cracked his knuckles. One knuckle made him wince.

"Anyone could have written this," Andrei said. "It's not even signed."

"*N'existe pas*," Gordov said.

"There are guards on the gate," Andrei said. "How did you get in?"

"Nobody will care about that when you have gone," Shtemenko said. "A car is waiting."

"Why?" Nikolai said. "Why does Petersburg want me? And why in such a hurry?"

Shtemenko said, "The ambassador sent us. He has his orders."

"No," Andrei said. "This is a British base. Go and show your bits of paper to the British government."

"As far as we are concerned," Shtemenko said, "the British government . . ." He gestured wearily to Gordov.

"*N'existe pas.*"

"It exists here," Andrei said.

"No, they are right. Petersburg must be obeyed." Nikolai said. "I'll come to Paris."

Andrei was astonished. In English, he said, "Don't be such a fool!" Nikolai smiled. "It's for the best," he said in Russian. "I'll see the ambassador. I suppose I'd better take my dress uniform?"

Shtemenko looked at Gordov, who shrugged. "A uniform is a uniform," he said, and yawned hugely behind his hand.

Nikolai opened his wardrobe and pushed aside a hanging greatcoat. When he turned he was holding a Lewis gun. Shtemenko managed to raise a hand and shout, but all Gordov could do was gasp. Then Nikolai cocked and fired and raked the spray of bullets from side to side, knocking the two men off their chairs and killing them again and again. When the battering racket stopped he turned and looked for Andrei. He was hiding in a corner. "*N'existe pas*," Nikolai said.

Woolley was the first to reach the hut. Andrei was wrestling with Nikolai for the Lewis gun. It wasn't a fight; Nikolai simply wouldn't let go, until Andrei saw his chance and kneed him in the groin, a rising blow that lifted him onto his toes. Nikolai shrieked like a girl. Andrei knocked the drum off the Lewis and kicked it into a corner. Both men were splattered with blood: a bullet had nicked one of Shtemenko's arteries and his flailing body had sprayed generously for the few seconds that his heart went on pumping. On the floor, pools of blood were spreading and joining. Woolley went in too fast, skidded and fell with a crash that knocked the wind out of him. He sucked in air that stank of cordite. Gerrish appeared in the doorway.

"Get the doctor," Andrei said. Gerrish turned and ran.

Woolley sat in the red muck and looked at the bodies. "They don't need a doctor," he said. Bullets had made a ruin of Shtemenko's face, and Gordov had been almost cut in half. Both men looked less like people and more like sacks of spare parts, casually dumped.

"This one needs a doctor," Andrei said. He was kneeling beside Nikolai, who was squatting on his haunches and shuddering so violently that they could hear the chatter of his teeth. "Can't you cover those bastards up?"

Woolley got blankets and tried to throw them over the bodies. His strength, and his sense of distance, were distorted by shock and he bodged the job. One blanket fell short, and left Shtemenko's shattered face looking over the edge. Woolley reached out and tugged the blanket higher and got bits of wet skin on his fingers. He went outside and threw up.

Dando arrived at the run. Cleve-Cutler and Brazier and the duty officer arrived, all holding revolvers. "Can't you stay out of trouble for five bloody minutes?" the C.O. shouted at Woolley. Woolley was sitting against the hut. He spat out the remains of his supper and licked his lips and said, "It's a bit slippery in there . . ." But by then they were inside.

Four men with rifles came out of the night, at the double, and guarded the hut. Curious pilots wandered up and asked what on earth was happening. "Aston Villa nil, Wolverhampton Wanderers three," Woolley whispered. He was strangely short of saliva. Two medics arrived with a stretcher and carried Nikolai away. Finally the officers came out. Woolley stood up. Dando shone a flashlight on his face and asked him how he felt. "Better than those two," Woolley said huskily, "but not much."

"Come," Cleve-Cutler said. They trudged in silence to his office.

* * *

"One of them kept saying *N'existe pas*," Andrei said. "As if it was some private joke."

"He knew they were coming for him," Cleve-Cutler said to Andrei. "You think."

"Probably."

"But you didn't know he had the Lewis."

"No. Hidden in his wardrobe. I never looked there."

"Of course not. Extraordinary weapon to use."

Andrei drank his coffee, laced with the C.O.'s whisky. He had told them all he knew. What he could not describe was the killing: the hammering racket and the chemical stink and the invisible bullets kicking the men and making them jump and squirm. One second they sat looking tired and patient, the next second they were frantic and acrobatic and dead. That, he could not even begin to describe, nor to forget.

"Any idea where he got it?" the C.O. asked.

"Anywhere. He had money."

"How did these thugs get in? They didn't come through the main gate."

"Plenty of holes in the hedge, sir," the adjutant said. "Plenty of hedge. Can't guard it all."

"I want extra sentries everywhere," the C.O. told the duty officer. "On all the flights, the petrol dump, the ammo store, the motor transport. Go." He went. "Now, Mr Woolley. What were you doing there?"

"Not much, major. I heard the merry rattle of machine-gun fire. Then I fell on my arse in the gore. Then I chucked a blanket over the dead. *Two* blankets. Then I puked."

Brazier sighed. "At the sight of blood?" he said pityingly.

"At the sight of innards, Uncle. First time I've seen two men cut up and ready for the butcher's slab. Lights, liver, kidneys, tripes, heart, lungs, all on display."

"That'll do," the C.O. said.

"And steaming hot, too."

"Alright!" The C.O. was prowling around his room. "This is a hell of a thing. Two civilians, probably got diplomatic status, shot to bits by a member of the squadron, I mean, what could be worse?"

"And with an illicit weapon, too," the adjutant reminded him.

"I know what could be worse," Dando said. "Two civilians shooting dead a member of the squadron. We found loaded pistols in their pockets," he told Woolley.

"Nikolai would never have reached Paris, let alone Petersburg," Andrei said. "There's no future for the thirteenth heir to the Romanovs. He'll just cause trouble."

"Yesterday he offered me the Ministry of Railways," Woolley said. "Five thousand dollars a year."

"*You?*" Cleve-Cutler exclaimed. "You couldn't run a three-legged race." He kicked the waste-basket. "Conniving little hound didn't offer me anything . . . What are we going to do, Uncle? What do King's Regs say about this sort of situation?"

"Refer the matter to a Higher Authority, sir."

Cleve-Cutler picked up the phone and asked for Wing H.Q., and was connected, and asked for Bliss. The windows rattled, and the line went dead, and they all flinched at a roar like a cliff face collapsing. "Bomb," Woolley said. "Air raid."

"Sweet sword of Satan!" Cleve-Cutler roared. "Will this day never end?"

* * *

The bombers droned around the sky. They were near the airfield, perhaps over it. They were too high to be seen and the confusion of engine noise made it impossible to track an individual machine. A bomb fell at least every five minutes; sometimes several bombs fell together.

Most of the pilots had never been bombed before, and they took it badly. They sheltered in old trenches and swore softly at the Hun swine strolling about as if they owned the damn sky.

A faint whistle led to a dull *crump*. The trench trembled and bits fell off its sides.

"Missed by a mile," Snow said. "I reckon they're bombing at random."

"So they're just as likely to hit us as not," Munday said. "Bastards."

"This isn't war," Simms grumbled. "This isn't a fair fight." Another distant explosion made the ground vibrate. "Yah boo sucks!" he shouted.

"Be reasonable," Paxton said. "We do the same to them. Oh Christ . . ." The whistle was shrill and swelling. They ducked their heads. The bang was like being in the heart of a thunderstorm, and the duckboard leaped beneath their feet. "That was unreasonable," he said. He was shaking like a wet dog. Yet when he looked over the top of the trench, the moonlight was serene. No sign of an explosion. It wasn't even close, he thought.

After an hour the bombers went away. Cleve-Cutler sent men to search the field for damage. He was chilled and dirty and angry from sitting in a foul-smelling trench. "I've been thinking," he said to Ogilvy. "Hasn't this been too bad to be true?"

"Don't tell Uncle, sir. He's been playing billiards all through it."

"I don't mean just the raid. Look: it came straight after those two bandits broke in. Maybe they weren't Russians. Eh? Maybe they were German spies, sent to signal to their bombers."

"They didn't have anything to signal with, sir."

"Hidden somewhere."

"Why would they do that? They wouldn't expect to get caught, so why hide . . ."

"Yes, yes, don't go on about it. My point is, we've never been bombed before."

"Well, we've been lucky. Bound to happen eventually. Fritz knows exactly where we are, doesn't he? He knows there's a big push coming. Obvious thing: bomb the aerodromes."

Reports came in: no damage. Craters nearby, but not on the field. "Jerry couldn't hit us, could he?" the C.O. said. "Jerry's not as clever as he thinks he is. Splendid. A hot toddy, then bed for me." But while he was sipping his toddy, Jerry came back, stayed longer and bombed more accurately. No buildings were hit, but the mess windows were blown out and one canvas hangar was blown down. When dawn arrived there were a lot of repairs to be done. There were still two corpses locked in a hut. And the telephone was still out. Cleve-Cutler drove to Wing H.Q.

*　*　*

Bliss was shaving. Nothing Cleve-Cutler said made him pause. The razor left his cheeks looking as polished as his Sam Browne. "Who else knows?" he said. "Provost-marshal?"

"No, sir. Nobody knows, outside the squadron."

"How's young Nikolai?"

"Shocked. Sedated. Otherwise intact."

Bliss rinsed his face. "People have been known to die of shock."

Cleve-Cutler was very tired, otherwise he would not have said: "The duke is in good hands, sir. Dando won't let him die."

"Dando will do as he's damn well told." Bliss turned his back and urinated noisily into the toilet. It gave Cleve-Cutler time to think. When he was sure the colonel's bladder was empty, he said: "Does this mean the fate of nations is no longer in my hands?"

"Use your wits, man. His Highness is now His Lowness. There's a new gang in Russia, very touchy. If London discovers that you've been machine-gunning a brace of . . ." Bliss's voice was muffled as he pulled on his shirt. ". . . we'll both get the chop."

"So what do you advise, sir?"

"Me?" Bliss seemed surprised. "Do your duty, of course. You've got yourself into a messy situation, major. Simple solutions are always the best. What if none of your Russians existed? Shouldn't be difficult. You've lost two out of four already . . . What's that dreadful smell?"

"French vermin." Cleve-Cutler picked at a stain on his breeches. "What you're saying, sir, is that after all the nursemaiding we've done, you don't care if they both go west."

"No, I never said that." Bliss concentrated on making a perfect knot in his tie. "You said that."

"It's a sickening idea."

"Of course it is, old chap. The very thought of it makes me quite unwell. Breakfast?"

* * *

Breakfast was porridge, kippers, bacon and egg with mushrooms, toast and marmalade, coffee. Cleve-Cutler fell asleep in the car taking him back to Gazeran. When the driver woke him, he looked out and saw men knocking bits of glass out of the mess windows. The sun was shining as if nothing mattered. "This is turning into a very shabby war," he said.

"Yes, sir. Here comes Mr Brazier."

The adjutant looked far from shabby. He had relished the perils of the night. He was brisk and erect, and the heels of his boots struck small sparks from the tarmac.

"Good morning, sir. A glorious day for the gunners."

Cleve-Cutler heard the barrage rumbling again in the east. "Bliss was useless," he said. "Pretend it never happened: that's his solution. Nobody gives a toss about Russia. Nobody cares tuppence about us, provided we don't cause a scandal."

"Excellent. Well done, sir."

Sarcasm was not Brazier's style. "I've done nothing, Uncle," the C.O. said. "What have I done?"

"You've given us a free hand. Now we can make the problem disappear. You remember Sergeant Lacey, the cheese and the bomb."

"That was make-believe. There was no cheese and no bomb."

"Correct, sir. Now we have two actual bodies and a genuine bomb. An unexploded bomb, lying in a crater only half a mile from here. The bodies go in the crater, sir. A friendly Sapper captain is waiting to explode the bomb. His name is Captain Duffin. An Irishman. He enjoys making loud bangs. You'll like him."

This was all too fast for the C.O. "Where is this convenient crater?"

Brazier pointed. "Would you like to see it?"

"Yes. No. Should I?"

"It's only a hole. The bomb is buried at the bottom. One hundred kilograms. Should do the trick."

"A *hundred?* God's teeth, that's a whopper . . . Alright, Uncle. Let's do it."

A truck was backed-up to the hut and the dead Russians were carried out, wrapped in blankets. Their limbs had stiffened into the twisted angles of their violent end, and the loads looked more like bundles of logs. "None too soon," the C.O. observed. The odour of smashed guts was ripe.

He and the adjutant followed in a tender. As it swayed and bumped over the fields, putting sheep to flight, Cleve-Cutler savoured the guilty pleasures of crime. Blowing corpses sky high, other than in battle, was irregular, it was wrong, it was not officer-like. But it was bloody good fun.

The crater was ten feet wide and six feet deep.

"Tell me: is it usual for a dud bomb to make such a big hole?" Cleve-Cutler asked. "And if it's buried itself, how d'you know it's a hundred-kilogram job? In fact, how d'you know it's there at all?"

"Splendid to meet you, major," Captain Duffin said. "Your lads are doing great work, so they are." He was not much taller than a jockey. His voice played hopscotch: harsh one moment, squeaky the next: a disconcerting combination. "I see you've brought the late lamented. D'you want to keep the blankets? No, I thought not. We'll just dump everything in, so we will."

The bodies tumbled and sprawled.

"D'you wish to say a few words, major?"

"God help them. God help us all."

"Neat but not gaudy. Nobody would quarrel with that." Duffin slid down the side of the crater. "You'll need to be a good hundred yards from here."

Ten minutes later, the explosion made a gratifying *crack!* like a tree being snapped. A dense geyser of dirt and human remains climbed vertically and slowly collapsed upon itself. "Smithereens," Duffin said. "You could strain the lot through a sieve and not get enough to feed your cat."

The adjutant gave him two bottles of Irish whiskey.

"Oh, you needn't have done that," Duffin said. "But seeing as you have, it won't be wasted."

Later, Cleve-Cutler asked the adjutant: "Where did you find that fellow?"

"Better you don't ask, sir," Brazier said. "As they say in Russia." He was very blithe. It was a long time since he had enjoyed a funeral so much.

* * *

Wing did not wait for the Push before sending the six Bristol Fighters on a Deep Offensive Patrol.

The British guns were once more groaning and grunting in the distance when Cleve-Cutler told his flight commanders that their orders were to cross the front at Arras and patrol the line Douai–Cambrai, a distance of about twenty miles, at fifteen thousand feet. Gerrish would lead. Take-off at 11 a.m.

"Douai," Gerrish said.

The C.O. showed him the signal.

"Douai," Gerrish said, more thoughtfully. "Well, sir, they won't have far to come and look for us, will they?" Douai had a large German aerodrome.

"That's not what matters. Believe me, we're not out to make a big score. Not yet. I just want you to give the Boche something to worry about. Knock down one, two if you like, and we'll all be very happy. Then you can go and do it again tomorrow. But today . . . no heroics, Plug. Let some Huns get home to tell the tale and put the breeze up their pals."

"What you want," Ogilvy said, "is restrained carnage."

Gerrish smiled at that. Ogilvy didn't.

"Just a bloody nose will do," Cleve-Cutler said.

The Biffs took off at eleven. They circled and formed up in line abreast and swept across the airfield in a shallow dive. Cleve-Cutler saluted, and lost his cap to the sudden tearing wash of the propellers. He let it go while he watched the fighters climb. They banked left, re-formed into pairs astern, kept climbing. A cumulus cloud of dazzling white reared magnificently behind them. Cleve-Cutler felt a tear of pride trickle down his face and he did not wipe it away.

The flight crossed the Lines at thirteen thousand feet, and was only spottily Archied. Two and a half miles below, smoke from the artillery bombardment drifted like dirty ground-mist, speckled with soft, small flashes. None of the crews paid it much attention. Most had seen it all before. It was a remote event, rather like a disaster in a coal mine, and nothing to do with the war in the air. They concentrated on searching the sky.

The sky consisted of great white galleons of cloud; a scrubbed blue backdrop; and sparkling sunlight everywhere. Good day for a scrap.

Gerrish checked the map strapped to his left thigh, and looked below. The little river Scarpe glistened, a wet thread that dribbled towards Douai. He looked between the wings, past the shining arc of the prop, and there it was, a pretty little town, terribly old no doubt, stuffed with glorious architecture, maybe a soaring cathedral, probably an ancient university. If it didn't get out of the way soon and the British attack succeeded, then Douai might be a smoking ruin in a week or so.

Douai's Archie shelled the Biffs. No luck: maybe the clouds got in the way, or shrapnel fell on the heads of the gunners and their friends; anyway, they quit. Gerrish turned the flight southeast, towards Cambrai. There was activity in the air but it was far off and not worth chasing. Five Albatros D-IIIs slid around the edge of a towering hulk of cloud. They were single-seaters, glossy red against snowy white. Gerrish fired a Very light.

After that, there was little for him to do but wait. The rest of the flight closed up and swung onto an interception course. They had done it a hundred times. It was automatic. Still, Gerrish looked around and checked that everyone was there. He turned so far that he could see his observer, Munday. "Ready?" he shouted. Munday waved.

The Albatroses made a broad arrowhead. Gerrish was always intrigued by the apparent silence of enemy formations. They weren't silent, of course; it was just that his ears were swamped by the six-cylinder Rolls-Royce roaring in front of him. But in flight the Albatros formation seemed so silent, so effortless. Red should burn very nicely, he thought. Now both flights were closing fast, as eager as lovers with gifts. I've got this for you, he thought, and signalled a turn.

The six Biffs banked and levelled out. Their gunners had a clear shot from a steady platform. The Lewis guns crackled. Yellow tracer leaped out and tried to touch the enemy. The five Albatroses split up as if stung.

The outer two soared away in a steep, flaring turn. The inner three fell, each diving in a different direction. Gerrish looked over the side and watched them pull out and use their speed to climb. The slipstream rattled his head. Freezing air tugged at his helmet and goggles. He loaded the Very pistol and fired, rammed the pistol into its holster and gently eased the Biff into the beginning of a roll and held it there so that Munday could fire downwards.

All the Biffs were canted over, and all their gunners were firing long bursts at the rising Albatroses. The tactic worked. The enemy got driven off and fell away. The Biffs levelled out, a little ragged. At once everyone searched for the other red scouts, the pair that had not dived. Munday poked Gerrish in the shoulder and he pointed dead ahead. Gerrish's eyes were still watering. He could see one blurred red silhouette, too low for Munday to fire at without hitting his pilot or his prop or both. Gerrish's thumb pressed the gun-button, and the Vickers sent bright pulses of fire leaping ahead. As the Albatros swerved, his hands and feet automatically moved to chase it. The Biff dipped and heeled, and he realized he was falling out of formation, so he abandoned the target, steered hard back towards the flight and over-steered.

From nowhere, Snow's machine rushed at him. Snow was looking high up, his gunner was firing vertically, the two Biffs were seconds away from collision. Gerrish cursed and dragged the stick across as he kicked the rudder and opened the throttle. The Biff did as it was told, did much more than Gerrish meant: it skidded into a clumsy roll and threw Munday out.

Some gunners strapped themselves in. Not Munday. Munday liked the freedom to swing his Lewis all around the cockpit. He trusted Gerrish to remember this. Gerrish glimpsed Munday's right leg and he actually tried to turn and grab it, and of course he failed and had to watch the man falling head-over heels until he was a blob and the blob got swallowed by a cloud. The Biff slowly righted itself. For a few seconds Gerrish was too shocked to know or care where he was: more than long enough for an Albatros to make a beam attack. The shots wandered around the cockpit. Three bullets punched a hole as big as his fist in Gerrish's ribcage. The impact flung him sideways. His fist carried the joystick with it. The Biff tried to perform circus acts as it wandered back through the formation, and that was the end of the formation.

Crabtree flew a circle, trying to marshal the others. While he was concentrating on firing off Very signals he couldn't watch the enemy closely enough. Heeley was his gunner, and Heeley did a very competent job of swinging his Lewis from left to right, firing short bursts to scare off prowling Albatroses. Even short bursts emptied the drum. Heeley was so excited that he tried to fit the new drum upside-down. While he was hammering at it with his fist an Albatros came up behind and blew his hand off. The same burst went through the fuselage and severed so many control cables that the Biff put its tail up and fell. A final burst hit its tank, and now it was burning too brightly to be worth chasing.

Snow found himself alongside Simms and together they turned for home. Their gunners, Charles Dash and Duke Nikolai, were unhurt; the tactics drummed into them might yet succeed. For three minutes – say five miles – they fought off attacks. One Albatros fell out of the fight and began gliding home, trailing a rich train of smoke. Then others made simultaneous thrusts from each side and above, and that left the Biffs' gunners out of ammunition. Soon Snow's engine was streaming smoke, and the smoke became flame, and the flame exploded. Simms saw this and dived away as steeply as possible. His airspeed overran his engine speed: the aeroplane was trying to outfly its propeller. Something had to go, and it was the prop that snapped. He was lucky to crash-land in a German wood. Nikolai, not strapped in, was found many yards away, neck and back broken; but that was hours later.

Ogilvy was intelligent enough to abandon the fight and hide in a cloud. He sneaked home, dodging from cover to cover, and landed safely. His gunner, Maddegan, had a small hole in his backside: nothing serious; the bullet passed straight through. At first Maddegan was severely shocked, too shocked to be able to speak; but that had nothing to do with the wound.

McWatters and Andrei escaped too, although their Biff fell apart when McWatters tried to put it down in a potato field behind the British trenches. Some nearby troops came running over to help. They pulled the crew out of the wreckage and gave them cigarettes. Somebody dropped a careless match and the Biff went up, just like that. Andrei was lightly singed.

Cleve-Cutler waited until two o'clock before he telephoned Wing H.Q. Even then he didn't fully believe what he was telling them. Neither did they, until it was jubilantly reported in the German press next day. Bloody April had begun.

EARTHQUAKE STRENGTH 8:

Chimneys and monuments fall. Cracks in wet ground.

Next morning, eight second-lieutenants walked into the mess. They wore the new R.F.C. uniform, called the maternity jacket because of its deep, double-breasted tunic. It looked dull and shapeless against the stylish regimental outfits of old sweats like Dingbat Maddegan. His uniform was already patched at the elbow and the seat, and faded in streaks where his servant had taken out oil-stains with petrol. The newcomers seemed to be on parade, whilst Maddegan was obviously at war.

He sat lopsided, with one foot on a chair. He was eating breakfast. Nobody else was there. "Which one is Snow White?" he asked.

They glanced uncertainly at each other. The tallest man said, "The adjutant told us we might find Captain Ogilvy here."

Maddegan munched some bacon and thought about that. "I'd steer clear of him if I was you. He's been acting a bit funny lately." Their shoulders slumped a little, and those carrying valises put them down. "Go to your rooms," Maddegan advised. "Have a nice lie-down."

"The adjutant said our rooms aren't ready yet."

Maddegan nodded as he poked a bit of toast into the yoke of his egg, and he went on nodding as he ate it. A bright yellow drip trickled down his chin and ran out of strength before it reached the point. The replacements watched with interest; they hoped to be offered breakfast. "When you get shot," he said helpfully, "and they ask you *where* you got shot, always say 'Five miles north of Cambrai'. That's what I did. It makes them laugh like a dingo. I've never heard a dingo laugh, but then neither have you, so we're quits."

"Did you get the Hun that shot you?" one of them asked.

Maddegan felt egg on his chin and tried to reach it with his tongue. "Wrong question," he said. His tongue wasn't long enough. He scraped at the drip with a crust of toast. Servants came in with pots of coffee and bowls of porridge, and the replacements thankfully sat down.

One catastrophe was no reason to ground the whole squadron. Orders arrived from Wing to put every available Pup into the air. The British artillery bombardment was being threatened by a ferocious counter-battery operation. Enemy guns were hunting for British guns, guided by observers in balloons or aeroplanes who plotted the flash of British shellfire and told the German gunners where to aim. Fighters patrolled above. Archie erupted in a dirty rash, and the tunnelling of big shells through the sky created small storms that bounced the aeroplanes like unseen humped-back bridges. Very rarely, the paths of a shell and an aeroplane met exactly, and the gunners picked off the machine as cleanly as a poacher with a rook-rifle. The shell was not fused to explode at height. It merely wrecked the aircraft and sped on its way. Long before the bits reached the ground, the shell had gone on to hit its target. Or not.

All day, Cleve-Cutler sent Pups in sections of threes to patrol the front. After such heavy losses, experience was at a premium, so Woolley and Paxton flew. Ogilvy flew. McWatters turned up with a bruise as blue as a pound of plums across his forehead. He flew; so did Andrei, his aching ribs generously plastered. Maddegan flew until his leg got so stiff that he couldn't feel the rudder-bar. The C.O. flew. By nightfall, everyone had done at least two patrols; most had done three. It had been an exhausting day of chasing Huns and being chased by Huns, and often feeling bloody lucky to get home, unlike some. A new boy called Tucker muddled his throttle and strayed away from his formation and got shot down in flames by an opportunistic Halberstadt who sensibly saw no reason to stay and fight the two remaining Pups. Another new boy called Drinkwater shot his own propeller off and forced-landed in a field and might be intact.

Cleve-Cutler called for a squadron party, but even as he was mixing the Hornet's Sting, a despatch rider came from Wing. First patrol at dawn. Short party. Early bed.

Fitters and riggers and armourers worked through the night, but only six Pups were fit for action by dawn.

The sky was as red as the glare from a forest fire.

"Will you look at that preposterousness?" Dando said to the padre. They were on the airfield, waiting for the flight to take off.

"What's wrong with it?"

"It's profligate. Can't your God curb himself? Bad enough we're to have a bloody battle without Himself turning it into Italian opera."

"I find it rather jolly."

"Jolly? There's more blood up there than you'd find in Cork slaughter-house."

"Yes? It's not a city I'm familiar with. I once had an organist who moved to Tralee, but of course he had no knowledge of slaughterhouses. Very few organists do, I imagine . . . Ah, good morning, sir. Although the good doctor here takes exception to the dawn. Too red for his taste."

"Mine too. Nasty piece of weather on the way. My knee's giving me gyp. Never been the same since I hit it with a barn."

"How did you sleep, sir?" Dando said.

"Like the dead."

It wasn't the happiest answer, but nobody blinked. In the R.F.C., when men died they were not spoken of again; not in general conversation, that is. The convention was to believe as if nothing had happened. Death was just a different posting. Of course the tradition sometimes defeated itself. When five out of six brand-new fighters got hacked down and eight men failed to return, that was a body-blow to the squadron spirit. Ignoring it just created a very loud silence.

The C.O. didn't look as if he had slept well. He certainly hadn't shaved well. He kept squinting, although the light was still soft. "What?" he said sharply.

"I didn't speak, sir," Dando said. Cleve-Cutler nodded, blew his nose, cleared his throat. "Come on, come on, come on," he said.

They watched the Pups taxi to the end, turn into wind, and take off one by one. "Pretty little bus," the C.O. said. "No bloody good against the new Albatros, of course. Well, I'm off to Wing. Damn great Committee of Inquiry. Bliss told me to bring my pyjamas, so you might include me in your prayers tonight."

"I always do," the padre said.

"Spud's in command in my absence. Failing Spud, it's Paxton. Failing Pax, it's the cookhouse cat." He got into his car and it left at speed.

"Fletcher," the padre said. "That was the organist. I haven't thought of him in donkey's years. Fine musician but he rejected the doctrine of Transubstantiation, so he got the sack. Went to Tralee."

"Hullo," Dando said. "Hullo."

"The next chap was frightfully devout but he kept pulling out the wrong stops. Made a shocking din."

"They're coming back," Dando said. A white flare raced away from the leading Pup: the wash-out signal.

Everyone landed. The pilots got out and gathered around Ogilvy. "Damn compass was duff," he said. "They're fitting a new one."

Nobody spoke. R.F.C compasses were a joke. No two compasses ever agreed, and the whirligig of combat usually left the compass spinning and useless. Today the sky was clear. Nobody needed a compass to find the Front, or to find Gazeran afterwards.

"Better check yours, too," Ogilvy said. "Check everything else, while we've got time. Better safe than sorry." There was something strained about his speech. He sounded breathless, yet he had done nothing.

They went back to their machines. Woolley and Paxton sat on the ground, leaning back-to-back.

"Spud never used to be such an old woman," Paxton said. "Duff compass, for God's sake!"

"Where I grew up, we only had one compass for the whole street," Woolley said.

Paxton half-turned his head. "After the war, old chap, feel free to ask me for employment. The estate can always use a good rat-catcher."

"Where I grew up, we had rats as big as Shetland ponies. I remember—"

"Woolley!" Ogilvy called. "Your prop's been damaged."

242

They went over, and he showed them a nick in one edge. "It was there yesterday," Woolley said. "It's nothing." But Ogilvy sucked his teeth and shook his head. "Suppose it caused vibrations," he said. While the propeller was being replaced, Ogilvy had a tyre changed on another Pup and he made the armourers check all the drums for oversized rounds. When the flight took off it was very late.

It landed two hours later.

As Maddegan couldn't fly, he had been made duty officer. He couldn't ride a bicycle either, so he authorized transport for himself. Now he told his driver to take him to the Pups.

He found Ogilvy waving a compass in his mechanic's face. "It's just no good, Collins," he said. He sounded very tired. "This is . . . this is a *Hun* compass. You understand? A totally dishonest, *hostile* compass. What is going on? I'm at a loss, Collins. And this bally compass is no help whatsoever."

"No, sir. I'll have it changed, sir."

"Splendid fellow. Splendid fellow." Ogilvy gave him the compass and turned away, his head and shoulders slumped with the fatigue of carrying a compass. "Hullo, Dingbat," he said wearily. Collins rolled his eyes and scuttled away. "Anything happen while we were up?" He yawned.

"Nothing much. Three new Biffs got ferried in from England."

Ogilvy straightened up. He was stiff with anxiety, but his voice was still weak. "I must see them. How many did you say? Where are they?"

"In the hangars."

"Come on." Ogilvy set off, striding heavily in his thigh-length boots. Maddegan limped after him. "This is important," Ogilvy croaked. "Why only three? Why in the hangars?"

"I thought it was safer."

Ogilvy stopped. "Why safer?"

"Well, one of the gun crews thinks he's found an unexploded bomb. It's in a ditch, but . . ."

"Oh, Christ. Where?" Maddegan pointed, and Ogilvy set off in that direction. "Mustn't forget those lousy compasses," he muttered, and suddenly stopped. "What's Wing got to say? When does the balloon go up?"

Maddegan could scarcely hear the questions and he didn't know the answers, so he said, "There's eight replacements waiting to see you in the mess."

"*Eight?* Where from?" Now Ogilvy was wheezing; he looked intensely worried; even shocked. "What are their names? Never mind." He turned towards the mess.

"Look here, Spud. I have transport." Ogilvy was silenced by this simple fact. They drove to the mess.

The replacements, feeling much better with an English breakfast inside them, sprang to attention at the sight of Captain Ogilvy in full flying kit. The fleece-lined jacket was open and he carried goggles and helmet and muffler. Oil and grease still decorated his face.

Spud had it all prepared in his head: Welcome to the finest squadron on the Western Front, bar none. All he produced was a cough, a long and rasping cough that did his voice no good and hurt his chest. He thumped himself on the chest, and tried to apologize. His throat wheezed. That hurt too.

A waiter brought a chair. Maddegan sent for Dando. Dando got the ambulance.

Half an hour later, Dando found Paxton shaving in the officer's bathhouse and told him he was acting squadron commander.

"Don't be absurd, doc. I've never even been an acting flight commander."

"Well, Spud's blown a fuse, so you're it." He described the symptoms.

"Sore throat. Give him a pill."

"Listen, Pax. I've been watching Spud for days. What's wrong is in his mind. It doesn't want to go to war any more. So it's stalled his engine."

Paxton stared at him in the mirror. "Well, that's bloody convenient, isn't it?" He trimmed his moustache.

Dando watched, and wondered. They're not normal, he thought. They divide their world into fliers and failures. You're either eagle or eagle-shit. Wings on their breasts and sweet fresh air between their ears. "We'd better go and see Uncle," he said. "Make it official."

* * *

Brazier reduced the situation to its military essentials. Scratch Captain Ogilvy, never mind how or why. That, according to Cleve-Cutler's orders, made Lieutenant Paxton the acting C.O. But now Paxton was standing here, chewing a corner of his moustache and looking like a vegetarian who's won a pig in a raffle. That, too, was of military significance.

Brazier telephoned Wing H.Q., managed to get Colonel Bliss, told him what had happened, said he simply wanted to confirm the appointment.

"What? Not bloody likely," Bliss said. "Captain Woolley is your senior officer, isn't he? He gets the job. Forget all that tomfoolery about a court martial. Right now, only one thing matters."

"The Big Push."

"After that you can court-martial Woolley for wearing his knickers back-to-front for all I care. Don't worry about Cleve-Cutler, I'll take care of him." He hung up. The adjutant did not. "Did you get all that, Lacey?" he asked. "Good man . . . Kindly send a runner to Mr Woolley. My respects, and can he spare me a few minutes. I'm infinitely obliged to you." Now he put the phone down. "Due to an indisposition," he told Paxton and Dando, "the part of Acting C.O. will be played by Captain Woolley until further notice."

"On the accordion?" Paxton said. He felt both cheated and relieved.

But before Woolley could arrive, Sergeant Lacey tapped on the door and announced two visitors: Captain Lightfoot from the A.P.M.'s office, and Mr Hennessy from the British embassy in Paris. Brazier waved them in. Hennessy was about forty, tall, with a face like the jack of clubs. He was dressed for the moors in a lovat tweed jacket and breeches. Lacey took his cape and deerstalker.

"I was hoping that Major Cleve-Cutler would be here this time," Lightfoot said.

"Alas . . ." Brazier spread his arms. "The demands of war."

Lightfoot leaned towards Hennessy. "This squadron can be unexpectedly . . . what shall we say . . . volatile."

Dando snorted. "Volatile isn't the half of it. *Feckless* is the word you're looking for. Yesterday half of them went west."

"That's quite appalling," Lightfoot said.

"No feck at all, at all." Dando felt the stage Irishman coming over him, and shut up.

"It wasn't the best of days," Paxton said. He stuffed his empty pipe into the corner of his mouth and gave the visitors a challenging smile.

Hennessy uncrossed his legs, and re-crossed them the other way: a small diplomatic prompt. "Nevertheless . . ." Lightfoot began, when Woolley came in. "Lacey says I'm acting C.O.," he said. "What's wrong with Ogilvy?"

"He took his bucket to the well once too often," Dando said.

"Ah. Poor Spud." Woolley noticed the civilian. "I know you." His voice was flat as stale beer. "You ran the Lamb and Flag in Leeds. Buggered off with the vicar's wife and the burial club funds."

Lightfoot stared, and then shifted his stare to the adjutant. Brazier busied himself with some papers. Paxton frowned at Woolley. Of them all, Hennessy was least impressed. He raised one eyebrow fractionally, then put it back.

"This is Mr Hennessy," Brazier said. "From our embassy in Paris. And Captain Lightfoot, who speaks for the assistant provost-marshal."

"Oh." Woolley became guarded; almost shifty. "Well, I've gone straight ever since the Brighton stranglings. I paid my debt to society."

"Of course you have, sir." Brazier winked hard at Lightfoot. "Anyway, I'm sure we're here to discuss military matters. Eh? Is it cheese again? Or jam?"

"Neither." Lightfoot said. "It's far more serious."

"Richthofen's a woman," Woolley said. "Wears a size ten girdle." But suddenly he lost interest. He leaned against the wall and let his eyelids droop.

Hennessy spoke. "You have two Russian pilots."

"One," Brazier said. "The count. You're two days late for the duke."

"Dear me." Hennessy had a voice that was accustomed to instructing servants. "Well, that alters the situation radically."

"But not entirely," Lightfoot said. "The duke was lost on active service?" Brazier nodded. "There are two assassins at large," Lightfoot said, "and they may be unaware of that sad fact . . ."

For the next ten minutes, he and Hennessy outlined a Bolshevik plot to destroy all relatives of the Tsar in the West. It was a complicated business. The conspirators might try to gain access by claiming to be journalists or Russian Orthodox priests or diplomats. They might use chloroform or cyanide or more straightforward methods of despatch. Kidnap was not impossible, Hennessy said, and described how it might be done.

"Jesus!" Dando said. "If I didn't know you were an embassy man, I'd swear you were in the Secret Service, whatever that is."

"Let me be clear why we're here," Lightfoot said. "It's a matter of criminal law." He took *King's Regulations and Army Law* from his briefcase. Slips of different coloured paper marked relevant passages. "Were your Russian officers ever attacked or threatened in any way?"

"I should have been the first to know," the adjutant said.

Hennessy produced photographs. "Have you ever seen these men?"

"That one looks a tiny bit like my batman in 1915," the adjutant said. "He copped it in the Festubert show."

"They call themselves Gordov and Shtemenko, or sometimes Gouzon and Sarras, or even Gimbel and Steinbrunner. Their appearance . . ." Hennessy had much to say about aliases and disguises. Brazier listened patiently, but Paxton and Dando grew restless. "In short," Hennessy said, "this pair is not only ruthless but also cunning. And tenacious. They don't know that Duke Nikolai is no longer here. They'll find a way in."

"They may be here already," Lightfoot said.

"Extra precautions will be taken," Brazier assured him.

"This isn't burnt cheese, captain. This is an international conspiracy. This is life and death."

"Oh, bollocks," Woolley said. "These two buffoons are dead. Nikolai killed them with a Lewis gun. Uncle put the bodies into a bomb crater. A little Irishman blew them up. They came down like confetti. A French farmer got married on the spot, just to save money. If you don't believe me I'll tell you his name: Pierre, after his father who was also Pierre. Good enough?"

"Excellent!" Brazier said jovially. "I especially liked the confetti." Woolley scowled at him.

"Count Andrei," Hennessy said. "You say that he has survived?"

"Heavily sedated," Dando said. "He took a nasty knock, so he did. We'll hear nothing from him for a week."

"Did Duke Nikolai leave a will?"

"That he did," the adjutant said. "According to Count Andrei, he left his soul to the Tsar and his boots to anyone they might fit. No takers so far."

"Very apt," Lightfoot said bleakly. "Nothing much seems to fit here, does it?"

"Ah, that's war for you," the doctor said. "High explosive can be terribly dislocating. Humpty-Dumpty isn't in it, so he's not."

The adjutant walked with his visitors to their car. "Just supposing your two ruffians turn up here," he said. "What should we do with them?"

"Shoot the blighters dead," Hennessy said without hesitation.

"Consider it done," Brazier said. Lightfoot gave him an odd look, but Brazier just smiled and held the car door open. He was bored with being an adjutant. He wanted to live dangerously again. Otherwise what was the point?

The temperature fell as the day wore on. The sky was a dirty grey but it refused to rain. A smoky bonfire always burned at the eastern end of the aerodrome, to show the pilots the wind direction; today the smoke swirled and wandered and misbehaved. There were no birds to be seen anywhere.

At eleven o'clock, the adjutant assembled all the officers in the anteroom. The replacements stood in a separate group; they looked as if they were waiting for a train. Nobody spoke to them. Nobody said much at all. It was exactly forty-eight hours since Plug Gerrish had led the six Bristol Fighters on patrol.

"Gentlemen," the adjutant said, and the lights went out. The power supply had failed. It should have been funny, but all it got was a tired groan. "It matters not," he said. "I simply wish to say that, in the major's absence, Captain Woolley is acting C.O." He stepped back.

"War is a balls-up," Woolley said. In the gloom his voice seemed more cheerless than ever. "This is a big war, so it's a big balls-up. People expect things to happen just because their plan says so. Not me. I know better. Now, Wing H.Q. wants us to do three patrols this afternoon. Don't expect success. Expect a balls-up, and you probably won't be disappointed, and you might even stand a chance of getting back here alive."

He put his cap on and went out. The adjutant went with him.

"I've been in the army thirty-odd years," Brazier said, "and I've never heard a commanding officer talk like that before."

"Well, they looked a bit brassed-off. They need bucking-up."

"Yes. Yes, they certainly need that."

"Now I've bucked them up. Now they know the facts of life." Woolley headed for the C.O.'s office.

Half an hour later, he was sitting in Cleve-Cutler's chair and reading a file marked *Woolley, S. (Capt)*, when Paxton came in without knocking. "What does 'scabrous' mean?" Woolley asked.

"Don't know." Paxton kicked the door shut. It bounced open again. He kicked it so hard that it splintered. This time it shut. "I knew you were a twat. I didn't realize you were such a prick." He wiped saliva from his lips.

"You've been reading my file."

"More jokes. That sums you up, Woolley, by God it does! Everything's a joke. Nothing matters, does it?" Paxton's forefinger kept poking holes in the air. "*We* are here so *you* can have fun."

"Look: stuff that thing up your bum, before I bite it off."

"Fine! Good idea! Go ahead. Do it." Paxton thrust his arm out until the forefinger was quivering an inch from Woolley's mouth. "Do it! Then I can report sick too."

Woolley used the file to knock Paxton's arm away. "Who's sick now?"

"McWatters. And Andrei. And Cooper, in 'A' Flight, and Griffiths in what used to be 'B' Flight, and several more. They all reported sick just after you made your stirring address. Funny, isn't it?"

Woolley waited for an explanation and got none. "They're scared," he said. "Is that it?"

"Of course they're sodding scared." Paxton dropped into a basket chair. "Scared of the Hun, after what he did to us. Scared of the machines, because they know the Pups are clapped-out and they think the Biff's a flying coffin. Scared of you, because you're an expert on how to make a balls-up of everything."

"That's not what I said."

"That's what they heard." By now Paxton's anger had worn out; he was empty, and almost indifferent. "Ever since we came here, you've behaved as if you don't care a tiny toss about the squadron. Well, now you *are* the squadron, and nobody cares a tiny toss about *you*. Why should they?" Woolley was in his usual position, slumped in the C.O.'s chair, watching the flies racketing around the cold light bulb. Paxton got up and went away.

*   *   *

Lunch was over. Almost everyone was in the anteroom, for coffee. The buzz of an aero engine cut through the soft conversation. The adjutant took his coffee to the nearest window and looked up. "It's one of our Biffs," he said. "Since everyone else is here, that must be Captain Woolley." They all went outside.

The cloud was starting to break up. It was still grey streaked with black, but the base was higher and there were ragged gaps where the wind made chasms of clear air.

Woolley was in a new Biff, with an airman strapped into the rear cockpit for balance. As soon as he saw the crowd, he put the Biff into a shallow dive and crossed the field, much less than a hundred feet up. He did a flick-roll as smoothly as if the thing were on rails. "Is that hard to do?" one of the replacements asked. The Biff climbed away steeply, its bellow echoing around them. "At that height, it's insane," McWatters said. "It's insane at any height. Biffs aren't built to be stunted."

Woolley found a canyon that reared to three or four thousand feet and was half a mile wide, and he used it as a circus tent. He looped, then looped again and half-rolled off the top of the loop and held that position while his speed decayed until the Biff toppled onto its wingtips in a great swooping side-slip. He flattened out, swung the opposite way, then swung back again, so that the Biff was fluttering straight downwards, the engine ticking over.

"Falling-leaf manoeuvre," Andrei said. "I did that once, by mistake."

"How did you get out of it?" Maddegan asked. Andrei shrugged. "Better you don't ask," he said.

Woolley had somehow managed to abandon the falling-leaf. Now the Biff was in a power dive. A ton-and-a-quarter of aeroplane, encouraged by 190 horsepower, created a startling turn of speed. Woolley let it plunge a thousand feet and he got both hands on the joystick and hauled. The Biff bottomed-out hard enough to flatten his rump and drag the blood from his eyeballs. Then it was soaring almost as fast as it fell. He enjoyed its momentum as long as he dared, and he used the last dregs to carry the Biff over the top of yet another loop.

"That's too much," Paxton said. "That's just not possible."

"He's in real trouble now," McWatters said confidently.

The Biff was spinning. Woolley had finished the loop in a casual, nose-high attitude and the fighter had stalled. At first the spin was a sluggish corkscrew. Then it got more violent, like a dog chasing its own tail. The Biff was no longer flying but falling, and trying to thrash itself to death as it fell. And doing its best to get rid of its pilot, too: every turn of the spin flung Woolley against his straps. His eyes were fogged: the altimeter was a permanent blur. His senses were struggling to keep up with the spin, and losing the battle. When he guessed the ground was less than seven hundred feet away, he switched off the engine. He centred the rudder. He shoved the joystick forward.

The elevators kicked the tail up, and the nose, heavy with its Rolls-Royce Falcon engine, obediently fell. Gravity did the rest. Spinning was hard work for the Biff; it was easier to dive. Woolley gave it five seconds to build up a rush of air over the control surfaces and he switched on the engine, eased the stick back, saw the horizon fall away. The Biff was on its best behaviour again.

Then he went back up and did it all again. He ended as he had begun: a flick-roll at less than a hundred feet above the airfield. He landed, and taxied over to the pilots. Switched off. Got out. The sweet smell of hot engine oil drifted in the breeze.

"It's a fighter," he said. "We fly it like a fighter. Not like a chorus line." He waited for some response; none came. "I haven't got a joke about a chorus line," he said. "Nor about the Biff. She's a killer. Let's turn her loose."

"With or without a gunner?" Paxton said.

"With. Your gunner guards your tail."

McWatters said: "How can he do that if the pilot won't fly straight and level?"

"Listen," Woolley said. "Flying Corps tactics said that crossfire saves your bacon. Maybe it does, as long as the formation lasts. No formation, no crossfire. No bacon."

He wiped his nose and let them think about that. "Anybody who wants to go on patrol using those tactics must be loony and I'll have him chained to his bed in case he bites someone in the arse. Meanwhile I'm looking for people to fly the Biffs as they deserve to be flown, as fighters and not as chorus girls."

Half the hands went up. Very quickly, the other half, startled by this confidence, raised their hands too.

"Mac and Pax and Andrei," Woolley said. "The rest get their chance soon."

"One question," McWatters said. "Exactly how did you get out of that spin?"

"Listen hard. I'm not going to keep saying this."

* * *

At three o'clock Woolley led a patrol of four Pups with the four Biffs, one of which was Ogilvy's fighter, its punctured wings neatly patched. The cloud base had sunk and visibility was less than half a mile. After twenty minutes, rain began stabbing at the cockpits and visibility got worse. Woolley gave the wash-out signal.

One Pup got blown onto its back when it landed. No damage to the pilot. Brazier was waiting with a fistful of orders. All further patrols had been cancelled. All ranks were confined to camp until 5.30 a.m. tomorrow. Then the P.B.I. would go over the top and the Battle of Arras would officially begin.

Spud Ogilvy had gone. He was in an ambulance train bustling towards Boulogne and a hospital ship and eventually a nursing home in Harrogate.

Dando drove him to the railhead. Ogilvy was so tired that he had to be lifted onto his bunk on the train, yet he could not sleep. He looked like a man who was being hunted to death. Dando discussed his case with the senior medical officer. "No visible wounds?" the man said.

"He's overdrawn at the bank," Dando said. "A man has so much courage in his account, and when the last little bit is spent, there's no point in asking him to pay more."

Dando shook hands with Ogilvy before he left. Ogilvy's grip was weak at first, and then fierce. He didn't want to let go.

*   *   *

There was no dawn. The night merely gave up and left, and grey daylight took its place with no enthusiasm. The cloud was higher than yesterday but it was blacker, and it leaked rain everywhere. The Lines were black, and the cloud was black. No barrage: the guns had been silent all night. The war had died in its sleep and gone to hell, where it was at least warm.

Four Biffs patrolled at fifteen hundred feet. McWatters ducked his head and glanced at the chronometer clipped to his dashboard. Five twenty-nine and thirty-six seconds. He straightened up and began counting. Too slowly. He reached fifty-seven when the barrage erupted. Fifteen miles of British artillery made a noise that cracked the sky. Within a few seconds it cracked the earth too. The British front trenches bubbled with men. They surged into no-man's-land with all the dogged obstinacy of an invasion of brown ants. They didn't run: the loads they carried prevented that; but they didn't walk either: they made as much haste as the heavy soil allowed. No man stopped unless he fell. What they were all so eager to reach was something that looked like boiling porridge.

Weeks of shelling had torn the German Lines into tatters, and then ripped up the tatters and chopped what was left into little bits. Now the barrage was pounding this devastation with such ferocity that the striking shells overlapped each other. Yet men still lived down there. McWatters saw distress flares arcing out of the German defences, calling for help from their artillery.

Within ten minutes the German Air Force arrived: six Pfalz scouts, escorting a pair of two-seaters which were undoubtedly there to spot for the guns.

The Hun scouts flew straight at the patrol. The Biff was a strange new design, long in the nose and wide in the wings, and they probably thought it was a bomber or maybe a photo-reconnaissance job; either way it looked like a juicy target. But when the formations clashed and broke up into separate fights, with a Pfalz and a Biff circling to get a shot at each other, the new design showed itself to be very lively. The healthy pull of the engine gave great grip to the wings and tail. In a vertical bank, the gunner had a fine view of the enemy trying to tighten the circle. One Pfalz went down in flames, another broke off the fight and found itself pounded by the forward-firing Vickers of a Biff and dived away, full of smoke but minus a propeller. The rest rapidly followed. The pair of two-seaters witnessed this brisk defeat and promptly went down to ground level and flew home.

There was more air fighting to come, against Huns who were less impetuous and more dangerous. Both sides were up in force. The weather blurred much of the action, but sometimes the glow of a falling flamer showed through the rain. And when a pilot had time to glance down he always saw another wave of brown ants surging across no-man's-land. The stretch of boiling porridge had moved on. The guns had increased their range. The infantry had captured the first line.

*   *   *

Danger was an unpredictable drug. Sometimes it stimulated the senses, sometimes it flattened them. McWatters flew on four patrols during the first day of the battle. Twice he landed in a state of high excitement. Once he found himself almost an observer in a combat that might have killed him at any moment: his body flew the Biff, and sweated and cursed, while his mind looked on.

The final patrol was cut short because driving rain brought an early dusk. When he landed, McWatters couldn't remember anything; couldn't even remember taking off. He was too tired to get out of his flying kit. He went to his hut and fell asleep as soon as he lay down. Forty minutes later he woke up so violently that he tumbled out of bed. Faceless devils were racing around the room, trying to kill him. He hadn't been so terrified since he was six and a nightmare made him wet the bed.

A hot bath did him a lot of good. He threw in plenty of bath salts and a dollop of some kind of lemony essence (sent by his mother) that created enough froth and bubbles to hide under. A glass of whisky was within reach. What more could a man want? Somebody walked past the bath-house, whistling. That's old Munday, he thought, and wished Munday would come in and chat. But Munday was dead.

The whistling faded. McWatters lay like a log and absorbed the shock of loss. Until now he had fended off the truth, but the truth had strolled past, whistling. Munday was gone. And Plug, and Crash. Harry Simms, too. Charlie Dash. Heeley, whose first name nobody knew. Nikolai, whose second name nobody could pronounce. That made seven. Who else? Snow, the Canadian. All gone west.

A couple of the replacements came into the bathhouse and McWatters couldn't stand their chattering. He got out and got dressed and took an umbrella and walked to the orderly room.

Sergeant Lacey was reading a Harrods catalogue and listening to a gramophone record of guitar music.

"Something's wrong with that banjo," McWatters said. "Needs tuning."

"The government of Panama has just declared war on Germany," Lacey said. "I'm playing this as a tribute to Panamese pluck."

The guitar went idly in search of its melody; found it; lost it; and lingered lazily over a few final chords. McWatters grew bored and took the catalogue from Lacey's fingers.

"I expect they'll wear straw boaters when they go over the top," Lacey said. "Boaters and blazers and creamy bags. Everyone flashing the most tremendous tropical smiles, and all encouraging each other with shouts of 'Remember, men, you are Panamanian!' as the Prussians flee in panic and—"

"Shut up, Lacey. Why have you got this?"

Lacey took back the catalogue and showed him an illustration of a croquet set. "A bequest from Duke Nikolai to the squadron. Perfect for those idle summer evenings."

"I'm damn good at croquet." McWatters played a full-blooded imaginary shot. "I can sock the ball until it begs for mercy." He turned away, and noticed eight valises stacked against a wall. "That reminds me . . . Mr Dash borrowed some letters from me. I wonder if . . ."

Lacey gave him a small bundle of letters. "Mr Dash left a note. He wanted you to have them if . . ." He shrugged.

"They're from a mutual friend," McWatters explained.

"Miss Legge-Barrington, I believe."

"Charles Dash was a damn good sort, Lacey."

He ran back to his hut. The letters were in chronological order. The latest was on the top. It gave Nancy Hicks-Potter's address. McWatters shut his eyes and dreamed of illicit sexual ecstasy. The prospect was as intoxicating as the idea of victory over the Boche, and now it was a damn sight closer.

*　*　*

Northeast France is mostly flat and dull. The ground is heavy and good for sugar beet, which thrives on water, but in 1917 it did not make good trenches for the British Army, who preferred a nice chalk soil that drained quickly. Because of the low-lying nature of the terrain, nowhere here drained quickly. This was not ideal cavalry country. Even so, given a long spell of drying weather, the area around Arras might conceivably have offered the British dragoons and the lancers a decent charge at the enemy.

In April 1917 the battle of Arras opened in driving rain and the weather got steadily worse. When the infantry went over the top they were slogging through mud. High above their heads was the perpetual scream of shells. It was Easter weekend, and the infantry prayed that the barrage had destroyed the German wire and smashed the German trenches and shattered the concrete strongpoints that were built into the Hindenburg Line which looked down on Arras and the whole fifteen-mile stretch of the Big Push.

The key was Vimy Ridge, only a few hundred feet high, just a long crease running north to south; but it was steep-sided and the German Army had it. Or, more accurately, they had what was left after the Allied barrage had pounded it. Now the guns were pounding it again. The bursting shells might look like boiling porridge from the sky, but what the infantry saw was a wall of smoke and flame that grew uglier and more raucous as they plodded across no-man's-land.

This was not a walkover, and nobody had ever supposed it would be. Some German machine-gun posts had survived. They chattered and stuttered and cut holes in the troops toiling up the slopes. Nobody turned back. To retreat was more dangerous than to advance. The safest place to be was in the enemy trenches. In many places, British soldiers rushed the trenches and met an enemy that the bombardment had entirely killed, or terrified into surrender, or driven insane. Elsewhere there was plenty of desperate fighting, especially by the Canadians. They were given the highest and hardest stretch of Vimy Ridge to climb, and they had to buy every foot of it with their dead. Attack and defence were reduced to a primitive ferocity. Rifles became clubs. A Mills bomb, chucked around the corner of a trench, was the best weapon. By noon on the first day, the Canadians were on top. Vimy was captured.

Soon, all the first-day objectives were taken. The battle of Arras had advanced the Front by a mile, sometimes two miles: the biggest gain since ... Nobody could remember when. Men hurried across no-man's-land and scrambled up the slopes to revel in the thrill of standing where yesterday the Boche had stood. Across the plain, faintly visible, were the spires of Douai. Douai, for God's sake! Until now, as remote as the far side of the moon.

It was a splendid start, a thumping victory, a crack in the Kaiser's armour. The newspapers all said so, and for once they were nearly right.

*   *   *

Cleve-Cutler was back in Taggart's Hotel.

The Committee of Inquiry into the loss of his Bristol Fighters had moved from Wing H.Q. to Brigade H.Q. After a gloomy session of many questions and few answers, the chairman sent Cleve-Cutler to England. He was to seek the views of experts at the War Office, the Directorate of Military Aeronautics, the British & Colonial Aeroplane Company in Bristol, and the curators of the British Museum, too, if he felt they might throw some light on the matter.

"Hullo," Taggart said. "You look fucked."

"Rough crossing," Cleve-Cutler said.

"I thought you'd be in Arras." Taggart poured two nips of brandy. "Up your kilt."

"Up yours." The brandy tasted like a small reward for long service and good conduct. "Since we're being so frank and bloody candid, you don't look unfucked yourself."

Taggart grimaced. "This lousy weather. Bits of bullet keep doing a route march around my body. Since you're not in Arras, I reckon you're here because your shiny new fighters took such a pasting the other day."

"Firstly, that's not true. And secondly, how did you find out?"

"Chap from 60 Squadron told me yesterday. I suppose you want a room. I'm full up, but . . ." He ran a finger down the entries in the register. "Snotty little captain in the Sherwood Foresters: I'll kick him out. Unless . . ." Taggart scratched an eyebrow. "A man's entitled to go to hell his own way. You might like to know that your old friend Lady Jaspers has a room."

The title fooled Cleve-Cutler for a moment; then he understood. A pulse began throbbing in his forehead, as urgent as a klaxon. "Well, that's a coincidence," he said.

"No such thing. She's kept a room here ever since . . . Well, ever since." Taggart glanced at the clock: almost noon. "Should be up by now."

Cleve-Cutler climbed the stairs with a kind of military stride, to hide the fact that he was both eager and reluctant to meet her. A very young man in a khaki shirt and officers' slacks opened the door. What Cleve-Cutler noticed at once was the way the light caught the golden down on that part of his cheeks left unshaven, which was the greater part. "Oh well," Cleve-Cutler said. "Damn it all to hell."

"Let him in," she called. "It's only grumpy old Hugh, he won't bite you."

"Don't be so bloody sure of that."

The young man closed the door behind them and tiptoed away. He was barefoot. Cleve-Cutler saw a tunic hanging on a chair. Second-lieutenant, Durham Light Infantry. Hell's teeth! he thought. A dribbling infant! He would have given a month's pay to punch the fellow in the teeth, but a major could not strike a subaltern. Not in a lady's bedroom. Not in the Royal Flying Corps. Not before lunch. "I'm looking for my umbrella," he said. "Did I leave it here?"

"Come and have some champagne." She was sitting up in bed. She didn't look like a million dollars, but she certainly looked like fifty thousand guineas. Even with the brandy inside him, he felt like sixpence by comparison. "Tell me all about this battle," she said. Newspapers lay on the bed.

"You know more than I do." He took a glass of champagne. "This is pretty rich, even for you, isn't it?"

"Well, everything else is so scarce. Taggart can't get decent tea or coffee, and Fortnums are always out of sugar, so I'm doing my bit for England like this."

He drank. Champagne merged with brandy to spread wellbeing. "Not one of your worst ideas," he said.

She topped up his glass. "You need it. You look as if you've *walked* from France."

"Bloody awful crossing. Hell of a sea, and we zigzagged like fury to dodge the U-boats." He drank. "My dinner's in the Channel. Breakfast, too." He drank again.

"I like you thin. Have you stopped feeling grouchy?" He nodded: he couldn't resist her. Nobody could resist her. "Good," she said. "Promise not to fight, and I'll introduce you." He nodded again. "This is Tommy. Tommy, this is Hugh."

They shook hands, very briefly, reaching across her bed. Tommy kept his eyes down and went straight back to the other side of the room.

"There," she said. "That didn't hurt, did it?"

"I'd better be pushing off," Cleve-Cutler said.

"Not before lunch. I'm hungry, Tommy's *always* hungry, and you must be *empty*. Besides, we're both stony broke, so you'll have to pay."

"I've got an appointment at the War Office at three."

"So have I. We'll share a taxi."

They ate at a nearby restaurant, Studleys, in a curtained booth. While he supped his soup, Cleve-Cutler took stock of Tommy and decided that he was a young eighteen. His collar was a size too big. He looked tired, perhaps drained of energy by a night of carnal excess, or several nights, or several days and nights . . . He did not have the face of a soldier. He took a second helping of soup. Perhaps he was still growing.

Nobody said much. They ate dishes of whitebait, and then mutton chops with redcurrant sauce, buttered parsnips and braised onions. Tommy had an extra chop and parsnips. He concentrated on his food. Obviously it mattered greatly to him.

The table was cleared.

"I take it you're on leave," Cleve-Cutler said. Tommy blinked a couple of times before he agreed. "When does it end?" Cleve-Cutler asked.

Again, there was a pause. "In a little while, sir," Tommy said.

It was such an unmilitary answer that Cleve-Cutler repeated it: "In a little while?" Tommy nodded, once, sadly. "I see," Cleve-Cutler said. "Well, we're not on parade so you can drop the 'sir'. I don't know your other name."

"Blanchflower."

"Oh. Bad luck."

"*You* can't be on leave," Dorothy said. "You just were. What brings you to London?"

"Can't say. Top secret."

"I'll ask my chums in the War Office."

"You're awfully thick with the generals, all of a sudden. What are you up to?"

"Can't say. Terrifically top secret."

He made a sulky grunt. "Whatever it is, it doesn't pay very well." He covered the bill with money.

"Poor Hugh," she said. "You're not much fun when you're jealous, are you?" He ignored that. He ignored Tommy Blanchflower. He ignored the waiter who gave him his hat. The surgeons might have hitched his face into a permanent, jaunty smile, but they couldn't stop him brooding if he wanted to brood.

Tommy went back to Taggart's. Hugh and Dorothy took a taxi to Whitehall.

"I suppose he's another trophy from your tea-dances," he said.

"Far from it. I met him on Waterloo station. We go to the races together, on my gold medallion. That's why we're flat broke." She said nothing more, and neither did he.

* * *

British and Canadian troops began a painful campaign for villages whose quaint names they soon learned to hate: Méricourt, Arleux en Gohelle, Willerval, Oppy, Monchy le Preux, and many more. Before long these places ceased to exist, battered into brick-dust by one side after the other, in a series of attacks and counter-attacks.

And still it rained. The British had tanks, but they bogged down or broke down or both. The British guns had to be dragged forward through a chaos of their own making, a pox of flooded craters and sucking bog.

Hornet Squadron, like every R.F.C. unit, was in the air all day.

"A" Flight went first, led by Woolley. Ten miles over and one mile up, they got into five or six fights within an hour, all without loss, all without success. The sky was a murky tangle of cloud, much of it leaking rain, and visibility was poor. Much tracer stabbed the gloom; much smoke got pumped from exhausts; nobody scored a kill.

They landed at Gazeran. One Pup was coughing so hard that it barely crossed the hedge; it would not fly again that day. All the machines were slick with rain. One Biff showed a stream of red from cockpit to tail: its gunner had bullet-wounds that bled down his arm and ran through a hole in the fuselage. He would not fly again that year.

"B" Flight left and came back with much the same to report, except that the casualty was a Pup pilot, shot in the foot. He was barely conscious when he landed, which he did with such a bang that the pain flowered into total oblivion and the Pup touched a wingtip and made destructive circles in the grass. The doc had to cut away his flying boot before he could be lifted out.

"Can you patch him up?" Paxton asked.

"There are nineteen bones in the human foot," Dando said, "not to mention seven in the ankle. He's broken most of them. What do you think?"

"Don't get shirty with me, old man. I didn't shoot him."

At lunch, Woolley briefed them about the afternoon patrols. "And I'm acting major until the old man comes back," he said. "You can cheer if you like."

They chewed their food.

"I've got a pain in the bum," Maddegan said. "That means there's rain on the way."

By 3 p.m. each flight had flown another patrol over the battle-field. Fierce counter-battery work was being done by both sides in an attempt to shield the infantry from the pounding of artillery. Two-seaters kept grinding up and down, their observers searching for the flash of an enemy battery, or for coloured smoke that would indicate a friendly infantry position. Mainly, they saw rain and shellbursts. If they flew low they got raked by machine-gun fire. When they climbed to escape, the rain blotted out all detail.

High above all this bloody confusion, a separate battle went on: a struggle between fighters. Hornet Squadron drove down a couple of Huns and blew a Pfalz scout to pieces, or maybe he just fell apart under the strain; it was hard to say. One Pup was a flamer. Andrei's Biff lost its prop when he flew into bits of an FE2d, fluttering down after a shell knocked its wings off. He glided halfway home, potted at by troops to whom he was an ominous shape in the rain, and made a clever landing on a farm track.

Woolley gave a third briefing at 3.30 p.m. The rain had stopped and enemy machines were flying low over the battlefield, strafing troops who had not had time to dig trenches. At 4 p.m. Hornet Squadron took off with orders to stop the strafing. After forty-five minutes they came back without one Pup. Nobody had seen it crash. Every machine was holed or ripped or bent or all three.

Four new Biffs, six new Pups and three replacement pilots had arrived. Woolley put Maddegan in charge of the replacements. "Kick their arses," he said. "Keep them flying until they're flapping their little wings in their sleep. I won't take them over the Lines until they've done at least twenty hours solo." Maddegan glanced at their logbooks. "You want me to turn deuces into aces."

"Oh, I don't bloody know." Woolley was wet and cold. His eyes were sore. His ears ached from so much climbing and diving. The stink of whale-grease filled his nostrils. He opened two bottles of Guinness and gave Dingbat one. "I didn't pick the bastards. Just get them out of the nursery, that's all."

The adjutant visited Andrei and told him that Duke Nikolai's death had been confirmed. "A Hun machine dropped a message-bag on one of our 'dromes," he said. "No doubt as to identity. His tunic was enclosed."

"He will be avenged ten times over."

"Yes, of course." Brazier was surprised to see tears streaming down Andrei's cheeks, although his face itself was stiff and stern and his voice was strong. "Your loyalty does you credit."

"He was a true Russian," Andrei said. "What more is there to say?"

Brazier remembered the Bible whacking Nikolai's head. "Naturally, you two didn't always see eye-to-eye."

"He gave his life for Russia! It wasn't his fault he was stupid. He was raised to be stupid. He didn't know how to live, but he knew how to die."

"I don't know whether you were aware of it," Brazier said, "but he urged the C.O. to have you shot for treachery."

"Magnificent." Andrei's face was shining with tears and pride. "In such a small body, such a big heart." He poured two tots of pepper-vodka. "To Nikolai! To Russia!"

Brazier drank, and shook hands, and left. Later he told the padre what had happened.

"Extraordinary people, the Russians," the padre said. "They couldn't raise a cricket team if you gave them all eternity. Still, I shall say a prayer for Nikolai. A gallant lad."

* * *

The inquiry got nowhere.

It identified four possible causes of the Arras Incident (as it was discreetly labelled). First, the Bristol Fighters might have underperformed or suffered some grave failure. Second, the observers' marksmanship might have been poor. Third, the pilots – especially the flight commander – might have been in error. Finally, the enemy might have been armed with some new weapon. Rockets were spoken of.

The trouble with all these theories, Cleve-Cutler pointed out, was the total lack of supporting evidence. The survivors spoke of "a classic interception, exactly as practised". There was nothing unusual about the Albatroses. Except their success.

Someone mentioned tactics.

The Director of Military Aeronautics was ready for that. He had brought a paper, summarizing the tactical situation vis-à-vis the Bristol Fighter. He reminded those present that this type had originally been conceived in the photo-reconnaissance role, to replace the highly vulnerable

BE2c and RE5 and their like, which were being lost in large numbers. That was why it was a two-seater. A single-seater could not defend itself while the pilot was taking photographs. The superb design of the Bristol Fighter made it well able to fight off such attacks. It was built to fly straight and level. A pilot who threw it around like a Camel placed unacceptable strains on the structure. But during testing it had been discovered that this apparent drawback could be turned to great advantage. A group of Bristol Fighters, flying in close formation, formed a multiple gun-platform whose crossfire was lethal to any enemy attack. This had been demonstrated again and again in trials. In fact its performance was so impressive that it was given the name "Fighter" and sent to the Western Front in that role.

The Director distributed copies of his paper.

Cleve-Cutler struck a match and held it to a corner. As the flames swarmed across the pages he let the copy drop into an ashtray.

"What do you think that proves?" the Director asked.

"I don't know. I just wanted us all to be aware of what actually happened to some of my men, ten thousand feet above the Western Front."

The flames, and the words, silenced the others; but silence brought a solution no nearer.

He got back to the hotel at eight o'clock. "I've shifted the fair haired boy to another room," Taggart said. "So you can stay with her, if you want."

"Good."

"They're not here. They went out, both."

"Oh well." Cleve-Cutler headed for the stairs, and then checked. "How long has he been here? The boy."

"Let's see . . . Ten days."

Cleve-Cutler went upstairs, wishing he hadn't asked, wishing his knee didn't ache so abominably. He had a bath, ate a bowl of Taggart's stew, drank some wine, went to bed. When he awoke it was daylight and Dorothy was in her nightdress, sitting on the bed, brushing her hair.

"What's this stuff about Lady Jasper?" he asked.

"Taggart's joke." She tossed the brush away and, with one easy roll of her body, got into bed. She dragged up his pyjama jacket and hugged him so hard that his ribs hurt.

"I say . . . Look here, steady on old girl." The embrace was a shock, but already his body was rising in approval of the idea. Where was discipline? Where was order? He was a major in the R.F.C., for Christ's sake! "Who's in command here?" he demanded. His pyjama trousers had gone. "Dammit, woman."

"Look! The height of fashion." She took a yellow hair-ribbon and, with one practised flick of the fingers, tied a bow around his penis. "I claim this height for King George and England! We shall now sing the national anthem."

"You're very frisky, for someone who's just had ten days of rumpty-tumpty."

"Ten days?" She fussed with the bow, making it neat and tidy. "You mean poor Tommy. I kissed him once, on the cheek, and he had palpitations. Tommy is one great big emotional booby-trap."

Cleve-Cutler tugged the ribbon. "What would happen if you did this to him?"

It was meant to be a joke, but she took it seriously. "He'd be a gibbering idiot for a week. What he doesn't understand about himself would fill a book."

"Ah. So you and he have not been fornicating like the beasts of the fields." Cleve-Cutler knew that that was excessive, but he felt entitled to a little excess.

"Would it make any difference if we had? I don't remember you making any pledge to be faithful as you trotted back to France."

"Well, you didn't ask for any." They ended up staring at each other. "Where did he sleep?"

"On the couch."

Cleve-Cutler undid the ribbon and dropped it, delicately, over the side of the bed. "What was it about him that appealed to you?"

"Oh . . . desperation, I suppose. He was sitting on a luggage trolley in Waterloo station, and everyone was rushing about except him, and he looked as if his pet rabbit had died."

"Pet rabbit," Cleve-Cutler said. "This is a commissioned officer in the Durham Light Infantry, in wartime, and he looked—"

"Don't be so stuffy. The first time I saw you, you were grinning like a baboon."

"Surely not."

"Like two baboons. Anyway, Tommy had no money and nowhere to go, so . . ."

"I see." He stretched. "Well, enough about him. More than enough. What about us? What's on the menu?"

"Rackety." She could see that he had forgotten, so she said. "Rackety-rackety-rackety. It's in code."

"*That* rackety. Of course. I remember it well . . . What does it mean?"

"It's the signal for the Big Push," she said, which made him laugh. After that, the morning improved rapidly.

* * *

On the third day of the battle, 11th April 1917, it snowed.

The Allied advance, already reduced to nibbling a few yards here and there, came to a halt. It left many troops in exposed positions. These had been expensively bought: the price lay scattered about the woods and fields. Having spent so much to win so little, the generals refused to think that the effort was wasted and so they kept on spending. It was a miserable existence for the infantry, chilled by the blizzard, chivvied by machine-gun fire, hounded by artillery.

All day, Woolley sent up units of two or three aircraft to patrol the battlefield and chase off any strafing machines. It meant flying low: dangerous work. The prop blasted snow at the pilot's head, and the horizon was a white blur.

A lieutenant called Drinkwater, flying a Pup, got shot at so often that he felt sweat trickling down his body. Flashes of small-arms fire caught his eye, but by the time he turned, whirling snow had spoiled his view. More flashes came from a different side, and a sharp scream as a round scarred the engine cowling. "Bastards!" he shouted. A hillock loomed, and then trees on the hillock. The Pup reared to miss them. Enough of this madness. Drinkwater went up a thousand feet.

He was alone. Two Pups had taken off with him; one turned back with a sputtering engine and he'd lost the other in this grisly weather. He flew wide figures of eight and waited for something to happen. Eventually the snow thinned and almost stopped. He could see for a mile. Two miles.

At once, enemy Archie began to seek him out and he climbed and turned, dived and turned and climbed some more. Drinkwater had been with the squadron for seven weeks; he was a veteran; he knew how to outwit Archie. The bursts made blots, like cheap ink soaking into cheap paper. A flight of six Sopwith 1½-strutters crossed above him, probably off to bomb a railhead or an aerodrome, and the Archie switched to this juicier target. Drinkwater saw activity on the ground and went to look. What he found was British cavalry, sheltering in a dip behind a wood.

This was so extraordinary that he forgot about strafing. Cavalry were not an unusual sight; their camps were all over northeast France, far behind the trenches. This was the first time he had seen cavalry at the actual Front, within striking distance of the fighting.

They were lancers. From two hundred feet he could clearly see their lances, looking like the sort of javelin he had thrown in the school sports. The men holding them were dismounted, standing in groups. They wore swords. Some of them waved to him. They looked as relaxed as if they were at a point-to-point before the start.

He circled. Nothing much happened. Maybe they were returning from action. If so, there was no point in hanging around. He climbed to five hundred feet and flew east, looking for trouble. In less than half a mile he found it. The ruins of a farmhouse were busy with men in field-grey. He sideslipped to get a better look and a machine gun opened up. "Bloody nerve!" he said. The Pup's Vickers was fully loaded. He hadn't shot anyone or anything since before breakfast. He put the nose down. A second machine gun began firing, and a third. He sheered away and felt bullets smacking into the Pup. He gave the engine maximum revs and curled his body into the smallest space and hared back to the wood.

The lancers were cantering past it. They were not going back to camp. They were heading for the open fields around the ruined farmhouse.

Drinkwater flew alongside them and waggled his wings and waved and shouted. They waved and shouted back. He could see their open mouths.

As the field widened, so the cavalry spread out and quickened their pace, kicking up a fine spray of snow. Drinkwater counted at least sixty men. He climbed and got a splendid view. Now they were into a gallop and the lances were being lowered for the charge. He kept climbing. They were aiming to sweep behind the farmhouse. The first row of horses went down as if tripped and their riders died with them. The next row raced into the bullets and now the machine gunners were hosing the rest of the galloping column, finding fresh targets as the leading horses crashed and made room for the bullets to hit the followers. In a minute it was over.

Before that, Drinkwater had dived at the farmhouse and kept his thumb on the gun-button until the Vickers stopped firing. He was fired at, but he was too angry to care. He climbed, and turned, and took one long look at the snowscape dotted with struggling animals and men, and many more not struggling, not moving, just lying in ragged rows, and a few who had turned in time and were racing away, trying to out-run the bullets. Then he stopped looking and flew to the west.

Something cracked loudly and the control column ceased to do much controlling. The Pup sank gently, in a powered glide, and finally found a bog on the outskirts of Arras. It skimmed the mud until its wheels stuck and it performed a very squalid cartwheel.

Drinkwater was filthy, and cut about the head and legs. A squad of Pioneers got a rope on the wreck and dragged it and him out of the bog. After that he remembered a middle-aged doctor, a glass of rum, and a deep cellar. An open-truck railway train came along and took him on a dark journey. It was like travelling on the London Underground, except it was different. He climbed a lot of stairs and was put in an ambulance. Then he was at Gazeran, being looked at by Dando. When Dando had finished, the adjutant questioned him about his patrol. "It seems you got Archied,"

Brazier said. "Was anything else noteworthy?"

Drinkwater shook his head.

Routine patrol, Brazier wrote. "Don't you remember the tunnel under Arras?" he asked.

"Why did they do it?" Drinkwater whispered. The doctor's stitches showed up stark black against his chalky face.

"That's obvious," Brazier said. "They did it to get the troops to the Front without being shelled by the Hun. The Hun blew Arras to blazes, but he couldn't touch our lads safe down below. And now we get the wounded out in the same way! Lucky you, eh?" He strode away. The door banged.

"I should have crashed the Pup," Drinkwater whispered. "Crashed it on the guns."

Dando slid a needle into his arm. "Count to ten," he said.

"More than ten." Now Drinkwater was anxious. "At least sixty. I counted sixty . . ." His eyes closed. The needle came out.

* * *

The experts had gone off to consult other experts. Cleve-Cutler had a free morning. "Good," Dorothy said, at breakfast. "You can come with me to Hammersmith."

"Hammersmith? That's an awful hole."

"My chums at the War Office don't think so. They've given me a frightfully secret job in Hammersmith. Go and fetch Tommy. He must come too. Otherwise he'll just skulk in his room."

Cleve-Cutler climbed the stairs. He was sexually content, and full of bacon and eggs, and rested by a good night's sleep; so his mind was relaxed and free to let the pieces of the puzzle drop into place almost without his knowing it. He tapped on the door and Tommy Blanchflower opened it. "You've deserted, haven't you?" Cleve-Cutler said.

Tommy was barefoot, and his toes were plucking at the linoleum. "Not really," he said. "I'm just a bit late. Lost my train ticket."

Cleve-Cutler went inside. "How late?"

"Um . . . two weeks."

"Then the military police are out looking for you, old chap. Anyone who overstays his leave by two weeks is a deserter in their books."

"Didn't overstay my leave."

Cleve-Cutler sat on the bed and waited.

"Didn't take any leave." There was a hint of defiance in the voice. "Did a bunk. Walked out. Got a train."

"Then you're definitely a deserter. And you can't spend the rest of the war hiding in here."

"I'm not going back *there*." Tommy sat on the floor. He used the minimum effort: just let his back slide down the wall.

"It's your best chance. Go and apologize to your C.O. Tell him . . ." He stopped because Tommy had slumped further, until his elbows rested on the floor. "Not going back," he said.

"I see. In that case, stop being so bloody Russian and tell me exactly what went wrong."

"Cub-hunting. I was in the mess one night and the chaps got a bit bored and decided to go cub-hunting. You know what that is?" Cleve-Cutler nodded: it was a kind of hide-and-seek played by young officers, an excuse for noise and bullying and broken furniture. "They made me the cub. I'd seen what they did to the cub if they found him too easily. Put boot-blacking on his balls, that sort of thing. So I found a very good hiding place. Too good, because they never found me. Bad mistake. I heard them getting more and more annoyed, and drunk, and I didn't dare come out. In the end I had to use the lavatory. Everyone had gone. I sneaked back to my room and they'd made an apple-pie bed. So I walked out."

"For an apple-pie bed? For a joke?"

"It wasn't a joke." Tommy hooked his big toes together and watched them wrestle. "They despised me. Ever since I told one of them I didn't want to go to France, and he told the rest, they were all against me."

Cleve-Cutler took a moment to consider that. One possible question was: why apply for a commission if you don't want to serve your country? But he knew the answer. Conscription at eighteen meant Blanchflower would be in uniform whether he liked it or not. Everyone went. "France isn't so bad," he said. Not so good, either, he thought.

"That's not what my brother said in his letters. He hated it. Got killed a year ago. A cousin got killed too. Knew it would happen. Said so."

"They died for England," Cleve-Cutler said. "What better sacrifice can a man make?" His hand covered his artificial grin.

For the first time, Tommy looked him in the eyes. "They didn't sacrifice their silly lives," he said. Something like contempt was in his voice. "Other people organized their deaths. Will you go back to France and sacrifice your life?"

"Not if I can bloody well help it."

"So we're agreed." That was that. Nothing more to be said.

They went by cab to Hammersmith, through steady rain that was flecked with sleet. Dorothy chatted easily, mainly about racing. The men did their conversational duty, but Cleve-Cutler was considering the fact that, by not having a deserter arrested, he was himself committing a crime. It didn't worry him so that was something else to wonder about.

The cab stopped at a large brick building, once a commercial laundry, now requisitioned by the War Office. "This is where the generals have asked me to do my bit," she said. "It's where the losers come to collect their winnings."

An elderly sergeant took their names and led them into the main hall. It still smelt of soap and flatirons. Sitting on benches, waiting with the skill of soldiers who have learned to wait, were about a hundred amputees.

"Now I begin to understand," Cleve-Cutler said.

"I have no medical qualification," she said, "but I can give hope."

An elderly doctor introduced himself. The hall was divided by canvas screens and there was a constant traffic of bustling nurses and men who would never bustle again. "I've got a rather interesting chap for you to meet," the doctor told Dorothy. "No legs, but what a heart! Name's Miller, so you can call him Dusty." He took them to a canvas cubicle, waved them in, and said, "I'll be back in half an hour."

A young man sat in a wheelchair. He had the milk-white skin that goes with red hair. His face was young and his eyes were old. He was holding an artificial leg as if it were made of glass.

"Thank God! A good-looking man at last," she declared. Without taking her eyes off Miller she said, "You two, toddle off, make yourselves useful. Vanish!"

The elderly doctor was waiting for them. He was bald and broad, with a cheerful mouth and untrusting eyes. "Let me give you the guided tour," he said. "We're rather proud of the Hammersmith Factory. Treating the limbless has made great strides lately." Cleve-Cutler glanced sharply, and saw no sign of irony. "Here's a lucky chap." They looked into a cubicle and saw a man whose right arm had been amputated above the elbow. "Today's the day he gets a new arm. Let me see the stump . . ." It was rounded and red as an apple. The doctor stroked it. He was a craftsman searching for rough edges, bodged workmanship; and finding none. "Do you still miss it?" he asked.

"Yes sir. I can feel it wanting to pick things up."

They moved from cubicle to cubicle: a man without a foot, a man without half a leg, without two-thirds of a leg, without both forearms. Lieutenant Blanchflower asked the doctor quiet, intelligent questions. Major Cleve-Cutler grunted occasionally and looked nobody in the eye. He wanted a drink. The doctor, pleased to have such an attentive audience, spoke about the problems of shattered joints and ravaged muscles. "Just last week," he said. "I found this in a patient's buttock." He rummaged in a pocket and produced a jagged bit of shrapnel, the size of his thumb. "That's what's wrong with this war, if you ask me."

Blanchflower did ask him. By now Cleve-Cutler wanted a large drink.

"Your biggest enemy in the field is not the Hun," the doctor said. He had stationed himself where he could watch the shuffling come and go. "Your biggest enemy is a tiny organism, *Clostridium welchii*, which lives in the intestines of animals and is transferred to the fields in the usual way."

"Dung," Tommy said.

"Quite so. Most battlefields were farmland, so *Clostridium welchii* is abundant. A soldier struck by a shell-splinter falls to the ground, gets his wound dirty, and infection follows as night follows day. Unless the damaged tissue is soon excised, gas gangrene sets in."

"Not in the Royal Flying Corps," Cleve-Cutler said firmly. The constant parade of stumps was making him queasy.

"Peritonitis and septicaemia are the airman's foes, in my experience. If shrapnel penetrates the abdominal cavity, or a bullet impels fragments of uniform into the body, especially if it impacts with bone—"

"Good Lord. Is that the time?"

"My grandfather was a surgeon at the battle of Waterloo," the doctor said. "He told me that the lance, the sabre and the musket-ball made the cleanest wounds a man could wish to see."

"Oh God," Cleve-Cutler muttered, as another amputee lurched past on crutches. "This is a dreadful place."

"There's nothing more stupid than a shell," the doctor said.

"It makes a chap think," Tommy said.

"I'll meet you outside," Cleve-Cutler said, and left without shaking hands.

He had to wait forty minutes until Dorothy and Tommy came out. "Aren't they doing splendid work?" she said.

"Don't ask me. This place is a chamber of horrors. It's worse than a zoo. People could pay sixpence to go in and throw buns at the limbless." His anger surprised her, so he persisted. "Christ knows it's hard enough to fight a war without coming home to this kind of freak show. It's obscene."

"Goodness." She widened her eyes. He realized she wanted to hear more.

"Told you Hammersmith's an awful dump," he said. "Look at the rain! We'll never get a cab."

"Poor Hugh. Never mind, here comes a nice big bus and it's going our way, what luck."

"Bus?" Cleve-Cutler hadn't travelled by bus since he'd left school. They got on. It smelled of shag tobacco and sweat. "I missed breakfast," Tommy said. "I hope you can pay for lunch." Cleve-Cutler said: "*What?*" The bus moved off. "Well, I'm jolly hungry," Tommy said.

"Where to, guv?" the bus conductress said. Cleve-Cutler turned, amazed that a second-lieutenant would cadge lunch off him. "What?" he said.

"Where to, guv?"

"Taggart's Hotel."

The conductress raised her eyes to heaven. Dorothy said, "Here, give me some money."

He felt better when they reached Kensington and got off the bus. "I apologize," he said. "Inexcusable remarks. Must have been a bit liverish."

"Champagne's good for the liver. We'll go to Studley's."

"Claret's awfully good, too," Tommy said.

"Shut up, you. And call me 'sir'."

"Claret *is* awfully good," she said. "We'll have lots of claret."

Lunch was, if not happy, at least convivial. He watched her and thought she must be the only person in London who was not troubled by the war, who actually looked forward to each day and enjoyed it. He found her buoyancy irresistible, infectious. When he took a cab to the War Office, he had to remind himself why he was in England. He was frowning as he walked into the meeting room. It was empty, except for an R.F.C. captain who was looking out of a window. "O'Neill!" he said. "Who let you in? This is no place for a thug like you. And where's my meeting?"

"I work here, sir. And your meeting's been cancelled."

They took stock of each other. They had not met since the summer of 1916. Both were survivors, in their different ways. Looks ten years older, Cleve-Cutler thought. Lost weight, O'Neill thought. "Colonel Bliss telephoned," he said. "The Committee of Inquiry is scrapped. New tactics for the Bristol Fighter. Close-formation flying and crossfire are out. The machine is now flown offensively. The pilot attacks—"

"That bastard Woolley's behind this, isn't he?"

"Bliss didn't say, sir. He just said your squadron has flown the Biff like a single-seat scout and got good results."

"Bastard. Right! I'll soon get back and sort him out."

"One other thing." O'Neill waited until the C.O. was looking at him. "You are commanded to represent the squadron at a memorial service in

Westminster Abbey for Lieutenant Simon Savage, M.P."

"When?"

"One week from now."

Cleve-Cutler thought hard and remembered what Savage had looked like. Bliss was right, of course. The Corps had its enemies in Government; it must put on a show, make friends, win votes. Savage would be a hero at Westminster Abbey; his C.O. must be there. "What about the battle?" he asked.

O'Neill shrugged. "We're not losing. We're not winning, either."

Cleve-Cutler rapped the table until his knuckles hurt, and he stopped. "On and on and bloody on. It's got so I wouldn't know a victory if I saw one."

* * *

Arras was a brutal slog, in the air and on the ground. Most R.F.C. squadrons were losing at least one pilot a day. At that rate, an entire squadron would be dead and replaced by the end of April. It didn't work out so tidily, because new boys got killed much faster than old sweats. Still, everyone was looking forward to the offensive promised by the French. General Nivelle had a masterplan that would, he promised, deliver *le dernier coup*, smash the Boche Line and end the war. If it also distracted the German Air Force, the R.F.C. would be very grateful.

"Meanwhile," the adjutant told Woolley, "this Arras show is doing a splendid job of bucking-up the French Army, which I'm sure you recall took a bit of a pasting at Verdun."

"That's bollocks," Woolley said. It had been a day of too much flying and too little success, in grimy weather. Now they were in his office, drinking bottled Guinness.

"Absolute bollocks, sir," Brazier agreed. "But the war has reached a stage when nothing less than absolute bollocks will do."

There was a tap on the door and McWatters came in. "You want to see me, sir?"

"Yes. Uncle says this Push will last until Michaelmas. Nobody can fly every day. Cut the cards." Woolley put a pack on his desk. McWatters cut, and showed the six of diamonds. "You win," Woolley said. "Take a day off."

McWatters poked his little finger in his left ear, which was still ringing and whistling two hours after descending from the height of a small Alp. "Orders from Wing are pinned up in the mess," he said.

"I did that. Damn clever, eh?"

"Every fit pilot flies, it says."

Woolley went to a corner of the room. He took an upright chair and walked towards McWatters. "Stand to attention," he said, and swung the chair and hit McWatters behind the knees quite hard. McWatters collapsed, making an oddly high-pitched moan. "You're not fit to fly," Woolley said. "Look at you."

"Yes, sir."

"At Bog Street School you wouldn't get in the girls' beanbag team."

"No, sir. Thank you, sir." McWatters limped out. His legs hurt but his left ear was cured.

"And when will you take a day off?" Brazier asked.

"Bog Street. . ." Woolley straddled the chair. "So named because of the bog. Clever, eh?"

Next morning the rasp of acro-engines woke McWatters early. He lay in bed, only half-awake, and as the engine notes changed in texture, he pictured the warm-up, the taxiing, the take-off. Later, his servant came in with a mug of tea. He meant to get up. Rain pattered on the windows. The next thing he knew a dog was barking, the light was bright, the tea was cold, his watch said eleven. He felt stunned with sleep.

The mess cooked him an early, solitary lunch.

Chlöe Legge-Barrington's letter to Charles Dash gave an address for Nancy Hicks-Potter somewhere near Bruay, a town about twenty miles northwest of Gazeran. McWatters set off in his car and tried to drive northwest. He met a mass of traffic. From the west, columns of troops marched towards the fighting. McWatters got out the map. This route to Bruay ran parallel to the battlefront. The whole damn road would be clogged. He cursed and went back, painfully slowly, until he met the main road from

Arras due west to St-Pol. From St-Pol he could pick up a good road north-east to Bruay. It meant a long, stupid detour, but at least the car would go.

St-Pol was a madhouse. It took him half an hour to get in and longer to get out. Now the map showed two miles to the Bruay turn-off. He followed a convoy of trucks. The Bruay turn-off appeared and it was blocked. Two limbers, parked sideways, sealed the entrance. A sapper sergeant leaned against a wheel and drank tea from an old bully-beef tin.

"What's the trouble, sergeant?"

"Wagon up ahead's caught fire."

"No reason to close the road, is it? *Sergeant?*" This time McWatters leaned on the rank just enough to make the man put the tea away.

"It's an ammunition wagon, sir."

McWatters checked his watch: 2.35 p.m. The world was full of idiots and they were all wasting time, wasting his day. He raged silently. "It's essential I get to Bruay," he said. "What's the next-best route?"

"Well . . . I wouldn't start from here, sir."

McWatters drove on. The sergeant picked up his tea. "Fuckin' officers," he said comfortably.

It was twenty kilometres to the next town, which was Lillers. McWatters didn't want to go there. Lillers was *north* of Bruay. At every crossroads he tried to turn right, but military policemen stolidly waved him away. He drove to Lillers (another confusion of men and horses and vehicles) and turned east towards Béthune. His backside ached. His stomach grumbled. The car needed petrol. Nancy Hicks-Potter was a bitch. No woman deserved this kind of attention. Then: a stroke of luck. A policeman with brains showed him a shortcut to Bruay. Eleven kilometres. In only forty bumping, halting, grinding minutes he was there, and she was not.

The address he'd got from the letter was an old sugar beet factory, now used to store medical supplies. "All the F.A.N.Y. girls have moved forward," a sombre Medical Corps captain said. "Gone to a new casualty clearing station at Bouvigny. You can come with me, if you want. You'll certainly never find it on your own."

McWatters sat beside him in a truck that shuddered and jolted over corrugated roads. The daylight faded and died. "Is this an official visit?" the captain asked.

"Sort of. I'm sort of . . . offering my services."

"Bully for you, lad." There was no encouragement in his voice.

Bouvigny was nothing: just a name for a village in ruins. The truck joined a line of ambulances whose dimmed headlights showed a cluster of Nissen huts.

"Busy," McWatters said.

"Busier inside."

The truck stopped and McWatters got out. "Thanks for your help."

"It was nothing. I shan't stay. As soon as we've unloaded, I'm off."

McWatters watched stretcher-bearers take wounded through a curtained doorway. The procession never stopped. Some of the men were crying out in pain. The stretcher-bearers walked with the long, patient stride of ploughmen. After a while McWatters joined them, not because he wanted to but because he could see no alternative.

The hut was big and bright and almost entirely taken up with heavy wooden tables. He went at once to a corner, so as to be out of the way.

The flow of casualties was fast and efficient. As one stretcher was lifted from a table, another was slid onto it. A doctor, perhaps two, made a rapid examination. Twenty seconds was typical; a minute was a long time. Then the bearers lifted the stretcher and moved away and another replaced it. The tables were never empty. The slick routine fascinated McWatters.

"Your first visit to a C.C.S.?" said the captain. "This is triage." He had the dull-eyed expression of a millowner watching his machinery in action. "You've heard of triage?"

"Um . . . no."

"French word. Dividing into three. Anyone strong enough for the journey is sent on to hospital immediately. That's one decision. Anyone not strong enough but worth the chance of surgery here goes straight into surgery. That's the second decision. No time for debate. Triage needs speed."

"Division into three, you said."

"Yes. Must I define the third category?"

"You mean they are . . ."

The captain pointed to an exit at the far right. "That leads to what we privately call the Moribund Ward. No visitor should leave without seeing it."

McWatters made his way between the tables, trying to look calm and official, trying not to look at the butchery being exposed on either side. His courage ran out when he reached the entrance to the Moribund Ward. He stopped and wiped his nose, checked his watch, wiped his nose again. And then, thank God, a F.A.N.Y. nurse came out of the ward, carrying two buckets of bloody water.

"I say! Let me take those for you," he said. Without a word she put them down. He picked them up and followed her through a different hut, into the night. She pointed, and he dumped the water into a pit. She pointed again, and he filled the buckets from a standpipe. While they were filling, he cleared his throat and said, "I don't suppose you happen to know Nancy Hicks-Potter, by any chance?"

She nodded. He carried the buckets back. The metal handles were thin and cut into his fingers. He spilt water onto his shoes and breeches. By the time they reached the ward he was gasping. "Wait here," she said, and took the buckets. Her face was punished by fatigue.

After ten minutes, another nurse came out, hunched as if against a cold wind. "I'm Nancy. Who are you?"

"Jack McWatters. Charlie Dash was my best friend. He made me promise to look you up if . . ."

She was shaking her head. "Don't know any Charlie Dash."

"Well . . . you met him at that nunnery near Beauquesne." She yawned. "You got along jolly well," he said.

"Not me. Can you carry buckets?"

"Of course. Dash had lots of freckles. He—"

"No. Don't remember. Come on, there's work to do."

For an hour, McWatters carried water to and from the Moribund Ward. It was softly lit and quiet; almost soothing. New patients were carried in, the nurses washed them and comforted them and eased their pain with generous doses of morphine. If a man felt hungry or thirsty, a nurse was swiftly at his side with food or drink. If he was distressed, she held his hand and talked or listened. But most of the dying had already slipped into sleep. Blankets hid their wounds. Occasionally a man cried out, and mumbled, and was silent. McWatters was reminded of his school dormitory, where sometimes dreams disturbed the sleep of homesick boys. Then he saw a stretcher being quietly taken out by the far door. The Moribund Ward appalled him. He was glad to wrap a torn handkerchief around his palms and escape with his slopping, bloody buckets. At the end of an hour he did not come back.

He was bone-tired and ravenous. He hung about until the sombre captain turned up with another truckload of medical supplies. "Seen enough?" he asked. McWatters nodded. "Not everybody's cup of tea, is it?" the captain said.

They went back to Bruay. McWatters ate half a sandwich. He could still taste the smell of the ward. He found petrol for his car. He got lost three times and drove into Gazeran at one in the morning.

The day had been a painful failure. He could cross off Nancy Hicks-Potter. That left Edith Reynolds. No thanks. He didn't care if he never met her, or any other nurse.

He went to bed, and woke up in a prison of blackness, feeling desperately sweaty and afraid. He went out into the cool night air, and promptly vomited the half-sandwich. That made his day complete. There was nothing left to lose.

* * *

Spud Ogilvy got his voice back. His wits, however, were another matter.

Cleve-Cutler took the train to Harrogate. Ogilvy was in a huge white hotel, taken over by the War Office for the treatment of officers suffering shell-shock.

"Which is what, exactly?" Cleve-Cutler asked a Dr Wallace.

Wallace took out a rubber band and stretched it. The band was strong, and it stretched a long way, but eventually it snapped. "I could tie the ends together, but it will never be the same," he said.

Cleve-Cutler looked at the remains of the experiment. "And that's the best you can do."

"We're talking about the best that Ogilvy could do. Were you there?"

"No, but I've read the report. He went on patrol. Had a bit of a scrap, nothing special, everyone got back. Lost his voice and went to bed. Sounds to me like laryngitis. Or a dose of 'flu."

"He has no infectious or contagious disease. Physically he's quite sound. Even his voice is almost back to normal."

"So how d'you know there's anything wrong?"

"Sudden noises frighten him."

"*Noises?* What rot! He's a fire-eater! Likes nothing better than sending a Hun to Kingdom Come with a loud bang!"

"Nevertheless, sudden noises frighten him."

"You've had your leg pulled, old son."

"You'd better see him," Dr Wallace said.

Ogilvy had a comfortable bedroom on the fourth floor. There was a fine view of a wide lawn. He was sitting on the bed, barefoot, cross-legged like a tailor. He was wearing grey flannel trousers and a heavy white sweater. His eyes were hidden behind a pair of aviator's dark glasses.

"You're looking well, Spud," Cleve-Cutler said. Dr Wallace sat in a chair in a corner.

Ogilvy took a long time to answer. "Not looking *well*," he said. "Been looking *hard*. Can't see the adjutant anywhere."

"That's not surprising."

"Of course it's not. Uncle's got very poor eyesight."

"Really? I hadn't noticed."

"Well, you wouldn't, would you? He's lost his glasses. You can't expect to see him from here when he's lost his glasses." Ogilvy's voice was quiet but firm. "It's a ridiculous idea."

Cleve-Cutler tried a different tack. "This place is awfully posh. Sure you can afford it?"

Ogilvy thought about that. "It's awfully kind of you," he said at last, "but I couldn't possibly accept a loan. Not in the circumstances."

"And what are they?"

"That depends. How much do you need?"

Cleve-Cutler lost patience. "Alright, Spud. That's enough flimflam. What I need is a good flight commander."

Again, Ogilvy gave the matter some thought. "That's because you keep losing them. You lost the last one, didn't you? Otherwise you wouldn't be here, looking for another."

"Has it occurred to you that you're letting down the rest of the squadron?"

"No," the doctor said. "Stop that."

"You lost them, too," Ogilvy said. "Time you got some new glasses. Get some for Uncle while you're at it."

Cleve-Cutler looked around, and nodded. "Very comfortable. *Very* comfortable." He went to the door. "After you, doctor." Wallace went out. As Cleve-Cutler followed him, he slammed the door as hard as he could. "Sorry," he said. "It slipped."

"Imbecile," Wallace said.

They went back in. Ogilvy was sprawling on the floor, propped up by his left arm. Blood was welling out of his lower lip and dribbling eagerly down his chin. The aviator glasses had gone; his eyes were almost shut. The left arm wobbled and gave way, and he collapsed. Wallace ran to the door and shouted; then ran back. "Get out of here," he said.

"He bit his tongue, that's all," Cleve-Cutler said. "Looks worse than it is."

A nurse and a doctor arrived in a hurry. "Throw this idiot out!" Wallace said.

"Worse things happen in France every minute," Cleve-Cutler said, as he backed away. "No need for all this melodrama." He was briefly tempted to slam the door; instead he kicked it as he left.

He went downstairs. All the men he saw looked perfectly fit. The nurses were pretty. This was a jolly place to sit out the war. He strolled past a

Guards captain who wore an eyepatch. "Beats Arras," Cleve-Cutler said cheerfully.

"Harris? How d'you do. Brocklehurst." They shook hands. "You got out too, did you?" He didn't wait for an answer. "Bloody liar. Nobody else got out. Just me. The rest are hanging on the old barbed wire."

Cleve-Cutler walked away.

"Bloody liar," Brocklehurst said softly. "All bloody liars."

Cleve-Cutler sat in what had been the hotel lobby. There was obviously nothing to be gained by staying, but he wasn't going to give that quack the satisfaction of thinking he had run away. After about half an hour, Wallace came down. "I put six stitches in his lower lip," he said. "You deserve the same for your stupidity."

"Every man would run away if he could. I want Ogilvy back. He's physically fit: you said so. He's malingering. The battle starts and he gets a sore throat: how convenient! I'll tell you something, doctor. You're treating the wrong end of the patient. A kick up the arse is what he needs." He stopped because Wallace had done an extraordinary thing. He had reached for Cleve-Cutler's wrist and was feeling his pulse.

After about fifteen seconds, Wallace let go. "You're standing still, major, but your heart is racing. Why is that?" Cleve-Cutler picked up his greatcoat. "I'm confident Captain Ogilvy will recover," Wallace said. "If *you* were my patient, I should be far less certain." But Cleve-Cutler was striding away.

* * *

Maddegan kept the replacements flying, and in much less than a week each man had done twenty hours solo in Pups.

"Plenty," Bliss said. "Ye gods! It's generous." He was on the telephone to Woolley. "We gave your squadron special treatment after you made a nonsense of those Biffs. That's history. Now that you're up to strength, I want every machine on patrol."

"Those replacements aren't ready, sir. They can fly but—"

"Listen to me, captain. The battle is in command now. Not me, not

Trenchard, not General Allenby whose Push this is. And the battle wants all your pilots *now*, ready or not. Clear?"

It was 6 a.m. The snow had blown away, but there was rain about. Woolley went back to the mess and told McWatters he was acting leader of "C" Flight. "You've got two new boys," he said. "If you lose them they'll be charged to your mess bill. You," he said to a replacement called Pask, "can you piss without splashing your boots?" Pask was too startled to speak. "No?" Woolley said. "You must be a bloody awful shot. Stick close to me. Do what I do. Are you a hero?"

Pask thought fast, and took a chance. "No, sir."

"Good. Heroes die young. I want you back here alive."

Woolley led a four-Pup patrol. He took them high over the battlefront, never below nine thousand feet, often as high as fourteen thousand, screened from Archie by tattered layers of raincloud. For two hours they wandered about, always changing height and direction, always getting jostled by the wind. Twice they fell into a steep dive; the second time there was gunfire. As they flew back to Gazeran they met a black squall that tossed them and soaked them. Pask was an unusually fit young man: he boxed and swam and played rugby and climbed mountains. When he landed he was so tired that his fitter had to help him take off his sodden sheepskin jacket.

He plodded over to the flight hut. The others were already there, getting out of their flying kit. From their conversation, he gathered that some Halberstadts had stalked them but a bunch of Camels drove the Huns away. Later, the Pups had dived on some Pfalz scouts, but these vanished into cloud. He hadn't seen these Huns either; he'd thought the Pups were testing their guns. He had done nothing but watch Woolley, while friends and enemies flew and fought around them.

As they walked to the mess, he fell in alongside Andrei. "How can you see anything up there?" he asked. "It's all so grey and empty."

"Fear helps," Andrei said. If Pask had poor eyesight, then nothing anyone said would save him. Besides, Andrei was hungry for his second breakfast.

* * *

Cleve-Cutler stayed in Scarborough overnight and got the train back to London: a slow journey, bedevilled by signalling faults and locomotive breakdowns. The air in London smelt of sulphurous coal and horse-dung, as usual. He went to the War Office, in case there were any fresh orders for him. Nothing.

"I've seen the newspapers," he said, "but they're all bullshit." That raised some eyebrows. "An Australian expression," he said. "We find it increasingly useful."

"Vivid, certainly."

"What's really happening at Arras? What's the weather like?"

"Bitter."

"And the fighting?"

"Bitter, also."

He went to the hotel. Taggart looked at him. "I said you wouldn't like Harrogate. Full of whores, conchies and doctors. There was a bloke here to see you. Name of Littleton. Littlejohn. Smallpiece. Something like that."

"Means nothing. Leave a card?"

"No. She's upstairs."

Cleve-Cutler went up, thinking how rotten it would be to go through life with the name Smallpiece. There had been a man in his regiment called Crapper. And another called Fluck. Always in trouble, Fluck. Perhaps people lived down to their names. Might explain Blanchflower. He turned a corner, and there was Tommy Blanchflower with a sponge-bag in one hand and a towel over his shoulder and a smile on his face. The smile had been there before they met.

"How was Harrogate?"

"Bloody. How was London?"

"We went to a first night. New comedy, terribly funny. And we're just back from Hammersmith."

"Not terribly funny."

"No, but Dorothy's awfully good at cheering them up." He made the sponge-bag spin on its string, and watched it spin back the opposite way. "Especially the ones without legs. But then, she knows what it's like to be shot. Even better than you do, probably."

Cleve-Cutler felt a surge of temper and forced himself to be calm. "What exactly do you mean by that?"

"You mean she's never told you? Well, well." Tommy didn't actually smirk, but his smile was dangerously near it. "How strange. It was a shooting accident, in Scotland. Her father was shooting deer. Dorothy was ten. He was helping her cross a stream when he stumbled, the gun went off, she was hit in the leg. Complications set in, the leg had to come off. He's never forgiven himself, of course."

"Of course. Look here: you really must go back to your regiment, you know. It's your only hope." Already Tommy was shaking his head. "They'll catch you," Cleve-Cutler said. "And some military bloody policeman will stumble and his gun will go off."

"So it's just a choice of bullets, then, isn't it? German or British." Somebody was coming upstairs. Tommy went into the bathroom. The lock clicked.

Cleve-Cutler went to his room, not knowing what to think or how to feel. Maybe she had lied to the boy. Anyway, who cared? But if it made no difference, why was he bracing himself to challenge her? But when he opened the door the room was dark. She was asleep.

He sat on an upright chair and listened to her slow, soft breathing. Cock-ups everywhere, he thought. I come to London for an inquiry that's cancelled. I go to Harrogate and Spud talks through his arse. The service in the Abbey will be bullshit. Christ alone knows what's going wrong in France, but my squadron's taking a caning, you can bet on that. And I'm in Taggart's hotel, sitting in the dark, waiting for what?

He got up and undressed, not loudly but not quietly, and got into bed. He hadn't realized how stiff he was until he relaxed. The bed was wonderfully welcoming. He thought he could smell roses, or maybe primroses, or daffodils; flowers were not his strong suit. It didn't matter. He was soon asleep.

The bastards weren't going to catch him. He kicked and punched and bawled his way out of what he knew was obviously a nightmare even while it was happening, but that didn't mean the bastards wouldn't harm you unless you escaped, until finally he got jolted into consciousness by some punches in the ribs. Real punches that caused real pain. "Kick me again," she said, "and I'll put my knee where it hurts."

"Oh . . ." His mouth was dry, his lungs were chasing air. "Bad dream. Sorry." He got up and found a towel and dried his face and head. He sat on the bed and waited for his body and brain to calm down. Her hand touched his. A finger tickled his palm. "Nothing's gone right lately," he said. "I don't suppose you'd—"

"Yes."

"That's awfully decent—"

"Yes."

"You really are the most—"

"Yes."

After that, there was nothing more to be said. As usual, at the beginning he felt gentle and kind, and at the end he was swamped by a rush of lust that left him feeling slightly betrayed because he'd hoped for a sweeter and more lasting pleasure. There was never enough: that was the trouble with sex. An hour later, when his courage had returned, he mentioned this. "That's God's little joke," she said. "He had to spoil everything."

* * *

Seen from eighteen thousand feet, the Halberstadt looked like a moth in a ballroom.

Paxton, flying a Biff, had been watching the Halberstadt for ten minutes. It was a mile below him and he was up-sun, which made him virtually transparent unless the enemy had eyes of iron. He circled and watched the Halberstadt cruise around. It was so tiny that a speck of oil on his goggles covered it.

Midday. He was hungry. He cracked a slab of chocolate against the rim of the cockpit. He turned his head and shouted, "Chocko!" and his gunner,

Griffiths, reached for a chunk. The air was Arctic, so the chocolate was like stone; but it tasted good.

Paxton was high in the sky because a gloomy lull had settled on the battlefield. He could have gone trench-strafing. No thanks. That was good sport during a noisy battle, when the Hun infantry kept their heads down; but not now.

At this height the sky was a bowl of shimmering blue. Actually the blue was rock-solid and any shimmering was taking place inside Paxton's eyeballs, which complained about being shunted three miles high and made to look into a glare like an open furnace. Paxton and Griffiths constantly checked the sun. Maybe one of the new high-flying Albatroses was hiding up there. The risk made the chocolate taste all the better.

Still the Halberstadt cruised about. Hunting for bunnies, no doubt.

In the end, the weather took a hand. A sea of cloud blew in from the west. When its fringes covered the Halberstadt, Paxton drove the Biff down into the muck and gambled. He throttled back and heard the wind howling in the wires and waited for the gloom to become light, and when it did he levelled out and broke cloud. Griffiths' elbow dug him in the ribs. "Left and down!" he shouted. The enemy was a thousand feet below, flying away. A two-seater. That made life more difficult. Paxton eased the Biff up into the cloud.

For the next seven or eight minutes he stalked the Halberstadt. Most of the time he was in or behind cloud, edging closer, drifting downwards, always trying to second-guess the other pilot's move, until he suddenly broke cover and there it was, dead ahead and slightly above, looking as pretty as a fat pheasant. Paxton whooped and nudged the throttle open and saw this bird spread its wings in his gunsight and he fired.

The usual boyish stammer from the Vickers, the usual faint whiff of cordite. The Halberstadt jumped aside as if kicked. Paxton banked to give Griffiths a wide view. The Lewis made an angry chatter that went on until the drum was empty. Griffiths had a new drum on in a flash, but the Hun was swallowed by a cloud. Paxton plunged in after it. Hopeless. Came out and got thoroughly Archied. Went home.

"This is a damnfool way to live," Cleve-Cutler said. "All this skulking about in hotels."

"I like it," Dorothy said. They were in their bedroom; she had bought a small gramophone and she was sorting out a box of records belonging to Taggart. "What's wrong with it?"

"It's so damned . . . what's the word? Hand-to-mouth."

"That's three words. I'm not complaining. Just counting."

He sat sideways in an armchair, legs dangling, and watched her read each label and then dust the record with a silk handkerchief. He thought she was the most delicate creature he had ever seen. "You can't call this *home*," he said.

"Good God, no. Home was frightful. I never want to live in a place like that. This is perfect."

"Suppose we got married."

She turned her head and gave him a cool, appraising glance as if he had suggested rearranging the furniture.

"Well, suppose we did," he said.

"You would hate it. You'd hate me. You'd want to live in a house, with a maid and a cook, and neighbours. I don't want any of that. I like hotels. I like hiding."

"Yes, you do. You like telling fibs, too." He hadn't planned to say that. It just slipped out.

"You can't stop now." She was amused.

"Your leg. You told me it was an accident with a pony-trap when you were six and living in Berkshire. Then you told the boy deserter it was a shooting accident in Scotland when you were ten. So which was it?"

"Neither. I was deformed at birth. Very dreary explanation. So I invented something more colourful. More entertaining."

He suspected she was mocking him, and he resented it. "Peculiar way to entertain people," he said.

"I did it to entertain *myself*, you booby. It's no fun growing up a cripple."

"Oh." Cleve-Cutler felt obscurely that he was in the wrong, but he was damned if he would apologize when she was the one who had lied. So he counter-attacked. "Maybe you'd better tell me all your other entertaining fibs," he said. "Then I'll know where we stand. Let's take little Tommy. Did you really find him on Waterloo station?"

"No. Met him at the tea-dance at Malplackett House. Same as you."

"And did he really sleep on your couch?"

"Yes. For a couple of nights."

"And then?"

"Oh, we shared the same bed. And we thoroughly enjoyed ourselves in it." Cleve-Cutler was silent. "Guess what I've found," she said. "'Poor Butterfly'. Shall I play it?"

"Why ask me? You'll do what you like anyway."

"Self-pity?" she said. "I expected better of you, Hugh." She put on the record.

Poor butterfly . . .
'Neath the blossoms waiting,
Poor butterfly . . .
For she loved him so.
The moments pass into hours,
The hours pass into years,
And as she smiles through her tears
She murmurs low . . .

There was a knock on the door. Cleve-Cutler heaved himself out of the chair and went and opened it. The boot-boy, a skinny fourteen-year-old, stood holding a brass tray on which there was a visiting card. "Waitin' downstairs," the boy said.

Cleve-Cutler took the card to the middle of the room, where the light was better. "Captain Ralph Lightfoot. Assistant provost-marshal."

"Sounds vaguely . . . religious."

"Far from it. The A.P.M. is the army's Scotland Yard. Law and order, crime and punishment. I'd better see what he wants."

He was in his stockinged feet. He slipped his shoes on and knelt to tie the laces, and therefore did not see Dorothy swiftly unstrap her artificial leg. She clipped him on the side of the head: a glancing blow that broke the skin and knocked him to the floor. He felt it as a burst of roaring white heat that receded as everything receded into blackness.

The artificial leg went back on as fast as it came off; she had done it fifty thousand times. The boot-boy watched with his mouth hanging open. The record churned towards its end:

The moon and I know that he'll be faithful,
I know he'll come to me,
By and bye.
But if he don't come back,
Then I'll never sigh or cry.
I just must die . . . Poor butterfly.

She gave the boy a shilling. Two days' wages. That bought his attention. "Tell Taggart he'll be down in ten minutes," she said. The boy ran. She headed along the corridor.

In fact it was fifteen minutes before Cleve-Cutler lurched downstairs, a wet towel held to his head.

"Don't tell me," Taggart said. "You slipped in the bath." This wasn't the first time that loving couples had left bloodstains on his carpet. "Sit here. No brandy. Brandy just makes you throw up." One stained carpet was enough for one night. "I'll send for a doctor. He slipped in the bath," Taggart told Lightfoot. "It's an awfully slippery bath, that one. People are always coming a cropper in it."

"I expect that's why he was wearing his shoes," Lightfoot said; but Taggart had gone and Cleve-Cutler wasn't listening.

The doctor came and put two stitches in his head and took a guinea and left.

"My apologies," Cleve-Cutler said. "Now then . . . fire away. Not too fast."

"Yes, major. The A.P.M.'s department is carrying out an investigation into a conspiracy to murder a Russian member of your squadron, Duke Nikolai."

"Too late, old chap. The Huns got Nikolai."

"Yes, sir. We realize that. But when the duke died, it seems he controlled a large sum of money, perhaps as much as a million dollars. This cannot now be traced."

"Well, you won't find it here. A *million?* Can't help you."

Lightfoot asked a few more questions, got nowhere and left. Cleve-Cutler climbed the stairs, both hands gripping the banister, his head nodding to the beat of his headache.

Dorothy was packing.

"Did you hit me?" he asked.

"Yes."

He sat in the armchair, carefully, so as not to knock his head against the back. "I withdraw my offer of marriage," he said.

"I wasn't going to let you take Tommy away." She was quite calm. "I don't care what your A.M.P. says or does."

"A.P.M. Get it right."

"He's not going to France, ever. I'm sorry I hurt you. Not sorry I hit you, because—"

"Please." He raised a hand. "Spare me the niceties."

"Anyway . . ." She closed the suitcase. "I only did it to make sure Tommy got a good head-start and they'll never catch him now."

"Fine. He can run slap into a brick wall for all I care, because the A.P.M. doesn't want him. The A.P.M. isn't looking for him. The A.P.M. came here about something totally different."

She leaned on the suitcase and looked at him. "That bandage suits you. It makes you look jolly dashing." It was true: the slant of the bandage matched the surgical twist of his smile. "I can't stay here."

"Stay or go, it makes no odds to me." He was feeling very tired. "Actually, I hope the little bastard does run into a brick wall. Several brick walls . . ."

Taggart sent a man up to get her bags.

The memorial service for Lieutenant Savage M.P. was a great success. Cleve-Cutler's bandaged presence was much appreciated. Dorothy was there, beautiful in black. She waited for him outside the Abbey.

"Back to France?"

"Yes. Back to Hammersmith?"

She nodded. She reached up and smoothed his collar in such a way that her fingers stroked his neck.

"Tell me honestly," he said. "When you said you shared the bed with that boy and . . . and so on and so forth, that was just another of your fibs, wasn't it?"

She raised her veil, and stood on the tiptoe of her one good foot to kiss him on the lips: a daring thing for an unmarried woman to do outside the Abbey in broad daylight. "Oh, yes," she said.

* * *

Every R.F.C. pilot and observer had his private way of coping with the mental stress of killing the enemy, and of living with the violent death of friends. Booze helped; so did witless, rowdy, destructive mess-night parties. The mind had its own way of releasing pressure: nightmares were commonplace. Sergeant Lacey, for all his bland professionalism, was not immune to the death toll. Long ago, he had found a way to deflect the brutal reality and thereby sleep soundly at nights. He assumed that every pilot would soon die. Death was part of his everyday routine.

He asked each new pilot to make a will. "A tedious chore, I agree, sir. But it makes the adjutant happy. A lot of gentlemen regard a will as a talisman, on the grounds that anything the army requires is bound to be superfluous."

When a pilot died, and his effects were collected for forwarding, Lacey put aside the chequebook. He used it to pay the man's mess bill; this made life tidier all round. After that, he only used it provided he knew there were ample funds in the account. And he made three other rules for himself. A cheque must be for a modest amount. It must predate death by at least a week. And it must benefit, not himself, but the squadron. This sometimes involved an oblique transaction. By sending a cheque for a mere ten pounds to a Baptist missionary charity, Lacey could clinch an agreement with a warrant officer at Brigade H.Q. which meant that a sergeant cook with prewar experience at the Ritz would be posted to Hornet Squadron. The warrant officer's mother was a Baptist missionary; Lacey knew he would keep to the bargain. The only question was which chequebook to use? April was a grim month; he was spoiled for choice. He chose D. G. T. Gerrish. Lacey found a signature in Gerrish's file and made a dozen copies before he was satisfied. He wrote the cheque and looked up. The adjutant was watching him.

"Everyone is a soldier, Lacey," Brazier said. "Look at you, fighting your little paper war against the banks."

"Good lord: *symbolism*," Lacey said. "We'll make an artist of you yet, sir."

"The A.P.M. will make mincemeat of you, one day."

"Surely, when everyone is happy and no-one suffers, there can be no crime."

"The army doesn't exist to make everyone happy. Quite the reverse," Brazier said, happily.

When Cleve-Cutler returned to Gazeran, there were many new faces in the mess. He sent for Woolley. "You've had your little moment of glory," he said, "and very expensive it's been. Now get back to your flight and for Christ's sake try not to lose any more men." But it took Cleve-Cutler only a day or two to learn that Hornet Squadron's losses were no greater than the rest of the R.F.C. The battle dragged to an end in mud and blood and misery and failure. By the end of the month, 151 of its machines had been destroyed, and many more had crashed as they struggled to get home. In all, the Corps lost 316 pilots or observers, dead or missing. The R.F.C. called it Bloody April.

This was the small change of carnage. The Allied armies' casualty figure was in the region of two hundred thousand dead and wounded. Unlike the R.F.C., the P.B.I. was not fastidious about counting its losses. What difference did 316 men make, one way or another? At any hour on any day of April 1917, a couple of hundred troops might vanish, drenched in the sudden annihilation of artillery fire. What mattered was the outcome. At Arras the Allies took Vimy Ridge and a few dozen gutted villages and no more. Vimy was a victory. The rest was defeat.

And it failed to distract any German forces from the French offensive a few miles to the south. Here, General Nivelle's troops were killed in such vast numbers, with such mechanical efficiency, that their advance wasn't worthy of the name: just six hundred yards on the first day. Nivelle had promised his attack would be *le dernier coup*, and so it was; but not in the way he intended. Nivelle quietly disappeared.

The Illustrated London News regularly printed maps of the war zones. Maddegan was in the anteroom, looking at a map of the Arras area, when the adjutant came in.

"That tunnel we dug under Arras, Uncle," Maddegan said. "How long did that take to dig?"

"Eighteen months."

"Reckon we'll dig another?"

"Unlikely. Pretty boggy ground ahead."

"Don't fret yourself, Dingbat," McWatters said. "The British Army is not about to tunnel its way to Berlin."

"Still, it was a brave venture," the padre said. "War's a bit like a cricket match, isn't it? You've got to keep changing the bowling if the batsmen get established. Bring on a bit of spin, swap your speed merchants about, toss the ball up occasionally. I've seen many a good bat bowled by a full toss."

"I had a subaltern in my battalion at Second Ypres," Brazier said. "Dotty about cricket."

"Not that I know anything about tunnels," the padre said. "Just a working chaplain, me."

"We had some good parties at Pepriac, didn't we?" Maddegan said. "I liked Pepriac."

"Second Ypres," the adjutant said. "This chap led his platoon over the top with a cricket bat and a bag full of balls. Out in front, clouting the balls into the German Lines! Cool as you like."

"It's all in the follow-through." The padre demonstrated. "Get your follow-through right, and you're halfway home."

"What was your follow-through like, Uncle?" McWatters said. "At Second Ypres, I mean?" But the adjutant was busy winding up the gramophone. "Blaze Away!" was on the turntable. One of his favourites.

EARTHQUAKE STRENGTH 9:

General panic. Conspicuous cracks in ground.

The R.F.C. had made the aerodrome at Gazeran in the autumn of 1914, when the war was young and the fields were stubble. The first adjutant had a passion for wild flowers. To his eyes, the French field was a drab desert. He sent for seeds and bulbs and plants.

Now, nearly three years later, as the warmth of May soaked into the earth, the fringes of the aerodrome began to show bright blue with English bluebells, and orange with Welsh poppies, and yellow with primrose. There were patches of white narcissus and red anemone. Marsh buttercups were springing up as densely as a crop.

Brazier disapproved. "Makes us look like Kew Gardens, sir."

"As long as it doesn't interfere with the flying, Uncle, I don't give a damn."

But something did interfere with the flying: the long grass. After such a wet spring, the sunshine created a lush growth, reaching up to the axles of the Biffs' wheels in places. Add to this a heavy dew, and the field became so slick that a pilot might find himself skidding like a duck landing on a frozen pond.

"Sheep," Woolley said. "About fifty. And a shepherdess. About nineteen."

Lacey was sent to search. Next day a very old man, dressed in rusty black, with a crook as tall as an archbishop, drove a flock of sheep into the camp. His left arm had been shot off in the war with Prussia of 1870.

The adjutant saluted him and gave him a tin of tobacco. *"Mangez les fleurs?"* he suggested, pointing out bluebells and poppies.

"Sale Boche," the man said, and spat.

"I don't quite see the connection."

"*Sale Boche.*" The man spat.

"He's completely deaf, sir," Lacey said. "But very sound politically."

The sheep did a fine job on the grass, clearing first the two main run-ways and then nibbling their way into the rest of the field; but the shepherd never let them near the flowers.

"A truly sensitive soul," McWatters said. It was early evening, and the officers were playing croquet on a well-cropped stretch of runway. "But not half as sensitive as me." McWatters was lining up a shot. "Watch this, Griff. I'm going to smack you into Belgium." His mallet made a sharp crack. The ball fizzed over the turf and was stopped by the rough.

"Just be careful what you do to Belgium," Griffiths said. "You don't want to upset the Hun." He set off for his ball.

"At school I won prizes for sensitivity," McWatters said.

"This silly sheep is eating my ball," Griffiths called.

The padre was umpire. "I think you get a free shot," he said. Griffiths hit the sheep, which bounded away. "Not quite what I meant," the padre said. Woolley strolled towards them, hands in pockets, looking bleak; but he always looked bleak. "The Huns are happy," he said. "Captain Ball's gone."

"Ah," Dando said. He sounded sick. He tossed his mallet at the box it came in. Nobody else spoke. "You wouldn't have said it unless it was definite," Dando said.

"It's definite."

"Well . . . that's an awful shame, so it is."

No more fun and games. They walked to the mess. The sunset became more splendid by the minute, but all the life had gone out of the day.

None of them had met Albert Ball; the man flew with 56 Squadron, and their field was miles away. Yet everyone knew what he looked like: not handsome, but good-looking, clean-shaven, eager, the unlined face of a young man who couldn't wait to fight. In a period when the R.F.C. was often outclassed, Ball made the enemy look second-rate. He never wore a helmet or goggles. He liked the wind in his hair. He tore into any Hun formation, no matter its size. He flew as if he didn't give a damn for anyone, and by the day of his death he had forty-four confirmed kills. He had rattled up his score at an astonishing speed: fast enough to earn him a Military Cross and a Distinguished Service Order, followed by a second D.S.O., and then a third. A Victoria Cross must have been in the offing. And he'd still been only twenty years old.

In Bloody April his mounting score had been a bright light in a gloomy battle. Now it was May, and Ball's luck had run out. Nobody lasted for ever. Still, it came as a shock to lesser men when even the best went west.

* * *

June wasn't altogether a bad month. Not brilliant, but not a blood bath like April. The squadron got a steady supply of Bristol Fighters, the new F2B with its even bigger engine, worth 220 horsepower; until finally all the Pups had been replaced. There was a price. Patrols went on. Six men died. Two were in a Biff that got lost in a fog and flew into a quarry. One was a sentry who saw what he thought might be an unexploded bomb and gave it a kick. The other three were pilots of Pups. Archie got one: a direct hit at twelve thousand feet: a good way to go, if you have to go. A clutch of Fokkers ambushed another and he was a flamer: not a good way to go. And the last, and saddest, was Andrei.

A dozen people were watching Andrei's Pup as it returned from patrol and came sliding down its glidepath towards Gazeran field. That was quite normal. Airmen will always watch any landing. The Pup was only fifty feet up when it toppled slightly to the left. The angle grew steeper, until the Pup fell off its glidepath. The bang panicked the sheep grazing at the edge of the field. An hour later, when the rescue team was shovelling the last bits of smoking wreckage into a truck, the shepherd was still collecting strays.

Cleve-Cutler ordered a squadron party that night. Nobody mentioned Andrei. Everyone played the usual violent games, poured drinks into the piano, smashed the furniture. The pilots and the observers tried to out-sing each other, bawling until they became hoarse and raucous and fought with soda-syphons instead.

Woolley was not there. He had made a token appearance and slipped away. Now he was in his hut, drinking Guinness and playing backgammon with Sergeant Lacey. The dice were not favouring him. Lacey had won six games straight.

They heard a distant cheer, and the tinkle of breaking glass.

"If one knew no better, one would suspect that they were celebrating," Lacey said.

"Well, Andrei's gone and they're still here. That's something to celebrate."

Lacey got a double-six. "The same applied when Captain Ball died, but nobody celebrated survival then, as I recall."

"Ball was different. We're just tradesmen. Ball was an artist. This isn't a war for artists, it's all about machinery. The machine always wins in the end." Woolley threw the dice. Five and two: exactly what he didn't want. "You have a mechanical smell to you tonight, Lacey. And a whiff of brimstone, too. I give up. What do I owe you?"

Lacey consulted a piece of paper. "Eight and a half francs."

"Blood-sucking parasitic louse." He paid.

The adjutant drilled the burial party next morning, and the funeral in the afternoon at Gazeran church was faultless. Volleys were fired over the grave. A Biff flew low overhead and the gunner emptied a bucket of white petals which drifted down like summer snow. A bugler sounded Retreat, then took up a trumpet and played a few bars of Tchaikovsky of such crystal clarity that when the last notes faded to silence, the air itself seemed to have been purified.

The officers chose to walk back to camp. Cleve-Cutler beckoned to Dando. "It was an old Pup, you know. Too many patrols, too many stunts. I expect something broke. A spar, a strut, an aileron."

"Indeed, indeed. Very true."

"Or you get a wasp in the cockpit. The pilot lashes out at it." He performed a panicky piece of flailing. "Over goes the joystick. Before you can say knife . . ."

"Nobody would argue with that, either, major."

"All it takes is a couple of seconds."

"I was watching. A couple of seconds is all it took."

Cleve-Cutler saw a pale blue butterfly on the path, resting its wings, and he stepped over it. "All the same, it's a shabby way to go, isn't it?"

"If I wasn't an agnostic, I'd think God didn't care."

A week later, there was a memorial service in one of the hangars. The padre ran it, brilliantly. He didn't make the mistake of invoking God too much; God was not a safe bet on the Western Front in 1917. He made sure the chaps had familiar, four-square Anglican hymns to sing – "To Be a Pilgrim" and "Onward, Christian Soldiers" and the like – which balanced the presence of a patriarch of the Russian Orthodox church. He was deeply bearded and splendidly robed. It was difficult to associate his massive pomp with little Andrei; but then, it was becoming difficult to remember the dead man's face. Difficult and pointless. Memories were like obsolete aircraft: just so much clutter, to be got rid of quickly.

Also paying their last respects were Captain Lightfoot and Mr Hennessy from the embassy in Paris. Hennessy wore a flannel suit of clerical grey and carried a black bowler. Cleve-Cutler resented the presence of civilians (other than the patriarch) at what was a squadron affair. After the service he said, "You must be the spy that my adjutant told me about."

"If I must be," Hennessy said, "then obviously I am not, and therefore your adjutant is wrong. Am I going too fast for you?"

"Oh, sod it," Cleve-Cutler said. "Come and have tea, both of you".

Mess servants set up deck chairs for them, far from the crowd of pilots and gunners. They served China tea with lemon, and cherry cake, and went away.

"The gang of assassins has been eliminated," Hennessy said.

"Well done. Did they put up much of a fight?"

"They went all to pieces," Lightfoot said.

The C.O. stirred his tea and watched a Biff charge across the turf and come ünstuck and make height like a hawk riding a thermal. Paxton was flying. The C.O. recognized his style. "Brazier said you had pictures of a pair of ruffians."

"*N'existe pas*," Lightfoot said.

"What does exist, somewhere, is the duke's money," Hennessy said. "Ten thousand dollars."

"Not long ago it was a million."

"Duke Nikolai misplaced the decimal point," Lightfoot said. "His arithmetic was fragile."

"Russian dukes have flunkeys to do their sums for them," the C.O. said.

"Still, ten thousand dollars is a tidy amount," Hennessy said. "If it's not in his bank account, where is it? Come to that, where is his chequebook?"

"Maybe he gave everything to Andrei."

"For what possible reason?" Lightfoot asked. "Nikolai didn't know he was going to die."

"Come, now. You mustn't be too sure of that," the C.O. said comfortably. He was on his home ground here. "It happens all the time. More tea?"

"If this money helps put the Tsar back on his throne," Hennessy said, "there will be a ceasefire on the Eastern Front within seven days. And we'll all be in deep trouble."

"Which reminds me, major," Lightfoot said. "The adjutant of 40 Squadron denies receiving two hundred pounds of raspberry jam from this squadron when it was at Pepriac. It would seem, therefore, that you are still in debit to the brigade quartermaster in the amount of two hundred pounds of raspberry jam. The A.P.M. is involved because the jam appears to be missing."

"Nikolai is missing, too," Cleve-Cutler said. "My theory is he took the jam."

"Very droll." Lightfoot collected the last few crumbs from his plate. "Excellent cake, sir."

"We've got a new cook," the C.O. said. "Absolute genius. You should see what he does with pigs' trotters."

* * *

July followed June with neither triumph nor disaster.

Hornet Squadron took a professional interest in the war beyond its patrol lines. Everyone knew that half the French Army had been teetering on the edge of mutiny after Nivelle's monumental cock-up of an attack. That wasn't good. Some reports said five hundred thousand Russians took to the streets in Petrograd – what had happened to Petersburg? – and demanded peace. Other reports said the Bolsheviks in Galicia, wherever that was, had persuaded half the Russian Army not to fight. That wasn't good, either.

Mutiny in the east, mutiny in the west. Who was left to fight the good fight? Why, the dear old battered, bruised and bloodied British Army, which would hold the fort until the Americans could raise an army and build an air force and launch a navy.

So July 1917 was not disastrous, but it was nothing to cheer about. It was midsummer, and summer meant campaigning. The war was costing the British taxpayer seven million pounds a day. For seven million quid a day you expect to get a pretty good show, with plenty of fireworks. What you won't accept is the British Army sitting on its arse, eating its bully-beef sandwiches and singing "Pack up your troubles in your old kit bag and smile, smile, smile". There would have to be another Big Push. The war was turning into one Big Push after another, with precious little to show for them. But maybe the final Big Push would be more of a Last Gasp that saw the only two surviving Allied soldiers killing the very last surviving Hun. It might not be a cheerful prospect, but where was the alternative?

* * *

The adjutant was in the anteroom, drinking his mid-morning coffee and listening to "The British Grenadiers" on the gramophone. He beat time on the sugar bowl with a spoon.

"Not an improvement," Paxton said. He had just eaten a second breakfast, after a D.O.P. of nearly three hours. Now he was deep in a big leather armchair and trying to nap. His sense of balance still remembered the lurch and bounce and sway of the Biff; his ears still buzzed to the thunder of its Rolls-Royce Falcon. Throw in the *tonk-tonk-tonk* of Brazier's spoon, and sleep was impossible. The record marched to its end. "Thank God," Paxton muttered.

A captain with a face as scarred as a chopping-block, and hair that was thin and going grey, came in and looked around.

"O'Neill," the adjutant said. "Well I'm damned." He got up and shook hands.

"I left a few replacements in your office, Uncle," O'Neill said. "Drinking your whisky. Lacey said you wouldn't mind."

"You probably don't know anyone except Paxton. He's the one with the so-called moustache. Try not to hit him. If you break him, you'll have to pay for him." He went out.

Paxton had been silent so far because he was impressed by O'Neill's face. "Somebody broke *you*, didn't they?" he said. "What happened? You look as if you walked through a revolving door going the wrong way."

"There was a bang," O'Neill said. "After that, it was all a bit vague."

He didn't want to discuss it. He'd told his story far too often, to far too many doctors, and now he wasn't sure what was truth and what was half-remembered dreams induced by morphine jabs. O'Neill had not been as lucky as Cleve-Cutler. The doctors were unable to find a jaunty grin in his ruined face. They tidied it up; that was the best they could do.

"We've got Biffs now," Paxton said. "I expect you saw."

"I can't fly. Bust eardrum. Other things."

"Really? Rotten luck." Paxton stretched and yawned. He felt pity for O'Neill, who was now nothing more than a penguin: wings but no flight. His useful life was over. "This is Griffiths, by the way. My gunner. Nearly as good a shot as me. O'Neill used to drive the aeroplane for me, in the old days," he explained. "He was my ghillie."

"Good for him."

"I like to think so. Come on, I'll show you my F2B," Paxton said to O'Neill. "Would you like a flip in the back seat?"

"Not in a thousand years." They went out.

Dando watched them walk away. "Those two used to fight continuously," he said. "Black eyes, bloody noses."

"What were they fighting about?" Griffiths asked.

"They were fighting about the best way to fight."

"Good Lord. Rather like Tweedledum and Tweedledee."

"Similar," Dando said, "but without the brains."

On his way to the orderly room, the adjutant heard the distant sound of fifes and drums, and pictured a battalion on the march. He envied them. The war was marching away from him. He should be at the Front, not shuffling bumf in a stuffy office.

The six replacements all wore the appalling R.F.C. maternity jackets. They looked like chauffeurs. He didn't care what their names were; he had seen them all before; they were forgettable.

"Welcome to this squadron, whose title escapes me at the moment," he said. His tone of voice was affable yet lofty; he liked it and kept it. "I trust you will find the amenities to your liking. If you play croquet, there is croquet to be played. If you prefer lawn tennis, we have a new tennis court. If it is cricket you seek, then look no further. A fine swimming pool exists. Our chefs are superb. After dinner, the squadron orchestra plays. Games of chance add to the entertainment. Life is one long round of gaiety. How is it done? Sergeant Lacey here takes all the credit. I leave you in his hands. I must go now and practise for the squadron ping-pong tournament." He squeezed out a tight smile and went into his office and shut the door.

"May I suggest you make your wills?" Lacey said. "A tedious chore, but it pleases the adjutant if you do." He distributed the forms.

"When do we fly?" Mackenzie asked.

"In the gaps between the gaiety," Lacey said.

* * *

Corps H.Q. restricted all squadron commanders to two patrols a month. This was the logic of accountancy: the less they flew, the longer they would live. Cleve-Cutler couldn't alter R.F.C. policy, but he made sure his two patrols a month were seen to be difficult and dangerous. This was one of them. He was leading "C" Flight along the patrol line Douai-Cambrai, the route where Gerrish and Crabtree and all the rest had gone down.

He flexed his buttocks and spread his legs apart, which made his hand twitch the joystick and the Biff rocked gently. McWatters, on his right, cocked his head, suspecting a signal. Nothing developed, so he looked away. Cleve-Cutler was restless because his left testicle itched abominably. It was stuck to the inside of his thigh by dried sweat, and it was also trapped by some twist in his underwear. Nothing he did would release it. He tried to forget the damn thing, but it would not forget him. It itched. What if the bus broke up? he wondered. There are worse things than an itchy ball. An F2B looked solid but it was only wood and wire and canvas. Bits had fallen off aeroplanes flown by his friends; he had seen it happen, big bits; seen the consequences, too. He checked his altitude. Just over fifteen thousand feet. If a wing crumpled now, how long would it take to spin down? And what would he be thinking as the ground came rushing up?

What else? Collision? The flight was six Biffs in a twin arrowhead formation, one behind and above the other. The C.O. put his experienced men beside him and new boys to the rear. *Follow, look and learn,* he'd told them. They'd all been churning along for fifty minutes, with no sign of Fritz. But he bullied his mind to stay alert. Anything might happen, in the blink of an eye. Someone might sneeze and jerk his throttle and surge forward and try to chew your tail off with his prop. A Hun might drop out of the sun and you'd never see him because you'd be shot through the heart. Or the left testicle. Or the petrol tank under your seat. Better through the heart. Flamers were the stuff of nightmares.

Now Cleve-Cutler was very awake. His mind went on frightening him. Archie was a rotten trick. Somewhere a scruffy Hun gunner might be ramming a shell up an anti-aircraft gun. Twenty-five seconds later you got bits of red-hot Archie whizzing through your kidneys. Decent, hard-working chaps, the kidneys. You didn't get them complaining and demanding to be scratched.

That was when McWatters rocked his wings and pointed. A cluster of dots grew into a bunch of single-seat Fokker scouts, toiling up to do battle. Or perhaps not. The Biffs met them halfway and much ammunition was sprayed about the sky, but the enemy was very wary and kept his distance.

After a few minutes of feints and wide circles and dives and zooms, Cleve-Cutler fired a flare. The flight came together. The Fokkers flew alongside the formation but kept well out of range. One pilot waved.

Cleve-Cutler felt excited and disappointed and tired, all at the same time. This patrol still had more than an hour to go, and he dreaded it; he wanted to go home and land *now*, something that had never happened to him before. The hour trudged by. The flight came upon an untidy scrap between a crowd of Camels and a mixture of Huns, too late to make a difference. The scrap dissolved into nothing, in the baffling way that scraps had. "C" Flight returned to Gazeran and landed. Cleve-Cutler got out and shook his left leg. The itch had gone. He was alive, which was something; yet he was dissatisfied with himself. He felt wrong. His heart was juddering and bucketing like a runaway train.

The adjutant was waiting. "Good news, sir. Six replacements. Three pilots, three observers."

"Give a pair to each flight."

"And Captain O'Neill is our new intelligence officer."

"Have him shot."

"Certainly, sir."

The C.O. had a day bed in his office. He awarded himself some medicinal whisky and went to sleep.

Fifteen minutes later he awoke, sweating and gasping, so convinced that the phone was ringing that he lunged for it. The harsh clamour still vibrated in his head. The room was silent. "Bloody hell and double buggeration in spades," he said. His clerk heard the noise and came in. "Mr Paxton is here, sir." he said.

"Who telephoned?"

"Nobody, sir."

"Change that phone. It's broken."

Paxton was standing in the doorway. "Major," he said. "You've given me Mackenzie. I know him. He's no damn good. I don't want him in my flight."

Cleve-Cutler's mind was emerging from the dungeon of sleep, but his office still seemed foreign. "You'll take what you're given," he growled.

"He's reckless, he's clumsy, he's too short."

"And he's yours. Goodbye."

Paxton stood and stared down. The C.O. squinted up at him. He shoved his head forward, challenging Paxton to challenge him.

The phone rang. "Don't answer that," Paxton told the clerk. "It's broken." He went away.

*   *   *

Later that day, Paxton interviewed Mackenzie alone in the flight office. Bits of German aeroplanes decorated the walls. "Let's get one thing clear," Paxton said. "You're a damned handicap to my flight. I've seen you try to fly and you're like a pregnant duck in a hurricane. I've seen you try to shoot and you couldn't hit the garden with the garden hose."

"That's a Rumpler." Mackenzie pointed to a ravaged tail-fin. "I knocked down one of those." He looked around the room and pointed to a wheel painted with a black cross. "Isn't that off an Aviatik? Got one of them too."

Paxton cupped his hand around his ear.

"Sir," Mackenzie added.

"Somebody has blundered and dropped you in the real war. If you want to do your patriotic duty, fall downstairs and break your neck. I don't want you. Now get out."

Mackenzie went, looking nowhere near as subdued as Paxton had hoped. He opened Mackenzie's file and worked backwards. A week in England, under training on the Bristol Fighter. Before that, a couple of months in France on RE8s, a newish two-seater used for reconnaissance. Before *that*, a few weeks on BE12s, an oldish two-seater with a bad reputation. His C.O. had written: *Tougher than he looks*. No mention of an Aviatik or a Rumpler.

*   *   *

The crews were glad to see O'Neill take over the job of recording their patrols. Uncle knew nothing about fighting in the air; he just wrote down what he thought they'd said. O'Neill had knocked about the sky, and had been knocked-about in return; he had his face and an M.C. to prove it. He knew what questions to ask.

Also he was a new joker in the pack. The squadron was tired of teasing its non-fliers: the doctor, the padre, even (if you had the courage) the adjutant. The new-fangled title of "intelligence officer" made an irresistible target in the mess.

"You know everything, O'Neill," McWatters said. "What about this weather?" A rainstorm was hammering the roof of the mess. All flying was cancelled.

"Passing shower." It had been raining solidly since the previous afternoon. "Lays the dust."

"That's official, is it?" McWatters was standing at a window playing noughts and crosses against himself on the condensation. "You're sure it's not a military secret?"

"I know a military secret," Mackenzie said. He was almost horizontal, sprawled in an armchair; only his legs were visible. He made everyone wait and said, "Damn, it's gone. Bloody good secret, it was, too."

"What about all that thunder, up at Wipers?" Woolley asked. "Is that a secret?" Wipers was what everyone in the British Army called Ypres.

"Thunder is not intelligence," O'Neill said. "Thunder comes under Acts of God."

"Don't ask me," the padre said. "Wipers is forty miles away. Not in my parish."

"Ask the Hun," Paxton said. "I'll bet he knows."

"Ask Mata Hari," McWatters said. "She told the Hun."

"D'you really think so?" Cleve-Cutler said. He looked up from his game of double-patience.

"The court thought so, sir." A few days before, in Paris, a French court martial had found Mata Hari guilty of passing military secrets to German intelligence officers. "That's all that matters, isn't it?"

"Oh, I can't agree there," the padre said.

"I feel sorry for the woman," the C.O. said. "I saw her dance, once, in

Paris. Wasn't wearing much. Quite delightful. Any man there would have walked through fire for her. And now they're going to shoot her."

"But she spied . . ." Paxton said.

"The Huns shot Nurse Cavell two years ago, and she *wasn't* spying," the doctor said. "Wasn't even accused of spying. You don't need much of a reason to shoot people in wartime." He had stomach ache: too much cherry pie for lunch. A doctor in pain never got any sympathy, so he kept it to himself. "Sometimes I think soldiers need a reason *not* to shoot anyone. It doesn't put such a strain on their brain."

"Woman's place is in the home," McWatters said. "Scientific fact."

O'Neill said, "If Mata Hari got anything useful out of a British staff officer, she's a genius. I never have."

"She went to Holland," Paxton insisted. "She met German officers there."

"Well, Holland's neutral," Drinkwater said. Ever since he witnessed the slaughter of the cavalry at Arras, he distrusted any official statement about the war. "I bet it's lousy with German officers. Anyway, she's Dutch."

"Mata Hari?" the doctor said. "Doesn't sound very Dutch to me."

"Stage name," the C.O. said. Dando grunted and went back to the *Irish Times*.

"Now I remember!" Mackenzie said. "My big military secret. The Huns are in Buckingham Palace."

"Nothing's secret in a war like this," Maddegan told them. He had been dozing. The discussion had disturbed his rest. He thought it was rambling and pointless, and he wanted to end it. "Everything's advertised, isn't it? The Hun never attacks us without putting up a hell of a great barrage first! We never attack him without shelling him for a week!"

"I know why she got court-martialled," the C.O. said. "They're embarrassed because she got half the G.H.Q. into bed, and it's easier to shoot her than shoot them. They'll shoot her because she's pretty."

Drinkwater stretched a leg and gave Mackenzie's foot a gentle kick. "What was that rot about Buckingham Palace?"

"Stuffed full of Huns, old chap. You thought you were fighting for King

George of England, didn't you? Not a bit of it. He was born George Saxe-Coburg-Gotha, so we've all been fighting for three bits of the other side. Not to worry – the family's just changed its name to Windsor; where the soup comes from. So that's alright."

"My real name's a military secret," Woolley said, "but I'll give you a clue. It's Cheddar. Stanley Cheddar."

"A word in your ear," Paxton said to Mackenzie.

"Where the cheese comes from," Woolley said.

Paxton took Mackenzie to an empty corner of the mess. "Don't make jokes about the royal family," he ordered. "It's neither clever nor funny. And it's in damn bad taste."

Mackenzie rolled his eyes. "Is there any *good* taste in this war, sir?"

"When in doubt," Paxton said, "shut up." He strode away. Rank had its privileges, and one was always having the last word.

* * *

The rain did not keep Lacey from his work.

He took a truck and drove around northeastern France, stopping at several camps or depots to collect or deliver the luxuries that made life bearable: toilet soap, gramophone needles, Canadian bacon, Indian curry powder, umbrellas, flashlights, fruit, tennis balls, wineglasses, carpet slippers, bicycle pumps. The biggest item he received was a billiard table, which he bought from a squadron about to be transferred to England. He gave them a cheque signed by J. T. N. Osborne, for five guineas. Lieutenant Osborne had inexplicably flown into a small hill at full throttle. Such things happened.

The adjutant was pleased to get a pair of elasticated knee-bandages; the damp weather was causing his joints to ache. He was unusually jovial. "We have a Kipling in our midst," he said. "Or should I say a Longfellow?"

"There will never be another Longfellow," Lacey said. "For which, God be thanked."

Brazier waved the remark away. "That piece of poetry you wrote for the major has turned up trumps. It's been printed in several newspapers. Now the johnnies at Corps H.Q. who deal with the Press want the rest of the poem."

"That's all there is. One verse, no more."

"Come, come, sergeant. Get your muse on parade. It *is* a muse you writer-chaps have, isn't it? Tell it there's a war on."

"Bloody hell," Lacey muttered.

"That's the spirit," Brazier said.

The rain stopped. The squadron flew again, always on Deep Offensive Patrols. It was a gruelling business that tested the nerves and the body, whether or not a patrol led to the whirling confusion of combat with its split-second escapes and sudden killings. Simply to spend a couple of hours in the thin air between ten and twenty thousand feet made the heart and lungs toil, and the neck and the eyes ache from searching. Sometimes the effort might send a few pinpoints of light drifting across the eyeballs; or perhaps that tiny flicker might be an enemy machine briefly catching the sun. Survival hinged on chances like that.

"B" Flight landed after one such patrol. O'Neill was waiting at the flight office. "One short, I see," he said.

"Finlay," Paxton said. "Engine failure. If he's lucky, he's a prisoner-of-war."

"You didn't see what became of him?"

"Too busy. A flock of Fokkers made a nuisance of themselves. You wouldn't believe how bloody cold it was."

"I have a vague recollection."

Paxton took a hot bath; but when he dressed, his hands and feet and ears were still chilled. He was walking to the mess, worrying whether his body was losing its ability to cope with assault by howling, freezing air, when Mackenzie approached.

"I have an idea, sir."

"So do I: whisky-soda and a pipe. Buzz off."

"We could fit twin Lewises to the Biff and double the gunner's firepower."

"Spare me your tactical brainwaves, Mackenzie. What you don't know about air fighting would reach from here to the back of beyond, and I wish you were there. Twin Lewises are too heavy."

"Remember the roller at Coney Garth? If I could handle that, sir, I could handle twin Lewises."

Paxton halted abruptly. "Now you're driving the bus *and* firing twin Lewises. *That's frightfully* clever. You couldn't drop a few bombs, could you? Then we can all stay here and play poker while you win the war."

"My gunner can fly the Biff, sir. I'll take his place."

"You'll go where you're damn well told, you insolent little tick. Now get out of my way before I put my boot up your miserable backside."

There was no more flying that day. The weather was fickle. Noise of the barrage far to the north reached Gazeran as a soft rumble, like a slow train crossing a steel bridge. O'Neill gave a short lecture on the state of the war. Cleve-Cutler attended. O'Neill said the news from the Russian Front was sketchy. The Italians seemed to be holding the Austrians, and the Turks were definitely getting thrown out of Palestine. Peru had broken off diplomatic relations with Germany, O'Neill added, and Brazil was becoming quite shirty with the Kaiser. Brazil, he reminded everyone, was much bigger than Peru.

"Bugger Brazil," someone said. "What about Wipers?"

"Ah, Wipers," O'Neill said. "On the subject of Wipers the best I can do is quote the words of our commanding officer." That got everyone's attention, especially Cleve-Cutler's. "A year ago he said, 'There is going to be a most enormous battle.'" O'Neill sounded like a provincial mayor opening a flower show. "Then he said: 'And the war will be over by Christmas. Which Christmas, God alone knows, and I don't care' . . ." Coarse laughter and shrill whistling silenced him.

"Quite true," the C.O. said. "True of the Somme, and now it will be true of Wipers! You have my solemn word." He looked at them, and they looked back, expecting more. He turned to the doctor. "What *is* my solemn word?"

"Drinks all round," Dando said at once. That got enthusiastic applause and foot-stamping. Only O'Neill remained silent.

The crowd thinned. Some went into Arras for whatever recreation its ruined streets might offer. Others made a poker school. Those with no money played tennis or swam in the pool. Maddegan, Drinkwater and Mackenzie went for a walk.

The countryside around Gazeran had emptied of troops after the Arras show stumbled to an end. Grass had sprung up to hide the rows of circles where bell tents had stood. During April and May, bugle calls had decorated the air, marking each stage of a soldier's daily life. Now the skylarks and the swallows were back in occupation. They had never really gone away; just been briefly silenced by the noisy soldiers. Here and there, a plough horse put its massive weight into turning the heavy soil. Each new furrow had a dull polish. It faded and began to crumble before the posse of crows had finished hunting for food. Sometimes an aeroplane droned overhead. The ploughman never looked up. French farmers ignored the war unless the shells were bursting nearby. Some had even been known to ignore that. Some had paid for their dedication.

The three airmen found a path alongside a small and wandering stream. Dragonflies jumped and sped and hovered, all without apparent effort. Lucky devils, Maddegan thought. "How long do they live?" he asked. Nobody knew. "Not long, I bet," he said.

"There are compensations," Drinkwater said. He pointed to a pair that was coupling while clinging to a reed.

"Desperately uncomfortable-looking," Mackenzie said. "But then, I don't suppose these two have had much practice."

"Have you?" Maddegan asked. Mackenzie simply smiled. The smile made him look even more like a boy in uniform, a mascot rather than a warrior.

They walked on, and talked of life after the war. Now that America was in, the Hun must lose; everyone said so; but nobody was putting money on it, not after the way the Hun had chopped up the P.B.I. and the frogs until they were mincemeat. Maybe Wipers would be different. The artillery could still be heard. Its endless rumble was like a smudge on the horizon. How could an enemy survive such a barrage?

They reached a wooden footbridge, just planks with no guard rails, and sat on it. Drinkwater took off his shoes and socks. His feet touched the water. Sticklebacks came up to nibble his toes, and he remembered a holiday in Scotland when he was ten. "Salmon fishing," he said. "That's the life."

"A pleasant enough pastime," Mackenzie said.

"Got a better idea?" Drinkwater was beginning to be irritated by Mackenzie.

"What matters is *now*. We're here to do the tasks that God has set us. We're here to kill the ugly Hun and fuck the beautiful women."

They were startled into silence. The word was often heard on R.F.C. camps, but usually in anger or blame. It was rare to hear it used in a literal sense.

"And I suppose you're an expert," Drinkwater said.

"Three Huns and five women."

"Fancy that," Maddegan said. "I don't suppose you remember the details."

"Vividly." Mackenzie closed his eyes. "Barbara was about twenty-five, brown eyes—"

"The Huns. I meant the Huns."

"Oh." Mackenzie's eyes opened. "An Aviatik, a Rumpler – both two-seaters – and a Fokker scout, rather old and slow."

"I've been here for months," Drinkwater said. "And all I've got is a share in an Albatros."

"I tell a lie," Mackenzie said. "Barbara had grey eyes. It was Pansy had brown."

"Sounds easy. What's the trick?"

"No trick. There's lots of them about, isn't there? *They* find *me*, usually. They see the wings on the tunic and they think I'm the Angel Gabriel, and they can't wait to get my bags off."

"Drinkwater means the Huns," Maddegan said.

"No, I don't," Drinkwater said.

They walked back to camp.

"All these Barbaras and Pansies," Maddegan said. "You really reckon you're doing God's work, do you?"

"I see it as a reward," Mackenzie said blithely. "I send a Hun to hell and I take a woman to heaven."

"Sounds like bullshit to me."

"Well, God has a place for bullshit, otherwise bulls everywhere would be terribly uncomfortable."

After that, Maddegan was silent. Mackenzie's fancy talk didn't fool him. He knew bullshit when he smelt it.

The anteroom was full and unusually quiet. The gramophone was silent. A crowd was standing around the poker table. Five men were playing. Nobody was joking. Maddegan saw the adjutant and whispered, "What's the score, Uncle?"

"Paxton's playing like a demon. Won a fortune and then lost most of it. Woolley's down, Dando's down, the big lads are up." The big lads were two Canadians, recent replacements. "Never play poker with Canadians," Brazier murmured.

Paxton played the next hand mechanically and he lost. A Canadian won. "That's me out," Woolley said, "and may the lot of you rot in hell, which is somewhere in Canada." He got up, and Mackenzie slid into the empty chair. "If nobody objects?" he said. He was holding a wodge of notes as fat as a sandwich. Paxton looked up, just far enough to see the money. Nobody objected. It was unusual for new boys to play with old sweats unless invited, but there was no rule against it. "Is there a limit?" Mackenzie asked.

"It's dealer's choice," Dando said. "Usually we've been playing a ten-franc maximum raise. But it's dealer's choice."

Play was slick and speedy. Mackenzie bet modestly and lost steadily. When he had to, Paxton moved his hands; otherwise he sat like a statue. Win or lose, he was inscrutable. Usually he lost.

The cards came to Mackenzie. He said, "Dealer's choice. No limit."

Silence. Mackenzie rasped his thumbs against the edge of the pack.

One of the Canadians closed an eye and peered at him with the other. "You sure your daddy would approve that sort of talk?" he asked.

Mackenzie smiled, and dealt. "Twenty francs to play," he said.

"You're just plain *nasty*," the other Canadian said. But everyone chipped into the pot. They picked up their cards, all except Mackenzie. He left his cards lying. "Dealer plays blind," he said. The tension in the room jumped a few degrees.

"We had a Russian used to do that," the doctor said. He was studying his cards. "Is this a hand you've given me, or an old leather glove?" He changed four cards. The Canadians changed two cards and three cards. Paxton, for the first time, looked at Mackenzie. "I'll play these," he said.

Mackenzie bet fifty francs. Dando quit. The Canadians stayed, and raised him fifty. So did Paxton. The watchers were shocked and excited: weeks and months of pay were lying on the table. Mackenzie stayed in, and raised a hundred.

"This ain't poker," one Canadian said, casually.

"Dealer's choice," Dando said.

"No complaints. But it ain't poker." He threw in his cards. So did the other Canadian.

Paxton had been given time to think. He had staked all his money; only a couple of francs were left. "See your hundred, and raise you a hundred," he said. He scribbled an I.O.U. and threw it onto the pot.

"I'll see that, and raise you five hundred," Mackenzie said.

Somebody said: "Christ Almighty." The words were spoken softly and they did not break the tension. A few men shuffled to get a better view of Paxton's face. Everyone knew what he was thinking. Paxton had chosen to play the hand he was dealt, but that didn't mean it was strong. He might be bluffing. He might be holding a load of old rubbish. Or perhaps not. Everyone was thinking the same thing: This man has played all afternoon, won big and then lost big. Now he could win big again, or go down the pan entirely. What would I do? Would I risk five hundred to discover whether Mackenzie's hand is shit or roses?

Paxton squeezed the point of his chin between thumb and forefinger.

He was no longer looking at Mackenzie. "Well, damn it all to hell and back," he said. "It's only money." He quit.

Mackenzie took the pot. The room was suddenly full of noise and movement. Paxton said: "It would be amusing to know . . ." He aimed a finger at Mackenzie's cards, still lying face-down.

"You wouldn't buy them," Mackenzie said, "so I'm not giving them away." He scraped them together and shuffled them into the pack. He looked calm, and slightly remote. He fished the I.O.U. out of the heap of notes. "Double or quits?" he said. That stopped a lot of conversations. Many people turned to look.

"Cut the cards? Sudden death, best of three, or what?"

"No cards. I'll bet you . . ." Mackenzie was toying with the IOU, rolling it around his forefinger. "I'll bet you I can fly a Biff *and* fire its twin Lewises *and* drop a bomb."

It was too absurd to be funny, and nobody laughed:

"And you will do all these things during one flight," Paxton said.

"Yes." Now almost everyone was listening.

"Done."

The poker was over. Mess waiters were bringing in tea and fruit cake. The gramophone was back in action, breaking the tension with ragtime. "I think that's called syncopation," Mackenzie said. "American invention. Jolly clever lot, aren't they?"

* * *

The next day was dull but dry. The entire squadron flew north, to an aerodrome at Poperinghe. This was less than ten miles west of Ypres. The crews noticed the difference as soon as their engines stopped. The Ypres bombardment boomed until the air itself seemed to be humming.

This trip was Cleve-Cutler's idea. Archie and aeroplanes fought a private war. Maybe Hornet Squadron could learn some tricks of the trade from British Archie and use them against the enemy. Wing H.Q. agreed. "Take a squint at Wipers while you're up," they said. "Get to know the landmarks."

Transport took them to the biggest anti-aircraft battery in the Wipers area. They trooped into the officers' mess, which was half a hotel. The other half lay in ruins. Coffee was served. A gunner introduced himself as Major Champion. He had eyebrows that signalled like semaphore flags.

"A good rule of thumb is this," he said. "If you cannot hear the shell explode, it's our mistake. If you *can* hear it explode, that's your mistake. And unless you do something very quickly, it's your funeral." He described all the things a pilot could do to help get himself shot down. Flying just below a bank of white cloud helped the gunners calculate his height. If the first bursts were at all close, then aerobatics greatly improved the chances of the next bursts. "I have seen Huns loop or spin to escape our fire," Champion said. "Looping and spinning is a slow way to travel but a fast way to eternity." He was pleased if one machine in a formation was damaged by shellfire and the others circled the casualty; that made his job much easier. Any machine which kept the same height and course for a minute or more was always a welcome sight, especially below ten thousand feet. He liked a nice tight formation. It made a better target.

"What's different above ten thousand?" Cleve-Cutler asked.

"Weather. Half a gale is enough to shove the shells a hundred yards sideways. Gunners don't want strong winds."

"And what else don't you want?"

Champion sighed. "Sudden changes of altitude. If you chaps go up or down several hundred feet, then we can't change the fuses quickly enough."

"I know the safest place to fly," Mackenzie announced.

Paxton closed his eyes and let his head drop. The C.O. said, "Share the fruits of your wisdom, do."

"Close to the Hun, sir. It's the one place enemy Archie never fires." Half the squadron groaned. "That's my experience, anyway," Mackenzie said.

"Thank you, major," the C.O. said. "Most enlightening."

"It's worth a try, anyway," Mackenzie said.

* * *

The adjutant enjoyed the squadron's absence. He even tolerated Lacey's playing records of Beethoven string quartets. "At least those blighters can keep in step," he said. "Not like that long-haired anarchist friend of yours who started the riot in Paris."

"Stravinsky. It was the audience who rioted."

"Wanted their money back, I expect."

"No, they wanted their childhood back."

Brazier didn't even try to make sense of that. He filled his pipe while he glanced at the paperwork that Lacey had put on his desk. "Well, well. Brigade quartermaster's got his jam back at last. How did you manage that?" Lacey said nothing. Brazier nodded. "Better I don't know . . . Two hundred pounds of raspberry?" He lit the pipe. "I thought it was straw-berry."

"Opinion was divided."

"Divided, was it?" Brazier blew smoke at the flies. They did not panic as they used to. Maybe they were beginning to like the taste. Flies were cleverer than Huns. A million dead Huns was a solid achievement, but flies seemed to thrive on death. "The Q.M. seems to have given up on the cheese."

"He was always more comfortable with jam . . . Some items here require your approval."

Brazier looked at the list. "A squash court?"

"Portable. It's wooden."

"Where in God's name did you find a squash court?"

"All it needs is a foundation. I can get racquets and balls from Harrods."

Healthy exercise, Brazier thought. Who could possibly object? "Approved. What's this? Silk flowers?"

"A genius in Amiens. I challenge you to tell his silk roses from the real flower without touching."

"Where do we put the bally things?"

"On the dining table at guest nights," Lacey suggested. "In patriotic colours."

"Get two bunches. We'll see . . . What's next? *Silk sheets*. Are you mad, Lacey?"

"Silk is very practical. It's warm and hardwearing. This is a cancelled order for a Paris bordello. Those people understand beds and bedding and—"

"No. Definitely no. Whatever next? Eunuchs in the orderly room? Lipstick in the flight huts?"

"Some French pilots wear lipstick," Lacey said. "Very effective against chapped lips, I believe." But he knew that silk sheets were out. Since Mata Hari, the Allied armies were taking no chances.

* * *

During lunch, Major Champion suggested that, unless Cleve-Cutler's lads had to hurry back to Gazeran, they might like to see what use the army made of the excellent photographs taken by the R.F.C.

They drove to a warehouse on the outskirts of Poperinghe. Champion got them through the guard of red-capped Service Police, and led them into a well-lit space as big as a ballroom. Aerial photographs lined the walls. Officers with magnifying glasses studied pictures spread on tables. The place smelt of developing fluid, with a faint aroma of coffee and chicory lingering behind it.

A shirt-sleeved officer introduced himself as Lieutenant-Colonel Kerr-Scott of the Tank Corps. He led them to a large table. Polished brass shell-cases held down the corners of a map. It showed the area of the coming battlefield, with the Ypres Salient in the middle, poking like a blunt arrow-head into enemy territory. "Beyond the Salient it's nearly all farmland," Kerr-Scott said. "A few very small villages – Langemarck and Poelcappelle to the north, Gheluvelt and Becelaere to the south, Zounebeke and Passchendaele to the east. In the piping days of peace, farmers hereabouts got fined heavily if they allowed their dikes and culverts to become clogged. What you are looking at, gentlemen, is a well-drained bog. This map shows how it looked ten days ago, when our bombardment began."

Kerr-Scott moved the shellcases and let the map roll itself up. Beneath was another map, spattered with blue.

"The same area, three days later. Thanks to your comrades performing photo-reconnaissance, we have been able to make a record of the destruction of the drainage system. Every time a shell destroys a drain, it creates a small swamp. Blue indicates swamp."

He moved the shellcases once more and revealed another map. "After five days of bombardment." The spatter of blue had spread and begun to connect up and form larger blue patches.

The next map showed lakes and rivers and blotched streams of blue. "This is the swamp map after seven days of bombardment," he said. Swamp covered so much of the planned battlefield that there were gasps of laughter. "I know," Kerr-Scott said. "But wait. There is more to come. Here is yesterday's swamp map, after ten days of bombardment." There were a few chuckles but they quickly died. The map showed scarcely any dry ground in front of the British Lines. Almost everywhere was blue; almost everywhere was bog. This was the ground the P.B.I. would be expected to take.

"We've also made a raised map, out of plasticine," Kerr-Scott said. "It might give you a better idea of what the area looks like from the air."

The crews strolled over to the raised map. Cleve-Cutler stayed to talk. "I take it our lords and masters know about all this, sir," he said.

"Yes and no. We sent copies of the swamp maps to G.H.Q. Yesterday we received orders to discontinue the practice."

Cleve-Cutler nodded. "A reasonable request. If you discontinue making maps, perhaps the gunners will discontinue making swamps."

"That's a pretty thought. But look here: we mustn't be too hard on G.H.Q. We'd probably do the same, if we were in their shoes."

Cleve-Cutler was startled. "Ignore all *this*, sir? Surely not."

"Yes, we would, old chap. How many rounds have our guns fired, already? Two million?" It wasn't an argument; Kerr-Scott's voice was gentle. "If you shoot off two million shells at the enemy and then you *don't* attack him, he's won a victory, hasn't he? The important thing to remember about G.H.Q.'s battle plans is that they have no reverse gear. Unlike my tanks."

Cleve-Cutler wanted to ask if the tanks would reverse out of the swamp; but he was only a major, and such a question might be tactless; so he said nothing.

"Please thank the pilots who took these photographs, if you have a chance," Kerr-Scott said. "Very brave men."

But the photographs are wasted, Cleve-Cutler thought. "I'll try," he said.

The crews filed out of the warehouse and climbed onto the transport.

"Not quite what I expected," Major Champion said. "Still, food for thought. Eh?"

"Perhaps the rain will hold off," Cleve-Cutler said. "Perhaps the sun will bake the bog and save our bacon."

"It never has yet, so it's certainly overdue."

The squadron flew back to Gazeran.

They took off and landed by flights.

Paxton's was the last flight to land, and Mackenzie was the last in the circuit. This meant that when Paxton touched down, Mackenzie was still half a mile away, three hundred feet up, and edging closer to the Biff in front.

It was flown by Drinkwater. He was a serious young man who always did his cockpit checks twice and who never forgot his first instructor's warning that most accidents happened during take-off or landing. He was scanning the aerodrome, looking for wrecks or ambulances or other obstructions, when something alarmed his peripheral vision, and he glanced left and saw the right wingtips of Mackenzie's Biff overlap his own left wingtips and create a six-inch sandwich.

Drinkwater's instinct was to escape to the right. But any bank or sideslip might cause the machines to touch. The thought frightened Drinkwater and he flew absolutely straight and level. He risked a look at Mackenzie. The man was without helmet or goggles and he was grinning. Now the pairs of wingtips were separated, but only because Mackenzie had let his Biff drift back a little and wander even further to the right. His propeller arc was only eight or ten feet from Drinkwater's wings. Both machines were shaking and bouncing in the combined turbulence. By now Drinkwater was so frightened that he did not think; he just whacked the throttle open and climbed. His mouth was dry and no matter how hard he swallowed, it refused to summon up spit. He looked down. Mackenzie, hair blowing in the wind, waved.

By the time Drinkwater had circled and lost height and lined up another approach, Mackenzie had landed.

Drinkwater got down safely. He spoke briefly with his gunner. They agreed Mackenzie had been insanely stupid; that left nothing more to be said.

When they entered the flight hut Mackenzie was there alone, sitting on the table, swinging his legs. He was obviously waiting for them. Drinkwater hung up his flying gear and gave Mackenzie time to apologize. His gunner busied himself and kept his mouth shut. Mackenzie combed his hair. The gunner got bored. He wanted his tea. He waved a hand and left, briskly.

Still Mackenzie was silent.

"I don't know why you're here," Drinkwater said. "You needn't be afraid that I shall report you to Paxton."

"You poor fish. You're not brave enough to report me to the man in the moon." There was a lot of vigour in Mackenzie's voice, and a little contempt. "You hate taking risks. You shouldn't be flying a fighter. You should be driving a tram."

"Awfully kind of you to care what I do."

"Do? You don't do a damn thing. You play safe. No risks! That'll get you nowhere except the grave. What are they going to say about you? Here lies young Drinkwater . . . um . . . he nearly took a chance once, but then he funked it."

"Look: that idiocy of yours upstairs," Drinkwater said harshly. "I don't care what you do to me, but you nearly killed both our gunners. That's intolerable."

Mackenzie jumped down from the table and strode over to him and punched him in the belly. Drinkwater was winded and sank to his knees, wheezing. "You swine," he whispered.

"Well, you said you didn't care what I did to you."

After a while, Drinkwater staggered to his feet. At once Mackenzie tripped him and he fell on his rump.

"I knew a very nice chap at school who said you should never kick a man when he's down," Mackenzie said. He kicked Drinkwater in the ribs. "Personally, I've always thought it was the best time to kick him." He put his cap on and went out.

*　*　*

The C.O. had got out of his flying kit and was heading for the mess and a cup of Earl Grey, when he saw the adjutant trotting towards him. This was a signal in itself: in Uncle's army, officers never ran, except when playing games or leading an attack. Then the C.O. saw two men in civilian clothes, and he felt a harsh tightening of his chest. Civilians always brought trouble. "If they're from the Paris embassy, I won't see them," he said.

"They're not."

"Russian embassy? Brazilian embassy? *Daily Mail?* It's been a foul day, Uncle. You look after them."

"They're Americans. Bliss said we must be nice to them. He was on the phone. Be charming, he said."

"What do they want?"

"They seem to be looking for the secret of success."

"Should have stayed at home, then. Come on, we'll pour Scotch into them. Perhaps we'll win a goldfish in a jam jar."

The Americans wore dark suits and Homburg hats. They stood near the biggest Buick the C.O. had ever seen. Brazier made the introductions. Mr J. J. Dabinett was tall and thin and cheerful. Mr Henry Klagsburn was stocky, and when he shook hands he looked hard at Cleve-Cutler as if memorizing his face. Both men were clean-shaven and about thirty years old. "How can I help you?" the C.O. said.

"Sir, we're here to sell the war to America," Dabinett said.

"You should have come three years ago. It was brand spanking new then. It's got a bit shop-soiled now, a bit tattered and torn. Been left out in the rain too long." Cleve-Cutler remembered that he was supposed to be frightfully nice. Sod it. Too late now. Like the Yanks.

"That's exactly why we're here, sir," Dabinett said.

He spoke quickly and clearly. A group of Chicago businessmen, all millionaires, were very concerned about the indifference, the apathy of many Americans towards the war in Europe. Enthusiasm was a weapon as important as any gun. So they had sent Dabinett, who was a journalist, and Klagsburn, a cameraman, to make a film about the war to be shown in the U.S. and thus boost morale there. For the past month they had been all over the Western Front, searching for suitable material.

"Seen Verdun?" Cleve-Cutler asked.

"Yes. Impressive but . . . not encouraging."

"The Boche say they had a quarter of a million casualties at Verdun. Same for the French, probably. Only five miles wide, you know. Five miles of battle, half a million dead or wounded, and stalemate."

"We can't find what we're looking for in the French Army, sir."

"Neither can the French Army, Mr Dabinett."

Pessimism made Brazier restless. "I think you'll find the British Army is made of sterner stuff. Listen to those guns. We'll blast the Boche out of Belgium, you'll see."

"We saw," Klagsburn said. "Belgium ain't what you'd call a pretty sight." He had a New York twang that stretched the vowels like chewing gum.

"You don't fly the Camel here, sir?" Dabinett asked.

"No."

"Too bad," Klagsburn said. "Very hot piece of machinery. Small bus, big guns. If Douglas Fairbanks flew a fighter, it would be a Camel. This Bristol Fighter is too big."

"It is not too big," the C.O. said.

"He means too big for the cine-camera, sir."

"Then get a bigger camera," the C.O. growled.

"Oh, sure," Klagsburn said. He walked away.

"I'm sorry, sir." Dabinett was calm. "My colleague has been filming in too many trenches lately. It cramps his style."

Brazier had only once been to the cinema, and its appeal was a mystery to him. "So . . . what are you looking for?" he asked.

"Action," Dabinett said. "We had high hopes of filming your cavalry in action, sir. The folks back home don't see this war going anywhere. If we can show them some movement. . ."

"Who the hell is *that?*" Klagsburn demanded.

"That's Mackenzie," the C.O. said. "He's just a pilot."

Klagsburn pointed, for Dabinett's benefit. "He could be the guy . . . Jesus Christ, what a face. Pray God he hasn't got a hare lip. Get him, get him."

Cleve-Cutler beckoned, and Mackenzie changed direction. "Is he an ace?" Dabinett asked. "Knocked down a few," the C.O. said. Bliss had ordered niceness. "He's a frightfully nice chap," the C.O. said. "Awfully popular."

"Will you look at that face?" Klagsburn said to Dabinett. "That's pure gold."

"He's a bit short."

"I'll stand him on a box. That face . . . They'll love that face in Chicago. Hell, they'll love it in Milwaukee, and Milwaukee's full of krauts. Pure gold."

"These gentlemen are from America," the C.O. said.

"Jolly good," Mackenzie said, and smiled.

"Thank you, God," Klagsburn muttered.

"Would you mind taking your cap off?" Dabinett said. "We'd appreciate it." Klagsburn was walking around Mackenzie, and grunting and nodding. "Perhaps you could ruffle your hair for us?" Dabinett said. Mackenzie did so, and laughed. "Pure gold," Klagsburn said.

Fifty yards away, Drinkwater leaned against the doorway of the flight hut and rubbed his ribs and watched. Maybe he's right, he thought. Maybe I should take more risks. Doesn't do him any harm, does it?

* * *

Lacey found a carbon copy of the original, which he'd used as a bookmark in his *Golden Treasury of English Verse*. He took it to the padre's little chapel. Nobody would interrupt him there. The air was heavy with a religious aroma: linseed, sacred balm of cricket bats. He sat on the stool of a portable organ which he had bought for twelve guineas using Harry Simms's bank account, and he read the lines aloud:

Now God be thanked
From this day to the ending of the world!
Blow, bugle, blow! Was ever . . .

He read the rest in silence. It was awful. It just brayed and clashed and fell over its own feet. He felt ashamed. Surely he could do better than this?

It took an hour, but in the end he was pleased, even proud. He took it to the adjutant, who read it and said: "It's too short."

"Were it longer, it would be too long."

"We'll see about that."

They showed it to the C.O. "It's a bit short," he said.

"Looked at another way, sir," Brazier said, "it's not too long."

"True. Well, let's hear it from the horse's mouth."

Lacey filled his lungs and orated:

Armed with thunder, clad with wings,
Men like eagles hunt their foes.
At home in the heavens, and Heaven's their home.
See! In the sunset their epitaph glows.

"Well, it certainly rhymes. Nobody can say it doesn't," the C.O. said. "You've put 'heaven' twice in the same line."

"That's irony, sir."

"Ah. Well, we can't have too much of that, can we?" He initialled the page. "Send it off, Uncle."

* * *

Steadily the squadron's original F2As were being replaced with F2Bs. The big difference was the engine. The F2B had a Rolls-Royce Falcon III. Its twelve cylinders created such a surge of power – half as much again as the Falcon I – that unwary pilots got a punch in the back if they opened the throttle too fast and too far. The F2B's maximum speed was 123 mph, an improvement of 13 mph. That might not sound much, but if it took a pilot inside the killing range of his guns, it was very useful indeed.

The fitters and riggers had serviced Mackenzie's Biff; now he had to air-test it. He found Paxton in a deck chair outside the mess. Half the squadron was there, idling away the hour before lunch.

"Double or quits, sir," Mackenzie said pleasantly. Paxton looked up. The sun was in his eyes. Mackenzie's face was a blank dark shape. "I'm air-testing my Biff, sir. It's a good time for our double or quits."

"Go to hell." Paxton pulled his cap over his eyes.

"Double or quits it is, then, sir," Mackenzie said.

Ten minutes later, Mackenzie took off. The Biff climbed and turned, and began a shallow dive towards the mess. It levelled out at fifty feet. Something round and red fell from the rear cockpit. A few deck chairs quickly emptied. It turned out to be a football, bouncing hugely and travelling fast.

"That's his bomb," Dando said. "Wasn't there some idiot pilot who used to drop footer balls on Jerry aerodromes?"

"A. C. H. Manton, in 7 Squadron," the padre said. "Opened for Somerset in the summer of '14. I saw him make a century before lunch, on a wicket with more devils in it than you'd find in Revelations."

Mackenzie came back and cruised by, and waved. So did his gunner, a tall young man named Tyndall, who had hair the colour of new straw. They climbed steeply away. The sky soaked up the engine's roar until it was just a buzz.

"Great sportsman, Manton," the padre said.

"We couldn't afford sportsmanship at Bog Street School," Woolley said. "Sometimes we had to take it in turns to cheat."

Mackenzie reached two thousand feet and turned into the wind, which seemed to be fairly steady. At an indicated airspeed of sixty-five miles an hour, the Biff was balanced and happy. It might hit the odd invisible bump or pothole which might make it twitch or wobble. Or it might not. Best not to think of that.

"Ready?" he shouted. He unfastened his seat belt.

"Any time," Tyndall answered. Their cockpits were so close together that when they leaned backwards their shoulders touched. An inch more, and their heads touched.

"Ready, steady, go!" Mackenzie shouted. Still holding the joystick, he raised his feet and hooked them on the front of his cane chair. At the same moment Tyndall stood and turned and swung his right leg out of the aeroplane. Mackenzie shuffled left and used his right hand to drag Tyndall's foot down onto the chair. With Tyndall's body fighting the gale, the Biff bucked and rocked. Mackenzie worked the stick and got the wings level again. "Come on!" he bawled. Tyndall groped for and found the spade grip on the top of the stick. Mackenzie let go of the stick, turned to face the tail and swung his right leg over the side. The airstream blew it on its way and it fell into the rear cockpit. For a long moment both men had a foot in each cockpit and both their bodies were shaken by the rush of air. The Biff resented their antics; it twitched nervously. Mackenzie grabbed the Scarff ring and heaved, and fell into the rear cockpit, head first. When he straightened up and looked out, Tyndall was disappearing into the pilot's seat. At once the Biff stopped complaining.

They let it fly itself while they congratulated themselves on being alive.

Tyndall was a gunner only because he had failed flying training as a pilot. He knew how the controls worked. When he took the Biff across the aerodrome he was careful to stay at least a hundred feet up. Even so, everyone outside the mess could see that Mackenzie was not the pilot. Neither man wore his helmet, and Tyndall's yellow hair was like a flag. What's more, Mackenzie was putting on a show with the twin Lewises, making them spin around the cockpit and aim high and low.

Everyone thought the whole stunt was very clever and very funny; everyone except Paxton.

"You're in Queer Street, aren't you?" O'Neill said to him. "You were broke before and now you've suffered a complex fracture of the wallet. You may never play the violin again."

"It was a cheap, childish trick," Paxton said. "No wonder you were impressed."

"Ask Lacey to lend you the money. He only charges 45 per cent."

"Get out of my way."

"And if you welsh on him, Dingbat breaks your legs."

Paxton did not go in to lunch with the others. He saw the Biff land clumsily at the other end of the field, and taxi towards the waiting mechanics, and he sent a mess servant to tell the crew to meet him in his flight commander's office.

When they came in, he had prepared a list of their offences and he read it out. It contained a lot of reckless endangering and gross irresponsibility and utter disregard and conduct prejudicial to efficiency in war. "Until these charges are heard in court martial, you are grounded," he said. "Now get out."

He went to the mess and ate a quick lunch. Nobody avoided him, but nobody came over and chatted, either. He was aware, from bits of overheard conversation and bursts of laughter, that the squadron had enjoyed Mackenzie's stunt. Go ahead, laugh, he thought. It's not your flight. It's not your responsibility. Wait till it happens to you. Wait till it all goes haywire. Not so funny then. Pulling bodies out of a wreck is no joke. He drank his coffee too fast and burned his mouth.

For the rest of the day he busied himself. Talked to the sergeant-fitters and sergeant-riggers. Looked at all the Biffs. Did an air-test. Informed the adjutant of his recommendation to court-martial. (Brazier asked for a full report.) Watched his gunners fire at the range. Reprimanded a mechanic for not saluting. Decided to have a bath. Walked to his hut, went inside and found a horse jammed in the bedroom door. Its tail swished at the eternal flies. Its rump stuck out like a tethered balloon.

As a flight commander, Paxton had two rooms. O'Neill sat in the other, smoking a corncob pipe.

"What the blue blazes is going on here?" Paxton demanded.

"It's a horse's arse," O'Neill said. "That's an expression the Americans use. London's full of them now. They say 'horse's *ass*'. Terribly genteel."

"Get your demented arse out of my chair, before I kick it out."

O'Neill pointed his pipe at the horse. "Take a good look. That's what you've become."

Paxton was tired, and tired of being lectured in his own rooms by a man who couldn't even fly. A flush of rage created a rush of energy and he tried to kick O'Neill, but O'Neill dodged and Paxton hacked the chair instead. Pain flowered in his foot and he lurched away, cursing.

"You're a horse's arse," O'Neill said. "You gambled and lost more than you could afford, and to a junior officer. Horse's arse! Then you took on a bloody stupid double-or-quits. Horse's arse! Now you've lost again, as everyone saw, and sooner than pay up you'll try to court-martial the fellow. Horse's arse!"

Paxton was red with anger and guilt. "What they did was a gross breach of discipline. I won't tolerate—"

"Gross breach of horseshit! When you were my gunner we didn't behave *properly*. We behaved like a couple of thugs. Air fighting is thuggery. Mackenzie looks like a china doll, but at heart he's a bigger thug than you."

"I had respect for rank. He has no respect."

"Mackenzie's a fart, but he's a brave fart. Don't expect a brave fart to salute a horse's arse. Christ Almighty, what an unholy mix of metaphors." O'Neill went out.

Eventually Paxton climbed in through his bedroom window and persuaded the horse to back out of the hut. Once outside, it deposited an impressive amount of dung. A well-behaved horse. He told a passing airman to take it to the guardroom. He went inside and sat in his chair until dusk fell. Then he switched on the light and wrote his report. And all the time, the Wipers barrage rumbled and groaned, far to the north. It never stopped, day or night.

* * *

Out of the blue, Edith Reynolds wrote to McWatters. Somebody in F.A.N.Y. had told her that he was looking for her.

He replied; they met for dinner at a restaurant in St Pol. She turned out to be stunningly beautiful, in a trim, athletic way. For months, the only women that McWatters had seen had been French, covered in shapeless black, bent double, doing something to sugar beet in a field. Faced with Edith Reynolds he smiled too readily and too much. He knew it, but he couldn't stop. The meal was pleasant and easy. Once she glanced at the wings on his tunic, which was encouraging. By now he had got his smile under control. He ordered coffee and Benedictine.

"I have an ulterior motive for meeting you," she said.

"I say! That sounds thrilling."

"No. Not thrilling." She reached for her Benedictine, and then pushed it away. "A couple of months ago, after the Arras affair, I went to a dance with some other F.A.N.Y. girls. It was at a big R.F.C. aerodrome, in the officers' mess, of course. Lots to eat and drink and a wonderful band to dance to."

McWatters had the unbroken pleasure of examining her face, because she was looking at her hands, palms up, fingers interlaced.

"I fell for a handsome young pilot. Sounds silly, but that's what happened. We danced the first dance and I was in love, deeply."

"Lucky chap." Oh fuck, he thought.

"Well . . . He liked me. I'm not un-pretty. We danced and danced. I'd never been so happy. I wanted to be alone with him because I hated sharing him with anyone, so we took a couple of bottles of champagne and slipped away." That was when she looked up. There was no trace of happiness.

"Slipped away," McWatters said flatly. "I see." He wanted to leave, now.

"We sat under a tree. I should never drink, I love the taste but . . . It's like an anaesthetic. Anyway, that's where I woke up, hours later."

"Under the tree."

"It was three in the morning. I found the guardroom and they got a car to drive me home. Now I'm pregnant."

McWatters was so shocked that he bit his tongue. He stared at her and swallowed warm blood. He was about to say *Are you sure?* but he stopped himself. She was a damned nurse. Of course she was sure. "What an utter rotter," he said.

"He's on your squadron."

"Don't tell me . . . Jesus Christ Almighty . . ." he sucked his damaged tongue. "It's bloody Mackenzie, isn't it?" She nodded. "I'll boot his tiny backside from here to Gretna Green!" he said. Other diners looked at them. "Sorry," he said.

"I don't want to be married to him," she said. "That's the last thing I want. Just . . . just make sure he knows what he's done."

"Yes." He rewarded himself with a long look at her delightful face. "Awfully bad luck." She shrugged, and took a very small sip of Benedictine. He said, "In the circumstances, I expect you've gone off men altogether."

"In the circumstances, yes, I have. But it was kind of you to ask."

* * *

Drinkwater had been captain of squash at school, unbeaten in his final term, so he supervised the erection of the portable squash court. Harrods had sent a dozen racquets and a box of balls. He picked out a racquet with a whippy cane shaft, and he was enjoying himself, playing some cracking drives mixed up with flicked boasts and cross-court lobs, when Mackenzie came in.

"Fancy a knock?" Mackenzie said.

Drinkwater was in whites and tennis shoes. Mackenzie wore red bathing trunks and he was barefoot. Drinkwater nearly said no. But he knew there were splinters in the floor and he saw Mackenzie holding his racquet like a frying pan. Revenge would be sweet. "Shall we warm up?"

"No. I'm ready. You serve."

Drinkwater won the first three points easily. All he had to do was hit deep drives down a side wall and Mackenzie fluffed the return.

"Bad luck."

"Don't worry, I'll soon get the hang of it."

Drinkwater served. He forced Mackenzie to the back wall and he was occupying the dominant position in mid-court, knees bent, poised for the kill, when he got hit on the backside by red-hot shrapnel.

"Sorry," Mackenzie said.

Drinkwater got a hand inside his flannels and rubbed his suffering buttock. "You hit that like a rocket," he said.

"I did get a decent swing at it." Mackenzie came over and pulled the flannels down and exposed a vivid red circle in the white flesh. "No bones broken."

"Didn't you see me?"

"You must have moved. Anyway, that shot would have been good, so it's my service."

Mackenzie hit Drinkwater with the ball twice more in the next three points. Both were full-blooded, painful blows, one to the buttock, one to the back of the thigh. "Try not to obstruct me," Mackenzie said. His next shot was a bullet. It whacked Drinkwater in the small of the back.

"You're doing it deliberately," Drinkwater said. "You're not playing by the rules." He had tears of pain.

"I'm playing by *my* rules," Mackenzie said. "And now I've won."

"Won what? You haven't won the *game*."

"Bugger the game. I want blood." He threw his racquet at Drinkwater and went out, whistling.

* * *

All patrols were cancelled.

"That means Wipers is coming to the boil," Cleve-Cutler said. "Boom wants everyone at full strength for the big day."

Ten minutes later, Colonel Bliss telephoned and asked him to lunch at Wing H.Q. "And bring your flight commanders," he said. "We keep a small mess, so I'm afraid you'll have to take pot luck. Pork pies and lemonade, probably."

Wing was not important enough for a château, but the staff lived in a fortified manor house with a moat and arrowslits. "Thirteenth-century, so I'm told," Bliss said. "Please make allowances for the plumbing. It's not handy if you've got the runs, and it's not comfortable if you haven't, so you might say it falls between two stools." He waited. They looked at him. "Between two stools," he repeated. "It's a joke. I've been working on it for weeks."

"Jolly clever, sir," the C.O. said. "Jolly droll."

"Too late now, Hugh . . . As it's not actually raining, I thought we'd eat outside."

The house faced inward, onto a paved courtyard. One wall supported a sprawling wisteria. Opposite it there was a magnolia almost as tall as the house. Elsewhere honeysuckle and roses were trained to the walls. Sprigs of lavender grew in cracks between the paving stones. The air was heavily patrolled by bees and butterflies.

"Of course you've met our friends from Chicago," Bliss said.

"Boston, really," Dabinett said.

"New York," Klagsburn said.

"I wasn't far out, then . . . Major, you sit next to me."

Cream of cucumber soup was served. Sunlight gleamed on silver cutlery and fine-stemmed glasses and bone china.

"Tell me, Mr Dabinett," Bliss said. "What's going on in the world?"

"Good Lord, sir, I don't know. I'm just a journalist."

"I know," Woolley said confidently. They all looked. "God's turned up in Portugal again. It was in the *Daily Mirror*."

"No religion in the mess, Woolley," Cleve-Cutler said.

"What's religious about it?" Klagsburn asked. "The Virgin Mary appears in a tree in the wilds of Portugal and talks to three raggedy-ass shepherd-kids, every month on the thirteenth prompt, that's not religion, that's a publicity stunt."

"Do we know what was said?" Paxton asked.

"It was all in Portuguese," Woolley said.

"Big mistake," Klagsburn said. "You got a message, you send it Western Union."

After the soup came scallops in cream sauce. "I picked out a white Bordeaux," Bliss said. "You need something to cleanse the palate . . . Isn't it strange to think they're running the Derby tomorrow at *Newmarket?*"

"It's safer there, sir," McWatters said. "The Hun's no sportsman. He can bomb London, so he wouldn't hesitate to bomb Ascot."

"He wouldn't get in without a grey topper," Woolley said. "I tried to bomb the Cheltenham Gold Cup in a brown bowler and they wouldn't give me the time of day."

"What d'you fancy in the Derby, sir?" Cleve-Cutler asked.

"I like Smuggler's Boy," Bliss said. "Intelligent ears. I go by the ears."

Kidneys in sherry sauce were served with duchesse potatoes and a rosé from Anjou. "We'll stay with the rosé to the end," Bliss said. "Very versatile stuff, rosé. Tell me, Mr Klagsburn, as an American, how do you feel about the idea of women getting the vote?"

"Oh, give it to them, for God's sake. Anything to shut them up. They'll take it sooner or later, whether we like it or not."

"Mr Klagsburn has had two wives," Dabinett said. The others looked at Klagsburn with sudden respect.

Lemon syllabub appeared, and more rosé.

"This is your first trip across the Atlantic?" the C.O. said. The Americans nodded. "And what has surprised you most?" he asked.

"The soldiers' height," Dabinett said. "So many are so small."

"Lousy beer," Klagsburn said, and shook his head when they laughed. "Come to New York. Taste some real beer."

A very sharp Cheddar was placed on the table, with pots of coffee and cream on either side. A bottle of brandy was added. The servants disappeared.

"The subject for discussion is Lieutenant Mackenzie," Bliss announced. "Your opinions, please." Nobody was eager to be first. "Come, come, gentlemen," Bliss urged. "Let's hear the pros and cons."

Woolley raised a finger. "Mackenzie's very free with his opinions, sir."

"Is that a pro or a con?"

"Sometimes it is," the C.O. said. "And sometimes it falls between two stools, sir." Bliss enjoyed that.

"Mackenzie's rather too impetuous for my taste, sir," McWatters said.

"He goes looking for trouble."

Dabinett leaned forward. "Isn't that desirable?"

"We encourage the offensive spirit," the C.O. said.

"What about you, Mr Paxton?" Bliss said. "Aren't you his flight commander?"

Paxton cut a sliver of Cheddar and captured it on the point of his knife. "Lacks respect for authority, sir."

"So did Davy Crocket," Klagsburn said. Bliss raised his eyebrows. Dabinett said, "Eminent American, sir. Highly regarded in Chicago."

"These peccadilloes," Bliss said. "Speaking out. Taking risks. Ignoring rules. Properly seen, these are exactly what we want of a fighter pilot! Confident! Flying in the face of danger! Keen as mustard! Now who best fitted that description? Eh? Captain Ball, that's who. Albert Ball, V. C., triple D.S.O. etcetera. Well, I believe we've found a new Captain Ball in Lieutenant Mackenzie. More to the point, so does Boom Trenchard. He's given orders that Mr Dabinett and Mr Klagsburn are to be guests of the mess at Gazeran for as long as they wish, and be given every assistance in making a cinema film of Mackenzie's achievements. I look to you, major, to do all you can to further their efforts."

There was silence while Cleve-Cutler tried to prepare a suitable reply, and failed, and fell back on the truth. "Hell's teeth," he said. "This is that bloody Russian nonsense all over again."

"On the contrary," Bliss said. "Mackenzie is a competent pilot with kills to his name."

"So he says. They're not on his record."

"Purely from lack of witnesses. I believe him."

"He's too short for a Biff, sir," Paxton said. "It's too big for him."

"Then put him in a single-seater! Ye gods! Where's your imagination? Haven't you got a Nieuport left over from those Russkies? Well, get him up in it!"

"Nieuport!" Klagsburn said. "Hey! That's a jazzy little bus."

"I'll do my best, sir," Cleve-Cutler said. "It won't be easy. He may look like an angel, but he behaves like a complete shit."

"You mean the man's a cavalier. Every squadron should have one. Bad for discipline, but good for morale."

"Pure gold," Klagsburn said. In his mind's eye he could see Mackenzie in a dashing little Nieuport, smiling like a younger Douglas Fairbanks.

Five minutes after they left Wing H.Q., Cleve-Cutler stopped the car. They got out and walked into a field, where the driver couldn't hear them.

"I suspected something as soon as I saw those scallops," Cleve-Cutler said. "When the kidneys came out, I knew it. We'd been bought and sold."

"Our goose was cooked," Woolley said.

"I don't believe he's shot down three Huns," Paxton said. "He's a lying little prick."

"Talking of which," McWatters said, "I've learned that he behaved abominably with a F.A.N.Y. nurse. Took advantage while she was intoxicated. Now she's in the club."

"Who else knows?" the C.O. demanded.

"Nobody. Just the girl and me."

"Right! Now listen: that story ends here. It's an official secret. Not to be spoken about."

Paxton cleared his throat. "Perhaps you haven't heard, sir, but I've recommended that Mackenzie be court-martialled."

"What for? Rape? Robbing banks? Wearing ladies' clothes? Come on, surprise me."

"Gross irresponsibility, sir." When the C.O. grunted and looked unimpressed, Paxton said, "And since you've raised the point, sir, I might add that Mackenzie's room-mate, Lieutenant Grant, has asked to be moved to a different hut."

"Mackenzie snores. Correct?"

"No, sir. Grant's complaint is that he is too often stark naked. And rather too friendly. Perhaps 'affectionate' is a better word."

"Grant's a miserable piece of piss," Woolley said. "Shake hands with Grant and he counts his fingers. I've seen him do it."

"Get Grant out of that hut," the C.O. ordered. "No scandal. And no court martial. God Almighty, Pax, you were as much to blame for that cockpit-hopping madness as he was. Anything else?" They had nothing to add. "Mackenzie likes hitting people," the C.O. said. "I'm not completely deaf or blind, I hear things, I see things. He picks on Drinkwater, heaven knows why. And he steals money. Goes into people's rooms and pinches their change."

"Not much of a hero, is he?" McWatters said.

"Don't tell Boom Trenchard," Woolley said.

"I doubt very much that Boom had much to do with this," the C.O. said. "It's Wing's idea. Bliss thinks Mackenzie looks like a hero, and it's up to us to complete the illusion."

They drove back to Gazeran. Cleve-Cutler had nothing more to say until the car pulled up outside the mess. "Mackenzie's buggered-up 'B' Flight quite enough," he said. "I'm switching him to 'A' Flight. I don't expect miracles," he told Woolley, "but for Christ's sake don't damage his pretty face."

"Yes, sir. If I find his hands in my trouser pockets, am I allowed to boot him in the balls?"

"Only if you're wearing the trousers at the time," Cleve-Cutler said, and went away feeling quite pleased with himself.

* * *

Next morning, Woolley walked into "A" Flight hut, carrying a small sack. "In here is the secret of eternal life," he said. He looked at the crews. Most faces were blank.

"Eternity's too late, sir," Mackenzie said. "My diary's full. Let's say Wednesday week."

"No, let's say you're a mouthy little shit who's in love with himself because nobody else is good enough." This was said so smoothly that Mackenzie flushed: a rare sight. "Now listen. I'm going to tell you Woolley's Ten Rules of Air Fighting. Rule One for pilots is never look back at the Hun who's trying to kill you. This sack holds the mortal remains of a Hun whose Fokker I blew to bits last year." Carefully, Woolley took out a calf-length flying boot, very scarred and scorched, and held it upright.

"I crept up behind him, fired, missed. He heard the bullets go by and he turned to see who sent them. This took him three or four seconds. You can fire twenty or thirty rounds in three or four seconds. I certainly did. Blew his head off. It was what he wanted, otherwise why did he give me a second chance? Healthy young Hun, in the prime of life." Woolley turned the boot upside-down and poured out a quart of blood. It hit the floor and splashed brilliantly. The flight jumped to save their boots and breeches.

Woolley tossed the boot into a corner.

"When there's a Hun behind you, and he's kind enough to miss, the last thing you need to know is the colour of his moustache."

He told them to recognize the different sounds of a Spandau and a Vickers. A Spandau made a fast, ripping *kak-kak-kak*. A Vickers made a slower *pop-pop-pop*. A Lewis rattled like a stick on railings. "If you hear *kak-kak-kak* and you can't see the Hun, he's behind you. Look back and you're dead. Turn hard!" That meant a vertical bank, then pull the stick right into the stomach and whack the throttle wide open. "Not Mackenzie, of course. Mackenzie's an angel, he can do what he bloody well likes."

They edged away from the spreading pool of blood.

"Rule Two: check your ammunition. Three: practise clearing gun stoppages. Do it blindfold. Four: get above the enemy. Height is a great ally. Five: don't fool around with deflection shooting if you can get behind him and shoot him up the arse. Six: don't shoot him up the arse if you can hit his head or the engine. Look at Dingbat: shot in the arse, but he got home. Seven: never follow a Hun if he dives out of the fight, even if he looks like easy meat. Let him go. If he's dead you can't kill him. If he's not, he might kill you. Stay with your flight. They need you, and by Christ you certainly need them."

He talked of the need to get close to the enemy. Anything over two hundred yards was a waste of bullets. Under a hundred yards was better. "If you can't see his oil stains," he said, "don't shoot. When you do shoot, fire short bursts." A new boy sees half a chance, bangs off a whole drum of ammunition and hopes for a hit; an old sweat aims straight and uses twenty rounds. "If you're on target, twenty is all you need," he said. "Save the rest. You'll need them later." Often a jumpy young Hun gave himself away by firing too soon and too long. "Concentrate on him," Woolley said. "Make him panic. Doom him."

They liked that. Some even laughed. Woolley saw nothing funny. He went back to Rule Two: always check your ammunition. "One fat bullet jammed up the spout and where are you? Wetting your bags at fifteen thousand feet, that's where. Don't expect the Hun to feel sorry. Any bollocks you may have heard about chivalry between foes is pure bollocks. If you get a gun stoppage and the Hun doesn't try to kill you, it's because he's out of ammunition, not because he's got the milk of human kindness like Mackenzie's got piles." Mackenzie coughed. Woolley glanced sourly at him. "Where I grew up, in Bog Street, we couldn't afford the milk of human kindness," he said. "We had to make do with Château Lafitte '93." Mackenzie shook his head, once. "And lucky to get it," Woolley said. "Alright. That's all."

They left, except Mackenzie, who picked up the boot and sniffed it. "Jolly interesting, sir," he said.

Woolley walked through the blood, already drying and tacky, and leaned against the doorframe. "The major's given you one of the Nieuports."

"Yes."

"Just like Albert Ball."

"That would be awfully nice, sir."

"Awfully nice . . ." Woolley laughed: an unpleasant, nasal sound. "You think what Ball did was nice, do you? How about slitting throats for a living? Is that nice?"

"Um. . ."

"Don't strain your brain, Mackenzie. Air fighting is a craft you have to learn. Mick Mannock is a far better fighter pilot than Ball ever was, and Mannock flew for two months before he got his first Hun. *Two months.* Bloody Richthofen crashed when he soloed. Took him a year to learn his trade. *A year.* Now some fat fart tells these Yankee comedians you'll be the new Albert Ball by the end of the month. That's a lie. Learn your craft!

Learn how to skulk around the sky, sneak up on some poor Hun's blind spot so he never hears the bullet that kills him. Bloody humane, that is, it's the way St Francis of Assisi would have done it, a nice quick Christian act of murder. Then bugger off home fast."

Mackenzie strolled over to the doorway. "Flying and killing," he said. "It's delicious."

Woolley felt that he had been talking to himself. "Delicious," he said.

"Yes, sir. Danger is the most wonderful part. I like being afraid. Fear is delicious. The more I get, the more I want."

"Jesus! See Dando. Get a sedative."

"Not flying is the biggest sedative I know, sir."

Woolley turned and looked at him. Each man was thinking much the same thing: what a bloody awful face to go through life with. "Well, you're probably right," Woolley said. "It's probably all a joke. You think you'll always win because you look like the fairy on the Christmas tree. That's a joke. Now you've got your own Nieuport, which is a little scout for little fairies, so that's a joke. And you're going to win the war in the cinema, so that's a joke."

"Talking of jokes, sir," Mackenzie said, "I honestly think you should drop the one about what you couldn't afford in Bog Street. Nobody's laughing any more."

"It's not a joke," Woolley said, "and I don't give a toss if nobody laughs. Get a bucket of sand and cover up this tomato soup."

* * *

Before noon, "C" Flight was on patrol.

Cleve-Cutler had briefed his flight commanders that the squadron was to keep up a series of Deep Offensive Patrols opposite Arras in order to distract enemy aircraft from Wipers. "Think how our generals would feel if they saw Fokkers poncing about the sky all day," he said. "Well, go and show your knickers to the Hun."

"Ponces don't wear knickers, sir," McWatters said.

"In that case, go knickerless. You'll be an even more terrifying sight."

But "C" Flight returned without having attracted anything except sporadic Archie. "We shot down a balloon," McWatters told O'Neill. "One of ours. Bust its string, I suppose."

"B" Flight took off and was slightly more successful. A pair of Albatros scouts shadowed them, probably hoping that someone would crack a piston and offer an easy target. The Biffs chased a few singleton Huns. If they got near, the Hun put his nose down and vanished: the sensible thing to do. Otherwise, it was a three-hour grind.

"Proves one thing," Cleve-Cutler said. "They're all at Wipers."

When "A" Flight left, just after 6 p.m., the weather was on the change again. Scrubbed blue sky alternated with cloud as scruffy as cotton waste. The Biffs flew through showers that came and went in seconds. Mackenzie's Nieuport tagged along at the rear. He had to work hard to keep up. The Lewis gun on the top wing made his machine look overloaded.

Five miles beyond the Lines, Woolley was at twelve thousand and still climbing. A sprinkling of dots showed up against cloud to the east; at least six, maybe more. Now came the old familiar clenching of the stomach muscles, and then a rush of saliva. What's the point? he wondered. Must ask Dando. He swallowed. Later his mouth would be dry. What good did that do? The body had some bloody silly ways of coping with danger . . . The Biff next to him was waggling its wings. More dots to the south.

Woolley swung the flight into a wide left-hand turn and kept turning and climbing. He had plenty of time: two minutes at least. There was cloud to the west, far below; that could be useful. Of course it was possible that these dots now taking shape were British or French. The Biff circled again and made four hundred feet. The setting sun picked out the first formation and showed purple, green, red and yellow. Hun colours. Seven machines. Woolley made a hand-signal. The flight spread out and each crew tested its guns.

By now the second bunch of dots had grown into four multicoloured Huns. As he watched, they veered left. He guessed they were hoping to get between the sun and his flight, and then attack out of the glare. Or perhaps just hide there, a lurking threat. He looked at the seven Huns. Only a quarter of a mile away. Amazing how rapidly a fight took shape. They were a mixed bunch of different types: probably a scratch flight. Good.

Woolley decided to tackle the four Huns first, maybe scare them off, then . . . Then he saw the Nieuport flying straight at the seven Huns like a child running towards the edge of a cliff. It changed nothing. He led his flight in the opposite direction.

Mackenzie saw none of this.

The moment he broke away he felt the same surge of fear and delight he had known as a boy when his father taught him how to ski by pushing him off the top of a slope. Everything was clean and fast and frightening. The air was too cold, the colours were too bright, and above all he was on his own. Free to terrify himself, to triumph, to be swamped by joy, to break his neck. He was a boy again.

The formation of Huns turned to meet him, but with a closing speed of more than two hundred miles an hour they left it late. Mackenzie picked out a two-seater on the leader's left because it was big and colourful. In the space of a breath it magnified. He glimpsed tracer criss-crossing around the Nieuport and ignored it. He fired both guns and rejoiced at the stabbing flames, leapfrogged the target and dodged through the formation as if it were tethered. Nobody fired at him. He looked back once, and saw an aeroplane spin slowly and spread a cloak of flames.

Three Huns chased him in a long dive to a bank of cloud that swallowed him. He turned left and right in the wet gloom and finally fell out of the other side. The Huns were in the wrong place. Just as well: the Nieuport was vibrating feverishly and strips of canvas were tearing off the left wings. The rudder moved grudgingly, too.

Just before he touched down at Gazeran, the engine quit, which gave cause for a final happy spurt of fear. At the same time, he realized why the Huns hadn't fired at him as he dodged through their formation. They couldn't. They might have hit their own machines. Splendid! That was worth remembering.

The mess was filling up for dinner. Mackenzie swaggered in, tossed his hat to a servant, and climbed onto the piano stool. "Flamer!" he announced, grinning like a bridegroom. "Exit one Hun, burning bright! Lovely flamer!" They applauded. Mackenzie jumped onto the piano keyboard and marched up and down. "Frying tonight!" he shouted.

Dabinett turned to Cleve-Cutler. "What did he say, sir?" he asked.

"Just a joke. It's a sign you see in fish-and-chip shops in England. Means they'll be open for business."

"Ah. So the frying referred to . . ."

"To the kraut," Klagsburn said. "The kraut in the flamer. I'd give a thousand bucks to have got a shot of *that*."

"I can't put 'frying tonight' in the subtitles," Dabinett said.

"You'll think of something. He'll think of something," Klagsburn told the C.O. "We can get away with murder in subtitles. I mean, who the hell knows?"

"'Down with tyranny!'" Dabinett said. "That'll do nicely."

Cleve-Cutler went over and shook Mackenzie's hand. "Well done, lad."

"I'm afraid I rather bent the Nieuport, sir."

"Who cares? We've got another! You're not hurt?" He pointed to a bullet-burn on the sleeve of Mackenzie's flying coat.

"Never felt better." It wasn't true. He felt flat. He wanted to fly again. Now.

* * *

While "A" Flight was up, the squadron's mail arrived. Lacey put Paganini's *Cantabile in D* on the gramophone and brewed some American coffee and started sorting.

From the usual intake he put aside three letters. One was from London, addressed to Major Hugh Cleve-Cutler in green ink with a woman's handwriting. He steamed it open and took out a snapshot of a slim young man at the rails of a ship. He looked very pleased with himself. Behind him was the Statue of Liberty. On the back, also in green ink, was written: *You fly. He fled.* It was initialled *PB*. That was all; no letter. Lacey put it back and re-sealed the envelope.

Next he opened a letter to Captain McWatters. It was from Nurse Edith Reynolds: her name and address were on the back.

Dear Jack,

I'm sorry I wasn't much fun. Still, you know the reason why. It was most awfully kind of you to want to see me again, in the circs. I wasn't very grateful at the time, was I? Too much self-pity! Nanny always said, "You pay for your pleasures" but I'm paying and where was the pleasure? Is it still to come? If you think it might possibly be, then shall we meet again? Soon?

Edith

"Saucy baggage," Lacey said. He replaced it and re-sealed it.

The third letter was from the *Yorkshire Post*. Originally it had been sent to The Minister for War, Whitehall, London, but it had been readdressed many times as it got shuttled from department to department until finally someone had stuck a label on it and sent it to R.F.C. H.Q. From there it had been forwarded to Hornet Squadron, marked *Attention: Adjutant.*

Lacey slit the envelope and took out a page torn from the *Yorkshire Post*, the "In Memoriam" page. Someone had ringed the death in action of a Lieutenant in the Royal Flying Corps. The notice included Lacey's epic verse, *Now God be thanked, From this day to the ending of the world . . .* It was said to be the work of "a brave British airman, somewhere in France".

Two notes were attached. One was from the literary editor:

Brave indeed! Or is plagiarism now a weapon of war?

The other note was a memo from Maurice Baring, Boom Trenchard's private secretary. It said:

Dear Brazier: I rather think you've been rumbled. My advice is, make a clean breast of it and appeal to the chap's sense of humour.

Lacey tore the notes and the newspaper page into little pieces.

"Baring has obviously never been to Yorkshire," he said to Paganini. "Humour has been extinct in Yorkshire since the fifteenth century."

* * *

Woolley told Cleve-Cutler that he had hammered into Mackenzie's skull the need to stay with the flight, learn his trade, wait his chance, do what he was told; and Mackenzie had rushed at the first Hun he saw like a dog after seven bitches. "I can't lead my flight with a loony in it, sir."

"Loony . . . That's a bit strong. He did get a Hun."

"Anyone can get a Hun. I never met Major Milne, but I'm told he made damn sure he got a Hun."

Cleve-Cutler thought about that. Milne had been C.O. before him. One day he had thrown an enormous party, and then taken off alone and deliberately rammed a Hun. Not a well man, so Dando had said . . . "Alright. I'll have a word with the lad."

The upshot was that Cleve-Cutler detached Mackenzie from "A" Flight, in fact from the rest of the squadron, and gave him permission to freelance: to fly when he liked, where he liked, and fight how he liked.

"Rather like Captain Ball, sir," Mackenzie said.

"Yes, I suppose so."

Mackenzie was enormously pleased. "Suppose I were to live in a tent, sir, next to the Nieuports? Awfully convenient."

"And also just like Captain Ball."

"Yes, absolutely."

The notion that Mackenzie was a bit of a recluse, if not a hermit, amused the squadron, all except the adjutant. "This sort of thing ruins discipline, sir," he complained.

"Bad for discipline, good for morale, as Bliss said. Remember?"

"It's irregular, sir. You won't find it in King's Regs."

"You won't find Hun flamers there, either, Uncle."

The spare Nieuport was not ready. While his bell tent was being put up and his kit transferred, Mackenzie wandered about the aerodrome, booting an old football from here to there. He reached the chapel and, because it was there, kicked the ball against a wall, harder and harder, trying to burst it. The padre came out. "You're turning the House of God into a bass drum!" he shouted.

"Am I really?" Mackenzie said. "That sounds like some sort of miracle."

"Spare me your ignorant jokes. I take my faith seriously, even if you don't."

"Funny you should say that. I keep having visions."

"No, you have delusions. There is a difference."

"Honestly, padre, I keep seeing the Virgin Mary up a tree. Look, there she is now."

"Profanity is not wit." The padre pushed past him and strode away.

"Look here, if three peasant kids can see her in Portugal, why not me?" Mackenzie called. No answer. "Damn, she's gone," he said. "See what you've done?"

He went into the chapel and knelt in front of the cross that the squadron carpenters had made from broken propellers.

"Signal," he said. "From Lieutenant Mackenzie, R.F.C., to St Hubert, patron saint of hunting. Subject: Flamers. Message begins. Keep up steady supply of above. Message ends." He almost stood, and then knelt again and said, "And if you bump into that poor bloody Hun I got, give him my regards." He got up. Drinkwater was standing in the doorway. "Come to say goodbye?" Mackenzie said.

"No. No, I've come to ask if you took my scarf."

"Ugly spotted green thing? Very nasty item."

"That's your opinion. My cousin gave it to me, for luck. I always wear it. Now someone's pinched it."

"Act of God. The Almighty doesn't like superstition."

"I think you took it." Drinkwater stared, but Mackenzie stared back. "Anyway, what's this about saying goodbye? Are you leaving?"

"No, but you might be. The old man asked me what I thought of your offensive spirit, so I told him. A chap's got to be honest, hasn't he? Ta-ta."

EARTHQUAKE STRENGTH 10:

Most structures destroyed. Large landslides.

Before lunch, Paxton and McWatters each led their flights on short patrols, escorting RE8s on photo-reconnaissance tasks in the Arras area. It was routine stuff, a chance to educate some replacements. There were few Huns in the air, and these declined to take on six Bristol Fighters. Enemy Archie was like a pack of dogs, always chasing, always barking. Two Biffs got ripped by shell fragments. One RE8 was shot down in flames.

Steak-and-kidney pie for lunch. Its pastry crust glowed like bronze and tasted like the glow and not the bronze: another triumph for Lacey's cook. Orders for the next day arrived by despatch rider. All leave was cancelled. The squadron was to be on stand-by from 3 a.m. onwards. That confirmed it. Third Wipers was about to begin.

A fine day had turned into a magnificent afternoon, with baking sunshine and more blue sky than you could shake a stick at.

No patrols had been ordered. The padre arranged a cricket match: pilots versus the rest. Klagsburn decided to film it. "Everyone likes a sportsman," he said. "War isn't all bullshit. Besides, we need a few laughs." He wandered about the wicket, shouting at the players to make it more exciting.

"Extraordinary fellow," Drinkwater said to Mackenzie. He very much wanted to ask him how he had got his flamer, without sounding envious or admiring, and this was difficult because he was, in fact, both. "Are all Americans like him?"

"I've known dozens."

"Really?" That was a fatuous reply. "Look: congrats on your Hun."

"Yes." Mackenzie's acknowledgement was so curt it sounded like a dismissal. "If you really want a Hun, don't wait for permission. It's not a bloody squash court up there, you know." He strolled away. Drinkwater stood with his hands clenched and hidden in his pockets, desperate to kill somebody and thereby prove something.

Dando was acting as umpire for the cricket match, mainly because standing quietly was the best way to get over the indigestion that raged within him. McWatters came and stood alongside. "I'm being punished, so I am," Dando said. "For a sin I never committed. Which proves there is no God and I wish to blazes He would go after the adulterers and the sons of bitches who covet their neighbours' oxen and leave my alimentary canal alone, for the love of Christ."

"I need your advice, doc," McWatters said.

"Has it to do with the bowels? That's the first question we doctors ask, so I'm reliably told. Who was it told me that, now?"

Harry Simms, McWatters thought, and very nearly said so. Harry Simms rabbiting on about Carter's Little Liver Pills and upsetting Spud Ogilvy. But that was not a fit subject for conversation and Dando should know better than to raise it. "Nothing to do with the bowels. It's about the way a girl gets pregnant."

"Ah, I know that one. It's called sex. We don't get a lot of it in the Royal Flying Corps. Boom Trenchard is strongly against sex, you know. He thinks it weakens your offensive spirit." The more Dando talked, the less his indigestion hurt. A cricket ball whizzed between them. "Trust the English to invent cricket," Dando said. "The only sport that's lethal and tedious at the same time."

"It may be a silly question," McWatters said, "but is it possible for a girl who's already pregnant to be made pregnant again? Say, a couple of months later?"

"No," Dando said confidently.

"Good. Thank you."

"I take it you're planning on having relations with a female two months gone?"

"I might. You never know."

"Very true. Even more true of the lady. Not every pregnancy goes the whole hog. Sometimes a lady's no longer pregnant and doesn't know it."

"Ah. So I might . . ."

"You might. Fortunately I can supply a device to prevent that. It's a protective sheath, illegal and totally sinful in Ireland but endorsed by the British Army and highly virtuous in France. God moves in a mysterious way, and not only in my alimentary canal."

Klagsburn wanted Mackenzie to do something heroic with the bat. He asked the padre to arrange five or six fielders behind Mackenzie. "When he hits the ball," Klagsburn said, "they all go hey! wow! terrific! and they point up high, and the nearest guy slaps Mackenzie on the back and the rest applaud, okay?"

"I've never seen anything remotely like that happen in a cricket match," the padre said.

"Trust me."

The padre organized the players.

"Big grins!" Klagsburn called. "Lotsa teeth. Mac, gimme some energy! Wave the damn bat!" He began filming. "Pitch the damn ball," he shouted. The bowler lobbed it invitingly. Mackenzie skipped down the wicket and whacked the ball hard and high. The fielders performed. "More excitement!" Klagsburn demanded. "He just won the damn game!" They cheered. A fat raindrop hit the lens. "Shit in spades," he said. "Sorry, padre."

They all walked away, the rain making dark dots on their shirts, but soon it was spattering hard and they were running. The storm chased them into the anteroom. The sky had a sullen look that promised plenty more where this came from.

"If it hits Wipers," Cleve-Cutler said, "God help the P.B.I."

"Join the army and see the sea," Paxton said. A servant gave him a towel.

"War is not a fair-weather pastime," the adjutant said. He hung his tunic on the back of a chair. "The British soldier can cope with a spot of rain. It's not going to kill him."

"Isn't it?" Maddegan said. "You didn't see the swamp map, Uncle."

"It's only mud. We know all about mud."

"I think the swamp's reached here," Maddegan said. Rain was being blown under the door and forming a pool.

Morale matched the weather. Nobody wanted to talk about Wipers. Nobody wanted to argue with Brazier. Rain hammering the roof made a depressing noise. The Americans looked around them, and decided nothing was going to happen here for a while. They got in the Buick and drove off to see the action at Wipers. There were rumours of tanks. Klagsburn thought they would make good pictures.

* * *

Cleve-Cutler sent for Drinkwater.

"I won't tolerate bullying in my squadron. What puzzles me is why *you* tolerate it, Drinkwater. You're bigger than him. Punch the silly bastard in the teeth."

"Wouldn't that reduce me to his level, sir?"

"No. You'd be on your feet and he'd be on his back."

"With respect, sir, it's not the Christian way."

"I don't know anything about that. I know what *works*." Drinkwater did not reply. He just stood, looking solemn. "Explain how your way works," the C.O. demanded. "Doing nothing."

"Sooner or later, sir, it will make him realize what an utter rotter he's been."

The C.O. used his sleeve to buff his buttons. "Well," he said, "it's a point of view. Alright, toddle off."

Drinkwater left. The C.O. watched him go, and took out an envelope addressed in green ink. He looked at the snapshot: the jaunty posture, the cocky grin, the heroic statue in the background. *You fly, he fled,* and PB stood for Poor Butterfly. It was all a lot of sentimental tosh. London wasn't in the real world. New York was just a name. The Western Front was where life was being lived to the full. And lost too, of course, but take away death and life had no point, no purpose. Cleve-Cutler looked at the picture again and was surprised to feel a brief glow of happiness. Poor young Tommy Blanchflower. Probably live to be sixty and die of gallstones. Serve the little bugger right.

* * *

"Damnfool deck chair," McWatters said. "Squashed my fingers." His right hand was wrapped in a handkerchief. "Can't write a bally word. Need to send a letter."

"Of course, sir." Lacey took up his shorthand pad.

"It's to Miss Edith Reynolds. Here's the address. Let's say . . . um . . . 'Dear Miss Reynolds. Thank you for your kind letter dated 27th July . . . um . . . The arrangements . . . um . . . suggested therein . . . um . . . are agreeable to me and . . . um . . . I suggest a further discussion . . . um . . . in the very near future. Yours truly, etcetera'. Oh . . . better put a PS: 'Subject to flying duties'."

Lacey watched him stride away from the orderly room. "Turgid," he said. He thought for a minute, and wrote:

Dearest Edith,

What a wonderful letter! I thought I might never see you again, and now it seems that you want us to meet! You spoke of your thirst for pleasure. If I can bring to your life a fraction of the joy you bring to mine, I shall count myself a lucky man. I'm told the Hotel Lion d'Or in St Pol is a cosy rendezvous. My stars! If I concentrate I can see your delightful smile from here . . .

Lacey signed it *Yours very affectionately, Jack McWatters.* Thirty minutes later he bribed a despatch rider to deliver the letter and wait for an answer. "And this goes with it," he said, attaching a red silk rose. The despatch rider cocked an eye. "Be prompt and courteous," Lacey said, "and you shall have one, too."

* * *

Cleve-Cutler telephoned ahead to Ypres, and when Dabinett and Klagsburn got there, a Tank Corps man, Captain Quigley, was waiting to look after them. They dined in his mess: oysters, braised pheasant and sherry trifle, with a robust Côtes du Rhône to help the pheasant along. "We always lay on a good spread before an attack," Quigley said. "Who knows when these chaps will eat again?"

"A shame about the rain," Dabinett said.

"Yes. The aim is to smash through the muck as quickly as possible," Quigley said. "We need to break out, and give the cavalry firm ground to operate on."

"What's morale like?"

"In the tanks? First-rate. Keen as mustard."

"How d'you reckon your chances?" Klagsburn asked.

"Zero. We'll bog down in less than a mile. We're not submarines. D'you play bridge? We've time to kill."

At half-past three they were in a dugout not far from the Front Line. Outside, the communication trenches were packed with troops waiting to move up. The barrage had stopped long ago. The dugout was crammed: a major, a captain, two lieutenants, batmen, runners, signallers. The Americans and Quigley sat in a corner; the others were always on the move, talking, joking, drinking rum, singing a line or two from a London show. The jokes were desperately poor, the singing was flat, and every minute somebody wanted to know the time. Far away, a solitary gun fired. It fired so regularly, about every third minute, that it was like a timepiece. Once, when the telephone rang, the major took the call and shouted for quiet. In the silence, the cracked music of a distant concertina trickled into the dugout. "Ours or theirs?" Dabinett whispered. Quigley just shrugged.

At three forty-five, Quigley said, "Jerry's unlikely to capture you now, so I can show you exactly where we are." He opened a map and pointed to the northern part of the battlefront. "Just beyond the enemy lines is Pilckem village – doesn't really exist, of course – and running south from it is Pilckem Ridge. That's the first objective."

"Can your tanks climb the ridge?" Klagsburn asked.

Quigley was amused. "It's not like Vimy," he said. "It's only a few feet high. In fact *nothing* is more than a few feet high out there."

"So what's beyond the ridge?"

"Just farms. The barrage got them long ago. Rubble, now. You couldn't hide a rat behind them. You can't even find them unless you know where to look."

"So it's all just . . ."

"Mud. Our tanks navigate by compass. The tank commander takes a compass bearing and sets off into no-man's-land and hopes for the best. Come on, we'd better get outside."

After the tobacco-fug of the dugout, the night air was cool and sweet. No stars. Heavy cloud. Quigley checked his watch. "Three forty-nine," he whispered.

At precisely three fifty, the barrage erupted and three thousand Allied guns fired.

Dabinett stumbled, and a soldier grabbed his arm. He felt as if the noise had blown him over. It made every thunderclap he had heard seem like a doorslam. The roar pounded his ears and numbed his brain. He lost control of his body, his knees were shaking, his feet were trembling. Then his brain caught up with reality. The *ground* was shaking, and he was shaking with it.

Now Quigley seized his arm. "Climb up!" he shouted. "See better from the top. Jerry won't harm us."

They went up a ladder. Shells were exploding all along the enemy trenches, making an unbroken line of spouting fire. Dabinett had to brace himself against the gusting wind. He was puzzled: a minute ago the night had been calm. Then he understood: the wind was made by the displacement of a thousand shells, all blasting holes in the air. He heard the crack and bark of field batteries, and looked behind him. Beyond the batteries was a horizon of gun-flashes like an army of signallers working the shutters of their signal lamps.

Klagsburn said something, and Dabinett turned and looked again at the battlefield. It was an earthquake releasing a volcano. Miles of the enemy lines were a blaze of orange light. Above this, hundreds of shrapnel-bursts sparkled. Higher still, burning oil fell like yellow rain from the drums of

Thermit flung by the artillery. And just to point up the magnificent, inhuman scale of the inferno, the enemy was sending up streams of delicate red and green rockets, his pleas for help.

"Look!" Quigley called, and gestured all around. The ground was moving, was running: rats were fleeing from the Lines. "Never seen that before," he said. "What you might call an unsolicited testimonial."

The barrage went on, devastating what it had already destroyed, but it made so much smoke and dust that soon it hid its own firework display. Now machine guns opened up, hundreds of guns, rattling like regiments of typewriters. It was a signal for the barrage to raise itself from anger to fury.

"Not long now," Quigley said. "And Jerry knows it. See?" Enemy shells were bursting in no-man's-land.

They climbed down. The dugout was empty except for the major, his batman and a signaller. "Have some rum," the major said. "They've gone over. Nothing we can do."

"When will the barrage stop, sir?" Dabinett asked.

"Not for ages," the major said. "Every four minutes, it lifts forward one hundred yards. In theory, the infantry just keep walking forward."

"In theory?"

"Nobody's perfect. Gunners make little mistakes. Have some rum. What time is it?"

"Two minutes past four, sir," Quigley said.

"Dawn in an hour. Full daylight in two. Then we'll know something. Maybe. Have some rum."

They waited. The barrage lifted, and lifted again, until its noise was a distant thunder. Now Quigley reckoned it was safe to go to the Front Line. Stretcher-bearers trudged back up the communication trench in an endless procession. Dawn was a red slash in the clouds; smoke from the barrage drifted across it. They reached the Front and climbed onto the parapet and looked across no-man's-land at where Pilckem Ridge was alleged to be.

"First objective taken," Quigley said.

"Is it?" Klagsburn said. "It all looks kind of samey to me."

The entire battlefront was a sea of craters. There were no paths or tracks; nobody walked in a straight line; men followed the rims of the craters. In daylight this was difficult; at night, with drifting smoke and bursting shrapnel, it must have been worse than a nightmare. Nightmares end. Men awake. Here, they could only plod on, from a world of mud and explosions into a world of mud and explosions.

"Jolly thorough lot, the gunners," Quigley said.

Dabinett nodded. He could see a few tanks tipped sideways in craters too steep for them to climb, but he said nothing of that.

They each helped carry a stretcher up the communication trench to a regimental aid post. Because Klagsburn was so much shorter than the man carrying the other end, blood ran down the poles of his stretcher and made the handles slippery. He dropped them before he knew it and fell forward, on top of the casualty. When he got up there was blood all over his sleeves. "Sorry," he said.

"Don't take it to heart, sir," the other stretcher-bearer said. "That one's not feeling any pain."

The Americans had breakfast. Then they took the film camera and went back to the battlefield.

* * *

At about the same time, O'Neill had a longer, much better breakfast. Then he returned to his hut and found it full of sheep. They were not as well-behaved as the horse. Droppings dotted the floor. He shouted for his servant.

"My compliments to Mr Paxton. Ask him to spare me a few minutes."

Paxton arrived, but not through the door; instead he looked through a window. "Dash it all, O'Neill," he said, "you really must curb this passion for farm animals. People are beginning to talk."

"I'm a reasonable man," O'Neill said, "and I'll make a reasonable offer. Get your woolly friends out of here or I'll smash your face in."

"I'd like to oblige you, but they're not my sheep."

O'Neill snatched a cushion that a sheep was chewing.

"I expect they just wandered in," Paxton said. "That one looks remarkably like you. Much cleverer, of course." O'Neill cursed, and hurled the cushion. Paxton had gone.

He found the French shepherd and gave him ten francs. "Infinitely obliged," Paxton said. "For a similar consideration, could you repeat the exercise, only this time with a small herd of goats?" The man grinned and nodded. "You are a prince amongst shepherds," Paxton said.

* * *

The squadron had been on stand-by from three in the morning. When the bombardment broke the silence of the night at three fifty, and the mess windows vibrated to the noise, everyone knew the infantry would be going over the top in a matter of minutes. Dawn came up, grey with rain, and no message arrived from Wing H.Q. Three hours later the crews were dozing in armchairs or eating a second breakfast or looking at the wet sky. Still no message. It was midday before orders arrived. Nine fighters – three from each flight – were to take off as soon as possible. The rain was heavier than ever; it was impossible to see across the aerodrome. Cleve-Cutler roused the crews and told them what was happening.

"The battlefield is lousy with Hun machines," he said. "Sooner or later they must fly home. Your task is to intercept them. Fly deep into enemy territory – at least twenty miles – and turn and patrol the area *beyond* the fighting at Wipers. With luck you'll dodge their Archie and you'll catch some Huns who are low on fuel and out of ammunition, and not expecting to be hit."

Forty minutes later the rain eased. The cockpits of the Biffs were soaked and slippery, but the engines had been covered and they fired willingly. Nine fighters climbed into a sky that flickered with lightning.

Woolley led the patrol, with Paxton as his deputy. The Biffs flew in three arrowheads of three. Orders were to stay in formation whenever possible. After a scrap, re-form at once. "Let's get a Hun if we can," Woolley had told them. "Let's get home if we can't. Watch your tail. Watch the next man's tail. And remember: a pint of pure water weighs a pound and a quarter, so have a good piss now."

He liked Wing's plan. It allowed him to climb through the rain cloud, emerge into glorious sunlight with heart-warmingly clear visibility in all directions, and keep climbing to fourteen thousand feet. Nobody was above them. The sky was spotless and speckless and blue enough to drive an artist to drink. The only machines below were little pencilled crosses, crawling over the ragged cloud. And down below the cloud sat the enemy Archie, blinded and baffled.

Woolley concentrated on navigation. It was a matter of dead reckoning: fly for so many minutes at this airspeed on that compass bearing, and you should arrive where you want. But speed through the air wasn't necessarily the same as speed over the ground. The wind was blowing them northeast. How hard? Only the wind knew that. And the compass might play tricks too, especially on a day when there were thunderstorms about.

Woolley looked on the map for a major road out of Wipers, and found one that went east for about twenty miles to Courtrai.

Perfect. Courtrai was the meeting place of five big roads. It had a river and a railway. Should be easy to identify.

Woolley wheeled the patrol north when he reckoned Arras was ten miles behind them. For the next thirty minutes they churned through crystalline air, sometimes gently rocking like boats in a harbour, enjoying what little warmth the sun gave at such a height. Then Woolley pointed down and they began the long slide to the clouds and through them.

They emerged in grey light, streaked with thin rain, and saw the sea, dead ahead, ten or twelve miles away. The wind had blown them far north of Courtrai. Woolley had guessed wrong. Immediately he made a wide half-circle and flew south. There was no road in sight. And now the rain fell heavily. Within a couple of minutes it contained hail.

There was half a gale in this storm, and its gusts shunted the Biffs like paper kites. The pilots opened out the formation until they were just blurred black shapes to each other. Hail battered against goggles. It was too dark to read the instrument panel, and in any case lightning glowed from time to time; so the compasses were probably thoroughly bewildered. The sky was full of traps and tripwires; Maddegan had to work hard with stick and rudder, so hard that he was sweating under his drenched flying kit. He couldn't see the ground, or the horizon. The sun was just a memory. He was flying on hope and instinct, like the rest of them: a dangerous combination.

The buffeting eased and within a minute they flew out of the storm, into a misty drizzle. The formation closed up again. Woolley saw a good, straight road off to his left. His map was soggy and unreadable. He took a chance and followed the road. Courtrai came in view so quickly that he couldn't believe his luck. Five roads fed into it, the river Lys went through it and headed west towards Wipers, and just outside town was an aerodrome.

Rising from it, like a hatch of flies leaving a pond, was an untidy parcel of German scouts. Woolley thought: Somebody saw us when we came out of cloud and turned south. Somebody got on the phone. The scouts tidied themselves up and made a box of eight, climbing hard. I bet they think we're bombers. They think we're easy meat. There was little Archie, and it was inaccurate: not easy to estimate height in wet weather.

Sudden waving by his wingman, Maddegan. Vigorous pointing to the right. Woolley raised his goggles and searched and found two large specks, no bigger than baby moths, far away and far below. Now the drizzle thickened to rain and he lost them. When he found them again he found two more, half a mile further away, all heading for the aerodrome. Back from the battlefield, with empty guns.

"Bunnies!" Woolley cried. "Rabbit stew tonight!" His gunner heard nothing over the Falcon's roar. Woolley fired a red flare, sending it racing and falling towards the returning machines: the signal to attack. All nine Biffs tipped and dropped.

The Huns were Halberstadt two-seaters. They did the only thing left to them: they dived for the aerodrome and the protection of its anti-aircraft guns. They were too late and too slow. Woolley's arrowhead caught the first pair and chopped them down in one rush of fire, the spray of the Vickers followed by the hammer and slash of the Lewis. It was easy to destroy an undefended aeroplane. You could get as close as you liked. Maddegan got so close that he saw the rage on the German gunner's face. The man actually flung an ammunition drum at the Biff. By then the Halberstadt was burning. Yellow flames as long as pennants were trying to lick the tail.

Paxton led the second and third arrowheads against the other pair of Huns, who did the sensible thing and split up. It delayed their ends by a minute or so. Each Halberstadt was hounded and harassed by three Biffs until, inevitably, it dodged and swerved and flew into somebody's gunsight. It wasn't a fair fight. It wasn't a fight of any kind. The Huns were shot while trying to escape.

Woolley didn't waste time trying to pull the formation together. The Biffs were scattered and someone on the ground was working a heavy machine gun or two: tracer kept nipping at the fighters' heels. And by now the eight scouts from the aerodrome had made enough height. They were single-seat Albatroses: fast. The nearest was only five or six hundred yards away.

They chased the Biffs towards the battlefield and although they failed to catch them they did not quit. It was a strange piece of highspeed stalemate. Exhausts were pumping streamers of blue smoke. The Biffs edged together. From time to time an Albatros fired a few hopeless rounds, and a Biff gunner did the same. Finally a fresh rainstorm blustered in from the west and stopped all their nonsense.

The rain was so dense, and the wind flung it so savagely, that all aircraft, friend and foe alike, lost sight of each other. Now the real battle was between the thumping downforce of the rain and the engine's power to keep dragging the wings through the air. There were storms within the storm, squalls that left propellers thrashing uselessly in air pockets or chewing at blasts that hit so hard the whole machine shuddered. Every crew member was banged and bruised. Some pilots found their strength being drained: the storm was so violent that their muscles ached from working the controls and the aeroplane flew crabwise, or nose-heavy, or worse. Some men were in tears of exhaustion. Some were close to despair.

The storm ended as sharply as it began. The Biffs burst out of a lashing blackness into a grey and watery daylight. It was as beautiful as a reprieve at the scaffold. The Albatros scouts failed to appear: turned back by the storm, if they had any brains. Woolley fired a white flare. As the scattered fighters re-grouped, he counted them. Eight, including himself.

The formation circled. Still no sign of the ninth Biff. One of Paxton's wingmen was missing. Lefevre. Gunner's name was Conway. Here comes Archie. No point in waiting. The battlefield was only a couple of miles ahead: he could see gunflashes and smoke, and the steely glint of light reflected on water. That was somebody else's funeral. Woolley gave Lefevre and Conway another fifteen seconds. Archie found their height with a five-shot salvo, all in a straight line, the last burst a hundred yards away, yellow-brown with a hot red centre. When you could see the red it was time to go. Woolley waggled his wings and dived two hundred feet. He turned left and flew for ten seconds, just to upset the Hun gunners, and went up again at max revs and into the cloud. Half an hour later they were back at Gazeran. By six o'clock Lefevre and Conway were officially missing and unofficially dead: turned upside-down by the storm and crashed, was the general opinion. The adjutant summoned Lacey to pack their effects.

* * *

Conway had owned an air rifle. Mackenzie took it from Lacey, borrowed Lefevre's raincoat, and walked to the far end of the aerodrome. It was evening, and crows were making hard work of settling down in the trees. The gusting wind sent them flapping and screeching, bits of black whirling against a sheet of grey. Mackenzie had shot three birds when Drinkwater joined him. "Watch out," Mackenzie said. "I'm not very accurate. I might accidentally get you in the eye."

"You'd enjoy that, wouldn't you?" This was not a challenge; it was a mild and reasonable suggestion. "You're a very destructive person."

"I smell a sermon." Mackenzie aimed at a crow, but the wind shook his body. "You stink of decency."

"What's wrong with that? Isn't it what we're fighting for?" Mackenzie yawned and strolled on. Drinkwater followed. "Look: I've done you no harm," he said. "I don't see why you should treat me so badly."

"Badly?" Mackenzie almost laughed. "You get what you ask for. You act like a virgin. Virgins get raped. That's what virgins are for, isn't it?"

Drinkwater watched Mackenzie aim, fire and miss. Crows scattered, clattering angrily. "Cobblers," Mackenzie said.

"You don't know anything about me, so how can you say ..."

"You *walk* like a bloody virgin. You walk as if you're afraid you'll drop something if you open your legs."

They moved on. Drinkwater felt aggrieved: his virginity was none of Mackenzie's business. He let a little anger out. "You seem to take a keen interest in other chaps' tackle," he said.

"So do you. So does everyone. The difference is, I'm not ashamed of it."

This idea made Drinkwater thoroughly uncomfortable. He looked for an escape and found the war. "When Woolley's patrol landed, one of the chaps had blood on his goggles. Did you know?" Fifty yards away, a young rabbit paused outside its hole. Mackenzie shot it through the head. "Hun blood, presumably," Drinkwater said. "They must have been extremely close." He sucked his teeth. "I'd give a month's pay to ..."

"Oh, go to hell." Mackenzie strode away. "You don't want blood on your nice goggles!" he shouted. "You'd like the glory, but not the gore!"

Drinkwater watched him go. Everyone talked about the wonderful comradeship in the R.F.C. He hadn't found any. Chaps came, chaps went. The camp was like a railway station: lots of bustle, nobody to talk to. And now it was damn well raining again. "Oh, bugger," he said, miserably, and felt fractionally better.

* * *

Rain fell all next day. It did not stop the squadron flying.

There had been a short party the night before to celebrate the squadron's four kills. Everyone was in bed by ten o'clock and up again at dawn. Breakfast was fuel rather than food. Nobody wanted to start a three-hour patrol with an empty stomach.

O'Neill got off the telephone and told the flight commanders that the German Air Force was all over the battlefield like birds over the plough. The infantry assault had reached a critical point. "The Hun is doing a lot of trench-strafing," he said. "Frankly, I suspect that 'trench' flatters what is more likely to be a scrape in the ground. The situation is fluid."

"We don't need your bloody silly jokes," Paxton said. "Rain isn't funny."

"I wouldn't waste my wit on you. The situation *is* fluid."

"That means you don't know," McWatters said. "If you don't know, don't guess."

"D'you want to do my job?" O'Neill demanded.

"A child of six could do your job," Paxton said.

"I wouldn't let you anywhere near a child of six."

"How touching. And I thought you preferred farm animals."

They stood and glared at each other.

"Where I come from, we couldn't afford sex," Woolley said. "We made do with rhubarb. Not as exciting, but it goes better with custard."

"For God's sake," McWatters growled.

"Where's the damn fighting?" McWatters asked O'Neill. "Or don't you know that either?"

O'Neill unrolled a map and showed them a red line seven miles long that wandered uncertainly, less than a mile to the east of what had been the German trenches. "That's where the damn fighting was yesterday. Satisfied?"

"Christ . . . The P.B.I. didn't get far," Paxton said.

"There were counter-attacks. And I don't suppose the weather helped."

"There you go again," McWatters said. "Guessing."

The C.O. arrived, waving orders from Wing. "They're very pleased with yesterday, so we're to do it again, one flight at a time. I'll lead 'A' Flight first. When I get back, Pax goes, then Mac. All clear?"

"The Hun will be waiting for us, sir," Paxton said.

"That's what we want. Every Hun machine on standing patrol is one less over the battlefield."

But the day did not work out as planned. Cloud reared much higher than the day before, and the wind blew at different strengths at different heights. Cleve-Cutler's navigation was bad. When he brought his flight down into the gloom of rain, he was lost. They roamed about for twenty minutes, failing to find any land-marks, attracting sporadic Archie, while the C.O.'s faith in his compass evaporated. He was lucky to catch a glimpse of the North Sea. He led his flight over the Belgian beaches and turned left towards the English Channel, where they got briskly Archied by a couple of British destroyers. He found Dunkerque by the elementary method of flying so low that he could read the name on the railway station; followed the line south; and eventually reached Gazeran, drenched and cold and in a filthy temper. He'd used up his ration of two patrols per month and got nothing out of either.

The squadron flew all day and had no luck. McWatters got so bored that he decided to descend on Courtrai aerodrome and strafe whatever was lying about. A storm of Archie chased his flight away; evidently Courtrai's guns had been reinforced. Woolley, patrolling just below the cloudbase, was about to give up when he saw a stream of enemy aircraft leaving the area of the battlefield. They were low, very low, just skimming the ground. He waited, and saw more of the same. He took his flight home. "Intercepting Huns at ground level in this weather is a mug's game, sir," he told the C.O. "They all took the same route. I bet they've got machine guns posted, just waiting for us."

"So where's their standing patrol?" Cleve-Cutler had a headache caused by his burning sinuses, or he wouldn't have asked such a question.

"Nowhere. Why play our game? They need all their strength at Wipers."

"Bastards."

Paxton was leading his second patrol of the day and thinking much the same thing. Wing H.Q. would soon take the squadron off this nonsense. Tomorrow it would be sent to Wipers, to help try to clear the sky above the troops: stop the strafing, chase away the Hun machines spotting for their artillery, do battle with the high-flying scouts that made possible the strafing and the spotting. Paxton was not looking forward to it. Something went bang in the Rolls-Royce Falcon and at once his Biff was gliding down, its propeller slowing to a useless *phut-phut-phut*. He had just enough time to wave to his deputy leader, and then the flight was above him and thundering away. They knew the drill. If any machine went down, it went alone. There was nothing the others could do to save it.

Paxton tried the likely things: changed the fuel tanks, changed the throttle setting and the mixture control, fiddled with the advance and retard lever. Nothing worked. He tried unlikely things: he worked the pressure pump, he switched back to the original tank. Nothing.

"Must be the electrics," said Griffiths, his gunner. Without the engine's roar, they could talk quietly. "Bust ignition leads, probably."

"Probably."

In less than a minute, the other Biffs had receded into a small, dark pattern, blurred by rain. Paxton's ears were adjusting to the strange quiet. He could hear the rain rattling on the wings. He could hear it sizzling on the exhaust pipe.

They had a little time before they crashed. Might as well make the most of it. He ate some chocolate.

* * *

Sometimes an engine packed up and then, a minute later, started again. Bit of dirt in the fuel pipe, perhaps. Cleve-Cutler knew it could happen; it had happened to him. So he allowed an hour after "B" Flight landed, and then another hour for luck, before he let the adjutant make the routine report that would result in a telegram boy knocking on a door somewhere in England next day. "And I want a mess party tonight," he added. "Lots of Hornet's Sting."

"Twice in two days?" Brazier said. "Is that wise?"

"Round up some guests. Canadians and Australians. Tell the band to play ragtime. Get that Scotsman with his bagpipes. Eightsome reels are what we need."

Brazier delegated most of the work to the duty officer. He collected Sergeant Lacey and two umbrellas, and they walked along duckboards laid on paths made boggy by the rain. "I'm getting tired of this job," the adjutant said. "It's grubby work. It's not becoming of an officer and a gentleman. It makes me feel like an assistant undertaker."

"We are all, in a sense, assistant undertakers."

"You're certainly good at writing epitaphs."

"It's a knack, that's all."

"Well, your latest effort is very popular in the Corps. Squadron commanders everywhere pop it into their letters to the bereaved. Bliss wants you to write another verse."

"No, sir. I can't—"

"Yes, sergeant, you can. I've told Bliss you will."

"The trouble with you, sir, is you think you can talk war to death."

"You're to blame for that, sergeant. I was just a simple soldier until you taught me your wicked ways."

The network of duckboards led them eventually to Captain Paxton's hut. Lacey opened the door. Brazier ducked his head and went in. "What the hell is this?" he demanded. The place was half-full of pigs. Lacey counted seven fat pigs, sprawled in a comfortable huddle. Most were asleep. The atmosphere had a rich, caustic stink. "The very picture of serenity," he said.

"Damn your picture. What's the game?"

"If pigs can live at peace, why can't men? Did you ever see two pigs fighting, sir?"

"Stop your nonsense, Lacey. What the devil's going on here?"

"A long-running feud. A vendetta."

Brazier prodded the nearest pig with his umbrella and made it grunt. "O'Neill and Paxton," he said. "Get O'Neill here . . . God in heaven! Is this army led by officers or imbeciles?"

"The two are not mutually exclusive." Lacey left.

Brazier found a chair and lit his pipe. The pig he had prodded got up and walked to the door. It peered at the rain, and came back and made itself comfortable. "You needn't look so bloody smug," Brazier told it. "You won't have bacon for breakfast tomorrow, but I shall." The pig was soon asleep.

By the time O'Neill arrived, Brazier had decided that understatement would draw most blood. "Maybe I'm old-fashioned," he said, "but this is a curious way to salute the loss of Captain Paxton."

"He put sheep in my room."

"Sheep. I see. And you replied with pigs. Why?"

"Paxton's a horse's arse."

The adjutant lost patience. "Paxton's missing, you great oaf! Went down behind enemy Lines. Certainly missing, probably dead. Shouldn't an intelligence officer know that?"

"He's not dead. He'll be back. You can't kill a fart like him." O'Neill's voice was harsh and unforgiving. "You wait and see."

"Get your stinking pigs out of here," Brazier ordered. "Do it now. I don't care where you found them or where they go. Pigs out, and hut clean and ready for the next occupant, even if you have to scrub it yourself. Christ! What a smell. What do pigs eat that makes a stench like that?"

"Apples," O'Neill said. "I gave them apples. And lots of plums."

Brazier and Lacey went back along the duckboards. "Extraordinary fellow," the adjutant said. "How the deuce did he get hold of seven pigs?"

"I believe it was the other way around," Lacey said. "The pigs won him in a raffle."

"It's no laughing matter, sergeant."

"Certainly not, sir. The pigs took a very grave view of the whole affair."

The adjutant knocked the ash from his pipe. "You're too clever for your own good, Lacey. The British Army does not like cleverness." That ended the discussion.

* * *

Griffiths saw the forest first.

It made a dark shape, large enough to disappear into the gloom of the rain. From a thousand feet it had a comfortable, cushioned appearance; but Paxton had seen what happened to aeroplanes that hit trees. "Risky," he said.

"So are fields. If you put her down in a field it's certain to be a bog, and then we'll go arse-over-teakettle."

Paxton thought about it, while the wind played sad tunes in the wires and the Biff lost another two hundred feet. The forest was dark green, almost black. Maybe it was all evergreens, like Christmas trees. Tall and thin and elastic. Maybe not. Maybe it was stuffed with oaks.

"We'll get captured if I land in the open. Somebody's bound to see the bus. We can hide in the woods. Get out of this lousy rain, too."

"You're the driver. I'm right behind you."

It was only when they were much lower that Paxton realized how strong the wind was. He could see tree-tops lashing. The entire roof of the forest seemed to be in turmoil. What's more, the storm was hustling the Biff along and it was far too late to attempt to turn into wind. He tugged the nose up, flirting with a stall, while he searched for a soft landing. Under the thin leafy branches thrashing about he saw swaying timbers that would welcome a fight with an aeroplane. He glimpsed something away to his left: a patch of giant Christmas trees. "Hold tight," he said.

The Biff had a tiny windscreen. As the wheels brushed the tree-tops, Paxton ducked below the cockpit edge. At first he heard a mild clattering: the wings were clipping the topmost branches. The Biff lurched and hit something big and hard; Paxton felt the shock through his boots and his backside. His waist-strap tried to cut him in half. His top-half was flung forward. His head whacked the instrument panel. The pain rose like a red tide and faded as the light drained from his brain. The last thing he remembered was the sound of trees being ripped apart. It sounded like he felt.

"Thank God for that," Griffiths said.

Paxton heard the words clearly, although there was a roaring in his ears. He couldn't see clearly, so he rubbed his eyes, but his hands were sticky. Blinking did some good. He took a close look at his hands and smelt chocolate.

"Thought you were a goner," Griffiths said, "until I heard you throw up. Any bones broken?"

Paxton wiped his hands on his coat and made them worse. "What a smell," he said. His feet seemed to be trapped so he tried to kick them free. Everything lurched and the gunner shouted in horror. "Keep still, for Christ's sake," he said. "We're fifty feet up." Paxton looked around. Nothing but branches and leaves, all moving. The roaring in his ears was the wind.

An hour later they were cold and wet and still trapped in the same shaky situation. The Biff had smashed the tops of several trees and now it was caught up in a tangle of broken branches. The light was failing and the storm was getting worse. Griffiths wanted to climb down. "We'll starve to death up here," he said. "Nobody's seen us. We'll freeze."

Paxton had a brutal headache that made it hard for him to think. "It's awfully dark down there," he said. "You'll get lost." He didn't want to be left alone.

"I'll get help."

"You'll get shot."

"I'd sooner be shot than starve." Griffiths climbed over Paxton and got onto the remains of the wings. This transfer of weight made the wreck sway. Paxton cried out in alarm. Griffiths was poised to jump for a branch but he hesitated, afraid that the thrust of his jump might be too much, might break the fragile cradle. "Bloody hell," he said miserably.

"Go on, go on," Paxton urged. "You can't stay there." The machine groaned and slipped, and dropped a foot or so. It was enough to knock Griffiths to his knees. He got up very slowly, and Paxton could see that his hands and head were trembling. "For Christ's sake, jump," he said, "or we'll be here all night."

But now the branch was further away. Griffiths sat down. "Just a minute," he said. "Just a minute." The minute stretched into two, and three. Paxton stared at him and could think of nothing to say. He had grown used to the roaring of the storm and the swaying of the trees. He paid no attention to a gust that howled like an express. Immediately behind it was a greater gust. It ripped into the wreck of the Biff and sent it tumbling. If Griffiths screamed, Paxton never heard him, nor saw him fall. He felt the wreck whirl, and his battered head bounced from one side of the cockpit to another, and the forest rushed upwards. A splintering crash destroyed the remains of his chair and left him dazed with pain. Leaves and bits of branches fell on him. All he could do was groan. It hurt to groan. Far away and high above, the storm kept up its stupid noise.

He dozed. When he woke up, the pain was no worse than a total ache. There was no light. He found a bit of branch poking into his neck, so he threw it away. It took a little time to hit the ground. He thought about that. He threw out another bit of branch, and listened.

No doubt about it. The ground was still a long way below him.

The night was long and wet. He slept a bit. Even in sleep he never moved in case he fell again. Dawn was in no hurry to penetrate the forest. When it reached him he saw that the wreckage was caught in the fork of a tree. The trunk of the tree was as smooth as a pillar. He was about thirty feet up. Griffiths must have been mistaken. They must have been more than fifty feet high. Not that it made any difference, especially to Griffiths, who was lying in that broken and twisted position which Paxton had so often seen when he flew low over the battlefield. This time it was someone he knew. Paxton gave up the unequal struggle. He lay back and let the rain pelt him. He didn't care.

*　*　*

The rain eased, but the wind grew stronger. All Channel crossings were postponed. In Paris, a church was blown down. Several Allied observation balloons were ripped from their moorings and last seen racing towards Germany, no bigger than beans. All along the Western Front, buildings already gutted by shellfire were tumbled by the gale. Throughout the R.F.C., signals went out cancelling orders for patrols.

Everyone at Gazeran enjoyed the rest, especially after the previous night's party. Paxton's replacement arrived before lunch: Captain Morkel, a South African. The adjutant took him straight to the C.O.

"Morkel, Morkel," the C.O. said. "Didn't we have someone of that name, Uncle? Also a South African?"

"Briefly, sir."

"It's a common name where I come from, sir," Morkel said. He was the opposite of the first Morkel: slim, and swarthy, with a permanent frown. Cleve-Cutler liked that frown. He wanted his flight commanders to worry. "I've given you a good flight," he said. "I expect you to work 'em hard.

What d'you think of this Wipers show?"

"Well, sir . . ." A blast of gale thumped the C.O.'s office and made it creak. "If this doesn't put the wind up the Hun, I don't know what will."

Brazier chuckled. "Damn right," Cleve-Cutler said.

They walked to the mess, clutching their hats against the wind. The Buick pulled up alongside them. "I guess nobody's flying, major," Dabinett said. "We've just had some of our film developed. If you think they'd like to see . . ."

"Yes. After lunch. Thank you."

Klagsburn put the Buick in gear and drove on. He said sourly, "It's all crap."

"No," Dabinett said. "Only half of it is crap. The other half is bullshit. There's a difference."

* * *

Hunger was worst.

The pain in his head had receded to an ache like wearing a hat two sizes too small. He was shaking with cold. Every time his clothes began to dry, another squall came along and soaked him. But hunger was the worst. It refused to let him sleep. It bullied him into trying to save himself. The infuriating thing was that half a block of chocolate was lying somewhere below him. It must be down there. He'd had it in the cockpit and now it was gone, like most of the cockpit.

The trunk of this tree was only about five feet away. He could probably reach it, but if he did, he knew he couldn't get his arms around it. Too big, far too big. Too smooth. Nothing to grip. Too far to fall. Thirty feet at least.

In the next tree, a squirrel ran along a branch, stopped, and looked. "I would welcome any suggestion," Paxton said, "no matter how fatuous." His voice was weak. The squirrel dashed along the branch, flung itself into space, found another tree, and raced away. "That's just showing off," he said. Something caught his eye, something swinging in the wind, hanging from the wreckage. It was a piece of control cable.

He kicked a hole in the cockpit. That was easy; everything was split or broken already. It was also stupid: suppose the cable got knocked loose and fell away? He felt sick. But the cable was still there, and he hauled it in. Ten feet, at most. Not enough. He searched, and found another length of cable buried in the shattered root of a wing. He tied them together. He tied one end to a branch. The cables were stiff, his hands were shaking, the knots were poor. "Best I can do," he said, and found that he was gasping for breath. He lay back and looked up through the space in the forest at grey sky a hundred miles away, and heard the moan and bluster of the wind. Then he slid down the cable.

With the help of his flying gloves he managed to slide fairly slowly. When he reached the end he was still a long way from the ground. While he was looking for a soft landing, a knot parted and the ground came up and hit him so hard that he folded like a jack-knife and beat his face against his knees. This was the third hammering his body had taken in less than a day. His brain knew the drill. Loud daylight faded to black silence.

* * *

"Another day dawns," Dabinett announced, "on a crack fighter squadron of the Royal Flying Corps, somewhere in France."

They liked that. They were gathered in the anteroom, curtains closed, fascinated by the flickering images of Gazeran that Klagsburn was projecting onto a screen. A pianist improvised sunny, tinkling music. Each clip of film got a roar of recognition: the Duty N.C.O. raised the flag; a despatch rider was met by the adjutant; pilots strolled to breakfast; the one-armed shepherd grinned at the camera. When he spoke and spat, everyone shouted "*Sale Boche!*" Troops saluted briskly.

"The intrepid aviators are eager to get to grips with the Hun," Dabinett said, and there were shots of flight commanders pointing at maps, of crews nodding vigorously and smiling broadly, of Biffs being started, Biffs taxiing, Biffs taking off. The pianist played bits from "The Entry of the Gladiators". Everyone cheered.

"Back from the battle!" Dabinett declared. "And victorious!" Biffs landed. Pilots and gunners shook hands, grinning. Mechanics cheered, silently. Dingbat Maddegan poked his finger through bullet-holes in the wings. A jubilant Mackenzie danced on the keyboard of a piano. More Biffs landed. The pianist played "Rule! Britannia": And still they cheered.

It was the shock of recognition that excited them. Nobody had seen himself on film before. The fact of being on the screen was reassuring: this must be a special squadron, and so membership must be special too. When Klagsburn began showing close-ups of men swimming and diving, playing cricket, singing at the piano, sprawling in deck chairs outside the mess, the feeling of pride grew even greater, until everyone knew that he must be a hell of a fellow and here were moving pictures to prove it. There was rather a lot of Mackenzie. In fact Mackenzie was rarely off the screen. Who cared? It was all a splendid stunt. It even made Uncle laugh.

There was a huge groan of disappointment when the screen went black. Then came warm applause. Servants opened the curtains.

Dabinett murmured to Cleve-Cutler, "You might like to see what we filmed at Wipers, sir."

"Might I?" Something about the American's tone of voice made the C.O. cautious.

"Then you could decide if you want the rest of your squadron to see it."

The C.O. kept his senior officers and told everyone else to clear off. The curtains were closed. Klagsburn fitted a new reel to the projector and began cranking. This time there was no jolly piano.

"Pilckem Ridge," Dabinett said.

It didn't look like a landmark. Every part of it was broken and pock-marked. Nothing grew. Rain flickered and made it more dreary. The film jumped to the top of the ridge. Stretcher-bearers picked their way across the ruined ground and grinned self-consciously as they stumbled past. The camera turned and showed them adding their corpse to a line of bodies. The camera took a closer look. Some of the dead were incomplete. None of the faces seemed at rest.

"See a dozen stiffs, you've seen a thousand," Klagsburn said. "Now here's where I nearly got myself killed."

The film cut to a view of the battlefield. Smoke from shellbursts appeared in the distance, looking no more dangerous than garden bon-fires. A line of duckboards wriggled between craters. Men carrying ammunition boxes walked slowly. "Step off those boards and you're a goner," Klagsburn said. "Drowned in the mud."

The film showed a ruined farmhouse, with troops sheltering behind it. "I needed a bird's-eye view," he said. "The stairs were sort of rickety, but . . ."

"You're mad," O'Neill said.

"Yeah."

The next shot was through a ragged hole in a wall. It looked down on a sea of craters. There was nothing but craters. They touched and sometimes overlapped. The camera slowly swung and searched, and everywhere it saw craters. The craters reflected the sky because they were full of rain. The entire picture was abruptly destroyed by a black explosion. Tons of mud raged upwards and outwards. "Time to quit," Klagsburn said. He stopped cranking.

Nobody spoke for a while.

"I never thought the swamp map would turn out to be quite as frightful as that," Cleve-Cutler said.

"Bloody frog weather," O'Neill growled. "Always lets you down."

"We made the holes," Woolley pointed out.

"What are you suggesting?" McWatters asked. "No barrage?"

"Got to have a barrage," the adjutant said. "Can't have a Push without a barrage."

Cleve-Cutler thanked the Americans. "You're welcome," Dabinett said. "That stuff's no use to us, sir."

"I suppose not. Still, the first film was jolly good, wasn't it?"

"Ripping," Klagsburn said. "Dashed ripping."

*   *   *

The sight of a German sentry, hands in greatcoat pockets, walking along a forest path, made Paxton feel a bit better.

When he came out of the daze caused by bashing his head on his knee, he lay and licked at the blood still trickling from his nose and wondered why the Huns hadn't caught him.

He guessed he was about ten miles behind the fighting; still, the area should be thick with Jerry troops in reserve. Probably the storm had hidden the noise of his crash.

He stood up faster than his heart liked and he staggered and went down on his hands and knees. It was a good position in which to search for chocolate. No luck. He found Griffiths, lightly covered with leaves. "Just like Goldilocks," he said. Griffiths' left leg looked wrong, so he tried to straighten it, and failed. He saw a splintered chunk of cockpit with his Very pistol clipped to it. Also a few signal cartridges. "Not edible, alas," he said. He put them next to Griffiths. "Must keep the place tidy," he said. "It wasn't Goldilocks. It was Hansel and Gretel. Get it right, for God's sake." His tongue hurt. He must have bitten it. He stopped talking and began walking.

Several other parts hurt: ribs, right foot, knees, head. Walking was terribly hard work. The forest floor was one long obstacle course of brambles and fallen branches. He was sitting on a log, getting his breath back and licking dried blood off his lips, when he saw the sentry.

Paxton was too tired to run. He didn't care if he got captured. He sat and let happen what was going to happen. The man never looked up. He had seen trees before. He had more important things on his mind. Food, probably.

Paxton watched him pass out of sight, and followed.

The trees thinned. The spaces between them had been cleared. Barbed wire channelled the path. Even before he saw the guard hut, he knew what this was. Ammunition dump. And, by the look of it, empty. All used up in the battle. That's why the sentry didn't care. Nothing left to guard.

Smoke streamed out of a chimney. Somebody laughed. At least two men were in there.

Paxton walked back into the forest and found the Very pistol and cartridges, and he walked all the way out again. He got lost, he tripped on thorny snares, he tore his hands and twisted his ankles. It took him an hour. Now all he had to do was go over to the guard hut and open the door and shoot two Huns. What for? For their rations.

Paxton knew that his brain wasn't firing on all cylinders. His growling stomach was doing the thinking. He sat down, leaned against a tree and told his stomach not to be so bloody stupid. Impossible to shoot two Huns. He'd have to reload the Very pistol. That took far too long.

His stomach sulked and he began to feel drowsy. He must have dozed off because the slam of the guard hut door awoke him. He peered around the edge of the tree. It was the sentry again, but now he was walking his beat in the reverse direction. Boring job. Anything for variety.

Paxton squirmed his bottom around the tree so as to stay out of sight as the man passed. Then the footsteps stopped. Paxton stood up. No sound. He did something very stupid: he peeked around the tree. You fathead, he told himself. What he saw was not a Hun pointing an angry rifle. He saw a Hun with his back turned, flexing his knees and turning his toes outward and going through all the motions of urinating against a sturdy pine. Paxton tip-toed over to him. Just as the sentry released a deep sigh of gratification, Paxton seized his neck and began to strangle him.

A pilot developed strong hands and arms, working a joystick for hour after hour. The neck was thin and stringy. The man struggled a little, and his helmet fell off. Paxton was looking at a bald head with a fringe of grey. Quite soon the sentry was a dead weight and Paxton had to drop him.

The guard hut was quiet. Nobody had seen. Why should they? Nevertheless, when Paxton had lugged the body away and put it out of sight he felt a great gush of triumph. What a risk! What recklessness! He looked at his fingers, and was astonished at their speed in killing a man. "Pip-pip, old chum," he said to the body. "If you'd gone before you left, this wouldn't have happened."

He put on the greatcoat and the helmet and took the rifle; also the man's papers. He was Ernst somebody, aged sixty-three. His false teeth were slipping out. Paxton shoved them back. "Don't mensh," he said. "Least I can do."

Now he was play-acting. None of this was real. He walked to the hut and opened the door. Another grey-haired soldier was standing on a chair, arms raised, about to hang an oil lamp on a beam. Paxton fired the Very pistol and a glaring red signal flare hammered him in the chest. It knocked him into a corner of the room and then it ricocheted loudly from wall to wall in a blaze of light and smoke. At last it smashed a window and escaped.

"Crikey!" Paxton said. "Never expected that!" The soldier was groaning and waving his arms, so Paxton shot him with the rifle, a thunderous bang. The soldier stopped waving but kept groaning. Paxton shot him again. The air was rank with the smell of cordite, tinged with something interesting. Paxton found a pot of stew bubbling on the stove. Saliva leaked into his mouth, and helped him speak. "Where d'you keep the spoons?" he asked the dead man.

*　*　*

At Gazeran the gale had blown itself out and there was even a promise of sunshine. The Americans seized the opportunity to set up some filming.

"You dash to the Nieuport, and your mechanic helps you get in," Dabinett said. "It's very simple, sir."

"Nobody runs to his bus," Mackenzie said. "Not in these boots and this coat. What's the point? You save twenty seconds. A patrol lasts a couple of hours."

"Nobody in America knows that, sir. Running makes it look more urgent."

"Huh." Mackenzie tied a spotted green scarf around his neck. "America doesn't seem to know much about this war."

Dabinett was growing tired of having to explain and defend his country. "America knows one thing, sir. The war is kept going by big dollar loans. If the Allies lose, a lot of American businesses will go bust." He could see that Mackenzie wasn't listening. "Chicago is in the trenches too, sir."

"Really? Well, I'm not going to live in America, so I don't give a damn. Ready."

He jogged to the Nieuport and climbed in. Klagsburn, standing on a stepladder, filmed him. The engine was ticking over: more urgency. "Stay there," Klagsburn called. "I want a close shot." Mackenzie opened the throttle, taxied away, turned into the wind, and took off. "Now where's the son-of-a-bitch gone?" Klagsburn said.

"Where d'you think?" Dabinett said.

Mackenzie was at eleven thousand feet when he crossed the Lines and fourteen thousand when he levelled out. At that height, in the blast of icy air, a flying helmet and goggles were essential; without them, his head would have been painfully cold and his eyes would have been clenched almost shut.

The sky was not busy, but it was not empty. Far to the north a scrap was taking place; machines were swirling at such a casual pace that they seemed like dancing insects, until one became a vivid spark and fell. "Ta-ta," Mackenzie said. He had no wish to get involved in somebody else's fight. Twice, British patrols changed direction to come and look at him, solitary Allied aircraft being unusual over enemy territory. He waved. They did not reply. They had no time for eccentrics, especially one flying such a lightweight frog bus.

He cruised around for twenty minutes until the enemy discovered him.

Five monoplanes came in sight. Only the German Air Force had monoplanes, so these must be Fokkers. Although they tried to outclimb him, Mackenzie knew that the twin wings of a Nieuport would always create more lift than the Fokker's single wing, and he wasn't surprised when they stopped climbing and flew at him.

With odds of five to one, he should have run away. He let the interception develop, and was irritated when three Camels came out of the sun and turned the tidy formation into wild confusion. Mackenzie flew into the centre of the confusion, banked steeply and circled, looking for trouble. All he saw was a whirl of Fokkers and Camels chasing each other. He flew through a squall of streaks of tracer, and a rush of terror pumped up his pleasure. A Fokker looped. Not a clever move. You got out of the scrap, but you lost a lot of speed. Mackenzie expected the Hun to half-roll out at the top of the loop and be right-side up, ready for anything. It didn't happen. He remained inverted, and fell. Mackenzie aimed the Nieuport at the bottom of the loop and got there only slightly later than the Hun. As they converged they were about a length-and-a-half apart. Later, the Camel leader's report said he thought they collided. Mackenzie saw useless details: neat canvas patches on the fuselage; engine oil on the pilot's face when he glanced back. Mackenzie began to fire and counted: "One elephant, two elephants . . ." He never reached three.

Streams of fire from the Vickers and the Lewis merged as they ripped through the Fokker and killed its pilot. His arms went up as his body was hammered forward. Mackenzie made a mental note of the time and place and he went home as fast as he could.

* * *

Paxton did not want to wake up, but the dream was unbearably sad. At first he thought he was at home in England, in the orchard. Birdsong, wind in trees. When he was a small boy, the orchard had been his favourite place to hide from grown-ups. He opened his eyes, and these were the wrong trees.

A fragment of his dream sidled into his mind: he had strangled his father and shot him and strangled him again. It sidled out, leaving the gloom of guilt. "No, no, no," he said aloud. "Not bloody true." That made him feel better. He had eaten the stew and half a loaf of bread. He had found a bowl of fried potatoes and some pickled beetroot; also a jug of milk. They went down too. Food had transformed him. He stopped wandering in never-never land and became a fighting soldier again.

The second guard's boots fitted him, more or less. He hid the body: heaved it into a bramble bush. The flying boots followed it. He tidied the guard hut, stuffed some rags in the broken window, lit the oil lamp, put a kettle on the stove. Sausage and cheese went into his pockets. Two grey blankets went over his shoulder. And still nobody came. But why should they? Who gave a damn about an empty shell dump? He walked until he found a hiding-place behind a stack of logs, and slept.

Now he was warm and dry, wrapped in stolen blankets. It made a nice change from the fear of falling from high trees. He curled up and enjoyed the comfort. His cheek itched, so he scratched it and saw scabs of black blood on his fingers. The fingers provoked memories of the tired old neck that had put up no sort of fight at all, and Paxton groaned. He didn't like the sound of the groan. "Him or you," he argued. "Him or you."

He was awake, and his scabby face kept itching.

He got up and found a stream. There was still enough light to make a reflection. What he saw shocked him. Bruises and dried blood were bad enough, but the eyes that looked up at him were frightened. Careful soaking got rid of most of the blood and muck. "What are you afraid of?" Paxton asked his face. "They're dead and you're alive." Water dripped onto his reflection and scarred it. The eyes were not persuaded; they still looked unhappy. He moved his head an inch and made the drips destroy the eyes.

With heavy cloud everywhere it was hard to judge the time. He guessed early evening. Better move before nightfall. The Very pistol went down a rabbit hole; he kept the rifle. A wide detour took him away from the guard hut and the ammunition dump. Sooner than he expected, the trees ended and he was looking at a river. Upstream, just around a bend, the tops of rows of tents were visible.

Paxton tried to go downstream and he walked into a bog. He backed out, mud to the knees. On the other side of the river was a road, with a lot of German troops marching or waiting or eating. A pair of Rumpler two-seaters flew overhead. Paxton felt very conspicuous. He walked upstream, trying to look like a sentry.

The camp turned out to be big. Going around the outside of it might look suspicious. He made for the middle. His rifle was shaking, pain was attacking his chest, his heart was pounding, demanding attention, until he gasped and realized that he had been holding his breath. His lungs pumped again and the pain faded. He was slightly encouraged by the sight of a lot of dirty, unshaven, weary men in filthy uniforms.

Some wore bandages, and moved slowly; a few were cheerful. They were all back from the fighting.

Paxton put his hands in his greatcoat pockets and let his marching degenerate into a slouch. He drifted through the camp, one survivor in a thousand survivors. Ahead he could see a dirt track leading to a bridge. Behind, he heard voices, not excited, nothing to do with him. He plodded on. One voice, crisp and curt, was persistent. Men turned and looked at Paxton. Obviously, this had everything to do with him. He wet himself: one brief, hot spurt down the left leg. He stopped and looked back. An officer beckoned, using that arrogant, economical flick of the fingers which Paxton himself had often used, and added him to a squad of twenty.

They marched to the bridge, singing. Paxton *dum-de-dummed*. Nobody noticed.

A railway track crossed the bridge. They sat by the line and waited. The soldier next to Paxton kept grumbling, and kept looking at him. Paxton shrugged. The man began to sound annoyed. Paxton lay back and shut his eyes.

If he got caught now he'd be shot. That's what the British Army would do to a Hun found walking about in khaki behind the Lines. Shot on the spot. Six rifles, and the officer's pistol to polish you off. "Awfully squalid," he whispered, and winced at his idiocy. After that he kept his jaws tightly shut.

It was dusk when a train arrived and came to a halt with much squealing of wheels and clanking of trucks. Unloading began: drums of fuel, crates of food, boxes of ammunition. Paxton dared not take his great-coat off and soon he was streaming sweat. He was shocked to discover that heavy labour was such damned hard work. The others made it look easy. He had no choice but to toil on.

They stacked the boxes, making a dump six feet high. By now it was night. Paxton picked his moment when the officer and an N.C.O. were checking paperwork by the light of a hurricane lamp. He took his rifle and sneaked behind the dump.

The train left. The squad marched away.

An hour later he was a mile further up the track and wondering what to do next. He had been very lucky, but now he was lost, physically weary and mentally exhausted. Too many life-or-death decisions; too much sudden death. Holland was neutral, and quite near. Holland would be good.

But which way? If he stayed in one place he'd die. Suddenly he had the odd sensation of looking down on himself, as if from a tall building. "This is no time to go potty," he said. But the experience was pleasant, and it lingered. He had to make a decision about something, so he ate some cheese.

It must have been about midnight when a train stopped a quarter of a mile away, and there was much activity. Lights bobbed about, men shouted. Paxton made another big decision. He went to see what was going on.

Hundreds of troops were lining up for food. It was a troop train made of cattle trucks. Two of the trucks were mobile kitchens. Paxton smelled soup.

He stood just outside the crowd and watched the lines shuffle past the kitchens. "Might as well be shot on a full stomach," he muttered. His head still felt occupied by strange pressures.

Nobody stopped him joining a line. Nobody told him he needed mess-tins or a bowl or tin mug or *something*, until it was too late and he was looking up at the cook, who called him a name which made everyone laugh. The cook stooped and lifted Paxton's helmet from his head and ladled soup into it. Everyone laughed at that, too.

Still, it was good hot soup, and the helmet didn't smell too bad if he didn't breathe as he dipped his nose. Two men watched him drink it down and they slapped him on the back and said presumably encouraging things. He nodded and grinned. The locomotive hooted. Everyone moved towards the cattle trucks. Paxton went too. Why not?

* * *

"What on earth is *that?*" Edith Reynolds asked softly.

McWatters ceased moving. He lay as a gentleman should, taking his weight on his elbows, and sighed. "It's me," he mumbled.

"No, it's not." She felt with her fingers. He found the touch quite thrilling. "It might be yours, but it's not you."

"Oh, well . . ." He kissed her, and got no response. "Look here: aren't we playing with words?"

"No, we're not. I'm playing with a length of bicycle tube, by the feel of it."

"Blast. I thought you wouldn't notice." He rolled onto his back. "I put it on when I was in the bathroom."

"Not notice?" She laughed. "My dear Jack, you know nothing about women."

"I only did it for your sake."

"Very gallant of you. But I don't find galoshes very romantic, so please go away and take off your galosh." She giggled, which annoyed him.

"There's no such word as galosh. So phooey to you." Nevertheless, he got out of bed and went to the bathroom.

When he came back, she said, "That's better."

He lay and sulked. After five minutes, she said gently, "This isn't fair, Jack. We haven't got for ever. I'm on duty at six o'clock."

"Why is it always the man who has to make the running? Anyway, you never waited for an invitation when Charlie Dash was at your nunnery, at Beauquesne. You just . . . helped yourself." He sniffed. "Not that Charlie complained. Lucky devil."

She was silent for a moment. "This happened at Sainte Croix nunnery?"

"Twice nightly, so Dash said."

"Well, it wasn't me. Not that it never passed through my mind, but . . . somebody else must have found him irresistible."

"Not you? Then who?"

"Does it matter?"

"Of *course* it matters."

"Why?"

"Because . . ." But he had no answer. "God speed the plough!" he cried. "Why can't something be simple, for once?"

"Once you get started," she said, "I think you'll find it's extremely simple."

McWatters thought of making a sneering remark, perhaps pointing out that you couldn't trust F.A.N.Y. nurses, they were all hopeless liars;

but he was tired of talking. "Nonsense," he said, and set about proving her wrong. In the event, she turned out to be absolutely right.

"Golly," he said, wheezing a little.

"Don't die on me," she said. "I see enough of that as it is."

* * *

After the rumours of mutinies in the French Army, there had been some talk in the mess of battle police. The adjutant had been happy to confirm that they existed, certainly in the British Army and probably in all armies. Their task, he explained, was to ensure that when the balloon went up and the infantry went over the top, nobody was left behind. "Some men need to have their bravery stimulated," he said. "I've known some very effective shots to be fired in our own trenches."

Paxton recognized German battle police as soon as he saw them, even in the dim light of the railhead. They were well armed and vigilant. When the train unloaded, they made very sure the trucks were empty. When the troops fell in and were marched away, battle police escorted the column. There was no singing, no talking. In the small hours of the morning, with the crack and shudder of gunfire and shell-bursts all too near, men had plenty to think of. Paxton was bitterly regretting the impulse that had got him on the train. He'd only done it because he was tired of making decisions and so he had trusted to luck, had gambled that the train would go eastward. He had no idea which way the tracks pointed, so it was a fifty-fifty chance. Now the bloody silly train had gone westward and he was marching into the battlefield. He could smell the drifting chemical stink of explosives. The bitch of a westerly wind was at work again.

They marched on a cobbled road until the cobbles became so smashed that marching was impossible. At some point they must have turned onto a track. The mud had been made liquid by rain and feet. Paxton listened to the suck and slop of hundreds of boots and found it most discouraging.

The track ended in a field. They sat in the lee of a slope and saw star-shells soar and droop and illuminate the night sky ahead. The glow was enough to show stretcher-bearers coming over the slope, stooping and hurrying, sometimes stumbling and spilling their loads. The odd bullet fizzed overhead and droned away.

Paxton chewed on his lump of sausage and tried to ignore the way the ground shuddered. After a while he found that he himself was shuddering, long after the vibrations stopped. He was glad nobody could see him. The next man nudged him, and offered a small flat bottle. "Schnapps," he whispered. Paxton gave him the remains of the sausage. The schnapps made him gasp, but it had a fiery charge that drove out the cold and some of the fear. He returned the bottle. They shook hands. Paxton wanted to embrace him. That drink was the first kind act in an age.

Much later, a sergeant came along the line and each man got two stick grenades.

The man with the schnapps took out his rosary beads and began a rhythmic murmuring.

Another sergeant came along. Everyone got a swig of liquor. It followed the schnapps like a rioting mob.

Then they were on their feet.

Paxton followed the others. If he kept walking he was bound to reach Wipers, and then Gazeran, then England.

They went around the side of the slope and waded through a stream. The enemy was firing shrapnel as well as high-explosive. He found them equally frightening: high-explosive blew you up, shrapnel cut you down. It was time to get into a trench, surely. They shuffled past a row of craters, all flooded. Paxton knew then that there would be no trenches. Anything deep enough to hide in would be deep enough to drown in. He was going to die. Hatred for his killers rose like bile.

They stopped. An order rippled down the line, and a metallic clicking followed. Bayonets were being fixed. Paxton had no bayonet. Serious offence, that. Fourteen days confined to camp. Paxton chuckled. The next man looked up and said something. It sounded friendly. *"Gesundheit!"* Paxton told him. It was nonsense, but nothing mattered any more. The schnapps bottle appeared. They emptied it.

After that, everything happened very quickly.

First, there was a charge. Paxton's boots were thickly caked with mud, so he lumbered rather than charged. There was a lot of firing and a hell of a lot of smoke. Paxton thrust his rifle, even though he had no bayonet, because everyone else thrust theirs, and he shouted because everyone was shouting. *"Gesundheit!"* he roared. Not much of a battlecry. He stretched it, made it last. Better!

But this bloody mud was a bastard. His legs were tiring, and he lagged behind, which was how he came to see his pal with the schnapps killed by a grenade. It blew him off his feet. Paxton went forward and looked at the pile of rags. This was all wrong, this was bad, this was just plain rotten . . . He was coughing and spitting from breathing these foul fumes, so he lumbered on.

Something had to be done. That was clear to him. Your pal gives you a drink, you can't just let him die. He was shouting, "Bastards! Bastards!" A wall of searing hot air hit him from the side and flung him far away. Then a roar deafened him. He lay on his face in the mud and knew that he would never breathe again. His lungs had quit.

That was only the beginning. Next he spent a long lifetime wandering about the battlefield. Or maybe it was five minutes. His lungs wheezed painfully, treacherous bloody things. First they quit, then they un-quit. Bastards. Something familiar stuttered, away to his right. It must be a Vickers. Good old Vickers! Never lets you down. Well, not often.

Paxton found a rifle with a bayonet and walked around behind the Vickers. Two-man crew, one feeding, one firing. He stabbed the feeder in the back and pulled the trigger. Enormous bang, and the recoil jerked the bayonet out. The gunner jumped up and Paxton bayoneted him too, several times. "Bastard!" he shouted. *"Gesundheit!* Bastard!" The man lost his tin hat. Paxton sat down and took off his coal-scuttle helmet, sticky with old soup, and put on the tin hat. Better. More dashing.

War is easy, he thought. You just kill people. Someone was trying to kill him. Bullets were fizzing past his head. He sat behind the Vickers and blasted off a long, scything burst. Now *this* was fun. He was still enjoying himself when three men in khaki kilts dived into the gun-pit. "Where the devil have you been?" Paxton said. "It's been frightfully lonely here."

"Thank God you held out," a lieutenant said.

"Gesundheit," Paxton said. He fired off the last of the belt.

EARTHQUAKE STRENGTH 11:

Railway lines greatly bent. Underground pipelines severed.

"Smuggler's Boy," Paxton whispered. "Did Smuggler's Boy make it?"

He was in Dando's two-bed sick bay, washed, shaved, hair brushed, dressed in fresh pyjamas, crisp white sheets drawn up to his chin, looking like a man who'd gone fifteen rounds with Gentleman Jim Corbett.

"Don't know," O'Neill said. "Never heard of him."

Paxton's eyelids came down very slowly. He seemed to lack the strength to lift them.

"You look knackered," O'Neill said. "I've got to write a report. There's a chance of a medal. Frankly, I wouldn't give you the skin off my rice pudding, but . . ."

Paxton licked his lips, once.

"Some Royal Scots Fusiliers found you. With a Vickers. Winning the war. At Wipers."

Paxton coughed suddenly, and dribbled a little. O'Neill wiped it away with a handkerchief. "Dando says you got somewhat knocked about. When you crashed. I need to know all that."

Occasionally the eyelids trembled; nothing else moved. After a while O'Neill went away.

* * *

Third Wipers went on and the losses were heavier than ever. The rain also went on. August was like winter. The drainage system of those Flanders fields had been wrecked and the rain had nowhere to go but down. Soon it was trapped by flat layers of clay and rock. The top-soil became saturated and then liquid. Even height gave no escape. A geological curiosity of this area was the fact that water collected on the ridges too, and stayed there. The soldiers didn't find it curious. Knee-deep in muck, sometimes thigh-deep, permanently soaked, at risk from slow death in a swamp as well as sudden death from high-explosive, the infantry had other words for Flanders.

Far from cutting their losses, the General Staff ordered more attacks. The original Push had involved only a hundred thousand men. Plenty more were waiting in the Reserves. Damn it, they'd been expensively trained and drilled; they were ready. It would be a criminal waste not to use them. It would mean that all those gallant lads who'd fallen would have died for nothing! God forbid.

The new attacks failed. The German Army had been ready for Third Wipers, and it had built a deep belt of concrete pillboxes. The concrete was very thick; sometimes even a direct hit only scarred it. The blast probably killed the machine-gun crew inside, but they were quickly replaced. Tanks were the obvious weapon against pillboxes. They struggled in the swamps, flooded and stalled. When British infantry tried to rush a pillbox they got cut down. If, at huge expense of blood and bodies, they captured a pillbox, its only entrance was on the enemy side. Hun guns pumped shells and bullets into the opening. Meanwhile, British artillery went on chewing up the battlefield. Each time Hornet Squadron flew over it, the ground looked more than ever like a flooded moonscape.

* * *

Dando's notes on Paxton began with concussion. He felt pretty sure about that, because any pilot who survived a crash must have whacked his head on something hard, and this head was badly cut. So were the knees and elbows. Dando suspected that a couple of ribs were cracked. There was heavy bruising almost everywhere. What worried him most, however, was the total lack of appetite and interest. Most patients got thirsty, even if they weren't hungry. Most patients talked, too. "Find out if he's in pain, if you can," Dando told McWatters. "I can't get anything out of him."

Paxton moved only his eyes when McWatters came in. His eyes looked tired. His skin was slack and shiny.

"Hullo, Pax." McWatters squeezed a foot through the blankets. "I hear you walked all the way to Wipers. Never realized you were so jolly fit. How are you feeling? Chap called Morkel is looking after your flight. Bit swarthy. Decent enough otherwise."

Paxton did not move. McWatters got a chair.

"You probably want to hear all the gossip, don't you? Let's see . . . The mess had pheasant for dinner last night, flocks of the bloody birds! Sergeant Lacey got them. *And* the wine, crates of it, spanking good stuff. The man's a magician. Of course we do D.O.P.s all day, usual grind. Remember Mackenzie?"

Paxton frowned. McWatters was startled at how old it made him look.

"Woolley got him kicked out of 'A' Flight. The little sod flies on his own now. Keeps getting flamers, or at least he claims he does, so the Yanks are happy . . ."

Paxton was struggling to get his arm out from under the blankets. McWatters helped him, and said, "D'you want. . . I mean, can I . . ." With immense effort, Paxton scratched the tip of his nose. His arm flopped. McWatters tucked it out of sight.

"Here's something to make you laugh. You remember that nurse who told me she'd been rogered by our little choirboy? All codswallop. Fairy tales. God knows why, she's an absolute stunner, I mean . . ."

Paxton's eyelids were falling.

"I'd better push off." McWatters stood up. Paxton blinked, and half-opened his eyes. "Smuggler's Boy," he whispered. "Did Smuggler's Boy do it?"

"Haven't the foggiest old chap. Better get some rest."

*　　*　　*

McWatters had never seen an enemy formation bigger than six until a dozen Huns came up through a hole in the clouds.

He laughed. It wasn't funny, but he had sucked in lungfuls of air and he had to do something with them. Now he felt tired; his limbs were heavy.

Fear did that. He was familiar with fear. It would vanish with action. He rocked his wings, test-fired the Vickers, made sure the whole flight was awake, and immediately dived into the attack. Why not? He was more or less up-sun and he had height advantage. No point in waiting.

They were Halberstadts, two-seaters with two guns, big strong beasts but they lacked a Biff's performance. They certainly couldn't climb as steeply as the Biffs could dive. McWatters heard his wires start to scream, glanced at the airspeed dial and saw it nudging two hundred, and looked up. The Huns were starting to scatter. Good! A spot of panic would even the odds.

Now he picked out a Halberstadt with commander's streamers on the wing-struts, made it his target and fired. For a few seconds the air was laced with tracer. Everything shook: the Hun, the Biff, McWatters himself.

It was not a good fight. Too many machines in too little space meant much wild flying and few clear shots. The flight went clear through the Halberstadts and used its speed to climb away, all except Drinkwater.

His place at the rear meant that he suffered most from the confusion. The few shots he fired went wide. No shouts of joy came from his gunner. Another blank. He tightened his grip and heaved on the stick just as a Halberstadt skidded across his path. He gave it a burst. He saw it wing-over and fall, smoke gushing from its engine. "Bull's-eye!" he roared. He thrust the stick forward. Bagged a Hun at last! he thought. He was going to make sure of victory if he had to chase the blighter right down to the ground, and that was what he had to do.

The Halberstadt was heavier than the Biff. Its exhausts kept pumping huge amounts of oily smoke but apparently its engine still worked. It kept Drinkwater out of range.

He was sure he could change all that when the Hun had to flatten out and the chase became a charge across the countryside. He was frustrated again. Obstacles got in the way: trees, hillocks, churches. The German pilot knew the land. When at last Drinkwater got the Biff lined up for a shot, swirling smoke hid the enemy. It was maddening. To make matters worse he saw tall trees racing past his wingtips. The Hun had found a gap in a forest. Smuts from his exhaust coated Drinkwater's goggles. When he dragged them off, the Halberstadt had vanished. A few seconds later the forest ended and he was skimming over farmland.

The Hun must have escaped down a turn-off in the trees. Left or right? Drinkwater guessed left. He banked hard and chased along the edge of the wood and met the Halberstadt coming head-on. He took a second to fire and that was a second too long. A burst from the Spandau hit his head. The Biff flew into the ground at about a hundred miles an hour.

An oil leak had caused the Halberstadt to make so much smoke. Its Mercedes engine seized-up while the pilot was circling the wreckage. He glided to a bumpy landing. Neither he nor his observer bothered to look at the bodies. They'd seen that sort of thing before, and it wasn't good for the appetite.

* * *

Tchaikovsky ended with a crash, and then threw in two more final thumps for good measure. The needle hissed. Lacey reached without looking and lifted the arm.

"I see *The Times* says we've captured another farmhouse at Wipers, sir," he said.

The adjutant was invisible in his office, but his door was open. He did not speak.

"It wasn't like this at the Somme," Lacey said. "All the talk then was of how soon we'd capture some real towns. Bapaume and Péronne, I seem to remember. . ."

No comment.

"We nearly got them. Nearly got Péronne, anyway. Then there was Arras, where we captured several important villages. Isn't that right, sir?"

More silence.

"And now we're two weeks into Third Wipers, and the news is we've taken another farmhouse. First it was towns, then villages, now it's farms. What next, do you think? When the next Big Push takes place, will *The Times* be applauding the capture of a vegetable garden?"

"Come here," the adjutant said.

"Or a large herbaceous border, perhaps." Lacey went in. Brazier was sitting, hunched at his desk. His great fists were clenched and rested on each side of an open file.

"You never wrote that poem you gave us. The commanding officer used it as a tribute. Now it turns out to be a fraud."

"More of a *collage*, sir. Perhaps a *mélange*."

"Colonel Bliss calls it a damn fraud. Line one is stolen from . . . Rupert Brooke." Brazier spoke heavily; he might have been naming a defaulter. "Whoever he is."

"Was, alas."

"Shut up, sergeant. 'Now God be thanked'. Brooke wrote that. 'From this day to the ending of the world!' Stolen from *Henry V*, would you believe! Shakespeare!"

"No mean thief himself, sir. Who is to say—"

"Shut your treacherous mouth!" Brazier roared like a drill sergeant. Lacey recoiled. He had miscalculated; the adjutant was in a rage. "Next you raided Tennyson. 'Blow, bugle, blow!' Stolen from a song. 'Was there a man dismayed?' Stolen from 'The Charge of the Light Brigade'. 'Who rush to glory, or the grave?' Stolen from the poem 'Hohenlinden' by Thomas Campbell, and no thanks to you the theft was disguised when the major changed the ending. 'Land of our birth, we pledge to thee' you thieved from 'The Children's Song' by Rudyard Kipling, no less. That leaves 'Dulce et decorum' etcetera, which is public property, I suppose."

"Horace, actually," Lacey said before he could stop himself.

"So five-sixths of your poem is stolen property. You've humiliated the C.O., you've blackened the reputation of the squadron, you have obliged me to apologize in person to the brigade commander. The editor of the *Yorkshire Post* has publicly accused the Corps of . . ." He searched in the file. ". . . 'of making literary sport out of its sacred duty to honour its dead.'" Brazier clenched his fists and rubbed the knuckles together. "Now speak."

"Oh, it was a joke," Lacey said gloomily. "I couldn't think of anything original, so I cobbled together some stuff I remembered from school. It was all so obvious, I was sure someone would see through it. It wasn't even good verse, it certainly didn't make sense, I mean I never expected anyone to *like* it. Quite the reverse."

"The editor of the *Yorkshire Post* claims he brought the whole shabby business to our attention weeks ago."

"I scrapped it, sir."

"You *destroyed* an official *signal?*" The adjutant's knuckles changed colour.

"Not a real signal. Just a note from the newspaper."

"Theft, insolence, failure to obey an order, and now wilful destruction of an official communication."

"Anyway, that first verse was superseded by then. You already had my second verse, sir. Nothing wrong with that. All my own work. Entirely original."

"Are you completely witless, sergeant?" Brazier took a paper from the file. "Or do you think everyone else has brains of cheese? Your second verse began, 'Armed with thunder, clad with wings', did it not?"

"Yes. That's what I wrote."

"That, sergeant, is what you copied."

"No! No, sir, that's not true." Now Lacey was outraged. "That second verse is entirely my work, sir."

"William Cowper." There was a sour twist to the adjutant's voice. "Wrote a poem called 'Boadicea'."

Lacey closed his eyes. "Oh no," he whispered. Brazier thought he was slumped in guilt. In fact Lacey was swamped by a golden memory of a classroom on a summer's afternoon, with chalk-motes drifting endlessly in the sunlight, and distant sounds of cricket mocking the pupils, and a boy reciting Cowper's imperial anthem. *Arm'd with thunder, clad with wings:* the line had been absorbed by Lacey's brain and, all these years later, blandly offered up as a true gift when it was really stolen goods. He didn't feel guilty; he felt cheated. Yet there was no dodging the truth. He was the victim, but he was also the cheat.

"What now?" he asked.

"Oh, you lose your stripes and tomorrow you report as sanitary man in the Front Line trenches, where you spend the rest of the war with a bucket, collecting the daily droppings of the troops." Brazier took a moment to enjoy Lacey's stricken face. "That's if it's up to me. Unfortunately it's up to the C.O."

"Oh." Lacey chewed his lip. "Perhaps he'll see the funny side of it."

The telephone rang. The adjutant answered it, and said, "Yes, immediately." He hung up. "You can ask him yourself, sergeant. The C.O. wants you in the sick bay. Take your pad and pencil. Go now."

* * *

When Paxton had been led out of the battlefield, he had not wanted to go to a regimental aid post to have his injuries examined. The doctor at the aid post had looked him over and decided he should go to a hospital by way of a casualty clearing station, but Paxton disagreed violently. He insisted on returning to Gazeran. There was a struggle, which turned into a fight just as fresh casualties were being hurried in. The doctor had told Paxton to go to hell and when he looked up from the bloody stretchers, Paxton had gone. Paxton got a lift to Poperinghe and found General Disinfectant's H.Q. there.

The doctor had a keen sense of duty. As soon as possible, he had telephoned Gazeran and talked to Dando. An hour or so later, General Disinfectant's car delivered Paxton to the aerodrome. Dando had never seen a man so badly bruised and still alive.

The C.O. had been impressed too. "Shouldn't he be in hospital?" he asked. "He may have internal injuries. Things you can't see."

"Yes, sir, he may have. But he crashed, he walked right through the fighting, he didn't rest until he got back to his squadron. Here is where he's determined to be, major. If we send him away now, it won't help him to recover."

From time to time, Cleve-Cutler visited the patient. Paxton never spoke, and scarcely moved. The C.O. always asked him if there was anything he needed; and finally Paxton responded. "Rum," he said.

Dando brought a bottle and everyone had a tot.

Paxton sighed. "Schnapps is the stuff." His voice was a husky whisper. "Awfully nice Hun shared his schnapps with me. What a pal . . . Best friend. Dead now. Some bastard threw a grenade and . . . foof. Some bastard killed my pal. No bayonet. Then I found a bayonet." There were tears dribbling down his cheeks.

"Wait a moment, Pax," Cleve-Cutler said. "Have some more rum."

When Lacey arrived with his pad and pencil, the C.O. said, "Start at the beginning. Start with the crash."

Paxton thought hard. "Couldn't find the damned chocolate. Found Griffiths, though. Poor Griff. Found the Very pistol. Shot the old man . . . No. Wrong." He sipped his rum. He was looking better; the skin around his cheekbones was pink. "Choked him. That's right. I had to strangle him because his neck was so small that I couldn't get his boots on." Lacey's pencil raced across the page. "Anyone can do it," Paxton said. "It's easy. I wanted to strangle the Vickers crew, but they had big feet. So I used the bayonet on them. Soon shut 'em up. Soon stopped their nonsense."

He talked for several minutes, always in the same hoarse whisper; and then suddenly fell asleep.

They went into Dando's office.

"Something godawful happened," the doctor said. "He didn't dream all that."

"He's hellish keen on strangulation, isn't he? Makes me believe he's done a bit. Eh? Is it as easy as he says?"

"Never tried," Dando said curtly. "Don't know."

"Give me your notebook," the C.O. told Lacey.

"It won't mean anything to you, sir." Lacey handed it to him. "I use my own private shorthand."

"Well, I'm going to burn it on my own private bonfire, so we're even. Have some rum, Lacey. You look like a piece of boiled cod."

An orderly tapped on the door. Mr Paxton would like to talk to the major.

When he went in, all the colour had gone from Paxton's cheeks and he was frowning hard. "Smuggler's Boy," he whispered. "How did he get on? Colonel Bliss said . . ."

"Gay Crusader won the Derby, Pax. Smuggler's Boy came nowhere."

"Pity." Paxton winced slightly. The eyelids came down.

*   *   *

Lacey went back to the orderly room, and found the adjutant chatting with Captain Lightfoot. "Here he is," Brazier said, "back from the wars. Well, I'm off to inspect the gun crews. No rest for the wicked." He took his black-thorn stick and went out.

Lightfoot sat at a desk and opened his briefcase. "I am here to take your statement," he said. "Are you, or have you been, in possession of five thousand American dollars belonging to the late Duke Nikolai?"

Lacey put his head on one side and thought about it. He had been bullied by the adjutant, and snubbed by the C.O. He worked hard for the good of the squadron, and his worth was not recognized. Now he was being chivvied by the A.P.M. Would it never end? Rot the lot of them. "I'm sorry, sir," he said. "Under the Official Secrets Act of 1911, I cannot answer your question."

It was Lightfoot's turn to think.

"Are you saying, sergeant, that you have, or you had, the money, but your possession of it is an official secret?"

"No, sir. What I'm saying is that anything I might say about that money, assuming it exists, *might* be in breach of the Act."

"*Might?* Don't you know when you're breaking the Act?"

"If I answer that, sir, then you will know that I am covered by the Act. Such information could be construed as officially secret. Therefore I cannot reveal that fact to you, sir. My answer, whether it be yes or no, would contravene the Act, always assuming it applied."

Lightfoot reviewed the idea. "So you're telling me that you can't even tell me whether or not your actions are subject to the Official Secrets Act."

"They might be, sir, or they might not. If they *were* subject to the Act, and if I revealed as much to you, then you would be in possession of a secret and I would be guilty of telling you."

"So you can tell me nothing." Lacey frowned.

"It's not as simple as that, sir. To tell you nothing might imply that there is nothing to tell, whereas—"

"Yes, yes, sergeant. Let's go back to first causes. When did you sign the Official Secrets Act?"

"If I were to answer that—"

"I know. I know. But for every lock there is a key. If you signed the Act, somewhere there must be a superior officer who was responsible for your signing. Who is he?"

"Always assuming such an officer exists—"

"Yes, I know all that. Please, let's take it as written."

"Hypothetically then, I should have to ask such an officer for permission to reveal his identity, because . . ." Lacey shrugged.

"Because it would be covered by the Act," Lightfoot said flatly. Lacey nodded. "Which you may or may not have signed." Lacey looked noncommittal. "So I'm wasting my time."

"That's not for me to say, sir."

Lightfoot closed his briefcase and stood up. "Sergeant," he said, "you make a fool of the army at your own peril."

The best answer was silence. Lacey said, "We live in perilous times, sir. We must gird our loins and baffle our foes."

That was a mistake. Lacey realized how bad a mistake it was when Lightfoot stood quite still and stared at him. He sat down and unlocked his briefcase. He took out a sheet of paper and read it. Lacey felt blood tingling in his fingertips. It was a strange sensation and he did not enjoy it.

"I don't go looking for trouble," Lightfoot said, "but if it comes looking for me, I am ready to meet it. This is a report from the brigade quartermaster. You sent him two hundred pounds of jam, labelled raspberry, actually plum. Those labels were forged. Printed in France. Stuck on the tins in France. I believe you were responsible, and I can prove it. It's not the only illegal extravagance originating on this squadron, nor is it the largest. I intend to investigate them all."

This time Lacey had the sense to be silent. Lightfoot left.

Fifteen minutes later, the adjutant came in. Lacey was watching a cup of tea grow cold. "Gone, has he?" Brazier said. "Good."

"You could have helped me, sir," Lacey said. "You know how to handle the A.P.M., you've got rank. Why did you leave me alone?"

Brazier hooked his thumbs in his tunic belt and rocked comfortably on his heels. "The Japanese have a saying, sergeant. It goes like this: *The nail that sticks up gets hammered down.*" He went into his room. The door banged shut.

Lacey unlocked a filing cabinet and took out bundles of chequebooks. He began burning them in the stove.

* * *

"How did you know?" Dando asked.

"Felt it in my water," Woolley said. "Got a spirit message from my dead granny, the Cherokee chief Read. it in Old Moore's Almanack. Who cares?"

"Ah, you're right, so you are. There's two drinks left in the bottle." They finished the rum.

Woolley went back to his hut and stuffed bottled Guinness into his pockets. He walked across the aerodrome and enjoyed the night, which was dry, and the breeze, which was slight. The stars were beginning to lose their glitter: dawn was near. The cookhouse cat, out hunting, came bounding towards him, its tail high as a flag. "Hello, Kitty," he said. "I see you've heard the good news. China's declared war on Germany. So we can all go home now." The cat escorted him. "I used to know a girl called Kitty. Wore a size fourteen shoe. She could drop-kick a goal from halfway, and barefoot too." The cat was an attentive audience, all the way to Mackenzie's tent. The tent was empty. This was no surprise. The Nieuport had gone.

Woolley lit the oil lamp and immediately attracted a large moth. It blundered about so much that he took his hat and knocked it into a corner. The cat trapped it and ate it.

"I didn't need that," Woolley said. "I really didn't need that." He opened a bottle and drank some Guinness. The cat came over and stood on its hind legs and tried to paw at the bottle, so he tipped a little stout into a bowl. "Finish that and you can have a small whisky," he said. He lay on the bed and watched the cat develop a taste for Guinness. When he woke up the cat was asleep on his chest and Mackenzie was standing, silhouetted by the dawn.

"What's going on?" Mackenzie asked.

"Don't just lie there, Kitty," Woolley said. "Explain yourself to the gentleman."

Mackenzie came in and flopped into a camp chair. He was in his flying kit. His face was as grimy as a coal-heaver's. He found a towel and rubbed at the oil-stains.

"Well, he's gone," Woolley said. He sat up, and the cat tumbled to the ground. "The major's not in a good mood. Don't go asking him for more pocket money. Big party tonight."

"Bang goes another piano."

Woolley took out a bottle of Guinness and looked at it. "Four o'clock in the morning, it was. Dando says that's the fashionable hour to go. God knows why. It's the arsehole of the night."

"Are you going to drink that?"

Woolley opened the bottle and gave it to him.

"What else did Dando say?"

"Shock. He said it was shock. Sometimes a man gets pushed too far and he can't get back again."

Mackenzie sipped his Guinness. "Dando doesn't know."

"That's right. Dando's guessing. Is that lipstick you're wearing?"

Mackenzie nodded. "Stops my lips getting chapped. Lacey got it for me. I have such delicate features, you see. Of course I never notice them, except in the mirror, and then they look ordinary enough. I got another Hun. Is that what you came to ask me about?"

"Confirmed?"

"Probably not. I went rabbiting. Went a long way over the Lines and hung about until the sun came up. It was dazzling, just like a searchlight.

Lit up an LVG two-seater. They never saw me, I was in the glare. What you call a Christian murder. Home for breakfast. Poor sport."

"I keep telling you, it's not a sport. It's a trade."

"For you, it is. Not for me. I do it for fun." He shrugged off his coat and pulled off his boots. Thick socks went with them. He pointed his toes at Woolley. "Silk stockings for warmth. Lacey again. You should try wearing silk, captain. It might get you out of Bog Street."

"Ah, don't be considerate, it doesn't suit you. You don't give a tiny toss about me." Woolley took the bottle and had a swig and gave it back. "You don't care about anybody. You're a shit. You get away with it on the ground, but believe me, that's not going to help you when you meet a Hun who's an even bigger shit than you are. Or worse yet, a pack of them."

"I'll do what I always do."

"Trust to luck."

"I charge straight into the middle of them, get so close to a fat Hun that his pals daren't shoot at me, and at that range I can't miss, can I?"

"It's what I said. Trust to luck."

"It worked for Ball."

"Oh, bugger Ball. Any stupid sod can give his life for his country. The real trick is to make sure the other bastard does it, not you."

Mackenzie went to the door of the tent and watched McWatters' flight take off. The Biffs closed up and droned away. "Anyway," he said, "as long as I knock down the flamers, why do you care?"

"I was an only child," Woolley said. "Dad always promised me a shit for a baby brother, but he spent the money in the pub, so I had to play with a pound of condemned sausages instead." He noticed an old, dented trombone lying in the grass, and picked it up.

"The Americans gave it to me," Mackenzie said. "Ball used to play the violin." Woolley put it to his lips and blew a sour note, and the cat fled. "I can't do anything with it, but that doesn't matter in the cinema," Mackenzie said. "It's just pictures."

"You're not going to listen to what I say, but I'll say it anyway," Woolley told him. "Don't trust to luck. Luck will always let you down."

Mackenzie finished the Guinness and returned the bottle. "Refreshing," he said.

Woolley was wrong; or rather, he was right in a way he had not meant. That afternoon he came back from a patrol in which "A" Flight got very briskly Archied. As he touched down, an undercarriage strut collapsed where a shell fragment had damaged it, and a wingtip ploughed into the field. The propeller hacked up lumps of turf and smashed itself to stubs. This dragged the nose down and the entire machine cartwheeled.

The rescue team got there very fast. The engine had been driven back, and Woolley was pinned in the cockpit. There was a heavy stink of petrol. They got him out by the vigorous use of axes and crowbars, not knowing that his feet were trapped. Both ankles were broken.

Dando packed him off to hospital. "Nothing very serious," he said. "Don't play the fool and you'll be back in a month or two. By then all this insanity at Wipers will be over." Dando was right about the injuries but wrong about the insanity.

EARTHQUAKE STRENGTH 12:

Damage nearly total. Objects thrown into air.

London in autumn had the right kind of weather: grey and cheerless. There was little to celebrate and the winter was nothing to look forward to. Russia was wobbling out of the war. A German and Austrian attack had just smashed the Italian Army. Zeppelins had bombed London yet again. And, as always, Third Wipers was toiling diligently at the business of losing an army in the mud. Sunshine would have been a bad joke.

Instead, London got the kind of greasy drizzle that was never strong enough to wash the smoke from the air. The wetness drifted into Charing Cross station and blackened the platforms so that thousands of bootprints left a brief record of troops in transit, until another train pulled in and fresh boots obliterated the old evidence.

Mackenzie hated it: hated the slick grey wetness, the crowds, the drifting smoke, the squeal and howl of locomotives. His luggage was one valise. He was first off the train, and first to the line of taxis. "Taggart's Hotel," he said.

"Sorry, guv. These cabs reserved for senior officers only."

"I'm a major. Acting major."

"Ho yes?" He was an old man, with a face that had long ago stopped looking interested in anything. "Looks like captain from 'ere."

"Give you a guinea."

"Rules is rules."

"Two guineas." The man hesitated, dazzled by riches. "Three," Mackenzie said.

"I'll lose my bloody licence, I will. Jump in quick."

It was mid-morning and the streets were full. Mackenzie was surprised how drab and gloomy the people seemed. In France, the troops who were out of the Lines were damned glad of it. They felt cheerful and they looked cheerful. These Londoners were a miserable lot. He thought: I bet a dose of strafing would buck you up. After that he stopped looking.

At the hotel he got out and gave the driver three shillings.

The man's mouth hinged open like a trap door. A string of saliva stretched and snapped. "What the bleedin' 'ell's *this?*" His voice could go no higher. "Three guineas, you said."

"I lied."

"It's a swindle." He was spitting. "I'll get a bleedin' copper. You're no officer, three guineas you said—"

"You're right. I owe you something." Mackenzie picked up a shrub in a small wooden tub and hurled it through the windscreen. "Keep the change," he said.

Taggart came out just as Mackenzie was going in. "I heard a crash. Was there an accident, or what?"

Mackenzie pointed to the space where the tub had been standing. "That brute of a cabbie is stealing your shrub."

"Bastard!" Taggart limped to the taxi and beat on it with his stick. "Come out of there!" The taxi shot forward and vanished around the first corner. "I got his number," Taggart said. "He'll be in the clink before nightfall, you'll see."

They went inside. "Why would a man like him want a plant like that?" Mackenzie asked.

"God knows. This town's full of thieves. It's the war. I suppose you need a room." He watched Mackenzie sign the register. "Ah, yes. I thought it was you. Your picture's been in all the papers. Mind, you've changed a bit since then."

"Bloody silly Albatros." Mackenzie wore a black patch on his left eye. A double row of stitches decorated the skin above it. Most of his left cheek was invisible behind dressings that were held in place by wide strips of plaster. When he spoke, a gap showed in the upper teeth on that side. "I blew it to bits, and some of the bits hit me."

Taggart touched his own eyepatch. "If you get any pain, I've a bottle of Norwegian aquavit that's strong enough to stun a moose."

"Are moose a problem in Kensington?"

"Not since I got this aquavit. They keep their distance. Before that, we were overrun by the buggers."

Mackenzie took his key. "By the way: Major Cleve-Cutler asked me to give you his regards."

"Ah. And how is he?"

"Absent-minded. Can't remember anybody's name. Between you and me, I think he's past it."

He had a bath, ate a sandwich and went to the War Office, where an old, thin colonel lectured him on the protocol of receiving a decoration from the monarch. "Don't speak unless His Majesty says something that requires an answer. No jokes. If His Majesty makes a humorous remark, you may smile. If His Majesty wishes to shake hands – highly unlikely – then do not crush his fingers. Do not squeeze. Do not pump. If you are given the wrong medal, or the medal has the wrong name, or His Majesty addresses you by the wrong name, say nothing. No alcohol before the ceremony. Do not faint. Do not stare. Do not scratch. Attend to your bowels and bladder well in advance. Make sure all your buttons are done up. That is all. Good afternoon, captain."

Mackenzie strolled down Whitehall, saluting and being saluted and returning salutes until he began to feel like a clockwork toy. He was looking at Big Ben because it was there to be looked at, when a cab stopped and emptied, so he took it because it was there to be taken.

The tea-dance at Malplacket House turned out to be a jolly affair. He danced with several young women, all of them cheerful, none of them so ill-mannered as to ask what he had done to his face. He was drinking tea when Dorothy Jaspers nudged his elbow and made him spill it. "Clumsy oaf," she said. Her smile grew wider and wider until it lit up her whole face. She took the cup and saucer and gave them to a passing naval lieutenant; he was so delighted that he thanked her for the slop. "Go and put it in the bilge," she said. "Isn't that right?" He hurried away.

"Come," she said, and took Mackenzie's hand.

"You're Miss Jaspers, aren't you? My C.O. said you would be here. He asked me to give you something."

"His burning love? His undying devotion?"

"No. A gramophone record."

"Dear Hugh . . . such a vagabond. How is he? Never mind, I don't care. Get your hat. We're going to a wake."

He stopped. "I've had enough of those in France."

"Don't be so damn picky. A wake is the only place a girl can get a decent drink in the afternoon nowadays. What else did he tell you?"

"Uh . . . Oysters. You like oysters."

In the taxi they were silent until Mackenzie said, "I suppose it's too much to expect that I'll know anybody at this wake."

"Just call yourself John and say you're a second cousin. Everyone has a second cousin called John. The deceased was a lieutenant in the Irish Rifles. I met his people at the funeral, so that's alright. Anyway, they'll all be well ginned-up by the time we get there."

The wake was in Belgravia, at somebody's town house. It was crowded and jovial, and it quickly absorbed them. An old and maudlin relative followed them around. "We shall not see his like again," he kept saying, with increasing emphasis. Mackenzie shook him off, but the words lingered.

Before long, he learned that the dead man had been a captain in the Connaught Rangers. He told her so.

"Then I went to the wrong funeral," Dorothy said.

"Do you go to many?"

"Heaps."

"Doesn't it get depressing?"

"Heavens, no. Funerals have replaced Ascot and Goodwood and New-market. Funerals and memorial services. It's where one meets all one's friends. I go to three a day, sometimes, just to stay in touch. And afterwards all the best drink comes out. Highly satisfactory."

"Not for everyone." When she blinked, he said: "We shall not see his like again."

"Oh yes we shall. We'll see his like buried every day of the week, with cocktails to follow."

"What good luck. So he didn't die in vain, then."

She straightened his tie. "You're bored, aren't you? You want to fight. Just like a soldier. Never happy unless he's picking a fight."

"I'm hungry. I do know that."

She took him to a small, dim restaurant. It was crowded, but she found a couple she knew and they shared their table. Mackenzie liked them; he was funny and she was pretty. There was no menu: food just arrived, and more food, and wine. It was all very easy and delicious. The other chap turned out to be a submarine officer: not only funny but brave. Occasionally, Dorothy stroked Mackenzie's thigh. She had a touch like fire, and he soared in his own estimation. When the sailor and his girl suddenly realized that they were late for the theatre, Mackenzie urged them to make haste, and to leave the waiter to him. They did. More food arrived: savouries, desserts, cognacs, nameless delights.

When he unfolded the bill, the room went quiet. Then blood pounded in his head, and the noise surged back. "I haven't got this," he said. "Jesus . . . I haven't got half this. Nowhere near."

"Pencil," she said. She signed the bill. The waiter brought their coats. Mackenzie wanted to tip him, but didn't know how, or how much. He went out feeling hot and humiliated.

The drizzle had stopped; the air was still. They took a stroll. "You could buy a Sopwith Camel for that money," he said.

"What's the point? You'd only break it." She took his arm.

"If you went to France, you wouldn't find the war so damn funny."

"I don't think it's funny. I think it's silly."

"Fighting and dying?"

"Quite absurd. And ludicrously expensive." Her tone was light. "You might as well throw five-pound notes at each other, for all the difference it makes."

Mackenzie felt that he was getting further and further out of his depth. He noticed her limp. "Doesn't your foot hurt?" he asked.

"How could it possibly hurt? It's made of wood."

One gaffe after another. "Where are we going?"

She stopped. "Be ready to be brave," she said. She raised herself on tip-toe and kissed him, quite hard, on the lips. "If we're not going to bed," she said, "there had better be a reason why."

"Look here . . ." His heart was pounding, and the damaged half of his face throbbed painfully. "Look here, this isn't right. I mean, you shouldn't have paid for dinner."

"Oh, you dear, sweet child. Somebody else will pay for it."

"Then . . ." But now Mackenzie was afraid to say more in case she mocked him again. He grunted, sulkily.

"There you go," she said. "Looking for another fight." It was the sort of thing his mother used to say, and it made him hate her.

She hailed a taxi and they went to the hotel.

"The police were here looking for you," Taggart said. "That bastard cabbie . . . Ah, it matters not. I told them you have an appointment with King George and they went away happy. I couldn't get the blood out of that carpet," he told Dorothy. "So there's a new one in that room." She gave him a smile that would have paid all her debts if he hadn't seen it before, many times.

They went upstairs.

Mackenzie sat on the bed. "What was all that about blood?" He was staring at the carpet.

"Who cares?" She pushed his shoulder, but he was as stiff as a plank. He refused to look up. "Oh God," she said. "You're not very good at this, are you?" No answer. "How old are you?"

"Eighteen," he growled.

"Don't get angry with me. I didn't make you a virgin."

"This is all wrong. Tomorrow morning I'm getting decorated by the king. It's my patriotic duty to . . . to get a good night's sleep."

"Oh, tosh and fiddlesticks! You're frightened. You're afraid I'll laugh at your pathetic weapon." There was a knock on the door. It was the boot-boy with a bottle of champagne. "Mr Taggart said you might like . . ." he began.

She took the bottle. She said to Mackenzie, "Give the king a big kiss, and tell him I hope you'll both be very happy."

He listened to her limp fade away along the corridor. He was still staring at the carpet, and wondering about the blood. She was right: he was frightened. Anyone as lovely as Dorothy Jaspers was frightening.

*   *   *

The king decorated Mackenzie with the Distinguished Service Order. "Two dozen Huns," he said. "Splendid, quite splendid. I thank you on behalf of all of Britain. Remember that this Order comes, not from Haig or Trenchard, but from me. This is my royal Order, in my recognition of your Distinguished Service. It is given sparingly. Well done."

Mackenzie stepped back and saluted. He felt buoyant. He felt as if weights had been removed from all his pockets.

The ceremony was in Buckingham Palace. The place was angular and charmless, a collection of rooms that were more like halls in a museum; but at least it was warm, and friends and relatives could watch from a gallery. There were many awards. When the king retired, the lines of officers broke up and there was a massive sense of relaxation. For the first time, Mackenzie felt free to look around and enjoy the occasion. In the gallery, getting to her feet, he saw Dorothy Jaspers. That red hair, so dark it was almost black, shone like a badge. "Bugger me," he said. Next to her, courteously helping her to rise, was Mr J. J. Dabinett. "Bugger me backwards," he said.

A tubby brigadier bustled up to him. He had a moustache that had been trimmed with a micrometer. "I'm Tunney, R.F.C. Press Office," he said. "Here's the drill. First you get your picture taken in front of the palace, for the newspapers. Profile only. No bandages in sight. Then be at Paddington station, 2 p.m., ready for a week's tour of munitions factories. Here's your speech. Memorize it. Same speech, five factories a day. Colonel Carr-Smollett will go with you. You met him yesterday."

"A week with *him?*" Mackenzie had forgotten he was talking to a brigadier. "He's pure starch. He'll drive me batty."

"Listen, lad . . ." Tunney's forefinger prodded him in the chest. "You're not the only D.S.O. in the Corps, nor the biggest. I've got a *double-D.S.O.* on the way and a possible V.C. after him. You're small beer, sonny. You'll obey orders and like it. 2 p.m. at Paddington!" He bustled off.

All the buoyancy was lost. Seven days; five factories a day. Thirty-five speeches, all identical. That was what this bloody medal had got him. He turned it over and read the engraving on the back. It said *Mackenzi*. He looked up and Dorothy Jaspers and J. J. Dabinett were facing him, smiling. "They can't even spell my bloody name," he said miserably. "Look. They've turned me into a bloody Italian . . . How the hell did you get in here?"

"Friends in the War Office," she said. "Did you sleep well?"

"That fat bastard . . ." He looked for Tunney and failed to find him in the crowd. "That fat bastard says I've got to spend a whole week making speeches at munitions factories."

"I drank the champagne. *Very* good."

"If I might intervene," Dabinett said. "I came to say goodbye."

"Oh. You've finished the film?" Mackenzie said.

"No. We decided not to make a film about the R.F.C., after all. Too many technical difficulties. You see, to convince the American people that the war is being won, we need to show action. Not just machines taking off and landing, but real fighting in the air. Alas, aeroplanes vibrate. Whenever we put a camera in a Biff, it shook. When the guns fired, it got worse. Everything blurred. A great shame."

"Damnation." Mackenzie touched his eyepatch. "And I don't suppose this thing can have helped."

"It created a difficulty."

"Well . . . God damn it all to hell." Mackenzie felt his day was falling apart. "Where are you off to now? Back to Wipers?"

"Oh no. Not the trenches. We're going to Palestine. Much more movement there, so it seems. Camels, and so on. And of course the light. . ."

He stopped because Brigadier Tunney was back, waving his clipboard. "Your mother is here," he announced. "I want a photograph of you both."

"She's in Scotland," Mackenzie said.

"Far from it. We notified her, the Palace invited her, and here she is." He pointed.

Mackenzie looked. His mother, wearing more furs than Genghis Khan, was advancing with her arms outstretched and a smile to match. "Andrew, darling!" she cried. "We're all so proud!"

"Get away from me," he said. "I don't want your pride."

"Now darling, don't be selfish. As soon as I heard, I couldn't wait—"

"*What?* You couldn't wait to blackmail me into uniform. You've never written, not even a postcard. There's only one reason you're here now. You're greedy for glory."

"I'm shattered," she said. Her head recoiled, and her eyes narrowed. "That my own flesh and blood could be so cruel."

"You're a vain and hypocritical bitch, mother."

She struck him. It was a sweeping slap, and as she was right-handed she hit the wounded side of his face. Pain roared like a fire in a wind. He flung a punch and hit her just below the cheekbone. Three bystanders went down with her.

The next thing he knew, he was being hustled through the crowd by Dabinett on one side and Dorothy on the other. They didn't stop until they were in the palace courtyard. Mackenzie was spitting blood.

"This won't do," Dabinett said. "We need to keep moving."

"That's her car," Mackenzie said, and spat again. "And her chauffeur. Know him anywhere."

It was a Daimler, one of a dozen limousines parked and waiting for their owners. He managed to walk to it. "Hullo, Tom," he said. "It's me. My mother wants you inside, in a hurry. Give me the keys." The chauffeur trotted off.

Dabinett drove. They stopped at Dorothy's apartment; she packed a suitcase in five minutes flat. On the way to Taggart's, Mackenzie said, "Sodding medal. Sodding factories. Sodding photographers. Sodding cinema. Sorry, Dabinett."

"I'm on your side, sir."

Mackenzie went in and packed his valise and paid Taggart and came out. Dabinett had left. "Where d'you want to go now?" Dorothy asked. She was on holiday.

"Scotland," he said. "And sod the lot of them."

The tank was full. Before nightfall they were far up the Great North Road, well into Nottinghamshire.

*   *   *

Next morning, deep inside Yorkshire, he said, "Well, that's two nights wasted." The words sounded bitter, almost an accusation, which was not what he intended. But he had been thinking about them for half an hour, as he drove and she read the map, and it was time to release his feelings.

The previous evening he had driven until his arms ached and he got cramp in his right calf. They had stopped at a hotel and registered as Captain and Mrs Mackenzie. The only rooms available were single rooms, on different floors. He was so tired that when he reached his room, he couldn't remember the number of hers. He slept badly and had many dreams, all bad-tempered. At breakfast Dorothy was fresh and blithe and each time he looked at her he felt cheated.

Now she put the map aside. "Only the working classes believe that sex is done in the dark," she said. "Has the army turned you into a peasant, Andrew?" He sounded the horn and scattered some sheep. "Perhaps you weren't talking about sex," she said.

"Yes I was. D'you realize I've got three sisters and I've never, ever seen a naked female?"

"French postcards?"

"Bits of cardboard."

"Still, they stretch the imagination."

"Not good enough. I want the real thing."

"Just show your stunning face. Girls are bound to come running."

He hunched over the wheel. "This bloody face of mine is a curse. I look like an angel, and the minute I don't behave like one, girls are shocked. They cry. They scream, they run away. It's damn difficult for a chap like me."

"You don't look terribly angelic now." She tickled his ear. "Anyway, it's time you realized that sex is a gamble. Take a chance."

"That's all very well, but. . . The point is, I don't know . . . I mean, how does one start?"

"Just ask."

"It's not that easy. What do I say?"

"Say what you feel."

"You mean . . . something like . . . May I have the pleasure of . . . the honour of. . ."

"Let's leave honour out of it. Pleasure, yes. Definitely. Positively. Without delay."

"Does that mean . . . um . . . now?"

"Yes, now."

He straightened up. "I'm not going back to that rotten hotel."

"We've got all of Yorkshire."

The moors rolled to the horizon. Compared with the wet plains of France and Flanders, this was wild, romantic country. Half the sky was bustling cloud and the other half sent bright patches of sunlight racing across the hillsides. He played a little tune on the horn.

"Well then, what about here?" He slowed.

"Too sunny."

He picked up speed. After a mile, the sunlight ended. He slowed again. "What about here?"

"Not sunny enough."

"For God's sake! What difference does it make?" He put his foot down. The Daimler charged uphill and down, hammering the bumps, lurching and swaying, and finally making Dorothy laugh. This was not fright or hysteria; something genuinely amused her. He let the speed fall away. "What's funny?"

"Look at you, Andrew. You're trying to fly. You've made me into one of your beastly Huns." She was still gurgling with laughter.

"Nonsense." He recognized his tone of voice: it was Brigadier Tunney's. Damn, she's right, he thought. Bloody women . . . They topped a hill. Far ahead, tucked away in the next valley, was a beech wood. "There." She pointed. "Go there."

Against all the odds, a cart track ran from the road to the woods. The beeches were in the lea of a hill and they soared like columns in a cathedral. "Frightfully noble," she said. Nevertheless, when they got out of the car, the breeze was chilly.

"More comfortable in the back seat," he suggested.

"No, no. This place was made for us. Everything's so tremendously phallic. Don't you find it wonderfully stimulating?"

"I don't need to be stimulated, Dorothy. I don't need to be frozen, either."

"Light a fire, darling."

It was one of the skills his father had taught him. In five minutes the flames had seized the kindling and small logs were beginning to crackle. "Done," he said. "Ready."

"Big decision." She had found a pile of travel rugs. "Do you want me with or without the woodwork?"

"Oh . . . With. I'm not going to be shortchanged." She liked that.

They undressed. Each stood, hands on hips, enjoying the sight of the other. "Not hairy," she said. "Good. I prefer men with silky skin. Your body is adorable."

"And so is y-yours. P-perhaps a sus-suspicion more hair than I expected." The stutter surprised him. He was trembling, too, and not from the cold. "I'm not com-complaining."

"French postcards never tell the whole story . . . Why are you shaking? What are you afraid of?"

"Dunno. S'pose I make a m-m-mess of it?"

She took his hand and they lay on the rugs. "Your parents didn't make a mess of it. Nor did their parents, and so on *ad infinitum*. It must be very easy. Think of all the stupid people in the world. No, on second thoughts, forget them. Forget everything. Especially the silly war. You're out of uniform, this isn't a battle. I've surrendered to you. Have you surrendered to me?"

"Yes." None of this made sense to him.

"Good, good. When nobody fights, nobody loses. That's something they never told you in the army." They kissed, and after that all conversation ended. The exchange of pleasure made a far better dialogue. Soon he was wondering why he had ever worried.

Above the beeches, a kestrel drifted, paused and hovered, searching the ground for food, and drifted on. It saw the glow of the fire, the gleam of the Daimler, the flicker of white flesh. It knew that this was no meal and it moved away at once.

A minute later it flew back, not pausing, not hovering, just sailing the length of the wood and vanishing.

* * *

They were lying in a tangle of limbs, half sweaty, half chilled, still slightly stunned by their achievement. It took a while for the breeze to awaken them. They got up, clinging to each other, and stood beside the fire. Its warmth dried the sweat and took away the chill. The flames had a fascination, and they were looking at them when a man gave an angry shout. He was striding down the track. He had a shotgun and a dog.

"Gamekeeper," Mackenzie said.

"Yes. Frightful moustache. Looks as if it died in the night."

The man kept bellowing at them. Every other word was an obscenity. He stopped when he was ten yards away. His face was thin and leathery and distorted by disgust. "What the bloody hell d'you think you're about?" he shouted.

"Fornication," Mackenzie said. "And it's far too good for the likes of you."

"And who the bloody hell d'you think you are?" The shotgun was raised.

"Excuse me," Mackenzie said. He went to the car.

"He is Viscount Haig, son of the Field Marshal," she told the man, and took a few steps towards him. "And I am his sister." The man gaped, and his gun drooped. "Not the usual effect I have on men," she said. Now he had

418

seen the wooden leg, and he was speechless. "My brother will be with you in a moment," she said sweetly.

Mackenzie got his Service revolver from his valise, cocked it and fired a shot well above the man's head. The crack-boom raised a panic in a hundred crows. The dog fled. "Be off with you!" Mackenzie cried and advanced, flourishing the revolver. Echoes were still reverberating. The man turned and ran. Mackenzie fired a second bullet into the treetops, and the man ran faster. He was two hundred yards away before he stopped.

"Well, he *was* surprised," Dorothy said.

"Probably never seen a Daimler before," Mackenzie said.

* * *

An hour after they crossed the border into Scotland, the damaged side of his face began seeping blood. He asked her to kiss it better, and she refused even to touch it with a handkerchief. "It's only blood," he said, and licked the trickle that had reached his mouth.

"I don't care. I don't care what pain men inflict on each other. Hack yourselves to bits, if you think it's fun. Just keep the blood away from me."

This angered him. It was, after all, an honourable wound. "So you'd prefer me intact?" he said. No reply.

He stopped in a town somewhere north of Glasgow and found a doctor. Dorothy came with him into the surgery. "There's bound to be gallons of gore," he warned.

"Don't care. I need some cream for my stump."

The doctor took off the dressings and the eyepatch and did not like what he saw. "Did all this happen on active duty?" he asked.

"Yes and no."

"His mother hit him," Dorothy said. "She wasn't satisfied with what the Boche had done. Very demanding woman."

"Well, she hasn't improved the situation. There may be some infection. D'you see?"

For the first time, she looked at the raw, battered face. "Jesus Christ," she whispered.

"If you must blaspheme, go into the waiting room." He re-dressed the wound. "What can you see with that eye?" he asked Mackenzie.

"Three of everything. Sometimes four."

"You need plenty of rest. Nothing else will replace that. No alcohol. And no strenuous physical exercise, of course."

The roads north became worse: narrow, twisting and stony; and he was weary. But he was determined to finish their journey. It was late at night when he stopped the Daimler in the gravel circle outside the high, iron-studded, oak double doors of Castle Mackenzie. He had to rouse the servants; they came bearing candles. "The generator gets switched off at night," he explained.

He was warmly welcomed. The warmth was redoubled when he introduced her as his wife. They stood in the hall while their bags were brought in and the car was garaged. The candlelight showed several large and faded Turkish carpets that covered less than half the floor. It showed parts of granite walls. It failed to show the ceiling, although Dorothy got a glimpse of hanging banners, which proved that there must be something up there somewhere.

They ate ham sandwiches and drank claret in the library, while a fire was lit in their bedroom. Mackenzie was so tired that he stumbled while going upstairs. She had to help him undress. He looked younger than eighteen. Maybe he wasn't eighteen. Plenty of youngsters lied about their age in order to get into the R.F.C. He lay naked on the bed. The firelight gleamed on his chest. She watched the pale gold skin being gently nudged by his heartbeat. "Why are we here, Andrew?" she asked.

"I forget." He looked at her with his one good eye. "We're going to get married, aren't we?"

"*No.* Definitely not."

"Why not?" His lips barely moved.

"There's more to be wed than four legs in a bed. Shakespeare."

"Well . . . I'm not going back to bloody old France."

She stretched out her arm and, with one fingertip, touched his heartbeat so lightly that the finger gave a tiny kick with each throb.

"You're too beautiful," she said. "If you grow old I'll kill you."

Next day it rained. He wore old, shabby tweeds, much patched with leather. "Belonged to my father," he said. They had breakfast in a room as big as the mess at Gazeran. They had the castle to themselves; his sisters were all in London with their mother. "Won't they come back?" Dorothy asked.

"Not in a hurry. Mother has a place in town. She probably thinks I'm skulking around Soho."

"You can't skulk in a Daimler."

He stood up abruptly, and wrapped some bacon in toast. "Don't tell me what I can and can't do." He went out. She heard orders shouted, doors slammed; then silence. She sipped her coffee and read some old newspapers. Mata Hari shot by French firing squad. More Zeppelins over London. Fierce fighting in Ypres Salient. Board of Trade appeals for less pleasure motoring. "Too late," she said. "Anyway, it wasn't all fun."

He came back three hours later, very wet and muddied to the knees, and holding a rifle. "Come and see," he said, and gave her an umbrella.

Standing in the rain was a horse with a dead stag across its back. "One clean shot. Halfway up the mountain. He dropped where he stood. Never heard me fire. A very Christian kill."

Blood dribbled down the horse's flanks. "What is this?" she said. "Some sort of Caledonian gift-offering?"

"It's supper. Fresh deer's liver, absolutely yummy. Thank you, Bobby." A servant led the horse away.

"Do you feel better now?"

"Better than what? Wait a second . . ." He saw a shape flying in the mist and aimed and fired. It veered away.

"God in heaven!" she said. "Can't you stop killing things?"

"Bloody heron. They eat our trout."

"What if I eat your silly trout? Will you shoot me?"

She was annoyed, but he was still very pleased with himself. "I might," he said, "if you were poaching."

* * *

He soaked in a hot bath. She sat and watched. They both drank whisky. "Tell me, then," he said. "The blessed woodwork. How did it happen?"

"Oh . . ." She looked away. "My mother wanted me to be a ballerina. Actually, she wanted to be a ballerina herself, but child-bearing had got in the way, which was obviously all my fault, so she pushed me into ballet school. I was about three, and very small and not nearly strong enough, but I had to dance and dance and dance, until one day the leg conked out. Some kind of paralysis. No way back. Better off without it, the doctors said."

"Hell's bells. Who needs a mother, eh?" She shrugged. "Still," he said, playing boats with the loofah, "they were probably right, weren't they? I mean, a conked-out leg is no use to anyone. You'd just end up a cripple."

She kicked the bath with her wooden foot. "I *am* a cripple."

"Yes, but not like a chap with a crutch."

She stood and kicked the bath repeatedly, until white paint flaked off. "When you can do that, you can lecture me on cripples." She sat down and gave herself more whisky. "Anyway . . . what smacked your face, apart from mother?"

"Shell splinters. They had to travel a long way to hit me, fortunately. Otherwise I might have lost this eye altogether."

"How awful. A conked-out eye is no use to anyone, is it? You're better off without it. They make very good glass eyes nowadays, you know."

"Oh, go to hell."

"That's the trouble with you soldiers. You never see the joke in war." She kicked the bath one last time. "You're too one-eyed. I'm off to lunch."

She had eaten and gone by the time he came down, so he ate alone. He thought of her, sometimes angrily, more often eagerly; until he couldn't wait any longer and he abandoned the meal and went in search.

She was at the window of a turret, looking out at three other turrets and two spires. "You might as well live in St Pancras station," she said. "Handier for the shops."

422

"The whole place is a fraud. It's a glorified shooting-lodge, put up by some Victorian grandee who went bankrupt and threw himself from this very window."

"Not possible. It's got bars on it."

"He was dreadfully thin. All that worry. Couldn't eat."

"Uh-huh." Obviously she believed none of this.

"It was a real castle, once. There's a genuine lump of the original stone underneath one of the lavatories."

"How interesting. A large fraud, surrounding a tiny bit of truth, which nobody ever sees. Why does that sound familiar?"

"It can't be me, so it must be you." It was a cheap remark, made in anger at her mocking jibe, and he regretted it. "Caledonian peace offering," he said quickly, and gave her the record from Cleve-Cutler.

There was a gramophone in the music room. As the needle made its preliminary hiss, he took her hands. "I can't dance," she said. "I haven't got the feet for it."

"Stand on my shoes. I'll dance for both of us."

Poor Butterfly,
Neath the blossoms waiting.
Poor Butterfly,
For she loved him so . . .

She hung from his shoulders, so that he scarcely felt her feet on his. When she began to sing, he knew that he had done something right, at last.

I know he'll come to me,
Bye and bye.
But if he don't come back
Then I'll never sigh or cry,
I just must die . . .
Poor Butterfly.

The record spun to an end. They were left in what had to be an embrace.

"I say," he said. "May I—"

"Yes."

"Have the pleasure. I was going to say—"

"You talk too much."

As they went upstairs, she said, "Hugh thinks I'm the Poor Butterfly, and I think he is."

"Were you . . ." It was too late to stop. "Were you ever . . . um . . . intimate with him?"

"Hugh couldn't be intimate with the Queen of Sheba if she wore nothing but his spurs and his Sam Browne," she said; which made him laugh, and that made her smile.

* * *

Next morning there was blood on his pillow; quite a lot of blood.

The castle had a telephone, but it wasn't working. One of the servants bicycled seven miles to the nearest doctor. When he came, a police sergeant was with him in his car.

The doctor changed the dressings. "This should have been done yesterday," he said. "I don't like the look of some of those stitches. What the devil have you been up to?"

"Oh . . . rest, and quiet reflection."

"Hogwash." He tested Mackenzie's heart and lungs and blood pressure, and shook his head. "A week in bed. Alone. If you don't lie down soon, you'll fall down." He scribbled a note. "Hospital in Edinburgh. See this man. He'll help you."

The sergeant replaced the doctor.

He said he had received a telephone call at the police station from Mrs Mackenzie in London. Of course it was an awful long way, and the line was all crackles and whistles . . . Still, it seemed that Mrs Mackenzie had lost her big car, the Daimler . . . It was a pity the details weren't exactly clear . . . And wouldn't you know it, she was cut off by the operator.

Military priority, or some such blether . . . There was no escaping the war, was there? Congratulations on your medal, sir. He said goodbye and rejoined the doctor. Mackenzie and Dorothy watched the doctor's car rattle down the long drive.

"That policeman knows the Daimler's here," Mackenzie said. "He's heard the gossip. He'll probably telegram my mother. She'll probably tell that fat-faced brigadier. We'd better leave."

"Where would you like to go?"

He tried to scratch his stitches, until she pulled his hand away and held it. "I haven't any money," he said.

"You own half of Argyll."

"I don't inherit until I'm twenty-one. I get an allowance, but I spent it all in France."

"Look around. There must be money here. Somewhere."

"Mother has a study. She always keeps it locked."

"Wake up, Andrew. If at first you don't succeed, *cheat*."

He went away and came back ten minutes later with a felling axe. She watched as he hacked away at the study door. The noise attracted a couple of servants. "It's alright," she told them. "A cat got trapped in there, that's all." They left. He chopped through the lock and the door swung open.

There was a massive bureau-desk, and it too was locked. "Mistrustful old bat," he said, and attacked it.

Inside was a cashbox. Also locked. "You miserable bitch!" he shouted. He stood it on end and swung the axe as if splitting a log. After three blows the lid fell off. They were forty-seven pounds richer.

"Where shall we go?" she asked. "Since you're not going back to France." He sat on the floor. His face was shining with sweat. Below the dressings the sweat was pink. "America?" she said. "I have friends there."

"That's desertion. I'm not going to desert." He spread the notes like a fan. "Forty-seven miserable quid. I don't know . . . What should I do?"

"That's easy. When in doubt, go to the races."

"I like being with you. I don't have to think. Thinking just makes my stitches itch."

They went to their room to pack. "Fresh underwear," he decided. "It's about the only thing I've got lots of." He undressed, and stood in front of the mirror, carefully brushing his hair. He cleared his throat. "May I have the pleasure?"

"Andrew . . . your affairs are your affair, but . . . Haven't you got a bank account?"

"It's empty."

"Well, empty it some more. Get an overdraft."

"Jolly good idea. *Now* may I have the pleasure?"

"Yes, of course." She fell onto the bed and lay spread-eagled. "Take me for all you're worth, Andrew. Including the overdraft."

* * *

The bank manager at Crianlaroch knew the Mackenzie family well and he valued their custom; all the same he could allow an eighteen-year-old an overdraft of no more than twenty-five pounds. Crianlaroch was a prudent place and the manager was only a year off retirement. Mackenzie took the lot in cash, on the spot, which was not at all what the manager expected.

"Perth," she said. "There's a race meeting at Perth."

It took them four hours to drive there. The weather was better, and Mackenzie was grateful for that because he was feeling worse. His face throbbed painfully and he was sweating all the time. The road was straight, even if it wasn't smooth. For mile after mile it ran alongside Loch Tay, and then it followed the Tay through Ballinluig and Birnam. "Where the beeches came from," he told her. Conversation was an effort. He was drowsy. At times it seemed to him that the Daimler was driving itself, and he was just there to fool about with the wheel. That was a dangerous idea. They had a flask, so he took some whisky to clear his head. "Darling, you just missed that cow, or whatever it was," she said.

"Did I really?" He squeezed her hand. "Goes to show what a bloody brilliant pilot I am."

They reached Perth too late for the first race. The bar was open. They ate smoked salmon sandwiches and drank whisky while they picked a horse in the second. "There's a runner called Total Wreck," she said. "No form, unknown jockey, poor draw."

"Back it!" he said. Total Wreck surged through the field and won by a length at thirty-to-one. They rejoiced, and went to collect a fistful of notes, and were still rejoicing when they came back to the bar and celebrated with more whisky. A big, pleasant-faced major strolled over and congratulated them. "You'll be Captain Mackenzie?" he said. "The D.S.O.?"

"No, no. Can't you see I'm in mufti? I'm on leave, old chap."

"Not so, I'm afraid. My name's Day. I'm in the APM's department."

"You're all bastards," Dorothy said. "Every last one of you."

"I'm not going to France," Mackenzie said.

"Of course you are. No fuss, old man. We'll forget the nonsense about the car. Forget all about the munitions factories. Up you get, old chap. If we go now, we can catch the London express and put you on tonight's boat train."

"How did you know I was here?" Mackenzie asked.

"Your picture's in all the papers. You're famous."

"He's not very well," Dorothy said.

"In that case he'll be in good company when he gets to Wipers," Day said. "Nobody's very well there at the moment."

* * *

Poperinghe wasn't a patch on Gazeran. The field was vast and bumpy; three squadrons were based here. The crews lived in draughty Nissen huts, eight officers to a hut. The mess was gaunt and cold. There was no escape from the wind; it rattled the windows of the orderly room. When two military policemen delivered Mackenzie there, they found the adjutant alone; and the adjutant was not Brazier.

"Where's Uncle?" Mackenzie asked.

"Moved on. I'm the new Uncle." He was balding and amiable, and he wore a faded Observer's wing. He scribbled a signature and the policemen saluted and marched away. "Spot of bother? I expect you're glad to be back. Blighty's a dangerous place, if you ask me. Too many beanos. Too many poppets."

"I'm not well, Uncle."

"See Dando. He's got some new hangover cure."

"Not hungover."

"Look . . . the C.O. wants everyone in the anteroom in five minutes. You'd better be there. You don't want to blot your copybook again, D.S.O. or no D.S.O."

"Oh, Christ."

"I must say you look pretty foul. Stay off the gin, old chap. That's my advice."

Mackenzie walked to the anteroom. He felt cold, but walking made him sweat. What he needed more than anything was a bath. Major Day had travelled with him on the express to London. Mackenzie had dozed most of the way. Occasionally he daydreamed about killing the major and running away, but the man was big and alert. Just to look at him made Mackenzie feel drained of energy. In London, Day had handed him over to a captain in the APM's department. They caught the boat train, and the boat. In France, the military policemen took possession. They had put him in a car and driven him to Poperinghe, hitting every pothole on the way. "Slow down," he'd said. "I'm not perishable goods, for God's sake. What's the rush?" They hadn't answered, and they hadn't slowed down.

There seemed to be a lot of new faces in the anteroom. He saw Dingbat Maddegan, and said, "What happened to Uncle?"

"Sacked. Jiggery-pokery. Something to do with jam. Lacey went too." Maddegan shrugged. "It's all bullshit."

Mackenzie noticed that Maddegan was wearing the three stars of a captain. "Congratulations."

"Well, McWatters copped it, so I've got 'C' Flight now. How was London?"

"Lousy."

"And King George?"

Mackenzie had to work hard to remember. "Very short," he said. "He couldn't spell my name." Maddegan was amused, but not greatly.

Cleve-Cutler came in with another officer, and everyone stood up and shut up.

"This won't take long," the C.O. said. "We're ordered to go ground-strafing again."

Total silence. Mackenzie tasted salt and wondered if it was blood.

"Corps doesn't give us these jobs just to keep us in flying pay," the C.O. said. "There's a reason, and this officer will tell us what it is. He's been in the thick of the fighting and he knows what's what. Major The Lord Delancey." Cleve-Cutler stepped back.

Now that caused a bit of a stir. Titled officers were a rarity. This one looked to be only a few years older than the average pilot. He wore the uniform of the Guards, and his right sleeve was pinned up. Those near enough to him could see that his left ear had been mangled. Delancey had paid for the right to be heard.

He asked them to sit down.

"I'm not an airman," he said, "so I'm not here to tell you how to fly. My experience has been on the battlefield. My job now is to act as liaison between the sky and the mud, and help you to help the infantry. I'll explain why you are being asked to do certain things, in this case: ground-strafing the enemy. I have seen your machines attack enemy troops and I know first hand how grateful my men were for your intervention. It saved the day. Well, here is another day. This time we're asking you to help us win it. At Passchendaele."

Now they knew the worst. There was a scuffing of boots and a mumble of curses.

"You've been there already, I know. More than once. What makes Pass-chendaele so special? It's our final objective. This has been a long battle. August, September, October, and here we are six days into November and still slogging it out with the Boche. Long and costly. The casualty figure I've heard is two hundred thousand. That's a big bill to pay, but if we can just take Passchendaele, we'll have got what we want and we'll have won this battle."

The C.O. was watching their faces. A few looked sick. That casualty figure was a bad blow. Personally, he reckoned it was on the low side.

"There's a terrible irony about Wipers," Delancey said. "The more ground we gain, the harder the battle becomes for us. We've advanced about four and a half miles since August, but most of the last two miles that we gained are now a swamp, if not a lake. When I tell you that we sometimes need sixteen men to carry a single stretcher out of the mud and onto the duckboard tracks, you'll appreciate the problems we face when we try to move our guns in the battle area. We lose them in the mud. I've seen artillery sink in a swamp. We're using pack-mules to bring up ammunition. We lose the mules too. Shells arrive covered in slime, and have to be cleaned. Usually it rains, of course, which helps clean the shells."

They laughed, briefly, glad of any reason to laugh.

"The enemy has no such problems," Delancey said. "Quite the contrary. They have reinforced their artillery behind Passchendaele, where the ground is firm and the roads are good. Not surprisingly, our troops are suffering severely from this mismatch. It will not stop them attacking Passchendaele, but I hope you understand now just how much they need your ground-strafing. Our guns cannot help them, but you can. To you goes the pride of place; yours is the vanguard."

There were no questions. Coffee was served. Everyone had something to say, but nobody had the nerve to say it to Major The Lord Delancey, except Woolley.

"You probably don't remember me, sir. Last March. A flying poacher took your deer, and you gave us the venison."

"My dear chap!" Delancey shook his hand. "How good to see you."

"Quite a coincidence, isn't it?" Woolley said. "Quite amazing. Almost unbelievable. After all, there must be a hundred squadrons in France."

"No coincidence. As soon as I was attached to Trenchard's staff, I looked through the list of pilots, just in case there might be an old school chum amongst them."

Cleve-Cutler, listening, said, "You went to school with *Woolley*?"

"No. But I remembered him as an unusually keen and combative officer, and when the need arose for a squadron to crack a tough nut, I suggested yours."

"How interesting," Cleve-Cutler said. "I don't think you've met the padre."

"I say, sir, weren't you second wicket down for Eton?" the padre asked. "Or was that another Delancey?"

They moved away, and Cleve-Cutler said, "You got us in the fucking vanguard, Woolley. Now you can have pride of fucking place; you can lead the fucking squadron."

"Yes, sir."

The C.O. braced his shoulders and grinned his rage. He had nothing more to say, but he was reluctant to move.

"Why did you get rid of Lacey?" Woolley asked. "He was a bit of a pansy, but at least we had comfortable toilet paper. And good grub. And ping-pong."

"The A.P.M. caught him with his fingers in all sorts of pies. Brazier had turned a blind eye, so he was as bad. They gave Brazier the option: court martial, or go back to the trenches. He chose the trenches, and now Lacey's his batman."

"And we're in this dump."

"You're free to leave, captain, just as soon as you've won the war. Is that Mackenzie? Tell him to come to my office. Now."

* * *

The adjutant saw Cleve-Cutler heading for his office and got on his bicycle. They arrived together. Cleve-Cutler had to kick the door open and the adjutant had to kick it shut.

"The usual bumf, sir. All it needs is your signature."

The C.O. worked his way through the bundle of papers. His signature became more and more illegible. Finally he stopped. "This letter," he said. "Who wrote this letter?"

"I did, sir. I'm afraid I never knew the officer—"

"That's painfully obvious." Cleve-Cutler got up and paced slowly around the room, taking care not to step on the cracks between the boards. The floor creaked and squeaked at every step. "They follow me, Uncle," he said grimly. "Hear them? They follow me everywhere. From Pepriac to Gazeran, and now here."

The adjutant put on a serious face and said nothing.

"All that tosh about the fellow's gallantry, Uncle. His conspicuous bloody gallantry. There must be something better to say . . . Anyway, the only conspicuous thing about Dobson was his raging acne."

"Not Dobson, sir. Jennings. This letter is for Jennings' next-of-kin."

"Where's Dobson's letter, then?"

"We've never had a Dobson on the squadron, sir. Not in my time."

Cleve-Cutler took the letter and tore it into quarters. "Send Jennings' people a two-pound tin of raspberry jam."

The adjutant made a note. "You think that will be adequate, sir?" he asked cautiously.

"It's all we can afford. Chuck in a couple of sandbags to make up the weight, if you like. I don't care."

The adjutant knew when to leave. Mackenzie was waiting to come in.

"Give the door a good kick," the C.O. told him. "Well, did you see her? Give her the record?"

"Yes, sir. She asked me to thank you."

"I'll bet she did. Stay at Taggart's, did you? What room did he give you?"

"Can't remember the number, sir." Mackenzie squinted at Cleve-Cutler's ferocious grin and it went out of focus. He rubbed the eye and made it worse. "He said there was no blood on the carpet. Didn't tell me that. Told her. Dunno why."

"I see. I see. Quite a beauty, isn't she?"

"Stunning."

"I hope she entertained you?"

Mackenzie was becoming weary from standing. He wanted to get the questioning over. "Yes, sir," he said. "She entertained me, and I entertained her, and we entertained each other, and that was that. We danced, and she sang, and it was all delightful. Sir."

"It sounds exhausting." Cleve-Cutler was circling the room again, frowning with concentration in order not to step on a crack. "Still, now that you're back you can have a nice rest at Passchendaele."

"I don't think I'm fit, sir."

"Fit enough to have a fight in Buckingham Palace, weren't you? A.P.M. told me all about it. Hellbent on a court martial, they were, until I persuaded them to let you go on patrol at Wipers instead. I leaned over backwards for you."

"I can't find the doc anywhere. He could—"

"Dando's gone to get a tooth pulled. You can see him when you get back."

"I can't see anything clearly, sir."

"Not surprised, with that bloody silly eyepatch on. Besides, you can't miss Passchendaele. Large village, full of Huns. Ah!" The C.O. knelt and put his ear to the floor. "Little bastards are listening," he whispered. He tiptoed to his desk and took out a Service revolver and fired at the floor. He kept firing until the gun was empty and the room was full of smoke. "Ground-strafing!" he said. "That's the stuff to give the troops." But by then Mackenzie had gone.

*   *   *

Woolley was talking to Dingbat Maddegan when he saw Mackenzie in the distance, going into the flight hut. He stopped a passing mechanic and took his bicycle and rode to the hut.

Mackenzie was picking through a litter of flying clothing. "Some bastard pinched my sheepskin coat," he said. "I've a damn good mind to tell the king."

Woolley went over to him and took a long look at his face, and walked away, his hands in his pockets. "How many fingers am I holding up?"

"Seven," Mackenzie said. He had found one flying boot. "Twelve." He heaved on the boot, but it was too small for him. The effort was exhausting and he had to rest. He sat on the table. "Six and a half?" he said.

"You're not fit to fly."

"The C.O. reckons I am. And Dando's got toothache."

"The C.O.'s off his head. Look at you: you've got the shakes."

"Uncle says it's a hangover." Mackenzie was shivering. He found a stained and ragged muffler, and wrapped it around his neck. "It comes and goes. It's come now, so it'll go soon. That's logic."

"Bugger your logic. You're not fit to fly. If you try to take off I'll shoot you."

Immediately, Mackenzie brightened up. "What for? To save my life? Bugger *your* logic."

"Alright, forget logic. And forget jokes. Passchendaele is no joke. I've been there already. Trench-strafing isn't funny, either. Too many Huns with too many guns."

"But think of the slaughter," Mackenzie said softly. He wiped his face with one end of the muffler and left smears of whale-grease. "Strafe a trench that's full of Hun infantry and you could knock over a brace of platoons in a single swoop. Wouldn't that be thrilling? If your luck's in, you might bag a whole company."

"It's not grouse shooting, for Christ's sake," Woolley muttered.

"Good God, no. It's much more fun than that." He smiled at Woolley; or, at least, half his face smiled. "That upsets you, doesn't it? Killing isn't supposed to be fun. Too bad. I like it. I didn't realize how much I liked it until you tried to stop me doing it. Flamers are fun, but you can only get a couple of Huns in a flamer. Whereas trench-strafing is one long glorious skittle-match. Huns by the ton."

"I had a dog like you, once. Never happier than when he was savaging sheep."

Mackenzie cocked his head. "You shot him."

"Somebody else did. Blew his stupid head off."

"I blame the sheep," Mackenzie said. "No sense of humour."

"Sometimes you get on my right tit," Woolley said. His voice was harsh; his face was sour. "Don't you *want* to live? You think the rest of us are turds; well, maybe we are turds. That's no reason to chuck your life away. Anyone can die, you know. It doesn't take brains. What's your damned hurry?"

"I like the taste," Mackenzie said simply.

* * *

The squadron took off thirty minutes before Canadian troops were due to assault Passchendaele.

Woolley led eleven Bristol Fighters, which was the most the squadron could raise. It had suffered badly since moving to Poperinghe. The Biff was a sturdy machine, but trench-strafing was the most hazardous kind of air fighting. The only way to do it was to fly low; very low. The enemy was all around, often well hidden, usually well armed, and eager to hack down an aeroplane before its guns could hunt them through their trenches.

Mackenzie flew the Nieuport. He'd had a bath and a nap, and he'd discarded the eyepatch. His fleece-lined coat had turned up. "I feel spiffing," he told Dingbat. "Show me the Boche and I'll doom him." His left eye was bloodshot and leaking tears, and it was slow to follow the movements of the right eye.

"That bus of yours," Dingbat said. "It's no good for strafing. Not rugged enough. Too . . ."

"Too frail," Mackenzie said.

"Yeah."

"But that's the trick. It's such a butterfly, the bullets go straight through it. They just make holes. Don't you see?"

Dingbat had no time to argue. He had a flight to look after. "Get in fast, and get out even faster," he said. "Don't hang about."

Woolley's briefing had been simple. The plan was to find Passchendaele, machine-gun the German trenches and gun-pits, kill as many as possible, force the rest to keep their heads down, and give the Canadians a chance to advance. That was the plan. As the squadron flew over Ypres, the weather began to interfere. There was mist all the way to the target. Sometimes it looked more like fog.

Woolley flew by dead reckoning. When his cockpit watch told him Passchendaele was below, he fired a red signal flare. At once the squadron split up and peeled off; each pilot went down into the mist and looked for trouble.

Mackenzie found it almost at once. The air was so murky that he could see little of the ground from three hundred feet. He sideslipped, making it easier to search. At two hundred feet, lines of yellow tracer stabbed through the mist, so close that it scared and elated him. He dived again. At a hundred feet he saw trees poking up, not real trees, just tattered stubs. The tracer was still chasing him. The gun was very near; he could hear its kettledrum rattle above the engine roar. He kept banking, losing height, searching, and through the swirl of mist he saw a line of ruins, thick with troops, and he felt like an angel. It was such an absurd idea that he dismissed it; but as he flew at the enemy the Nieuport was Mackenzie and Mackenzie was the Nieuport. Only gods could fly. He switchbacked along the lines of ruins, rising and swooping, hammering the panicky soldiers with bursts from the Vickers and the Lewis. The ruins came to an end and so did the taste of bliss. He climbed hard to escape the rattle of groundfire. The mist closed in. Slyly, his memory offered a picture of a crackling fire in a Yorkshire beech wood, offering the comfort of warmth when what he had felt was sadness after triumph and a thirst for even more triumph.

He was climbing when the heavy machine gun, firing blind, spraying bullets, hosing the mist in hope, got the reward for never giving in. It splashed a dozen bullets across the Nieuport. Every fourth bullet was incendiary. One incendiary hit the tank. The tank was one quarter-full of petrol vapour. The Nieuport exploded like a firework display with a stick of dynamite in the middle. Mackenzie saw nothing; not even the flash.

Woolley saw the flash through the thin top of the mist. It was a mile away and yet it was so bright that he blinked. When he looked again there was a brief, soft glow; then nothing.

On all sides, thin white rockets soared and died. The Canadians were attacking; the Hun troops were calling for help. In a few seconds, German shells would be drilling holes in the air and smashing gaps in the attack. Woolley dived back into the mist and shot off the rest of his ammunition.

The squadron landed at Poperinghe in ones and twos. Several had got lost in the mist; after so much violent banking and turning, their compasses were haywire. Every machine had been hit. A gunner had a bullet in his chest. A pilot had a shattered hip. One Biff was missing, and the Nieuport.

O'Neill asked his usual questions. Nobody had much to say.

"Fog," Dingbat told him. "Can you spell fog?"

Captain Delancey stayed at the aerodrome long enough to get official word that the Canadians had taken Passchendaele. By then it was nightfall and Cleve-Cutler was already mixing Hornet's Sting in a wooden tub. The adjutant came into the mess and Cleve-Cutler summoned him to taste it. "More rum?" the adjutant suggested.

"Excellent." Another jar of rum went in.

Woolley was playing "Colonel Bogey" with one finger on the piano. He kept hitting a dead note. "This wouldn't happen to Richthofen," he told the adjutant. "His circus has a Bechstein double grand."

"You don't say."

"Tuned daily," Woolley said. "By Beethoven's grandson."

"Do me a favour, old chap. A couple of rooms have to be cleared out. A bit of moral support would be welcome. Frankly, it's not my cup of tea."

They went to Mackenzie's room first. His valise was on the bed, unopened.

"We'd better have a look inside," the adjutant said. "Last week I found a small Stilton in one chap's bag." They spread the contents of the valise on the bed.

"Nothing special," Woolley said. "The usual junk. All very forgettable."

They began repacking. "I'll keep it in the orderly room for a couple of days," the adjutant said. "You never know."

"Bully for you," Woolley said.

The adjutant fastened the straps, and looked around. "Right," he said. "Ready for the replacement."

"You'll never replace that one, Uncle," Woolley said. "Here: let me carry that." They stepped out into the night. "Peaceful, isn't it?" Woolley said. The rumble of gunfire had ceased; the moon was up. "Never mind," he said, "we'll soon put a stop to that."

AUTHOR'S NOTE

Hornet's Sting is fiction based on fact. The reader is entitled to know which is which. My account of the war as it was fought on the Western Front in 1917 is fact, whereas most of the characters are invented ("Boom" Trenchard is an exception). I have tried to relate the facts of what happened in 1917 to the day-to-day life of a (mythical) squadron of the Royal Flying Corps.

Thus the descriptions of aircraft – especially the Sopwith Pup, the Nieuport Scout and the Bristol Fighter – are as accurate as I could make them. So is my reference to pilots' skills, or lack of them. Flying training was still a pretty hit-or-miss affair in the First World War. Twice as many pilots were killed in training as died on active service. How to get out of a spin was widely regarded as a mystery. For example: two of the R.F.C.'s most successful pilots were James McCudden and Mick Mannock. When Mannock first arrived in France, in 1917, he asked: "What do I do if I go into a spin?" McCudden said, "Put all controls central and pray like hell." That was the general state of knowledge, and I applied it to Hornet Squadron.

"Boom" Trenchard commanded the R.F.C., and he preached the gospel of the offensive spirit at all times. His policy pervades *Hornet's Sting*. There is evidence that German morale suffered from the presence of British machines, constantly patrolling behind enemy Lines. Equally there is evidence that morale in British squadrons suffered because deep patrols were always carried out at a serious disadvantage. Lieutenant A. S. G. Lee flew Pups with 46 Squadron in France for most of 1917. (He reached the rank of air vice-marshal in the Second World War.) Although he supported Trenchard's offensive spirit, he attacked the way it was applied. Trenchard's offensive strategy, Lee said, was "in effect, a territorial offensive", in which Trenchard believed that "for a British aeroplane to be one mile across the trenches was offensive: for it to be ten miles over was more offensive". Lee argued that this was nonsense. Treating the air like the land – as something to be captured – was a fundamental mistake, and Trenchard's crews paid for it.

Deep patrols were handicapped by the prevailing westerly wind. If a pilot was wounded, an engine failed, or a gun jammed, the crew was probably lost. Without parachutes (which were never issued to the R.F.C.) the likelihood was that the machine would be destroyed and the crew killed. There were times in 1917 when, according to Lee, British air losses were almost four times as great as German – and this when the R.F.C. was far below strength in men and machines. In his book *No Parachute* (Jarrolds, 1968), Lee described the R.F.C.'s distant offensive strategy as one of "sending obsolescent machines deep into German-held territory" and said it was "incomprehensible even at the time". In any war, soldiers (and airmen) gain experience by fighting, but Trenchard's stubborn insistence on Deep Offensive Patrols was so costly that the question must be asked: what profit is experience to the dead?

The Western Front was a cosmopolitan place. I have tried to reflect this, and not only in the make-up of the squadron. Chinese labour squads worked behind the Lines; there was a Portuguese division in the trenches, as well as a Russian regiment. Russian officers occasionally visited the R.F.C. There is no evidence that they served with a squadron. The Bolshevik assassins are my invention.

The introduction of Bristol Fighters was as disastrous as I describe. In April 1917, on their first patrol, the tactics of close formation flying protected by intensive crossfire proved to be a complete failure. Five Albatros D-IIIs led by Richthofen shot down four out of six Bristol Fighters and badly damaged a fifth. Tactics were quickly changed; thereafter the Biff was flown aggressively, as a fighter, and it proved to be a great success.

Captain Albert Ball's astonishing career is accurately summarized in the story. One of Ball's many skills was his ability to penetrate an enemy formation and fly his Nieuport so close to his target that other enemy machines were afraid to fire at him. After that, the problem was how to escape. This kind of air fighting called for enormous courage, but courage was not enough – as Ball and Mackenzie discovered. They also needed luck.

Details of the battles of Arras and Third Ypres – the bombardments, the tunnel under Arras, the swamp maps made by the Tank Corps, the casualty figures, the persistent bad weather, and so on – are all based on records of the fighting. Passchendaele was taken by Canadian troops with the help of ground-strafing by the R.F.C. The village (or rather its ruins) was about five miles from the Allied Lines at Ypres, where the battle had begun more than three months earlier. All this gain in ground, and more, was lost six months later.

I have tried not to exaggerate the appetite in R.F.C. squadrons for destructive horseplay and violent games during what the crews called "binges". But records show that exaggeration would be difficult. Pianos really were destroyed, furniture was smashed, revolvers were fired, much alcohol got drunk, occasionally blood was shed, and sometimes farm animals were found in bedrooms. None of this is surprising. Life was short; while it lasted, it was celebrated strenuously.

Which brings me to the episode where Mackenzie and Tyndall swap cockpits while their Biff is airborne. The late Squadron Leader Wally Wallens (who won a D.F.C. in 1940 for shooting down three Me-109s in one day) told me that in 1937 he and another trainee pilot performed the cockpit-swapping trick three times in succession, always without wearing parachutes. They were flying an Audax, an open-cockpit biplane not unlike a Bristol Fighter. They landed after each swap. Their purpose was to annoy an unpopular flight sergeant whose job was to record aircraft movements. He became increasingly confused when the pilot who landed was not the pilot who had taken off.

Mackenzie himself is not a model citizen. In some respects he is similar to Cattermole, a fighter pilot in my novel *Piece of Cake*, about the Battle of Britain. Some retired RAF officers found Cattermole unacceptable.

Others did not. Group Captain Myles Duke-Woolley, D.S.O., D.F.C., commanded a Hurricane squadron that fought in the Battle of Britain. "I go along with all your characters," he told me; and added that when he was asked if a squadron should get rid of an especially maverick pilot, he advised them to keep him. "He was bad for discipline but good for morale," he said. "Every squadron should have just the one."

The presence of Dabinett and Klagsburn in France is an echo of the visit by an American film crew to the Western Front in 1917. They came to make a film that would stimulate enthusiasm in the American people for the war. What they saw in the trenches was not encouraging, so they went to Palestine, where the British Army was visibly winning a war against Turkey.

One of the most difficult things to capture in a story of this sort is the outlook of the people. We know now that the United States joined the Allies in 1917, and that the war ended in 1918. With hindsight, it's tempting to see 1917 as a year of hanging on, of summoning up the strength for one last Big Push. But that was not how most people felt at the time. It was a very bad year, all blood and mud: colossal bombardments, huge battles, appalling losses, and virtually no change. Three years of massive effort had failed to break the deadlock on the Western Front. Most soldiers thought the war would last for years, perhaps for another decade, perhaps even for a generation. As late as September 1918, Lord Northcliffe, who owned the *Daily Mail*, and had led a mission to the US in 1917 and so might be expected to see the big picture, declared, "None of us will live to see the end of the war." So when Hornet Squadron held its smoking concert in Trenchard's presence, McWatters' sketch about how the war had lasted in the 1920s or 1930s was not just gallows humour. Many men could see no alternative.

It is not easy to enter the mind-set of young pilots whose expectation of life was measured in weeks, perhaps only days, in a war that threatened to outlast everyone. This knowledge was yet another test to be added to the everyday strains of the Deep Offensive Patrols: fatigue, bitter cold, ceaseless searching of the sky, sudden frantic combat, the sight of a flamer, the loss of a comrade, the frequent arrivals of replacements. To fly with the R.F.C. was to fight a separate war with one's own fears, and to stretch one's endurance to the limit. There was no science of post-operative trauma in 1917. Shell-shock was barely acknowledged. In keeping with this, I have tried to describe the treatment of mental casualties, such as Spud Ogilvy, according to the very narrow understanding of the day. If *Hornet's Sting* comes across as an account of just one damn thing after another, such is the nature of war. 1917 happened to be a worse year than most.

THE ROYAL FLYING CORPS QUARTET

WAR STORY

Fresh from school in June 1916, Lieutenant Oliver Paxton's first solo flight is to lead a formation of biplanes across the Channel to join Hornet Squadron in France. Five days later, he crash-lands at his destination, having lost his map, his ballast and every single plane in his charge. To his C.O. he's an idiot, to everyone else – especially the tormenting Australian who shares his billet – a pompous bastard. This is 1916, the year of the Somme, giving Paxton precious little time to grow from innocent to veteran.

HORNET'S STING

It's 1917, and Captain Stanley Woolley joins an R.F.C. squadron whose pilots are starting to fear the worst: their war over the Western Front may go on for years. A pilot's life is usually short, so while it lasts it is celebrated strenuously. Distractions from the brutality of the air war include British nurses (not much luck); eccentric Russian pilots; bureaucratic battles over the plum-jam ration; rat-hunting with Very pistols; and the C.O.'s patent, potent cocktail, known as "Hornet's Sting". But as the summer offensives boil up, none of these can offer any lasting comfort.

GOSHAWK SQUADRON

France, 1918. A normal January day on the Western Front – no battles, and about 2,000 men killed. Behind the lines, at an isolated airfield, Major Stanley Woolley, R.F.C., commanding Goshawk Squadron, turns on a young pilot who has spoken of a "fair fight" and roasts him: "That is a filthy, obscene, disgusting word, and I will not have it used by any man in my squadron." Woolley's goal is to destroy the decent, games-playing outlook of his public school-educated pilots – for their own good.

A SPLENDID LITTLE WAR

The war to end all wars, people said in 1918. Not for long. By 1919, White Russians were fighting Bolshevik Reds for control of their country, and Winston Churchill (then Secretary of State for War) wanted to see Communism "strangled in its cradle". So a volunteer R.A.F. squadron, flying Sopwith Camels, went there to duff up the Reds. "There's a splendid little war going on," a British staff officer told them. "You'll like it." Looked like fun.

But the war was neither splendid nor little. It was big and it was brutal, a grim conflict of attrition, marked by incompetence and corruption. Before it ended, the squadron wished that both sides would lose. If that was a joke, nobody was laughing.

THE ROYAL AIR FORCE QUARTET

PIECE OF CAKE

In 1939 the R.A.F. was often called the best flying club in the world, with a touch of the playboy about some fighter pilots. That soon changed. *Piece of Cake* follows the vapour trails of Hornet Squadron as it takes a beating in the Battle for France and regroups for the Battle of Britain, which is no piece of cake either. The Luftwaffe is big in numbers and confidence, and patriotism alone cannot save a man in a spinning, burning Hurricane.

A GOOD CLEAN FIGHT

North Africa, 1942. Dust, heat, thirst, flies. A good clean fight, for those who like that sort of thing, and some do. From an advanced landing field, striking hard and escaping fast, our old friends from Hornet Squadron play Russian roulette, flying their clapped-out Tomahawks on ground-strafing forays. Meanwhile, on the ground, the men of Captain Lampard's S.A.S. patrol drive hundreds of miles behind enemy lines to plant bombs on German aircraft. Cue revenge.

DAMNED GOOD SHOW

When war pitches the young pilots of 409 Squadron into battle over Germany, their training, tactics and equipment are soon found wanting, their twin-engined bombers obsolete from the off. Chances of completing a 30-operation tour? One in three. At best. The hardest part of any war is not winning but slogging on to avoid defeat. Bomber Command did that. A wickedly humorous portrait of men doing their duty in flying death traps – fully aware that in those dark days of war there was nothing else to do but dig in and hang on.

HULLO RUSSIA, GOODBYE ENGLAND

After a stint running guns for the C.I.A., Flight Lieutenant Silk, a twice-decorated Lancaster pilot, rejoins the R.A.F. to fly the Vulcan, a nuclear bomber. This is probably the best aircraft in the world. It makes sex look like gardening. But there's a catch. The Vulcan exists to retaliate against a Russian nuclear strike. Silk knows that if his squadron gets scrambled for real, there will be no England to return to. In the mad world of Mutual Assured Destruction, the Vulcan is the last – indeed the only – deterrent.